THE HERO GAME
AND OTHER
DUBLIN STORIES

JAMES MANNING

James Manning

11 Southside Books

Copyright © 2019 Estate of James Manning
All rights reserved.

Cover photo – the author with his first wife Margaret and son Maurice in O'Connell Street, Dublin in 1951.

CONTENTS

PREFACE	4
THE HERO GAME	8
THE GREEN IN DUBLIN	119
NO CAKES FOR DANNY BOY	154
POPPY AND LILY	180
STRAIGHTEN UP AND FLY RIGHT	204
DISCIPLINE	254
THE WINDOW	295
A CASE OF CONSCIENCE	310
AGNES	341
THE HARD COLD WORLD OF THE O'KENNEDY ACCOUNT	375

PREFACE

James Manning (1917-1984) was a gifted English teacher who wrote two novels, a number of short stories and plays, as well as some poetry, all whilst engaged in a busy family life and demanding teaching career. Some of his early stories were published in various periodicals in Dublin in the 1940s and 50s and his story in Irish, *An Fear gur Dhein Crann de* (*The Man Who Became a Tree*) was anthologised in *Nuascéalaícght* (New Stories) 1940-1950 (published by Sáirséal Agus Dill 1952). All the stories here, published for the first time, were written in the 1960s and 70s when he had already been away from Ireland for a decade or more. They have their roots in the years of his childhood and youth, growing up in the Dublin of the 1920s through to the 1940s, the son of working class, Roman Catholic parents who ran a grocer's shop. Such shops and shopkeepers feature in several of the stories, as does the commercial world of salesmen, which Jim (as he was known to his friends) was forced to become to help support himself and the family after the death of his father in his late teens. He remained a salesman throughout his twenties, before obtaining the degree at Trinity College Dublin in his early thirties that allowed him to pursue a teaching career. The Republican movement features in these stories too. His father Patrick had been involved in the Easter Rising of 1916 and later helped smuggle IRA guns around the city during the Irish War of Independence. Jim himself as a three-year-old came under fire at Croke Park in 1920. He was in the crowd at the Gaelic football match there when British forces opened fire. This was Bloody Sunday and he remembered hearing what he thought at the time was a man hammering on a tin roof, but was actually machine gun fire.

As one would expect, Catholicism looms very large too, several stories exploring the dynamic between religious belief, morality and the demands and temptations of the material world. There is an earthy quality to these stories where characters wrestle with the call of the flesh and the rigour of the spiritual, but also more intellectual matters are explored - the need for personal freedom in opposition to the rules of religion and society, the advent of communism, Irish nationalism and the relationship between church and state. Throughout, the character of the Irish is examined with a critical eye - but also with a passionate heart. For a man who had long since rejected Roman Catholicism he shows great compassion for and understanding of his characters as they struggle to balance the demands of their lives with the strictures of the church. Dublin itself is central to all these tales - there is a wonderful sense of place, the action permeated by the sights, sounds and smells of the city - and these stories are clearly a love letter to the Fair City where Jim spent the first thirty years of his life and which he carried within him on his travels to England, Egypt and Italy. There was to be another love letter to Dublin too, a novel called *Liffey My Love*.

The voice that tells these stories is unmistakably Jim. He was a great anecdotalist and that comes through in the way he tells these tales. He takes his time, painting in lots of detail, but nothing is wasted and all the while we are being taken inexorably toward often quite unexpected and moving destinations. He captures the Dublin expressions, rhythms and patterns of speech of his characters wonderfully. Those who knew him well will recognise in some of the characters depicted here members of Jim's family and people he knew in his youth in Dublin. The shopkeeper in *Poppy and Lily* who says "I want the space your rotten feet is contaminatin'" is repeating a phrase Jim's father would use in the shop to encourage people who were irritating him to leave. And in *No Cakes for Danny Boy* Paddy's sister's warning that he would find himself "running thirty miles after a crow on the last day to snatch a crust away from it" is something Jim's mother would say to him as a boy when he didn't finish his dinner. To which Jim once replied, "If I was that hungry, I'd eat *you*!"

The main character in *The Hero Game* – presumabley an older version of the boy in *Poppy and Lily* - is named after one of the heroes of the Easter Rising, Padraig Pearse. Perhaps this is because Jim himself almost bore the name of another leader from the Rising, MacDonagh, as his middle name, but when he came to be christened at the font the priest refused to allow it. MacDonagh (who, like Pearse, was executed by the British) had been the commanding officer at Jacobs Biscuit factory where Jimmy's father Patrick was stationed, loading rifles and tending to the wounded.

Jim's first wife Margaret died in 1960 in Cairo and so,

finding himself alone to bring up their five children, he returned to England and settled in the West Country to be near his in-laws. It was during the ensuing years that he began to write these stories. He remarried in 1967, his new wife Thelma taking much of the burden from him of running the home and looking after the five (and quite soon six) children. This freed him to devote more time and energy to his writing, which he did increasingly. However, he died of a heart attack at the relatively young age of sixty-six - less than a year into his semi-retirement from the teaching career he loved - and much of his work remains unpublished. When it came to his writing he was something of a perfectionist and these stories might have found their way out into the world during his lifetime had he not been so. He was forever tinkering with them, making small adjustments, revisions and corrections. Be that as it may, they're out in the world now where they deserve to be and we are able to explore the streets of a bygone Dublin like Pearse, the protagonist of the longest story *The Hero Game*, who wanders the city at night "drunk on the wild blood pounding through his veins."

Jim Manning (March 2019)

THE HERO GAME

It surprised him that there were some fellows still sitting on the steps below the heavy black door of the college for the last clock he had glanced at showed twenty past nine and that was some time ago. As yet he could not be sure who they were because the black, iron railings fronting the basement area of the tall, Georgian house gave his view of the group the jerky, flickering quality of an old film. But some of them were certainly from his own class as was evident from the flash of white in their midst, a sure sign that Brian Davitt was there in one of his usual, impossibly clean shirts. Why were they not at lessons he wondered coming abreast of the railings in the brisk, military tread, so suited to his erect, broad-shouldered figure, he had adopted since his release from the Bridewell where, with the force of a living voice speaking out of the flea-hopping darkness, it had come to him that he should sit for the Cadetship Examinations and devote his life to the service of Ireland in the green uniform that looked so smart and so natural on Padraig Pearse the national hero after whom he was named. "Did you never think of joinin' the or-gan-is-ation?" One of the I.R.A. men sharing his cell had asked him, but he had been discouraged from giving that matter any serious consideration by the scorn they had poured on him when, to induce a dreamy mood for sleep, he had gone on, despite their growls and groans of protest, reciting Tennyson's *Ulysses* quietly to himself - "Bloody English pome!" - though one of them had almost made up for that later when he confided: "The rest of us left our mark on the rotten, red-necked guards but it was you who's got nothin' at all to do with us that did the only real worthwhile bit o' damage o' the whole night." Was that before or after he had the idea of sitting for the Cadetship Examination, he was still trying to recall as he swung right at the steps into a wild cheer and an alarming onrush of bodies, huge and dark in the clear, spring light, clattering down to engulf him.

Smiling he raised his arms in an attitude of mock surrender and suffered them to clump him on the back, slap him on the shoulders, and tug him so eagerly up the steps that he sank on one knee - the hero in his hour of triumph shot through the back by an assassin, but still game - so that he had to be hoisted and hauled to his feet. All the while the raucous voices broke in his ears: "Good old Pearse!", "The Felon of our Land!", "Another martyr for ould Ireland!", "What time's the hanging?

He returned a patient smile on their flushed faces burning with secret joy at the crude grasp of their hands on his, the playful punches they landed on his shoulders and arms, - was it from Brian Davitt, his class rival, he had had that knuckled dig in the small of his back as they tugged him up the steps? In spite of that their reception of him was proving to be some sort of recompense for his unhappy years in that place where his quiet manner, his invariably good examination results tended somehow to isolate him from most of his classmates who for the most part seemed genuinely unaware of his existence as he sat at the back of the class, an ace tennis player warding off with the unerring racquet of his mind everything in the Brothers' droning lessons that offered no gift to his imagination. He allowed them to clump and punch away to their hearts content, for only a fool would refuse their adulation now and fail secretly to revel in it.

"And how are things at I.R.A. Headquarters today?" Gilmore asked, lounging against the door, unmoved by the general excitement, still working hard at modelling himself on the Bounder in the old *Magnet*. And making a good job of it too!

"I hear they're going to shoot their way into the courts today to rescue you!" a voice called from behind.

"I'm sure they won't do that," he replies airily over his shoulder. And said to Gilmore:

"How would I know what goes on in the I.P.A. when I'm not even a sympathiser with that organisation?"

He joined in the laughter which followed their hoots of disbelief.

"Course you're a member," dark-eyed O'Doherty said, "otherwise you wouldn't have been where you were to get yourself lagged, would you?"

Fat little McDermott, the middle button of his grey flannel jacket still hanging by its frail thread, pranced about in a jig of delight: "But you haven't heard what's happening at our headquarters here, have you? The Cock's sick again. Being prayed for - we hope with no success - and so we've no classes all morning and only

McCleary's history and his rotten oul leather to worry about in the afterbloodynoon!"

Dev Murphy, bright-faced and gay, broke away from a restless group by the railing and shouldering McDermott from the position of honour in front of Pearse, held him at arm's length by pressing the flat of his hand hard against his face.

"Hey, Pearse," he cried excitedly, "some of us are thinking of doing a bunk and coming with you to the courts!"

"Oh please don't do that, " he started in alarm, "I-I wouldn't like anyone to get into, trouble on my account."

Brian Devitt's sharp, handsome face appeared over Dev's padded shoulder.

"Riddle," the face said, "Why does the Cock get sick so often? Give up? Why else but for the desperate need of a nice little hen. But tell the court, sir, have you now come straight to college from the Bridewell?"

"Oh no, I got out just before the week-end, I had to spend the last few days seeing about a solicitor and so on. I just dropped into college today to give Doddier my comp and to tell the Cock what's happening. Oh, that'll have to be Franco now, wont it? Anyway, although my mother's sent in a note she says it'll be appreciated better if I come in and explain things in person and say why I have to be away today as well."

"Or maybe for the next ten years" Brian's face grinned, the chin coming down to rest lazily on Dev's shoulder.

"Well, we won't have long to wait to find that out," he tried to stare the smile down, "Herman Cowan the soli-

The Hero Game and Other Dublin Stories

citor says the whole thing will be over before lunch."

McDermott danced in front of him again. "Did you know that Doddier's away too? In bed with 'flu or whatever her name is."

"Sweating it out," Brian's foxy face leered, "with a bottle of old Irish whiskey and the young landlady."

"Any work for him has to be left on his desk," McDermott said, "Do you want me to take it up for you?"

"I'll do it myself, thanks very much all the same," He tapped his hand against his jacket to reassure himself that the two pieces of writing on which he had laboured so long during the past few days were still there. "I suppose I'd better see Franco and get it over with." he said, filing with them into the hall past a near-life-size statue of the Blessed Virgin standing on a small table against the wall from which in places the mould-green plaster was peeling. Patches of damp seeped greyly through the pinned-up notices, timetables, and group photographs that included one of the Archbishop, his palm resting flat on his bald pate, looking solemnly down at one of the juniors of some years back on the occasion of his one and only visit to the college. As they went past, Gilmore nodded towards the photograph and said: "It must have been a great surprise to his Grace that the first-year kid could piss so high." Several of the fellows glared at Gilmore who was always coming out with remarks like that possibly less because of the influence of the Bounder than of his sister who was in some kind of scruffy, workers' organisation and was rumoured to have left the church.

With a pang of envy he realised that Flora Gilmore's

trial was over. A few weeks ago she had appeared on a charge of inciting a gang of slum dwellers to attack a rent collector's car which they overturned and set on fire. According to the account in the greyish, blotchy labour paper Gilmore showed him at the back of the class, what she said in court was the sort of wadgy, boring stuff that meets your eye when you flick open a textbook on economics in the public library and flick it shut again almost in the same action. Who did she hope to interest, to convince, to inspire with all that dull-as-dishwater twaddle about Ireland being run for the benefit of the rising Capitalists, who robbed both their own workers and the public at large; for the big landowners who preferred cattle to people on the land; for the vested property interests who were as avaricious as the old landlords and who sent off a small fortune in ground rents to England each month? It was in that disconcerting, unreadable way the labour paper reported what she said. Real mind-paining stuff, about as far as you could get from a rousing, ringing speech from the dock about right and truth and liberty and freedom such as Robert Emmett and John Sheares and Wolfe Tone made when they stood there and stared unflinchingly into the squinting eyes of their accusers. And of death itself! Flora Gilmore had got six months he recalled with a cold shiver, but in a way that was unimportant now, almost a minor detail, for the really big thing was behind her - the ordeal of stepping into the dock, of standing there above the stares and sneers of the ignorant, uncomprehending mob, of enduring second by second agony of clinical, cold-blooded cross-examination by specialists more you would imagine in surgery than in law.

The group moved away from him and for an unreasoning instant he feared they were reading on his face the secret dread tightening about his heart. To his relief he saw they had begun to mount the broad staircase leading to the form classroom. Brian, looking down at him, sawed the side of his hand along his Adam's apple leaving him to go alone past the science lab to room 7 where Franco was always to be found at that time. He made his way down the dim corridor, hating the trembling in his legs which brought him almost to a halt in his efforts to control it. How stupid he had been a moment ago! How could a sentence of six months be unimportant, a mere minor detail? A day-and-a-half in the Bridewell had been like an eternity-and-a-half in the outer reaches of Hell. And though his classmates in their excitement would not have been likely to notice any signs of nervousness in his manner or appearance, Franco with his hacksaw look would certainly miss nothing. And when had Franco ever passed up the chance of giving a fellow a bitter, discouraging word, particularly at the moment he needed it least? Setting on his face the mask of calm courage to be seen in photographs of Padraig Pearse - he was more sure than ever now that Gilmore had made it up when he said that Pearse always had himself photographed in profile to hide the broad cast in one of his eyes, "the guy with the radio eyes" as he called him - he raised up his hand and allowed his knuckles languidly to knock on the door of the classroom.

A voice wailed from the other side as from the grave. Which always cropped up somewhere or other in your mind whenever you thought of Franco. Taking the wail for an invitation he entered the classroom where

Franco stood with his back to him gargling away at the class in Conemara Irish. Without turning round to see who it was, the Brother continued gargling: "And to think that a great poet like O'Rathaille, the man who wrote this poem, one of the greatest aislings in the mother tongue should have had to spend his latter days in miserable poverty. Ah, boys, the English have so much to answer for when you consider how badly they have always treated us! It was due to their policy of murder and rapine that the clergy and the nobles and the poets and the ordinary people of Ireland were made to suffer so much for so long. A sorrowful history indeed, but with the help of God we prevailed in the end. All right then, I want you to get the whole of this poem off by heart for the first lesson tomorrow morning. And I won't take any excuses. Anyone who fails to recite any part of it will be in dire trouble. Do you all understand that?"

In the still hush he turned his large, squared-off face to Pearse who with a faint hitch of surprise marked again its resemblance to Boris Karloff in his marvellous make-up as the monster in Frankenstein which had been showing to packed houses round about the time Brother Morrow was posted to the college. Mr. Dodd had once confided to him that the brother was secretly delighted with his nickname believing he owed it to General Franco whose victories against the Reds in Spain - who as Brian sneered fell mainly in the plain - were in the newspaper headlines every other day.

"Please, sir," he said in Dublin English, resting his gaze on the spot above the brother's half-clerical collar where in the film the bolt had protruded from the monster's neck. "I've come to tell you I have to be absent again today because my case is being heard in the courts this morning. My mother wrote so I'm sure that Brother Cox knows all about it already..."

"And so does half Dublin!" The lines on Franco's face shifted about and settled into a new pattern greyly illuminated by a glint of low cunning, a look which Pearse over the years had learned to interpret as Franco's version of a lukewarm smile.

"People these days," he glinted at Pearse, "are talking of nothing else but the terrible disturbances of that night. And how a boy from this college got himself involved in that sort of reprehensible behaviour I'm afraid I shall never be able to understand. And also I'd no idea your mother allowed you to stay out so late at night at a time when all good Christians are in bed."

His voice came out at Pearse like the creakings of the Old Dark House in the storm that marooned the travellers there making them the prisoners of Boris Karloff in a different make-up. And of course of the blood-chilling mad Saul as well!

"Wait outside a minute," Franco creaked, "I want a private word with you."

Pearse went outside and heard through the closed door a series of creaks and gargles that told him the class was being set some lugubrious task or other in the *Aids of Irish Composition* or some other horrifying book like that. He peered down the dim corridor to the staircase wondering just to break the monotony how he would react should the Mad Saul appear there gliding down the banisters his bright dangerous knife sharp in his hand. You had to work your imagination really hard in that college to make the bloody place even tolerably interesting. He longed for all this waiting about to be behind him leaving him free again on the night streets of the city where he would move in the murmur of the living crowds past shop windows warm with yellow lights, past intriguing hall doors leading to what mysteries beyond their flickering fanlights; past the shadow-crowded recesses of beckoning alleys and laneways, following as always a plan he had devised shortly after his father's death of travelling by train to one or other of the route terminal and on the return journey swinging off the conveyance into whatever street sent forth its secret cry to him and from thence finding his way home by guess and enquiry through the emptying streets of the beloved late-night city.

He almost jumped straight out of Swift's Alley where he was mooching at that moment when with uncanny simultaneity the door clicked shut behind him as Franco's metal-hard, friendly hand fell on his shoulder, a gesture he was surprised to find himself thinking might be the latter-day equivalent of the kiss on the cheek in the garden. From which you could tell they were all a bunch of nancy-men as Gilmore once whispered to him during a homily by Franco on that unfortunate incident.

"We're all very much concerned about you, Bolton" Franco said, looking less concerned than plainly disgusted.

"Yes, sir. I appreciate that very much, sir. Thank you, sir." Would that make him go away? He wondered what Franco was really concerned about and began to drift off into one of his ever-handy dreams in which a huge, black undersea creature almost the size of a cinema screen moved in slow, sedate dance around its victim, a harmless, merry little creature with delicate fluttering fins.

"Very concerned indeed," Franco went on shaking his box-like head, "You've given us no indication at all, nor do you seem to be interested, in what you're going to do after you leave college. Your spiritual director tells me you've had no call to the religious life and when your mother came in to see Brother Cox and myself after your fathers death - may God rest his soul - we learned that the poor woman wouldn't be able to afford to send you to the university even supposing you had a wish to go there."

"There's always Uncle Sam, sir."

The steel trap of Franco's mouth snapped shut on the misfortunate air which wriggled out through his nose in a tired sigh.

"Bolton' Bolton! You're being stupidly facetious again, aren't you?"

"Oh no sir! By that I meant my Uncle Pat. Oh look, just as you told us a few weeks ago, an example of internal rhyme. My mother is thinking of writing to my uncle in New York. For help. Well, actually for money for that's what help means. Uncle Sam is the name my sister and I have for him.

"Do you now? For your poor mother's sake I hope you haven't instilled into your sister the airy attitude you seem to take everything in life, especially to your future role in it - if you're ever going to have any at all!

Nearly all the other boys here have some idea by now of what they want to do and I'm pleased to see the College is putting in more candidates for public posts this year than ever before - the Junior Executives, the Clerical Officers, the Customs and Excise, the E.S.B, The Milk Board and so on."

Desperately he was struggling again to clamber up out of a giant, sour-smelling milk bottle, his constant fear that his mother might one day get around to writing to that distant cousin of theirs whom she claimed had some influence with the Milk Board!

"I'm going to sit for the Cadetship Examination, sir." He brushed from his sleeve the dried milk curds still adhering to it.

"The Lord be praised, decision at last, "Franco's face glinted greyly. "Good, Bolton, good. In fact very good. A little more work on your maths and you'll walk that examination. However...." He paused, as if to allow a kind of grey glee to begin glimmering deep in his eyes, "....I hate to have to say this but you'll understand it's my duty to point out that you will have to go before an interview board following the written examinations and who can tell how they're going to look on this trouble you're in at the moment, this charge you have to answer to in court today. The Defence Forces always take a most serious view of civil disturbances and of illegal organisations and of course the slightest hint, the merest whisper that a prospective candidate of theirs has been associated with political marches and street disorders is bound to make them very chary about accepting him into their ranks. However, for your poor mother's sake, and for that matter for your own, I'll offer up a special prayer for your intention."

"Thank you very much, sir." His knees shook with an impulse to have him fling himself on them and implore Franco not to pray for him. It was most embarrassing to think that the Almighty, who had so much else of real importance to occupy His attention, would on his account have to leave for a moment such a task as keeping all the constellations dead on course in order to listen to Franco creaking and wailing and gargling at Him in Connemara Irish - possibly the worst publicity the language could have. It would be enough to get a fellow hanged! And what a task to lay even on God, to figure out those idioms and proverbs he was always coming out with like, "Nature breaks out through the eyes of the cat!" or "He found it in his mouth like the dog found the scraping of the pot!" A language made up of one unpronounceable enigma after another. No wonder the language was nearly dead.

"And when you're in the courts, "Franco edged closer, his breath steaming with a warm, foody smell as from the buckets of pig swill collected from house to house by urchins after dinner on Sunday with their ringing cry of "Slop! Slop!" through the streets. Franco paused and swallowed down something, maybe another of his impossible idioms. "Try as I know you will, to see that the name of the College is not brought into this case in any way. Certain people might use that as an opportunity to attack our order, even our own dear Catholic faith itself. They might say that this proves the college encourages hooliganism, supports illegal organisations, and rejoices in the destruction of property. Certain evil people are still very strong in this country of ours - the Protestant Ascendancy crowd, Free Masons, so-called free-thinking intellectuals!"

Pearse swallowed on a lumpy constriction in his throat, an obscene Dublin idiom heard on the night streets shrieking to get out - and stared hard at the nail studded floor - in a barrack square Lieutenent Bolton conducted the execution by firing squad of certain evil people each of whom had the face of Franco and heard a voice out there, he just about recognised as his own, mumbling: "I will try, sir! I will do my best for the college, sir." The ragged volley ripped out. The figures fell forward - the firing squad! All the Franco's remained where they were. As they always do, creaking, wailing, gargling prayers and enigmas.

"Good luck then so," Franco moved his hand smoothly over the involuntary shudder in Pearse's shoulders and went in a black creaky slink back into the classroom.

Pearse stared at the floorboards a moment longer. How viciously the nails must have been hammered in to leave them winking like that below the level of the floor, right through the palm of each of his hands as he stared up at his tormentors from the shaft of the recumbent cross. Shaking free of the vision he clumped noisily down the corridor towards the stairs wondering about Gilmore's remark of a few weeks ago that every second fellow in the college thought he was Jesus Christ. But that wasn't surprising for just five minutes with Franco was equal to about an hour sweating blood in the garden. And what a bright piece of information to impart on a day when a fellow had so much else on his mind! It had never occurred to him that there would be an interview following the examination and that, to put it mildly, it might prove to be awkward. Yet, then again, what else could you expect when the Mad Axeman, Life, was out and about, probably as a member of the interview panel. He was always lurking somewhere out there wasn't he, awaiting his chance, watching for the unguarded moment when you thought you were safe to let you have it smack on the neck? Were they to be all in vain, the exhortations he had made to himself in the black stench of two nights in the Bridewell, that he take a detached, scientific look at his life and circumstances to discover how he could wrench free from the alluring dreams and fantasies that rose night and day from the floor of his mind to draw him deeper into them with their insistent lover's arms? During the brief spell in which he almost managed to see himself from the outside as if through a probing Martian telescope, he was appalled at the endless supply of fatuous fantasies he allowed himself to indulge in and in some exalted moods to accept as if they were hard, solid scientific facts. To take just the few days before his arrest alone, he had been the next Hollywood screen idol discovered one night on the city streets by a hawkeyed talent scout; the great scientist who would one day discover some new cheap source of energy in something ordinary like seaweed or cow-dung or body odour and in his spare time invent something to dry up the perpetual drizzle that falls over most of Ireland, particularly during the summer holidays; the daring motor-cyclist on the Wall of Death who also doubled for the driver behind the wheel of the car with its powerful engine running all the time that waited for characters like John Dillinger to emerge shooting from yet another bank bearing funds that in some unspecified way found their ultimate destination in the pockets of the poor; the half-drowned sailor with the broad shoulders washed up on the beach of a mysterious, unmapped island in the South Seas inhabited only by roving bands of sex-crazed beautiful girls of about seventeen or eighteen. What kind of mind could have revelled in such mad, stupid, childishly foolish, embarrassing nonsense? In the stinking dark cell he had willed himself out of that soggy bog of unreality and onto the solid rock of a definite decision about himself and his future, using as his guide a formula of insistence and rejection he had found a short time before in an article in Business Digest, a magazine with unfortunately sharp, glossy paper his mother had brought home from work for use, sheet by sheet, in the lavatory. According to the article on that fateful page, rescued at the last possible moment, success in life lay in the rejection of all unreal, unprofitable inessentials that swallowed up valuable time - which is money - and led nowhere. Painfully he realised that among the inessentials that swallowed up so much of his time were his continual speculations about the nature of reality and truth, the essence of beauty, the magnanimity of God, the reality of eternity, the magic of language - stuff like that which, he had to admit, showed no immediate profit at all and consequently would have to go. Instead, following the sound advice of the article, he determined to insist that he commit himself to what was available to him on a short, remunerative list of immediate and practical opportunities which offered a career as one of the following: An executive officer, a corporation clerk, an official in the Turf Board, a counter assistant in the Irish Tourist Association - and so on through the whole bloody dreary but essential list. And after his long, agony of self-sifting, having finally chosen a career as an officer in the Defence Forces, a career not first on his list, was it all to go for nothing now because of what he had done in an insane instant on that crazy night when he moved more in a world of dreams than among a screaming mob on the streets? In the dark, heaving recesses of his mind the Mad Axeman nodded grim assent. God, he's everywhere!

And where in fact was he himself? Part way up the stairs groping in his inside pocket for the Irish essay he had written with such care for Mr. Dodd on the storytelling art of Padraic O'Conaire as revealed in his collection of stories about Easter Week, *The Seven Virtues of the Uprising*! What a thrilling book that was! It would do Franco the power of good to read in it the story of the bishop who yearned so earnestly to share the lot of the dying heroes in the blazing heart of Dublin. For, in spite of his waily creaky voice and unfortunate appearance, Franco taught Irish History and Christian Doctrine in such an inspiring and persuasive way it filled your heart with love for Ireland and for God and as a sort of natural contrast, a pervasive distrust if not indeed hatred for the traditional enemy and all her works and pomps. Yet, after all that, when one of the pupils who had absorbed his teaching was on his way to stand trial accused of having accomplished, what in appearance anyway was a violent act of protest against the national foe - which in fact was how the Irish Press saw it - his sole concern was not for the poor victim heading to be picked on and prodded in the courts but for something as abstract and intangible as the good name of the college, a mere idea incapable of feeling! It was enough to make you want to spit! Of course Franco had promised to say a special prayer. But what did that mean? Nothing at all! What else did he do all day but say special prayers for this, that, and the other? In a way, it was what he was paid to do, and it meant no more than blowing your nose. By now God was probably so fed up with hearing nothing from him but special prayers He had probably delegated some angel who wasn't behaving himself quite as he should, to listen to them as a sort of penance. So, to hell with the good name of the college and to Franco's special prayers as well! Grim-faced peasants armed with pitchforks and scythes, their faces contorted with hatred like the mob in the square that night, thrust Frankestein's monster into the crackling flames. Yes, that's what Franco needed to have his logic straightened out for him. A good burn up in the heart of Dublin! Climbing towards the next landing he sensed all sorts of subtle movements going on beyond the verge of his consciousness, vague pulse-like motions on the point of resolving themselves into ideas, an uneasy welter on the surface of which he discerned faintly the suggestion that through this ordeal several things might be straightened out for himself as well, that this whole experience might become a sort of test not just for him but for all who knew him and for everything he believed in. He recalled the strange sense of being driven towards some inexorable fate that had descended on him in the Bridewell the moment the cell door slammed shut behind him with the crash of the Mad Axeman's weapon finding its mark once again. He paused on the stairs as if compelled to contemplate the ideas flitting about in his mind like creatures in a shadowed rock pool. Shaking himself free he went on up towards the classroom. A test for all he believed in, was it? Yet what exactly did he believe in at that moment standing there before the paint-pocked classroom door over which not even a damp cloth was ever run by the caretaker, a sort of walking turnip the brothers had imported from some Gaeltacht or other, a hen-faced man who gobbled trivialities about God, the saints, and the weather in a dialect not even Mr. Dodd could understand properly. He blinked at the sordid door and off-hand believed in God and in Ireland and in some ability or talent at present not yet apparent to him that one day would enable him to serve both with honour and dignity. And, since things were as quiet as death on the economic front at home, with some profit as well. As part of the design on the flyleaf of one of his schoolbooks was the legend: For the Glory of God and the Honour of Ireland. Yes, that is what he felt sure he believed in, as he groped about in his inside pocket for the six pages of his essay of which he wanted to keep separate from his speech from the dock on which he had worked so long and so lovingly, practically from the moment he staggered away from the horror of captivity which was mostly a pervasive, unidentifiable stench breathing out of the darkness, threatening to topple the balance of his mind into one long scream of terror. It was frightening to suspect that to escape from that unnerving smell he would have confessed; to anything they wanted him to, signed any paper they set before him. Extricating his essay at last he thrust open the door and strode into the classroom.

Everyone clamoured around him at once, smiling and calling encouragement. Gilmore away to one side, sitting on top of a desk, beckoned him towards him and asked quietly: "How did you become a member of the I.R.A. anyway? I never knew you took even an academic interest in that futile gang of outmoded gunmen. Did they recruit you at some public meeting in Foster Place or what?"

"Well..." By the narrowest margins he overcame the temptation to tell a deliberate lie. "I'm not - you know - really a member of that..." Another howl of disbelief went up from Brian and some of the others who had drifted over and he bent his head making sure they could see he was hiding a secret smile. After all he had done exactly what the newspaper report of his arrest said he had and who could blame him if his classmates drew whatever interpretation pleased them from it? He looked beyond their smiling faces to the window. Far to the south, beyond a vaguely geometric jumble of grey slate roofs and red chimneys the sun gleamed on the tip of one of the Dublin mountains - he really must consult a good map one day and try to figure out which - a pale cone rising into the early sunlight, gently swelling like the breast of a reclining goddess. "The brightness of brightness met me on a way so lonely," he repeated to himself, the opening of O'Rathille's poem in Mangan's reworking of it in *Poets and Poetry of Munster*. All the real poets saw Ireland as a woman, a goddess of unutterable beauty. His heart ached with love. Ireland was so beautiful! No wonder there were always heroes ready and willing to lay down their lives for her! Yes, what greater destiny could a man have than rise to the challenge of his time and become a national hero? Maybe that's what he believed in most of all!

In a slithering clatter of feet the boys were scrambling frantically from around him. To his surprise he saw that Mr. McClery, the history teacher, had come into the room and was striding towards the head of the room where he waved the red-covered book he was carrying and brought it down with a loud bang on the top of the desk.

"What's all this, eh?" McClery lunged with the spine of the book towards McDermott who slid quickly into the desk nearest to him from which he was rudely elbowed by Dev Murphy pressing in from the other end. "Where do you pack of lazy bostoons think you are? In some haunt of wasters and idlers like the Kildare Street Club? Get out your history notes there. Brother Cox may be absent but you'll not idle about in here disturbing my class. I'm next door until lunchtime and don't forget it! Get this into your fat heads - when I come in here in the afternoon anyone who fails anything in chapter ten of your Irish History, especially Poyning's Law, will find himself reliving that part of your European History known as the Reign of Terror."

He wheeled about in the flushed delight of his own power and discovered Pearse near the door towards which he had been quietly and quickly making his way.

"Who's that over there?" McClery came in a rush from the head of the class and stood before the door, "Can I credit my eyes?" He skipped back an over-amazed step, "Is it the famous political agitator we have here, the active patriot aptly named and all? We're honoured, sir. Indeed we are, all, all honoured!" He mocked an arm-flourishing bow. "Although until now I always laboured under the misapprehension that great national figures were to be seen only by appointment. Or in wax museums."

Pearse stared back at him careful to avoid meeting his eyes in which he sensed a gleam of mixed amusement and scorn.

"I came up to leave an essay for Mr. Dodd," he said unclenching his fingers on the sheets of foolscap and teasing the papers smooth behind his back.

"That's a very wise precaution, to hand it in before you go to the courts, when is it, today, tomorrow, next week?"

"Today, sir."

"Today!" With a sneer-tinged smile he invited the class to share in the joke he was about to make. "Oh, you've just made it in the nick o'teen, haven't you? For if they ship you off this evening to Mountjoy Jail, or Dartmoor, or Devil's Island or to whatever other holiday resort is favourite today with political activists and public enemies, your last deathless message to your college might be lost forever to posterity and the annals of Dublin."

Thrusting out his baggy bottom in a mincing bow he held out his hand into which Pearse in a wrench of revulsion placed the teased-out foolscap sheets of his essay. McClery held the sheets at arm's length frowning at them.

"These look as if they were stuffed between the bars of the cell to keep out the draught. But tell me, are you sure this is the right document you're handing me?" He stirred the sheets idly back and forth in the air, "Due to the strain you're under you haven't made a mistake, have you, and handed me instead of your essay your speech from the dock which as Macauley and every schoolboy knows is something every martyr for ould Ireland carries about with him as a woman does a handbag?"

"I'm quite sure. That's my essay.... sir. " Pearse stared hard into the hateful eyes.

"Ha! So, there was a mistake there to be made! So you have got your speech from the dock with you! Is it any good?"

McClery leered silently at him as if in triumph at the blush tingling along his forehead and flaming on his cheeks. How had the swine guessed? Had the rotten country mug seen him coming out of that fascinating newsagent's in Capel Street whose window was always crammed with sensational booklets such as *John Lee the Man They Could not Hang, Sweeny Todd, the Mad Barber of Fleet Street, Ned Kelly the famous Australian Bushranger, Maria Marten and the Murder in the Red Barn, The Songs Our Fathers Sang, Speeches from the Dock*. He pressed his elbow against his inside pocket where neatly written on foolscap paper were notes for his defence and a long speech full of ringing phrases and carefully balanced sentences adapted - no, not really copied - from Robert Emmett, which he would fling with the careless scorn of Michael MacDiammoir, in *The Old Lady Says No*, right in the teeth of the judges who in the booklet of speeches from the dock sat packed and bewigged on the bench, glaring dark, blotched hatred from their shapeless inky faces at the firm-lined figure of the patriot in the spike-bordered dock. He always hated the way Gilmore said: "Irish History is a dead bore. It's all about Patriots!"

"Of course," McClery said, "they'll never let you make that speech." His snigger was like a bicycle tyre rubbing against the fork of the speeding machine, "they'll shut you up - in all senses I suppose - in case the speech'd have an electrifying effect on the public gallery and send bodies of our good citizens running mad through the streets waving blackthorn sticks, old chair legs, umbrellas, betting slips, interview forms from the Labour Exchange, and copies of *An Phoblacht*, your pal's, the I.R.A.'s republic, that is, not Plato's."

His laugh ripped out loud and alone before the class which sat expressionless and silent, most of them with their arms calmly folded. McClery's face flushed scarlet.

"All right, then!" He crashed the book down on the desk narrowly missing Brian Davitt's hand which didn't stir, "You may think this fellow is a hero now, but just wait till the Justice down in the courts gets busy on him. He'll reduce him to that size," he held his thumb and forefinger a fraction apart, "He'll rub his fingers together and never notice he was there at all. So, get busy there on some real history. Fail any part of chapter ten this afternoon and by Golly! The tumbrels will roll. And a few fat heads as well!" He turned to the door and wrenched it open.

"Well now, Mr. Idler, mischief-making Bolton, I know you're real hot at public disturbances, but you're not going to disturb any more classes here today. So, go on, boy! Walk out of here. Your public's waiting impatiently for your appearance in your latest comedy. Queues are already forming for the early editions of both the *Evening Herald* and the *Evening Mail* which may well turn out to be collectors' items. You know what collectors are, don't you? You see them driving around in their big lorries from dustbin to dustbin. Out, boy! Out!"

Pearse sidled out past him - Jesus, if he touched against him there'd be a short-circuiting explosion in a shower of blue sparks! - and began to walk calmly, and with dignity he hoped, down the broad staircase. Two landings down, in spite of his firm resolve, his legs responded to his urgent wish to hurry fast and far from the hateful encounter and he found himself skipping, stumbling, clattering headlong to the ground floor.

In the hall he turned and stared with stinging eyes back up the stairs through the galaxies of dust drifting in a pale beam from the skylight under which McClery was undoubtedly lurking, the inevitable leer of glee on his thick farmer's handsomish face at having heard the painful clatter of the descent. "Slinky dung-booted bogman!" he whispered to the dusty silence of the staircase. "What will you ever do to have history remember you, even as a footnote - dole out three on each hand to some poor, harmless bugger for missing one of the prohibitions in Poyning's Law?" He drew on himself the arch dignity of a fully-betrayed French marquis walking with measured tread from the portals of his prison to the awaiting tumbrel before which slouched a mangy old mule with the thick face of McClery. As he passed the statue of the Blessed Virgin he muttered a quick prayer for her guidance and protection in whatever lay before him and in a fierce tug pulled the heavy door shut behind him. In its loud crash both Franco and McClery slumped to the ground in a barrack square drilled through the heart by Lieutenant Bolton who at the last minute, a gun in each hand, had stepped forward to take the place of a soldier whose nerve had failed him. No firing squad fiasco this time!

He moved with the ease of a swimmer into the morning hush of the sedate square passing the tall, stern houses whose high haughty windows returned on him the blank uncomprehending stare of women he drew close to in the street the better to caress his eyes over their unbelievable beauty. But the windows were far more discouraging than the unfriendly glances of the adored goddesses for behind the blind glass of any one of them might be lurking the Mad Axeman waiting and watching for the most unguarded moment to strike. He persuaded the raw, lonely drift of dismay through his heart that at seventeen a fellow is too big to cry and shouldn't even want to. And he would hold back the tears now just as he had at breakfast when the large, grey drops formed in his mother's eyes and bounced from her cheeks into her already over-watery porridge. He crouched under the barrage that followed her squall of crying, admitting ruefully to himself that the besieged in the Alcazar down in Spain didn't know how well-off they were with only shells and bombs and snipers bullets and falling walls to contend with. Bring his mother to bear on the place and the seige would collapse in a day! The sound of her voice was as unnerving as a shell dead on target - you! - its message almost as devastating: "Trouble is all you are to me, do you know that, trouble, trouble, nothin' but trouble. And to think of all I had to go through bearin' you an' rearin' you an' slavin' for you an' prayin' for you an' in the end, all I wind up with is trouble!" In full cry she filled his head with the wail of a banshee she could easily replace outside the walls of some haunted, condemned castle with her interminable theme of trouble: " I've had nothin' else but trouble since the day you and your sister were born, trouble, trouble mornin', noon, an' night to keep you clean-livin' an' respectable, an' nicely-dressed an' well-fed; to make sure you go to regular mass, confession, and holy communion; to warn you an' warn you to keep away from bad company on the street an' at school, and all the time havin' to work my fingers to the bone to give you a good education an' me with no husband to help me! And then in the heel o' the hunt what do you go and do but turn around an' get yourself arrested. God, think o' the disgrace o' that! May God in his infinite mercy look down on us! An' what'll the neighbours say?"

He crouched as one of the besieged over the table balancing the black crust of a Kennedy's loaf on the chipped edge of his bowl wondering was it because he, too must have had a mother like her that Sherlock Holmes took that leap with Moriarty down the Reichenbach Falls? An interesting theory to brood on, but later when there was no wailing going on his head. Listening to her, he fought down the dismay writhing within him, begging to be released in a howl of tears. He was on the point of crying out: "O.K. I admit everything! I'm alive and breathing so I must be as guilty as hell. Of whatever it is! So put the rope around my neck and get it over with," But just in time she turned in to another station which was a relief even though it was only a repeat of the old boring programme of: "Ah, well, if that's what Almighty God has in store for me, I suppose there's nothin' for it but to accept His holy will! I always thought my life would turn out so differently, that my children would be a blessing to me. But no! That wasn't to be! So let His holy will be done and eat up your stirabout there, it'll put the red neck on you for the day that's in it." The crust tipped off the edge and went hurtling down into the breaking waters far below. He fished it out of his lumpy porridge and laid it on his plate. Why couldn't the whole gang of them leave him alone today? - his mother, the fellows in the class, Franco, McClery, the Mad Axeman? He threw back his broad shoulders and listened to the rhythmic thud of his new shoes on the wide, rain-greasy pavement. He was well shut of them! The happiest moments of his life were those wrapped in his snug aloneness as he moved as an all-seeing, recording eye through the bustling night streets of the city, the Eyes and Ears of the world, looking at everything, missing nothing, storing everything up to be used for some great, unspecified task in the future. And so in the aloneness of his soul he moved on towards his ordeal which he would face alone with courage and dignity. On one plane, with the cold scorn of Parnell, he would fling his speech from the dock into the teeth of a hostile world while on another he would observe all that happened in the courts with the technical detachment of a kind of all-seeing photographic intelligence.

In the distance voices calling. His name on the wind! Swinging round he saw several figures running down the square towards him. With sinking heart he recognised Brian, Dev, and - he could hardly believe it - his twin sister Kathleen in her navy-blue school mackintosh, her hair, as she ran, streaming out like black smoke behind her. God, what were they doing here? Surely Dev wasn't in earnest when he said some of them were thinking of doing a bunk and coming with him to the courts? He couldn't have that. He wanted no one who knew him to be present when he made his speech from the dock. Although of course it would be quite in order for the judges to hear it, how could he stand up before his school mates and roll out such phrases as: "to the vindictiveness, the arrant cruelty of the sentence the law in its crass ignorance has seen fit to lay upon me, I have nothing whatsoever to say that would not be redolent with contempt. But as to why my character should be cleared of the foul slanders laid on it by the lackeys of the Law and as to why my motives should remain unencumbered by the deliberate misinterpretations inflicted on them by those who claim that they seek only to arrive at the truth, I have much, yes very much indeed, my Lords, to declare...."

Should Kathleen be present for the likes of that her piercing laugh would shrivel him up before he was even half-way through the opening paragraph of the speech. So what chance would there be of getting to the grand climax?

They came up with him, bright-eyed and disturbingly shrill, sparkling with a restless abandon that shook the foundations of his resolve to remain calm and clear-thinking for the tests of the day. He might have guessed he would not have got very far before the Mad Axeman sent for reinforcements. Something Kathleen did made him particularly uneasy. Her sharp, dark features were alive with subtle nuances of expression as if a mature woman of wide experience of life and the world was striving to divest herself of the disguise of girlhood.

"You never told us you had a sister!" Dev said in the hushed tones in which he recited the Hail Holy Queen!

"Louser!" Brian joked in a sneer, his cold eyes hard on Kathleen, "You were keeping her a secret, a real priceless treasure of a secret!"

"I knew right away," Kathleen's voice held that vital throb he loved to listen for in the voices of women heard on the tram or on the streets late at night. "I knew them from when you pointed them out in last year's college photograph."

"But what - what are you doing here?" He looked anxiously at her, "Ma will throw a fit if she knows you're mitching from school."

"But I'm not! I told the Reverend Mother I had to go to the dentist and the old eedjit believed me. When Ma said she couldn't get off work to come to the courts, I knew I just had to come so that someone from your own family would be there to give you encouragement and support. Sure you just can't go on your own."

"Oh yes I can. And I wish you hadn't told a lie at school on my account." He hated that Brian and Dev should learn his mother had to go out to work to support his sister and himself. He shook his head in admonition.

"You don't seem at all glad to see me, do you?" Kathleen's resemblance to his mother became more pronounced, which was always a bad sign. Brian sank on one knee before him.

"Let me plead for the hand - I mean for the right of your sister to accompany you to the courts, sire!"

"Don't be making a laughing jackass of yourself, " Dev looked down on him in scorn, "And in addition you've got the knee of your trousers on a sticky sweet paper."

"I just didn't want you to feel all alone, that's all." Tears glistened in Kathleen's eyes. God the heavy artillery already! "Sure what could be more natural than that and we twins as well which everybody knows we're closer than most. What real objection could you have against me going to the courts with you anyway?"

"Nothing at all!" Even as he was saying it he knew she could tell he was lying. One of the disadvantages of being closer than most! Her moist eyes gleamed with sharp sorrow in the clear air. Any second now her tears, large grey and terribly wet would start to bounce off her cheeks just like his mother's at breakfast. As if her porridge wasn't salty enough already!

"Alright!" he said quickly watching her eyes in dread, "I'll let you come with me if you agree to do everything I tell you. You will appreciate that I need all my wits about me today and so I can't afford to let anyone or anything distract me."

"But I'm only trying to help!" Her phrase filled him with foreboding.

"Of course! I know that." He hated the insincerity of his reassuring gesture of patting her clumsily on the back of the hand as if trying to keep back the dreaded outflow of tears.

Brian shouldered his way past Dev.

"You see, Kathleen," he said, his hard eyes narrow and gleaming like a predatory animal awaiting the best moment to spring, " I was right when I said he wouldn't really mind if we came with him."

"Do you mean you two are coming as well?" Just in time he managed to switch off his look of alarm.

"Why do you think we're after bunking out of college?" Brian asked, "We wouldn't miss this show for the world, would we, Dev?"

Had Brian's voice lingered a little scorn on the word 'show'? Later, when it was all over, he would have to return to that moment and listen to the voice again.

"In coming with you," Brian wore a kind of amused sneer, "We're proving who your real friends are, aren't we?"

That's what Brian's chin when he was speaking reminded him of, a downy, spotted peach being bobbed up and down on the end of an absurd string.

"Thanks very much, " he lowered his giveaway gaze, "but I'm not keen to be standing in the dock by people who know me. It doesn't feel right somehow."

"You're, not afraid are you?" Delight shone from Brian's eyes.

"Of course not! Each time I become aware that people I know well are in court looking at me, I'll get distracted. That's all I'm afraid of, for I need all my attention to concentrate on the charge, the evidence, the cross-questioning and so on."

To his shrivelling shame Kathleen took both his hands in hers and looked into his eyes in a manner he was pleased to allow her in the privacy of home when she was coaxing him to agree to something or other as if he were a sulky child. He tried to tease his hands out of her surprisingly hard grasp, hating this new view of him being afforded gratis to his school fellows.

"If I thought for a moment we'd distract you," Kathleen said, her face so close that the fresh warmth of her body enveloped him as an intimate breath, "I'd turn round and go back and persuade Brian and Dev to go with me. But honest to God, we won't distract you. The fact that we're there will be a support for you. You'll be glad of that when you're standing all alone up there in the dock."

He tugged desperately against the unyielding grip of her hands. He felt Brian and Dev crane forward the better to see what was going on. The sun flashed a blinding yellow message from a brass plate below the letter-box of a door on the far side of the street. The dead weight of doom in the pit of his stomach told him no rescuing troop of cavalry would see the signal for help and come their way at the gallop. Nothing would now prevent the grinning savages from tying him to the stake.

"All right then!" he said, at last drawing his hands free from her grasp, "But this is not a show" - the unfortunate word slipped out - " I mean, just a day off from school. So let's have no horsing about or any other kid stuff like that. That is a very serious matter to me."

"Oh we can all see that," Brian said startling him by shooting away from him walking backwards down the square.

The others surged forward one on either side of him and he stumbled into step between them, a silently screaming James Cagney being dragged by prison guards towards the electric chair.

"Hey, Kathleen!" Below Brian's beady eyes his mouth moulded a gormless grin, "Know the forst thing popped into my head when you said you told the Reverend Mother you were going to the dentist? I thought: at last! at last I see the light! At last I know what job I want to do in life. So Franco can stick the lie I told him about wanting to be a Civil Servant up his jersey. Oh, brothers probably don't wear those, do they? Anyway thanks to you, Kathleen, I've decided to be a dentist."

Pearse caught a hushed groan and a whispered "Oh Christ!" from Dev. On Kathleen's face there was a wide, almost lewd grin of anticipation, disgustingly larger than life, disturbingly older than her years.

"Marvellous job!" Brian said skipping backwards away from them, "Imagine, beautiful girls like you Kathleen coming in to see you all day and you with nothing else to do but sit them down comfortably, put them at ease and be really nice and kind to them."

"Especially," Dev jeered, " When you dig your knee in their chest and start to drag out their front teeth."

Kathleen turned a cold, expressionless profile to Dev her eyes warm on Brian skipping gaily down the road, his head coming gradually into direct line with the green grooved pillar of a wrought-iron street lamp. Pearse licked his lips,

"Look out!" Kathleen called out, unfortunately just in time. Brian burped a laugh and swerved round the lamp standard and into the roadway from where in a series of short skipping steps he swung behind them in an adroit move that brought him between Kathleen and Dev.

"Great view from here, isn't there?" He chatted into

Dev's white set face. Kathleen seemed to have grown taller swaying beside Brian in the sensuous flowing movements of a dancer enchanted by the sensations of her own body. In a hitch of surprise he saw she was wearing high heels. She'd obviously smuggled them into the convent in her school satchel and slipped them on in the lav on the way out. He sighed his surprise envy of this new Kathleen beside whom, he was humiliated to discover, he felt uneasy, distressingly juvenile, foolishly awkward in his movements, feelings, and thoughts. He hardly recognised in her the mild, characterless young girl who flitted hardly perceived on the periphery of his mind in which he always maintained a firm division between the world of his home and that of the college. Those two worlds had now come unexpectedly together in the taut group beside him about whom the air vibrated with disturbing, unspoken suggestions. Brian in particular exuded the air of sleazy sensuality which always hung over the group that gathered each lunchtime outside the back lavatory in the college to tell the latest round of dirty stories or some of the older filthier ones if the new stories weren't crude enough. God, as if he hadn't enough on his mind today! Why oh why hadn't he been more firm with Kathleen? If the others hadn't been there watching, he would have snatched his hands from her grasp and ordered her back to school. He should have done that anyway which would have raised his status with them and shown in no uncertain manner he wished to go to the courts alone. But the moment had passed. Now he would have to endure the unease of their presence not only in the courts but in the journey there as well during which he had planned to rehearse in his mind some of the more complex, convoluted sentences in his speech from the dock.

At the end of the square Brian surging ahead crossed to the far pavement, the other two close behind and entered a laneway, a short cut to the quays. The blind wall on the right of the long narrow thoroughfare was cluttered with various pieces of second-hand furniture set on the pavement opposite a terrace of dowdy shops, their windows crammed with an assortment of objects from that nebulous area between worthless junk and genuine antiques - brown-gravy pictures, crudely cheery vases, brash brassware of uncertain function, weepy china ornaments and other types of bric-a-brac. His mind sheered away from them, shuddering at the ugliness of the souls that had produced them, the shallowness of the souls they would appeal to.

"Hey, get a load of this!" Brian sprang away from them and flopped onto the striped mattress of a double-bed, raising a shriek from its springs and a succession of bell-like tinklings from its brass fittings. He mouthed an enviably good imitation of Mae West: "Come up and see me sometime, Buster, when I've nothin on but the radio!"

Kathleen's delighted laugh bit into his mind like the Axeman's favourite weapon.

A voice bellowed out from the dark cave of the facing shop,

"Hould on there, mae girril, I'm comin'!" On the instant a sinewy man in a grey cloth cap and grease-shiny muffler bustled into sight and swung at Brian's legs with the rusty, curved scabbard of a cavalry sabre.

"Gerroff me good bed there, you rotten little neck-stretcher! If I get near enough to you there's one ting you won't have on an' that's yer big ignorant head."

Brian bounded from the bed and stumbled into a headlong run from the flailing scabbard. The man swung round, paused redeyed and came towards Pearse, the scabbard thrust forward towards his face.

"You put him up to that, didn't you? You tink if you stay quiet with that long face on you I won't know you're the leader o' the gang!"

Ducking in alarm from the thrusting scabbard, Pearse clutched Kathleen by the arm and broke shamefully into a run followed by Dev whom he saw conducted an elaborately leisurely, show-off retreat that went unnoticed by Kathleen whose face bore a grave look of concern for Brian who waited for them nonchalantly at the farther end of the lane.

"What the hell do you think you're doing?" Pearse panted at him and went on in spite of Kathleen's gasp of disapproval, "Do you think I'm in the mood for this sort of kid's stuff today?"

"Was only trying to cheer you up," Brian sneaked a look at Kathleen, "You know, to keep your mind off what's ahead of you. You're probably more worried than you realise about how the thing may go today and the kind of sentence you might get. Most of the guys they've tried so far have all gone off to the clink."

"You see, he was only trying to help," Kathleen said, the peevishness, the bitter impatience of his mother in her voice, "That oul fella didn't hurt you, did he?"

"Only as much as Mae West might have," Brian leered

a smile at her, which she acknowledged in a shrill, ringing laugh. Pearse gritted his teeth, "I can manage quite well without that kind of cheering up," he hated the way a large, passing woman with bright red cheeks looked with expressionless curiosity into his flushed face, "I want no more of it." He saw that the woman was looking back at their little group, "Are you listening at all?" He asked Brian, "Do you understand what I'm saying?"

"Ja, mein General!" Brian, beady-eyed, sprang into the air and brought his heels together in a metal click, "Your faithful followers obey!" He shot his arm forward in a stiff Nazi salute, his thrusting fingers passing so close to Pearse's cheek he felt the wind of their passage, Pearse stepped back surprised at his sudden expression of overwrought consternation.

"O mein gott! What's happening to me?" Brian wailed. With his other hand he took hold of his saluting arm, just below the elbow, and clowned an immense, luridly-anxious effort to bring it down lower, "I've been taken over by Hitler!" he gasped and sprang into a brisk, slanting march as if the rest of him was being pulled forward by the power of his extended arm. "Help! Help!" he called marching into the street at the end of the lane and turning right into the morning crowds.

"You ought to be in a circus," Dev sent a sneering call from behind, "preferably one on tour abroad. In some country where they still have cannibals."

"You don't understand the joke," Kathleen's nose aimed at some point way above Dev's head, "Don't you see how clever he is?" She called after the stomping figure: "Don't mind the remarks, Brian, that's a great game you've got going there with the hand."

"Yeah - I mean Ja!" Brian, still saluting, slowed until she came up with him, "You know, Kathleen, you'd be amazed at all the great games I can get going with this hand."

Pearse winced at his tone of deliberate over-innocence and looked away from Dev to conceal his expression of horror. As he walked along behind them - Brian at the salute, Kathleen trilling out silly laughs, Dev pounding the pavement as if to break it - he began to nod his head in tempo with the insistent, muttering monologue in his mind that kept on producing example after example to support the basic contention that for some unknown reason fate had a hell of a grudge against him. And there was no doubt at all that you had to be eternally on your guard against the plots it was always hatching against you as if it were the brains behind some organisation of psychopaths dedicated to the propagation of despair and despondency. That was even more true when things were going well for on those occasions, unfortunately rare, when you went humming your happy way round the corner who were you certain to walk slap into but the Mad Axeman, the grim reality of life itself, waiting for you as if by appointment.

Like that evening last summer that started out so well. He allowed the others to move on ahead of him, holding on to their mere movement and noise as a sort of afterthought, while he allowed his heart to suffer again a pang of love for the beauty of the girl's face floating into memory like a living vision superimposed on the sordid ordinariness of the common street, a vivid, pleading vision wordlessly telling of love that appeared often in the orgies with himself which in the morning he refused to think about regarding them as something performed by a being with whom he was only tenuously connected. Imprinted on his soul forever would be the magic of the moment she came towards him from out of the midst of his beloved city crowds. At first he was speechless that such a beautiful creature should choose to speak to him above all the rest considering all the times he had come up to girls, looked longingly in their faces and turned abruptly away from their blank or hostile stares. "I want to be with you," she said, laying her gentle hand on his elbow. No she didn't! You had to stick to the truth and nothing but the truth, today of all days, so help me God! "I hope you don't think I'm being cheeky in speaking to you in the street," is what she said - or was quite close to it - in a clear accent very like McSwiney's who came from Donegal. Surrounding the points of red, like two paint splashes on her cheeks, her skin had a distinctly bluish tinge especially where it verged on her jet-black hair. "You see, I've lost my bus fare," she said, "and I don't know my way on foot back to Leeson Park where I'm staying with my aunt. Can you help me, please?" Could he help her! At that moment, had it been raining, he would have whipped off his jacket for her to walk on. Even though that fellow was an Englishman.

He walked beside her through the evening crowds thrilling again to her intimate accent - it was honest and direct like the touch of a friendly hand. Gradually, as his shyness fell away, he allowed himself to revel in the good fortune of walking beside a meltingly, beautiful girl of about his own age not too tall and a little broad where other girls were slim, with marvellously well-developed breasts. His fingers tingled to touch them. To his annoyance, Brian broke through his reverie with a cry for help. He saw he was holding his extended arm pressed hard against a brick wall, his feet noisily stamping time. They were on a corner.

"Kathleen! Kathleen!" Brian called, "For God's sake take hold of that mad arm and lead it into the next street or we'll be stuck here all day."

Pearse hovered in a limbo of waiting in which he recovered from early childhood his impression of that place as a vast overcrowded hall damp with un-baptised babies wailing forever outside the back door of heaven. And moved on again on the leash of Kathleen's increasingly maddening laugh which this time he determined would not intrude on the magic of the moments in which he walked in the warm dusk across the length of the city talking to the girl about what he couldn't remember now, but whatever it was he had carried it off with an amazing confidence as if he were used to going about with girls all the time, instead of just gazing at them with shy longing from afar. What would she have thought of him if she knew that like a hunter, itching to pounce on his prey, he spent hours trailing girls and full-figured women through the lamp-lit streets longing to stand in front of them and open his heart and say mad things like: "When I look at you I see all the beauty of creation!" or "Your beauty goes through me like flashes of lightening!" or "Your legs move through me like dreams!" Mad things that if overheard by some guard would be enough to get him locked up for life. But he never spoke; he walked into the stone wall of their hostile stares and limped away. He determined she would never find out these things as he walked nonchalantly with her through the city dusk, her legs in point of fact moving through him like dreams. It was at the top of Kildare Street where a lounging guard ran his cold eye over them that the ground pitched beneath him and he had the sense of things returning to rotten old everyday usualness, of the Mad Axeman lurking about somewhere ahead sharpening with gleeful anticipation his dread weapon on the flagstones of the street. But how nice, how beautiful to linger now over the events of the brief interval after that before the axe swung down, dead on time. Why couldn't memories like those be real, lingering minutes and not just flashes in the mind no sooner glimpsed than gone? Above all, those sweet minutes on the doorstep of her aunt's house when he looked down into her smoky grey eyes and knew with a certainty he never questioned that he could take her in his arms and kiss her! He put his hands lightly round her waist resolving that no matter how sorely the devil would be sure to tempt him, he would not be led by even such a tender beauty as hers into really serious sin like the missioners were always blasting off about in the pulpit. Definitely no upstairs or downstairs business. Who had called it that? Who else but his mother, leaning over the backyard, wall, his father's old bedroom slippers on her feet, gossiping with scaldy-eyed old Mrs. Wilson about the unmarried girl down the road who was about to have a baby. "Sure that wan'd let any fella in downstairs an' not even bother to ask him his name." God forbid he should ever be involved in anything like that! In the brownish dusk he hovered in a cloud of joy with the girl whose moist red lips slowly parted as she brought her face close to his. His arms tightened about her drawing the yielding joy of her soft body firm against him.

He looked up as if for a rest and saw that Kathleen and Dev were still following on behind Brian who was sending a strain of his usual corny wisecracks back over his shoulder, drawing that idiotic shrieking laugh from Kathleen, He returned to the girl taking up his memory at the point where she began to raise her face towards his, her moist lips slightly parted. You might as well enjoy the good part of it for as long as you could. He bent his head once more towards the lure of those lips unsure of exactly where to move his head to avoid ramming his nose into hers. And then their lips came together, hotly, sinking into each other in a sweet heart-bounding DRRRNNNGGG! shrilling, shrieking through his nerves, a demonic DRRRNNNGGG! blasting out of the old dark house as if every burglar alarm and Mad Saul in the city was scampering down the stairs trying to drrrnnnggg their way out of there. He sprang away from the girl and saw that her back had pressed against a vertical metal panel on which there were about eight or nine white push buttons each with its printed card beside it bearing the name of the occupant of each flat into which the doorbell had sent its mad summons. He flung away from the house to an outburst of angry voices, the winching open of upstairs windows, the thin wail of the girl's voice growing fainter behind him as he fled: "Don't leave me! Me aunt'll murder me!" With his unerring sense of timing the Mad Axeman had struck again. As no doubt he would later in the courts. He peered out of his reverie and saw they were walking along by the grey, gritty wall of the river. He must have spent longer than he thought dwelling on the beauty of that poor girl. What a rotten thing to do to have run away! Whatever else he should never have done that! Shame seethed in him all over again as it did through the weeks following that night when he had gone about with a blush of shame permanently on his face, like sunburn. In Dev's slouch just in front of him he detected a muffled, smouldering anger against Brian who clumped along beside Kathleen one foot on the pavement, the other scattering to the winds the usual rash of litter in the gutter. Both arms were swinging by his side. Was it a leg game now?

"Arrh, Jim 'awkins laad!" Brian spoke in a harsh English accent, "In the same broadside as ol' Pew lost 'is deadlights, I 'ad me leg carried away! Arrh! It lets the draught in at the other side something woeful! Fifteen men on a dead man's chest, yo ho ho and a bottle of rum!" He changed to his everyday voice, "If you'd just drunk a whole bottle of rum and fifteen guys with wooden legs hopped up and down on your chest in a sailor's hornpipe, you'd be good an' dead too!"

Kathleen's laugh - at such tripe! - trilled out like the bells shrieking from the dark bulk of the house, slicing through him like Saul's knife. What a mean, cur-like turn to leave the poor girl to face the consequences of her aunt's anger all alone! He should have stayed and apologised to the aunt for leaning his elbow on the bell buttons in a moment of abstraction. Running away was the sort of low-down act you'd expect from a sly fellow like Brian - God, why hadn't he remembered that before? - who was rumoured to have gone all the way with a girl guide at a week-end camp in Powerscourt the time he was in the Baden Powell Scouts before the brothers found out he was a member and got him to leave. Fat little McDermott knew all about it and every time he used to repeat the story with a hush of horror in his voice: "And she was only fourteen-and-a-half!" Brian came back out of the gutter laughing beady-eyed into Kathleen's adoring face. Pearse's soul shrivelled in dread. Was he no better than that fellow? Surely that's what his running away had shown him! That night, before he had realised what he was doing, he was in full flight away from her, borne along by his desperate limbs which seemed to have a mind and a will of their own. Why had he done that? He shuddered, loath to go over all that old ground again. It had something to do with the suspicious way the policeman had eyed them at the corner of Kildare Street. And of course with the delightful feeling that surged through him when her soft body merged in joy with his. To experience those kinds of feelings was bound to be as deep into mortal sin as you could get. And with the first shriek of the bells came a vision of his mother's hard, angry face screaming condemnation at him. Yet bad as his running away had been, hadn't he more than made up for it in the other situation which was far more dangerous? He had stood his ground when all around him grown men were running away on all sides some emitting the sort of mindless screams you hear from terrified children of a wet Saturday afternoon in Woolworths when their hard-eyed mothers turn on them with angry shouts and swinging blows about the ears and face. An enduring national pastime as his own ears and face well remembered. Maybe it would make up for the cowardly act of running away when in the courts he would stand firm and unafraid in the dock returning glare for glare with his accusers! He squared his shoulders and swung into a military stride which almost brought him full tilt into Dev's slumped back.

Brian broke away from Kathleen and curled his arm around one of the saplings growing within its iron corslet at the margin of the pavement. He looked back at her in a cheery confident grin that held a hint of contempt in it. In an over-ripe, fruity tenor he sang out: "Aye font to kaarf yor name on hervery three."

"Oh I love Richard Tauber, don't you?" Kathleen drooped her head sideways her eyes large and dreamy, "Lilac Time was such a lovely fillum, me mother an me cried all through it."

"You can do that any time on my shoulder," Brian said coming back to join her, a hard glitter in the slits of his eyes.

Pearse looked over the river wall and wondered were he to vomit up the disgust of his heart would he hit the lone swan bobbing on the brown swell of the incoming tide. But that wouldn't be fair to that fellow Gogarty who vowed to the river as he swam for his life across it that if he escaped the assassin's bullets he would provide a pair of swans to grace its dark waters. Across the road, the bookshop he had never managed to find open for business had boxes of jumbled books on frail-looking stands before each of its grime-scribbled windows. Through the shadowy gap of its part-opened doorway he saw wavy tiers of volumes leaning against each other like old campaigners. A tall, young man in a fawn raincoat lounged against the nearer stand moving his lips above a leather-bound book as if tasting its contents. How marvellous it would be to have nothing else to do all day but lounge over there free of the apprehension of time moving through you like the progress of a relentless spear! They turned their backs on the river and went on towards the courts. He allowed his eyelids to droop, filtering out the hard grey light, and listened to the fall of his foot steps one after the other on the blurred pavement.

"We're nearly there" Dev said at his side breaking in on the list he was compiling of the books he had read in the past few years. He must read H.G. Well's *The Food of the Gods* again. It made you aware of your mind expanding in your head like a brilliant globe of light powered by knowledge, wisdom and intelligence that raised you to a giant's height above the pointless, scurrying life of puny men. Who were no longer scurrying about beside or ahead of him as they had been since they joined him in the square but were walking slightly behind in a meek, cautious silence in which neither of his schoolmates paid any attention to Kathleen. With sinking heart he saw they were already in the shadow of the courts. So soon? Just a couple of dreams and a few haphazard memories and half your life's gone! Two policeman stood silent and grim on the steps above him. What had they against the tremulous beauty of the world that they stood dark and no doubt armed against it? People were moving in and out of the great doorway leading into the courts with the unpredictable dashes and pauses of fish in some far-off shadowed river - where he wished with all his heart he could be at that moment. Head high he went up the steps of the scaffold, another martyr for old Ireland, steady and serene, completely unmoved by the sight of the awaiting noose, the big zero of life. And tripped against the basket of a cat-faced woman in a valentia straw hat, calling out in a throaty belch: "Bunches of violets!" Lovely bunches of violets, sor!" He had the uncanny feeling of being part of a play, the wrong play, something like *The Old Lady Says No*. To hope! He drew deep on the trembling air, as if laying in extra supplies against suffocation and despair and headed on into the building. In the cramped hall, loud, bodied-tanged air swept warm over him. Against the sick-green walls people lounged, some alone with despair, others in tight, anxious groups, all of them wearing worry and concern like scare-healed scars on their faces. Self-important personages - solicitors, clerks, hardened criminals - bustled in and out of the several rooms leading to the hall, their manner embarrassingly reminiscent of McDermott and himself when they played the English spies out to capture Red Hugh O'Donnell in the college play last Christmas: "Irish dog, we have you in our power!" Ah, yes, but who was the Irish dog today and what dungeon in Dublin Castle would he find himself in before the day was through? In *The Old Lady* it was Robert Emmett but he had a shrewd suspicion that In the Mad Axeman's play he was to be the chosen victim. A man in a dark, greenish uniform came over and snapped his fingers at him.

"Got your summons there, young fella?"

He fumbled in his inside pocket and carefully separated his summons sheet from his speech from the dock which with all the traffic it had experienced already must be fairly ruffled by now.

"That's to be heard in there" the man said nodding his

head more than you'd think necessary at a door the colour of a coffin.

Brian came over and nodded at the man in the same loose-headed manner.

"Who's trying the case?" he bobbed his head like one of the mechanical Santa Claus's or gnomes in a Christmas display shop window.

The official stepped back from Brian aiming a suspicious under-lidded glare at him.

"Oul Sour Belly's on the bench," he said "and as you seem to be so mad for information let me tell you that he's in rare oul form this mornin'. He's galloped through each case in about five minutes and so far no one's got less than six months. So I don't suppose I'll see you or your pals noddin' around here again for some time, eh?"

Pearse yearned at the semi-circle of sky he glimpsed through the fanlight above the door. Or was it above Reading Gaol? He had never allowed his imagination to wander beyond that historic moment in the courtroom when the dying falls of the closing phrases of his speech would echo through the vast amphitheatre lighting like a soft, persuasive caress on the rapt faces of the audience who in the long swoon of silence following the speech would sit stunned and astounded, their hearts overflowing with amazement and admiration that a person so young could be at once so brave, so noble, so strikingly handsome. A voice tolled now from the heart of that rapt silence - "Six months!" God, were he to get six months that would really finish him with the army interview board. There would be no point in taking the examination, and for a bit of the Axeman's good measure he would miss the summer holidays as well.

"In if you're going, son," A solicitor festooned with papers looked impatiently at him and passed into the courtroom, Brian and Kathleen were both staring at him with that expression of mingled horror, apprehension and glee that is reserved not just for the dead but for the well dead.

"Where's Dev? he asked, suddenly missing his presence.

"Pagin' Dev Murphy! Pagin' Dev Murphy!" Brian intoned moving with a robot's stiff-legged clump about the hall, "Pagin' Dev Murphy the notorious associate of Doctor Crippen, Al Capone, Genghis Kahn and Mr McCabe the murderin' gardener of Malahide!"

Thankfully no one in the sick-green worry of the hall paid the slightest attention not even to Kathleen's idiotic laugh trilling out to remind him again of the metallic throb of the bells from the black bulk of the house in Leeson Park. Yes, it was perfectly despicable! But somehow he would make it up to her in the way he would conduct himself in the courtroom. Casting a long, lingering look behind in preparation for his departure from the hall, the world, he saw Dev shuffling past a group at the door.

"Wher'n the hell have you been? We've got crowds out looking for you, dragging the river," Brian pretended anger, "Were you collecting names for a petition for Pearse's release? Or selling ringside seats for the hanging?"

"It's always been a mystery to me, " Dev spoke in the

awed, hushed voice he used for reciting his favourite poem *The Convent Bell*, "how these women you see sitting in nooks and crannies all over the city manage to make a living from selling little binches of flowers? Sure who in Dublin ever stops to buy flowers? Even for their mother's birthday? So I went over to that woman in the Spanish hat out there on the steps and bought this." He raised his cupped hand from his hip and presented Kathleen with a bunch of violets.

"For me? She took the flowers in her hand, hardly glancing at them, fluttering her eyelids. Where had she learned that? Her eyes played over Dev as if he were some wondrous and significant object she had unexpectedly come upon. Rather like the occasion in the Daily Market when his mother was examining a floral chamber pot and saying: "Isn't that just gorgeous! Who'd have thought there was such beautiful things as that in all the world?" Dev looked like a man assailed with incurable toothache.

"Oh for Christ's sake!" Brian was surprised into real anger, "Let's cut out the fecking...." he mimed a violinist bowing an excruciatingly sentimental melody, "and get into the bloody courtroom with Pearse." Who sighed in exasperation at the blaze of raw anger in Brian's eyes, at the ridiculous experiment in psychic communication. Possibly it was blasphemous - alright, it was - but surely something like this lay behind Christ's agonised cry in the garden: "Could you not watch one hour with me?" He opened the door of the courtroom assailed by the uncomfortable thought that in spite of all the attendant inconveniences Christ must have been bloody glad to get up there at last onto the cross safe at last from the useless crowd who had been following him around, driving him half-crazy with their efforts to cheer him up, to keep his mind off the fate he had already prophesised for himself. "I wonder what sort of religious art we would have had if the electric chair had been invented in your man's day?" Gilmore had once whispered in his ear in the Long Room nodding at the crucifix on the wall beneath which Franco was sweatily at work doling out three on each hand to Hegarty. It was obvious that Gilmore was the sort of bad company his mother was always warning him against. Yet why was it he felt strangely drawn to the fellow, to a point not far short of the intimacy of real friendship? If only he could stop day-dreaming and spend all the time he would, thus save in the useful, creative and above all profitable ways set out in numbered sequence in that fateful article in Business Digest, there was so much he might get to understand about the twists and turns of his own mind and learn how best he might use it to live his life here on earth. On the other hand he always secretly feared that heaven might turn out to be a colossal disappointment inhabited by such good-living, religious people as his mother, Franco, Dev and McClery, a chillilly, healthy laugh-less place run by a sort of divine Axeman from a vast office full of files and forms in triplicate, and lists of vacancies for jobs in the celestial civil service.

  He paused inside the door of the courtroom and swallowed on his disappointment. What a dismally small place it was, totally unlike the Old Bailey as it appeared in court-case films! And, worse still, it was sordid with the presence of ordinary, everyday, nondescript people - the kind you saw all over town but never really noticed - nearly all of them well over thirty years of age - at least! What a dismal gang! Long gone over the hill and rolling down real fast on the far side! How could you expect - how could you even contemplate looking for - sympathy, understanding, and adulation from such a crowd of nonentities? Directly in front of him, huge and detailed as in an oil painting in the National Gallery, was the heavy weary face of the Justice on the bench - just a kind of raised-up desk - a cobweb of wrinkles stretching tight over his dry, grey skin. God, who else could he be but the hanging judge himself! A face straight off the cover of *Speeches from the Dock*! Cobra-green eyes flickered sickeningly into his and ranged over the murmurous bustling behind him where he discovered Brian and Dev were attempting to remain on either side of Kathleen as they worked their way through the crowd at the door. Hermann Cowan nodded to him over the back of a bench beneath the Justice and beckoned for him to come and sit near him. He began to weave his way towards the solicitor wondering about the layout of the cramped courtroom. Everything seemed to be on ground level, so where was the dock, the witness stand, the press table, the public gallery? He despaired that any manner of Justice could be done in a place as constricted and crowded as the lower deck of a tram during the rush hour and as full of rustling, scraping, scampering noises as the monkey-house in the zoo. As he edged his way between two of the benches murmuring apologies whenever he knocked against outstretched feet, the unsuspected barrier of brief-cases and parcels and at one point a gold-chained stomach, he heard a voice reading from a charge sheet and he listened intently more to the quaint phraseology than to the substance of what was being said. The clattering behind him made it difficult to concentrate on the full meaning of the words as Brian and Dev struggled for the privilege of sitting next to Kathleen who was following close behind him.

"We'll be on after this one," Herman Cowan smiled, his eyes narrowing shrewdly as they played over Kathleen who sat down with Dev - the winnah! - red-faced and ecstatic on the other side of her. In exasperation Pearse looked from Brian's angry face to Dev's glow of rapture, as if he had just received holy communion. Or was secretly sucking a bull's eye in class. He heaved a sigh of despair: had none of the three a thought to spare for him and for the coming ordeal he was about to endure the dread of which was already present in his legs which he feared would refuse to bear him to the dock, wherever that was, when they called his name?

"We've heard the charge against Conlin," he started at the boom of the Justice's voice, so deep and loud it seemed to emerge from beneath the bench, "So what in heaven's name are we waiting for now?"

He cringed at the harsh, no-nonsense Dublin accent which seemed specially created from rapping out such phrases as: "Six months!", "Life Imprisonment!". "Hanged by the neck!" With a start he realised that what the Justice meant by the charge was what had been communicated to the court in the quaint phraseology he had just heard. And now re-heard in horrified memory. He straightened poker-backed in his seat, his skin prickling in a goose-flesh of embarrassment.

"Kathleen," he whispered, "I think you ought to leave the courtroom for a bit. I don't think this case is suit-

able for you to hear. You know it's about.... It's about...."
He sought for the least shameful way to express the substance of the charge.

"It's about an oul fella who's charged with allowing his vehicle of public hire to be used for the purpose of prostitution."

Her matter of fact tone shocked him.

"I don't think you ought to stay to hear it," he said.

"I'm not going to leave you, so that's that," she said aloud attracting the flicker of the cobra-green eyes, "I don't care what else is going on here."

The Justice rapped on the bench until the hubub in the room lessened a little.

"What's the delay may I ask?" he enquired of the ceiling, "Our excellent police are commendably prompt in bringing charges against our good citizens. I wish they would be equally prompt in being present in court to substantiate them."

Pearse saw to his left a group of the usual, depressingly nondescript, everyday type of men sitting at a long table with notebooks open before them. God, were they what the generic term called the Press? Were they to be the channels through which his words would be conveyed to the columns of the newspapers? One of the men began to pick his nose and he quailed imagining the lurid, McClery leer that would most assuredly crease that broad red face as the reporter copied down the phrases of his speech from the dock. Somewhere a door slammed,

"Sorry, sor" A tall guard with rabbity front teeth and

squinting eyes shouldered his way towards a type of raised packing case around which a small group was standing for all the world like the groups you saw having a quiet chat about the previous night's debauchery after twelve o'clock mass on Sunday. He had given up attending late mass because of the embarrassing content of the chuckling conversations of the men near the street door which broke in on his efforts to follow the mass in his Roman Missel and improve his Latin at the same time. That article in Business Digest was literally crammed with useful ideas.

"But, Kathleen..." he tried again.

"Shh!" She gave him a small girl's jab with the point of her elbow. Hard as a flint and right in the solar plexus.

The Justice rapped curtly on the bench. People moved about the room apparently at random. Two of the reporters leaned back and giggled into each other's eyes like lovers on a bench in the Phoenix Park. Everything was so confusing he caught only some of the words in the brisk vocal rattle in which the guard was sworn in. A rift of silence followed in which - God, what was happening - something soft, was it fingers, began to caress his leg just above the knee. Startled he turned his head and found his face brushing against, almost snuggling into a tremulous, perfumed swelling which in a throb of terrified delight he knew to be a woman's bosom. He jerked back his head swooning in the candid gaze of an overpoweringly large woman of about thirty whose heavy make-up lent her an exaggerated, crimson smile. Soft hazel eyes enquired into his.

"Any chance of movin' up in the bed there a bit, mister," she whispered her eyes insinuating secret demands into his, "an' lettin' another poor lady in outa the cold?"

He hung in a stasis of numb delight until the great curve of her bosom with its shadowy cleft of rosy flesh heaved towards him again. He shuffled his bottom on the bench knocking against Kathleen who snatched a look at the woman and in a quick recoil stared pointedly in front of her as if studiously ignoring a shouted insult. Pearse tingled all over as the soft roundness of the woman's body pressed against his hip as if embracing it, the blood began to pound in his head, hammering fiercer still when the woman's motions in crossing her legs caused her tight black skirt to climb with a soft whisper up her enormous thighs revealing the black, lacey fringe of an undergarment. God, think of all the nights he had tracked woman across town like an F.B.I. agent on overtime and never once came as close as this to something really exciting - called life! Except of course on the night of the crazy bells when the Mad Axeman was on overtime as well. Is that the sort of thing Mr. Dodd meant when he sniggered to himself in class and said: "You will of course have noticed the dramatic irony in that?"

"Proceed, Guard Horan!" With an effort he wrenched his attention back to the Justice.

"I'm sorry for the delay, yor worship," The guard was saying as if gnawing through the phrase with his rabbity front teeth.

"Mr. X is present now here in court?"

"We have him now, certain sure. No mistake about it this time. On the last occasion you see..."

"Leave that for now, guard; and proceed please!"

"Right you be, sor!" The guard ran a finger round the rim of his stiff upright collar and rubbed it along the surface of the witness stand. The perfumed softness of the woman's breast wobbled against Pearse's shoulder as she leaned towards him to whisper into his ear,

"A mean oul screw tha' fella Guard Horan! To look at him you'd never tink that in his house it's his oul wife that wears the trousers. Even in bed they say. He'd lag his own mother just to keep in practice."

It was breathlessly impossible to escape the perfumed presence of her soft body although he knew Kathleen was darting suspicious glances round at him. The guard's voice rasped out again over a continuous undertumult of coughing, whispering, nose-blowing, foot-scraping against the grainy floor, all punctuated by the abrupt slamming of doors both in the restless room itself and in other parts of the agitated building. The sort of up-rush of noise you hear in church between the arrival of the priest in the pulpit and the opening broadsides of the sermon: "Tonight, my dear brethern, we shall deal with the brute lusts of flesh." He teased his shoulder away from the woman and with a soft, surrendering sigh eased it back again into the delight of her vast, comforting breast.

"....on the date in question was on me beat which covered Clare Street when the defendant drove up in his horse and cab and hiked to a halt outside Greene's Bookshop."

"Ah! A literary man!" The Justice glanced towards the reporters who grinned down into their notebooks.

"And where exactly were you stationed at the time, Guard Horan?"

"I was outside the door of Merrion Hall, sor."

"Waiting for the evening service to start?"

"No, yor worship," the guard said above the laughter, "It was so that the notes I was makin' should not get too wet. It was a showery night which was unusual for that time o' the year when you consider the fine spell o' settled weather...."

The woman's whisper was warm and moist against his cheek,

"A right sleeveen Horan is, A real peepin' Tom of a rotten oul scut!"

He nodded to her words, his scared reticence unclenching even more as he sagged sideways, deeper into the seemingly unending softness of her inviting body,

"The cab was stopped for some little time outside the bookshop," the guards voice rasped at a distance, "an' all the while the defendant, Conlin, was up there on the box obviously on the look-out for someone an' then the woman, Devrill came along and gave him a sign."

"Even though she wasn't far from the gospel hall, am I correct in assuming it wasn't the sign of the cross?" the cobra-green eyes flickered in the direction of the guard who tugged nervously at his collar.

"It wasn't, sor. Certain sure! She jus' stuck her thumb up in the air and waved it about."

"Just waved it about!" The Justice with a flicker towards the press table bent into his papers to make a careful note, "Is the lady in question present in court?"

he asked, looking up,

"Here y'are, your honour," called the woman moistly into Pearse's ear jolting him out of the melting delight of her contours. Sick with shame he saw her wave her hand in the air, the thumb pointing upwards.

"I see!" The justice played his suspicious green gaze over Pearse. As if most discouraged by what he saw, he returned to his papers. "Continue, Guard Horan!"

"Then Devrill went away, I think into Lincoln Place, and came back almost at once with Mr. X. and after some - er- some..."

"Speak up, Guard Horan! Haggling, did you say?"

"Consultation," the guard said as if he were meeting a difficult word in a reading lesson, 'After some time at this they seemed to reach an agreement and they got into the cab together. Devrill immediately drew down the blinds."

"How do you know it was Devrill?"

"She was bare." The guard blushed and struggled on through a hurricane of laughter, "I mean, her arm was bare to the elbow and she was wearin' a bracelet."

"For decency's sake no doubt!"

To Pearse's shame the woman too joined in the knowing, raucous laughter that rolled round the courtroom, encouraged it seemed from the press table where the reporters lolled about on their chairs like a drunken group in a privileged box at a low variety show in the Queens. Where was the dignity of the law you read about in detective stories?

"After she drew the "blinds," the guard wiped his sleeve

across his mouth and continued, "The cab proceeded away from me and went up the west side of Merrion Square past the National Gallery, in the direction of the other public buildings, the Natural History Museum and Leinster House."

The Justice paused over his notes,

"Did you say the Natural History Museum in Leinster House?"

"It's the government that's there, sor," The guard's puzzlement was not helped by the gusts of laughter beating with the steady rhythm of rain settling in for the day, "then the cab swung left and proceeded along the south side of the Square in the direction of Upper Mount Street...."

"....and the Pepper Pot! Guard Horan, while I'm sure that you're a godsend to tourists in the summer, please remember that most of us here know our Dublin. Delete all this guided tour information and get back to the bare facts of the case."

The woman yelped with delight and nudged Pearse in the ribs. One of the reporters bent over the table his head on his folded arms as if in a paroxysm of grief. Stealing glances to his left he saw that Kathleen was still staring red-eyed in front of her and that both Brian and Dev were leaning way back in their places, craning their necks the better to see the loud, laughing woman. Had they known before this that such things went on in the city at night? In his own interminable wanderings through the dark streets were things like this going on nightly right under his very nose, things he failed to comprehend because something prevented him from realising the significance of what he saw? It was like trying to crack a code to which you hadn't got the key. He had often seen men accosting women usually outside bright, noisy public houses and after a brief exchange of words walking away with them to the nearest dark, odorous lane in a brisk businesslike stride as if setting off for a long hike in the fresh air, an activity Franco was always recommending as terribly good for your health. And whether or not it was good for the health of the couples he had watched striding towards the nearest dark lane, he was only now beginning amazedly to admit to himself that he had always guessed correctly at the true nature of their business together but never allowed his mind to dwell on it. "You must keep your thoughts pure always" was a message dinned into him day and night by his mother. And he always did. But in the mean-time what was he missing? That really practical article in Business Digest stressed that you must be eternally vigilant not to pay too high a price for things which, though they look good in the catalogue, don't show any real profit at all.

"After a while," he returned his attention to the guard, "I saw the cab coming towards me along the north side of the square, on the park side,"

"Well it would need to be on that side, wouldn't it? Otherwise Conlin would be here on a traffic offence as well. So it came towards you, past Oscar Wilde's old home."

"Beggin' yor pardon, sor, there's no one o'that name in me notes."

"No, the Justice sighed, "Another case, another time."

Pearse hated the reporters' delight in noting down the remarks of the justice as if they believed he was trying the case expressly for their amusement. His fingers, hot and somewhat moist, pressed against his jacket feeling for the outline of the papers in his inside pocket. How could he ever make his speech from the dock to such an audience?

"Then the cab swung left again and went up the square past the National Gallary and...."

"Please! Not the tour again! Am I correct in inferring that the cab went right round the square a second time?"

"That's right yor worship,"

"And once again after that?"

"Oh no! He only did it twice in all."

"Was Conlin driving the hearse fast or slow?" the Justice's voice boomed out above the knowing sniggers. He leaned forward, frowning.

"Slow, sor."

"Was he walking the horse?"

"No, sor! He was drivin' in a sort of slow, jiggy trot." A squeal of delight broke from the woman and listening to the laughter rolling around the room, Pearse was reminded of an evening he had spent at the Royal with Brian who explained with arch amusement the subtleties of some jokes that were lost on him. "You seem to have led a real, sheltered existence," was a remark of Brian's from that night which rankled for weeks.

"In a sort of slow, jiggy trot" the Justice repeated, noting the remark down with great care. Or pretending to do so, A very dangerous man the Justice as was plain to see. A man after the Mad Axeman's own hard heart!

"Guard, are you familliar with *Madame Bovary* at all?" The Justice's brows were knitted as if he were involved in an intricate calculation like one of the aweful sums Franco set ten minutes from the end of the last lesson of the day.

"Sor...? Unless she's one of the Madames that go around with Madame Maud Gonne McBride who I detained last year during a protest outside Mount joy Prison."

"No, Guard, this is another kind of madame altogether. Pray continue!"

Who was the Madame Bovary he was talking about? Was she too part of the night life of the city that in all his wanderings he had failed to discover? He began to seethe with shame at the extent of his own ignorance. And wasn't there another mysterious lady his mother had once spoken about to a neighbour in a gobbling whisper, someone called Honour Bright whom Gilmore too had once mentioned and then clammed up having said: "It's well known in some circles who murdered her that night in the Pine Forest." God, to add to all the other mysterious goings-on, crimes as well, murders in fact! From now on there was nothing in the dark life of the surging city his searching eyes would miss, not a single detail, no matter how sordid, how sickening, how sinful!

At this point, the guard was saying, "I had stationed myself in a doorway near the bookshop from which I was able to observe Mr X and the Dervill woman descend from the cab. Mr. X was staggerin' about so I took it he was the worse for drink."

"The worse for what?" The Justice cupped his hands to his ear. The reporters grinned.

"Drink, sor. And so he was as we discovered later in the station. At this point however an argument developed between Mr. X and the Dervill woman, a loud, roarin' argument as to which o' them should, pay the cabman. "I thought it was you who was goin' to take care o' him", I heard Mr, X say, to which Devrill replied: "We agreed didn't we that the cab'd be a separate transaction."

"Liar!" the woman hissed against Pearse's cheek and crossed her legs in reverse order with a thrilling creak of cloth, a flashing glimpse of the top of her stockings and a strip of black suspender. Something in his throat threatened to choke him.

"Give'm a quid," Devrill said and Mr. X went on protestin'. At this point Conlin got down from the box waving his long whip and he asked Mr. X the followin' question:" The guard consulted his fold-over notebook, "Are you goin' to cough up the goino or am I goin' to have to get some bowsies I know to start draggin' you asunder? An' if I let these fellas loose at you they'll have to be dug outa you, do you realise that?" His very words. Then Devrill stuck her hand inside Mr. X's topcoat pocket and took out his wallet. "Why you rotton oul sight," she said, "You've a small fortune in there. If I'd known you were that flush I'd have charged you more. Give Mr. Conlin two pounds. He has that big oul horse to feed, not to mention the other oul mare, his wife could drink Lough Erne dry." Conlin then took the wallet from her and drew some money out of it, I couldn't see how much because Mr. X was staggerin' about all ways, wavin' his arms and protestin'. "For the love o' heaven" says he, "Leave me somethin' to take home. My wife will kill me if I leave her short of her housekeeping money." Devrill laughed at him and pushed him away with the flat of her hand. He's not a very robust man. "Go on back to your dreary oul Jane," says she, "It's because she leaves you short o' somethin' else that you come out lookin' for the likes o' me. An' not for the first time either. And put this in your pipe and smoke it, I was just as respectable as her once until I ran into the likes o' you! I bet you don't argue over money with her that leaves you nothin' sweet to remind you of her when you're out slavin' from dawn to dusk in your good corporation job to keep her offa the streets! Well, I'm not to be had for choice an' neither is Mr. Conlin. G'wan! Get Goin! If you put your skates on you'll be home in time to join her in a couple o' decades o' the rosary before yous get into your nice cold bed together with the picture of the Sacred Heart lookin' down on the two o' yous to make sure you behave yourselves," Her very words! An' I was real shocked by them. Anyway, Mr. X wouldn't go away. He kep staggerin' about until I feared he might fall down under the hoofs o' the horse. "Yous have robbed me," says he, "If there was a bobby about I'd get the two of yous lagged." His very words! At this point I came out of the doorway and accosted the three of them. "I want yous to accompany me to the station, " says I to which the woman Devrill replied, "How can I when I left me oul banjo at home? But you sing away an' Mr. Conlin can go round with the hat." Mr. X then agreed to press charges an' so we all proceeded to the station."

"And how exactly," the Justice rapped for silence, "did

you proceed to the station?"

"In the cab of course, sor."

It pained Pearse to see his own solicitor join in the general laughter and tap himself on the cheek with a folded document on which more than likely was set out the charge he had been summoned there to answer. He felt the intimidate nudge of the woman's soft hips.

"A real caution isn't he, oul Sour Belly? I always love been up before him for if nothin' else you get a real good laugh out of it." She bent the regard of her candid eyes on him. "Terrible quiet chap, aren't you?" Her make-up exaggerated her look of sympathy to tragic anguish, "Ah, an' sure that's why, isn't it? You're up too. I shudda guessed. That's what's worryin' you, makin' you so quiet."

He nodded in a turmoil of shrinking from her desecrated body and of an almost unbearable longing to be enfolded swooningly deep in its perfumed depths.

"Well, whatever you done," she said, "jus' remember you're as good as the next fella an' you jus' stand up there an brazen it out."

Her hard, calloused palm caressed over the back of his hand. A hard ball settled in the back of his throat. Certain other changes were beginning to afflict him elsewhere as well.

"And does that conclude your evidence, Guard Horan?" he heard faintly in the ringing distance.

"Except to say that when he was questioned in the station Conlin denied all the charges."

For the first time Pearse noticed the head and shoulders of a man he realised was Conlin raised above a densely packed group off to his left. It was as if the crowd were bearing him aloft so that the world could read the mean, cadging guilt flitting about on his grey pink-flecked face.

"Very well," said the Justice, "we'll hear from Mr. X now if you please. He's agreed this time to give his evidence, has he not, Guard Horan?"

"Oh indeed he has! Certain sure. He says it's his sacred duty as a good citizen to protect men under the influence of drink from the likes of Devrill and Conlin."

The woman pressed sideways into him. "That lousy sleeveen Horan! It's from the likes of him the rest of us need to be protected. The long, gropin' hand of the law he's known by in Clare Street. Doesn't know where to keep his hands when he arrests us girls, so he doesn't. And when it's men he arrests, which is very seldom I can tell you, he carries them into the station bashin' all the doors open before him with their heads."

A door slammed somewhere and Pearse saw a red-faced guard, shoulder his way through the crowd to confer with a man he hadn't noticed before sitting at a table beneath the bench, probably the clerk of the court. With much nervous fluttering of hands the man shot to his feet and whispered something up the Justice.

"What!" The Justice's shout brought a hush over the room. Horan tugged at his collar with the fingers of both hands and stared dismally at, the floor.

"Guard Horan!" The anger in his voice was terrible, "I had your solemn assurance that Mr. X would appear today, had I not?"

"Certain sure! Isn't he out there now ready to go through foire and water, as he says, in the interest of seein' justice done!"

"No he is not out there!"

"Sure didn't I talk to him just before I came in?"

"Well, " the Justice brushed impatiently at a sheaf of papers with the back of his hand, "maybe he's going through fire and water after all but in a way he didn't intend. I am informed that his wife has just put in an unexpected, if not dramatic, appearance in the waiting room and she has left just now bearing away your sole witness. By the ear according to our informant. It seems she had no knowledge of her husband's involvement in this case until informed by the usual well-intended neighbour or some other virtuous party dedicated to the revelation of truth at all costs, even to the break-up of a happy home. What would our venerable city do without such good citizens as these?"

Conlin cringed over the crumpled lapels of his brown overcoat picking at loose threads and flicking away invisible specks of dust.

"Am I still correct in assuming that your entire case rested on the evidence of this absent witness?"

"I'm afraid so, yor worship!"

"Very well then, since we've had one adjournment already and since it now seems highly unlikely that you'll ever get your witness to take the stand, I have no option but to pass judgement on the facts of the case as I see them. Case dismissed. So let's have the next case and hope that no more of the court's time will be wasted.

The woman snuggled cosily against Pearse.

"That was a rare oul suck-in Horan got, wasn't it?"

"Yes he did," he smiled at her. In spite of what he had learned of her sinful way of life he felt unaccountably at ease in her presence as if the simple fact of their bodies touching against each other had turned them into old friends. He blushed aside the annoying niggle of an urgent voice somewhere close by.

"An' what does a fine-lookin' chap like you find to do with yourself of an evenin'?"

"Nothing much."

"I haven't come across a nice boy like you since...." Her sudden wistfulness brought a lump to his throat. A rough hand grasped and shook his shoulder.

"Great God, Bolton boy, aren't you listening at all?"

He startled, dismayed that it was Mr. Cowan's voice he had been refusing to listen to.

"I'm sorry, sir."

"Well then go boy! Go!"

"Where to, sir?"

"Where do you think? To the box, where else? And for God's sake look sharp about it. Old S... the old boy's fit to be tied after that last fiasco. And watch what you say. Remember what we discussed!"

He blundered to his feet brushing against the woman's soft open knees. In trying to hold fast to the thrill of delight this new contact burned into him he lost his sense of direction. Where was the bloody box anyway?

The Hero Game and Other Dublin Stories

He moved in one direction, then another, through an intoxicating faintness in which his thoughts shuffled about without definition or focus mostly it seemed over the sticky sweat that was breaking out all over him. He saw Conlin hovering like a scavenging bird across the room and he went in that direction. He had the sensation of moving sponge-limbed through some other dimension of time and experience where everything was so alien he had no idea who he was or what was happening to him. He climbed into the air and looked down as from an aircraft on a speckle of featureless faces which of one accord turned their merciless alien's gaze back up at him. He half expected to find brilliant, pencil-thin rays of malignity parallel towards him from each pair of hostile eyes. Twice through the haze of his confusion he rapped out answers to some comedian's rapid patter about his name and his occupation. The tone changed and he wondered why a louder, more nasal voice had succeeded the first droning through the almost comforting haze that had settled over his mind, and some sort of malicious damage to a window in the offices of the British Commercial Centre in Merrion Square.

"Good Lord, are we back there again?"

The deep, penetrating no-nonsense voice of the Justice swept the haze from his mind leaving him in the stark immediacy of the courtroom where every shape and form was so clear and intimidatingly detailed it set him wondering how that quotation ended which said that nothing concentrates a man's mind more than the knowledge that what? Mr. Dodd had sniggered when he reached the end bit and he had been so intent on watching how his nose wrinkled up all one side that he lost the final few words of the quotation. Taking a deep breath he gave himself the air of a tourist inspecting an historic house - the ceiling could do with a coat of paint - and declined his head to rest his chin nonchalantly on his cupped palm which wobbled so distressingly on his trembling elbow, his head and shoulders jerked out over the edge of the box. "Not Guilty!" he called at that moment guessing this was the statement needed to fill the gap of silence that ensued when the hurried voice of the court official suddenly ceased to assail the air with its low Dublin whine. Across the room a figure rose into view as from the depths of some slimy bog, its close-cropped head and elfin ears floating disembodied in the air. With a start he realised that Horan was no longer in the witness box and that the guard who had arrested him had taken his place. A vague loneliness seized him for the sight of those rabbity front teeth. From his inside pocket he sneaked out the folded, sheets of foolscap on which he had written the notes for his defence dictated by Mr. Cowan, and his speech from the dock with its long, rolling complex sentences that even Mr.Dodd would have difficulty hanging on to as they twined and twisted on their sonorous way. He held the papers in his sweaty fingers well out of sight of the hostile aliens surrounding him and yawned grandly, tapping his clenched hand against his lower lip, all through the swearing-in of the guard. Still tapping he looked about the unfortunate room, one of the heroes of '98 with the manner of the Scarlet Pimpernel showing contemp for the minions of the law, the packed jury, and the hanging judge. He would have raised his snuffbox to his nostrils only the hand for that was already engaged in the task of keeping his foolscap sheets out of range of the cobra-green eyes of the Justice, who regarded him with some indifference. Across the room he saw the woman rooting in her handbag into which Kathleen was peering covertly ignored by both Brian and Dev who craned forward to stare unashamedly at the woman's garish beauty. He tapped his speech against the knee that had touched hers. He had sat next to her, felt her flesh warm against his, won from her the wistful admission that she would like to meet a nice boy like him. Let them look!

"....it was about eleven thirty p.m."

He turned, his attention to the guard who kept glancing nervously from his note-book to the justice.

"There were about three or four hundred people, men and women, assembled there in the roadway causin' an obstruction to traffic and creatin' a great disturbance by shoutin': "Release the prisoners! British murderers! Down with British justice; An...."

"I think we can dispense with the slogans, Guard. I accept they were creating a disturbance."

"They were indeed, sor! An' gettin' more and more agitated by the minnit! A speaker tried to address them from the steps of a house, callin' on them to burn the British buildin' down in retaliation for the hangin' of two Irishmen for plantin' a bomb in a suitcase in the left luggage depot at Victoria Station."

"Poor Oscar! We keep on meeting him at every hands turn. Is there a season of his plays on anywhere?"

"Neither o' the two men was called Oscar, sor. Their names...."

"I know their names, thank you, Guard Flaherty. I'm an avid reader of court cases."

In the joyful din that arose, Pearse watched the reporters shake helplessly in their chairs and he realised that he was witnessing what some of them would describe in the evening editions as "Laugher in court", usually in italics between brackets. He stared at the Justice's mouth dreading what would come forth from it when his turn arrived. His fingers were growing so moist with sweat it was as if they had been dipped in butter.

" I called out several times to the mob," the guard said, "to move along there but they kept on shoutin' and makin' threatenin' rushes towards the office of the British Commercial Centre where there were only two guards on duty. I then saw Inspector Woods and some o' the boys - the constables - from Store Street drive up and he made every effort to get the roadway cleared, even speakin' politely and reasonably to the mob. But sure this had no effect at all and fightin' broke out all over the place an' got very intense because the crowd kept on gettin' bigger all the time. And then at what I would judge the most critical moment in the struggle I saw the defendant there, Pearse Bolton, sort of stroll out from the middle o' the battle lookin' as calm and as cool as you like. He picked up a large, empty wine bottle from the roadway and stood there as if he was thinkin' about somethin'. I tried to get to him for we were under strict instructions to protect the buildin' at all costs. Before I could reach him though, he looked up, very casual like as I remember, and let fly the bottle right through the window of the ground floor of the centre, the one to the left of the doorway. When I got to him I told him he was under arrest and that I was goin' to take him to the station. He replied, and I quote: "That suits me fine, Inspector, it's on my way home anyway." When cautioned at the station he replied that he had nothin' further to say."

"That suits me fine, Inspector, it's on my way home anyway" he heard the Justice say, a sentence that had a familiar ring, and meeting the thrust of the cobra-green eyes he felt his legs wobble beneath him. "A witty chap, aren't you?"

"Not usually, sir. The police station I thought he was going to take me to is not far from where I live. I was just pointing that out, being polite."

His tongue was enlarged and misshapen, the inside of his mouth as dry and grainy as a sandpit. More perspiration broke out all over him as if driven forth by the fierce beating of his heart. He tried to dry his fingers by twitching them on the sheets of foolscap held down by his side. He felt most of the sheets slip to the floor. Alarmed, he ducked to retrieve them, knocked his head hard on the edge of the box and dropped the remaining sheets.

"What on earth are you doing there, boy?" The Justice looked across at him in astonishment,

"Nothing at all, sir. Just - er - slipped."

He loathed the rippled laughter that went round the room.

"Have you anything to say on any point in Guard Flaherty's evidence?"

"No, sir. That's exactly the way it happened."

"Yet you pleaded not guilty to the charge?"

"That is correct, sir." How did Emmet and Tone and John Sheares and the Manchester Martyrs manage to think straight in the dock with their legs wobbling, their tongue sticking to the sides of their mouths, their sweat threatening to drown them?

"What did you say your occupation was?" The Justice raised papers and dropped them at once as if they were contaminated.

"I'm a student, sir."

"Indeed! And at which of our two august universities are you pursing your studies?"

"At neither of them, sir. I'm at school still..."

"Oh I see!" The Justice leaned back comfortably in his seat and locked his fingers over the hard ball of his stomach.

"Why didn't you say right away you are a schoolboy. I asked you about your occupation, not your aspirations."

A man's laugh mocked from the back of the room. Stealing a glance he saw that both Brian and Dev were grinning up at him in the way they did in the history class during his frequent altercations with Mr. McClery - "I teach history, Bolton, a subject you would seem to confuse with melodrama, mythology, romance, and plain utter rubbish!" Kathleen sagged almost out of sight, her head in her hands. The woman - he sensed the tug of habit in her action - had turned to identify the owner of the rich male laugh. The Justice was regarding him with quiet intentness and with a sense of doom he knew he had become a mere object to be studied, prodded, reflected upon. The Mad Axeman was about to have a gala day. Oh yes!

"You were arrested about eleven-thirty, I see," the Justice said, "That's very late for a schoolboy to be out and about, isn't it?"

"I'm seventeen."

"As old as that!" The Justice swelled in painfully obvious mock astonishment. Where was his speech? He began to feel about for it with his foot on the floor of the box, but as he dared not look he might, for all he knew, be rubbing it to shreds on the smooth boards. The Justice frowned down at a document before him.

"And does your mother approve of you being out so late?"

"Well...." There was a white blob of dried porridge on his tie and he began to scratch at it with his fingernail. How could he tell of the tears, the wails of despair, the heart-rendering cries to God, His blessed Mother, and a troupe of long-tried saints which invariably greeted his return from his nightly meanderings about the city.

"A sore point, I should say. Tell me, as a schoolboy who has just turned seventeen, I notice, don't you have a certain amount of homework, of study to do of an evening?"

The woman was frowning beneath her heavy mask of cosmetics following the interchanges with an intent professional interest rather like a fan at a boxing bout in the National Stadium. To the screams of the bloodthirsty crowd Battling Bolton, battered but unbowed, decided to weave in with a left hook and a deft right cross.

"My homework" he said airily, "I always knock off in the lunch-hour and I get through most of the studying on top of the tram on the way home from school." Right on the point!

"Do you indeed!" The Justice sat backed amazed. Rather too amazed. "And to think that Einstein had to slave away morning, noon and night for years and years and years just to work out that one very simple equation! But to return to the time at which you were arrested, are you usually out as late as that, close to midnight?"

"Yes, sir. Frequently."

"And what does a schoolboy like you find to do in the streets of the city at such a very late hour?"

The silence of the room sang in his ears with the lonely humming of telegraph wires on wind-swept mountain roads.

"Nothing, sir. I - er - just sort of wander around."

The green eyes prying deep into his appeared much larger than when he noticed them. Were they growing even larger still? Like someone with strange, mysterious powers or like one of those mad professors you were always reading about which left you with the impression that too much education and not the other thing eventually drove you mad, was the Justice engaged in hypnotising him, coldly sapping his will, breaking down the barriers behind which lay the secret life of his soul? Under the pressure of those eyes, any moment now, surely his head must burst! The lonely mountain roads hummed in his ears. He looked out into the greyish haze, soft as gauze. God, was there no power now that could prevent him from blurting out how he passed his evenings on the street? How night after night he paced through the streets repeating to himself "I'm alive! I'm alive!" drunk on the wild blood pounding through his veins, singing in his ears, tingling like sharp fingers all over his expectant flesh? How in the sauntering crowds he sought continually for the image of the as yet unseen one who was always eluding him, slipping always away round the corners of his mind which shimmered in the fragrance she left behind? How as Mr. Hyde, his face painfully contorted, he shambled down narrow streets like Long Lane, his hairy knuckles knocking against his knees, looking for children playing on the pavement or on the steps of old dark houses at whom he could snarl like a vicious dog to scare them out of their wits - and be scared out of his own in turn if their shrieking mothers put in an unexpected appearance as happened on two occasions? How he burned like a naked flame with an obsessive passion for yearning at women's legs, bosoms and bottoms as if they were maddening magnets drawing the yearnings of his heart out through his eyes? Maybe even there was someone in the very courtroom who had seen him loitering on the Ranelagh side of Charlemont Bridge round half-past five in the evenings and guessed rightly he was there because the bridge was steep and the wind usually for the south-west so that when the women and girls came cycling over you almost never failed to get a generous eyeful of white thighs and sometimes even colourful undergarments. Were he to blurt out any of that it would certainly get him locked up not just in

James Manning

Mountjoy Gaol but in the criminal lunatic asylum out in Dundrum from which there is no getting free. Ever! And that was just a mere fraction of what he got up to night after night! The soft gauze fell away and he saw that the Justice was staring before him, absorbed as if following the course of play. He tingled with the temptation to provide a dramatic climax by throwing wide his arms and declaiming: With as firm a conviction as I have that Jesus is present in the Eucharist, I believe that in some intangible though real way I am part of all these things in my wanderings that bring a shiver up my back and make the tears start from my eyes - simple things like the endless wavelike movement of mortal people along dark pavements, the voices hoarse and human drawling out of steaming public houses; the stinging smell of fish and chip on wet nights: the brown fog blowing my own breath back at me as if returning a precious gift; the rain pinging on the dark, light-laced roadway; the glory of girls sailing through the golden light of street-lamps and vivid shop windows as if they bore with them all the beauty of the world; the moon dancing in the river of my blood dividing the living city.... Someone coughed and he saw the whole room was waiting for his answer. He nodded his head frantic to find somewhere in its depths the words that would make the Justice desist and bring all this to an end. The Justice shifted in his seat and scratched his grey cheek.

"Come, come, boy! We haven't all day. Surely you do more than just wander around?"

"But that's all I do. Honest."

"Well, you weren't just wandering around the night you were arrested, were you?"

"But I was, sir. That's the point. It's all I was doing."

"Didn't you take part in that reprehensible march through the city the consequences of which are being dealt with in this building ever since?"

"I had nothing whatsoever to do with that sort of thing, sir."

Beneath him he saw Brian and Dev exchange a quick glance. And sneer! That was unfair for he had never lied to them, never pretended that he took part in the march or was a member of the I.R.A. either. It was they and the rest of the fellows who had maintained those fictions. Not that he had grown hoarse contradicting them!

"You can't deny you were in Merrion Square, can you? You must have been there to get yourself arrested, mustn't you?"

"No I don't deny that at all. However Merrion Square just happened to be the place I had reached at that time."

"When you were just sort of wandering around, as you put it?"

"Yes, sir. That's exactly it. I had just wandered up from Holles Street and before I knew it there were crowds all round me, shouting and waving placards. And the rozzers...."

"The rozzers?"

"I mean the police, sir. The Garda Siothchana. They came in among the crowds with their batons drawn and there was fighting all over the place."

"But surely you saw the crowds were there before you

found yourself in the middle of them?"

"I didn't pay much attention at first. I just thought the street was more crowded than usual as if a concert or something had just finished. I admit that as soon as I saw the fighting I realised that something serious was going on."

What would they think of him were he to confess that his first impulse on hearing shouting, the soggy thump of fists on flesh, the sickening thump of flailing batons was to throw up his arms and utter a loud SHH! so that they would not wake up the babies with which the maternity hospital in Holles Street was probably crammed - like Limbo - so that they would all start crying at once and be a great burden on the nurses among whom was a girl whose marvellous legs had led him to trail them one night all the way across town to the door of the hospital.

"At which point did you join in the fighting?"

"Oh I had nothing to do with that at all. I don't believe in illegal, disorganised violence."

"Really?" The Justice with a smirk invited the press not to miss what was about to ensue, "Am I to infer that on the contrary you are a believer in legal, organised violence?"

"That's exactly right, sir. Any fighting that's to be done for Ireland should be left to the Irish Army which is organised and trained for that purpose.

The Justice sat back and uttered a little gasp.

"A nice point. However, it's a pity you didn't bear that in mind on the night in question."

"I quite agree, sir. But in a way I did"

If only he could gather his thoughts together and stop them from bounding away like scared rabbits into convenient burrows! A mistake to mention the army! If Sour Belly knew from the document before him or from Hermann Cowan that he was thinking of sitting for the cadetship examinations he might, out of the badness of his heart, shoot out a straight left bang on the nose of his hopes. So much for Battling Bolton, caressing the canvas!

"What do you mean by that last statement?" The Justice enquired.

"I'm not really sure, sir. For when I found myself in the middle of that mob I got very confused not so much because of the actual fighting but because of the shouting and the terrible screaming more than anything else that some of the men were making. Yes I think it was the screaming more than anything else that got me all confused for it reminded me of the kind of squeals you hear from the pigs when they're been driven into Fennelly's Bacon Factory. I heard that once and it confused me very much. I haven't eaten bacon since."

"Indeed!" The Justice rustled through the papers he had before him on the bench as if vainly seeking the key to some insoluble mystery.

"Yes, sir. So all I wanted to do was to get away from the mob and wander home."

He saw Brian make a knowing sour mouth at Dev.

"I see. And pick up an empty bottle on the way and do what no one else succeeded in doing that night, inflict considerable damage on the window of the British

Commercial Centre?"

"Yes, that is correct, sir."

"Why did you do that?"

"I - er - I - er - I'm not really sure."

"What again? I'm beginning to wonder if you're sure of anything at all. Any minute now you'll have me as confused as you claim yourself to have been - and apparently still are. For instance, I'm at a loss to understand why you plead not guilty to the charge when you've just admitted to the charge. But as to your motive, surely you don't expect me to believe you threw that missile just on impulse? Surely by that time you were aware of the nature and purpose of that unruly gathering?"

"Not really, sir. Naturally from the shouts and the curses I got the impression they were not very friendly towards the British Government. But what it was about I didn't discover until the other prisoners told me in the Bridewell."

"You were in the Bridewell?" The Justice seemed to be about to ask Hermann Cowan something. Instead he said:

"You must have been there. However, if you knew the demonstration was against the British Government, you didn't throw the bottle just on impulse, did you?"

"I - er - I think I did, sir. "On impulse" describes it very well. But then again I can't ever be completely sure about that for I was thinking of something else at the time."

The Justice sat back in amazement and began to repeat the statement in the general direction of the press table. But was that the whole truth either? He couldn't be sure because the howls of laughter breaking out like minor explosions all around were so loud it became ever more difficult to think straight. The angry pounding of the gavel didn't help either. It drew his fascinated gaze. Just like in a Warner Brothers film! In which the next sequence would reveal some state penitentiary the shadow of which he felt already darkening his spirit. For if the Justice were to ask next what exactly he had been thinking about when he flung the bottle, what could he answer? Wasn't it enough to have admitted flinging the damn thing? Wasn't it enough to have been scrupulously honest about everything - or almost everything - to the point of having the mob laugh at you? Your secret thoughts and dreams weren't on trial so holding back them couldn't be classed as perjury. Or could it? In such an atmosphere how had Tone and Emmett and the rest of them managed to stand up there and roll out their long, complex balanced sentences full of those figures of rhetoric Mr.Dodd was always mumbling about? Because they got them off by heart before they came there? In any case they didn't get confused and forgot their lines, nor drop their notes and speech on the floor and grind them to mummy under their nervous feet.

"Come, boy!" The Justice gave another green glare across the room at which the last giggles faded into comparative silence. "No matter where your thoughts were at the time of the incident there is not a shred of doubt - you have admitted it - that your hand was holding a large, empty wine bottle which I suggest you flung as an act of protest against the British Government. After all, it was against their property."

"I suppose it looks like an act of protest now. At the time though it wasn't in my mind at all. I know this is hard to believe but it's true nonetheless, that at the very instance the bottle was leaving my hand I knew I was doing wrong because, my Lords, let my voice ring through the length and breadth of this dear land of ours to state with all the emphasis at my command that I most certainly do not hold with riotous gatherings, assaults on the forces of law and order, the wanton destruction of property either public or private."

"You don't? Even though you destroyed - let me see - one pound, nineteen, and sevenpence half-penny worth of private property that was being put to public use? And who are those Lords you mentioned? And what's that about the length and breadth of this dear land of ours?"

"Lords, sir? What....Lords? What Land? O, did I...? I don't really know, sir. I can't help it if I sound a bit mixed-up. That's because I was so confused by what was happening all around me that unfortunate night. When I think about it, the mixed-up feeling comes back, all over again. For some reason loud shouting and jostling crowds always has that effect on me."

"Mixed-up, confused? That's putting it mildly. You mentioned the Irish Army just now. Do you realise what a menace you would be on a battlefield? To both sides? Just wandering around, in and out of the fighting, not really knowing why it's going on! And then on a confused, mixed-up impulse when you're thinking of something at the time, shooting off your rifle, or your mortar, or your field-gun and telling your superior officers, who of course would be delighted in the circumstances to hear it, that you're totally opposed to the destruction of property both public and private at the very moment when you're in the act of destroying as much of both kinds as you can manage! Good heavens, boy, you'd be such a danger to your own side they'd have to treat you as one of the enemy. A bit mixed-up? Yes, indeed. I quite agree. A lot of what you've said here this morning was exactly that. Yet in spite of it all, I must say I'm favourably impressed by the honesty and the candour with which you answered to the charge when you're being mixed-up and confused didn't make that any easier, I can appreciate that."

"Oh thank you very much, sir!"

"That may be very premature indeed, boy!" The cobra-green eyes raked over him and then sought out Hermann Cowan who came to the bench apparently to elucidate some points in the papers the Justice had before him into which he kept on jabbing his index finger. Bad omen! He risked a look at Kathleen who - was that because of the distance? - bore the frail, crumpled look of a little girl who has come to the end of weeping herself dry of tears. Brian and Dev stared at the floor their eyes dirty with betrayal. But where was the woman? He found her at the door accompanied by Conlin whose long, creased overcoat flapped down his back like moulted wings. He met the woman's eyes and the lurid mask of her face contorted, merrily in an encouraging wink beside which her jutting thumb waved in a gay, triumphant circle. She went out and he stared at the closed door allowing a warm surge of sympathy for her to flow into his heart which responded with a wild cry of desire for her warm, perfumed flesh. That was something you never thought about, never found, in *Speeches from the Dock*, a woman standing there abandoned and alone before the cold, contemptuous scrutiny of the mob, the colder deliberations of the unsympathetic judges. It must have been terrible for Flora Gilmore. Who got six whole months! Yet when you got used to it, standing in the dock wasn't really all that bad! You couldn't really call it an ordeal. More like a subtle kind of game or the goings on in the Thursday afternoon debating society Franco was always trying to get speakers for. And in spite of all the confusion which first greeted you, in which you couldn't even isolate the dock and the witness box from the rest of the room, though they were staring you in the face, there was behind it all a firm sense of order, a feeling for truth which set everyone in his rightful place, scrupulously separating the innocent from the guilty, the false from the true or the almost true, the friend from the seeming friend. He lounged in the box, yawning up at the ceiling, Bolton the Bomber, calm, cool, and collected waiting for the usher, or someone like that, to bring in the judge's black cap adorned with which he would launch into his; "the sentence of this court is that you be taken hence to a place from whence you came and be there taken to the place...."

"Bolton!" He turned to the Justice and was vaguely surprised to see he wasn't wearing a black cap, "I have had convincing proof of your good character and from what I learn of your scholastic ability, the high hopes of your widowed mother places in you are not likely to be disappointed. Consequently, I have decided to apply the probation act to you. The window of course will be paid for. And if you must just wander around this city of ours, boy, do it to some purpose, will you? Study the glorious Georgian architecture, train your powers of observation as Dickens did when wandering the streets of London. Set yourself some definite aim like that, because in your case it might be said that the devil found work for idle feet. I believe you have important examinations coming up, so I should advise you to do more than just knock off your home-work in the lunch-hour and most of your studying on the top of a tram on the way home. Try staying home some nights for a change. Real sustained study never did harm to anyone. And please remember," the eyes sparkled greenly into his, "you will always get more from a book than you will from a bottle."

As he left the box and hurried out into the hushed sunlight, the raw laughter of the court crowd still mocking in his ears, he bore as a treasured gift the unexpected warmth, the open friendliness of the Justice's smile which - it began to itch at his mind - might also be conveying some message that only those who stood in the dock to receive it would ever understand. And could not that message be that in some secret even mystical sense - a real Mr. Dodd word that second adjective - the judge and the accused, the innocent and the guilty were ultimately and indissolubly one, specially chosen actors with a kind of priest-like function - not just anyone stood in the box or sat on the bench - in a ritual drama, solemn and serious beneath all the laughter, a ritual concerned with seeking the truth, the whole truth and nothing but the truth? And was it part of the secret, mystical meaning of the drama that all the roles were interchangeable, that each actor was capable of being both innocent and guilty at one same time? Was that what Sour Belly - a typically, cruel and unfair Dublin nickname - was conveying in the green twinkle of his smile? Was that what the woman meant in her lurid wink from the door? He stood on the steps stretching his muscles - the Fox, notorious saboteur and seducer of women wanted on all five continents, especially by women, beating the rap yet once more - and drawing into his lungs the tide-tanged air yet unable to make space enough there for the magnitude of the revelations unfolding within him. It was just like when ideas come flashing at you out of the heart of the dark city and you have to hammer through the streets to keeppace with blazing excitement which makes you forget, sometimes for hours on end, that all around you are ravishingly beautiful faces, well-furnished bosoms, wiggling bottoms and shapely legs crying out to be swooned at and carefully and craftily trailed. How the woman's breast had wobbled against his shoulder! Desire burned in him like an urgent flame in the chill air.

"Well, anyway you got off." Brian's voice reached him from a cold distance and he saw that his classmate was staring down at the new shoes his mother had bought him for the occasion, as if their brash shoddiness gave off a bad smell.

"Yeah, we're real pleased." Dev sounded as if he wasn't.

Well, let them go! And secretly he was glad. It was amazing that though he stood within arm's length of both of them, neither had the faintest hint of what the experiences of the courtroom were beginning to mean for him. Those two were millions of light years away from him now, on a totally different orbit, and they would remain there forever while the heroic Flash Gordon zoomed onwards into brave new worlds of experiences and ideas that had no inkling of the daily futility of their Mutt-and-Jeff lives.

"Well then," Mutt tapped Jeff lightly on the elbow, "Let's go Dev, or we'll have no chance to eat our lunch before McClery comes in with his dreary *Poynings Law* act."

"See you back at Dotheboys Hall" Dev gave him a long look as if wondering how he would react to something really unpleasant in the not-too-distant future.

"Yes, he replied wriggling round the shaft of the pin that held him impaled on the classroom wall for all his shrieking schoolmates to aim their darts of scorn at. Brian shot an arch glance at Kathleen and without a word to her set off with his companion down the steps. They slinged to a halt at the edge of the pavement where a horse and cab was drawn up and went slowly along by the side of the vehicle casting furtive glances inside. As if in response to their curiosity, the woman from the courtroom leaned over the window ledge leering in the direction of the steps.

"Eh Horan! Horan!" Her street voice was as raucous as a sheet of corrugated iron being dragged over cobblestones.

"G'wan, Horan," don't be lettin' on you can't hear me when you were swearin' in there you could hear every word of a conversation that was goin' on about a mile from the shop door you were stuck in."

A tall figure in blue uniform detached itself from the group it was part of and began to slink away in the direction of the quays.

"Ah, don't be like that, Horan!" The woman waved a coloured object. "All I wanted to know is would you like us to give you a jaunt back to the station. Mr. Conlin's just reminded me of how much you like ridin' in a cab."

Jeering a laugh she sank back out of sight and the cab, swinging out into the middle of the road, went with a whisper of wheels behind its trotting horse off towards the heart of the city. Conlin sat high up on the box, flicking his long whip and grinning back over his shoulder at the amused crowd at the door of the courts.

"Did you see what that awful creature had in her hand?" Kathleen asked, "She had my bunch of violets which she must have nicked up off the seat when I wasn't looking."

"Would you like me to buy you another bunch?"

"No! I hate the very idea of flowers now. I'll never let one near me ever again."

"Ma gave me two bob. Would you like to come down to Savino's in Capel Street for a cup of coffee and a sandwich?"

"If I ate anything now I'd just throw up and you ought to know the reason why. Christ I - God forgive for saying that - I've never been so ashamed in my whole life as I was in that courtroom."

She began to walk on, towards a tram-stop he saw, and he fell into step beside her waiting for the storm to pass. The book shop was closed again. One day a famous millionaire inventor - inventor of Bolton's binoculars with which you can see through solid objects like cab bodies and clothes - would turn up at the book shop in a furniture van to buy up the entire stock of books and take them home to peruse at his leisure. Kathleen rested her forehead against the green, iron tram standard.

"It'll be a relief to get back to bloody Latin and Algebra after all that." She shivered as if she stood in a cold draught and he sought on her face in vain for the vibrant young woman he had discerned there earlier. In silence they boarded a tram and at once he sank into a drifting fog of shapeless, muttering images like those he encountered each night on the threshold of sleep. As if endowed with a rebellious life of their own, the grimy facades of the riverside buildings and the tram-reflecting shop windows rocked and rattled past his drooping eyelids. It was a relief that she had fallen silent. Yet that wasn't enough. He longed to be away from her, away from everyone in the whole world. Like in one of those moments of pure isolation when after a dive from the high board at Clontarf Baths, you rose with weightless leisure up through a long shaft of silent green towards the muted light speckling the high, distant surface. Gradually the hushed dreamlike state left him to be succeeded by vivid instants from the events of the day flitting through his mind without sense or sequence. Amazed at their energy he attended to their pulsing life like one enraptured in a cinema until he heard Kathleen's heels scrape on the floor and he too rose and followed her out of the tram. Coming round the corner into C'Connell Street, a restless wandering came over him, rather he supposed like an alcoholic's craving for a drink, came into him from the sight of the moving crowds, from the feel of the very flagstones under his feet. Maybe one night he would meet that

Donegal girl again and beg her forgiveness!

"I'll never get over that experience back there," Kathleen clicked clumsily along in a charmless, dumpy roll reminiscent of his mother's walk, "I thought I'd feel better when I got a breath of air, but not a bit of it, I feel even worse now. You looked a real right fool back in that courtroom, do you realise that? You made a complete show of yourself. I'll be ashamed of what happened there for the rest of my life."

"It's all right for you to talk. You weren't in the cursed-God dock."

"You don't have to speak to your own sister in the sort of language that awful creature Devrill would use. I'm so glad Ma wasn't there to see the shameful exhibition you made of yourself. And it's not just the idiotic things you said to the Justice - if you only saw the ridiculous look you had on your face when you were answering him - it's the way you were drooling over that woman and lying sideways towards her to get even closer to her than common decency permits. Disgusting that was! Wait'll Ma hears about it! It showed me something about you I never realised before."

"Ah, what the hell! I was only being polite as Ma is always telling me to be. What was I supposed to do when she spoke to me?"

"Ignore her for the filth she is! What else? And the intimate way you we're talking to each other, at one point like old friends! That nearly turned my stomach."

"It was your own fault anyway for staying in the courtroom. After all, I begged you to leave. And come to think of it you didn't need to have anything explained to you. You knew exactly what everything was about. It only goes to show the kind of interesting information there's to be picked up by nice girls attending a good convent school!"

"It's not just the school. Ma has had.... talks with me. There's lots of things a girl needs to know more than a boy."

He looked to see if she was blushing and could discern no change in colour on her hard, child face. What had his mother been telling her? Was there no end to the things he either didn't notice or didn't understand that went on right under his very nose not just in the city but in the heart of his family as well? He trudged on beside her. God, would he ever get to the end of all he still had to ferret out about life, about people, about himself? A few minutes later, just a few streets from her convent school, she turned on him, her teeth bared and sharp as if to bite.

"And tell me. whatever happened to your famous speech from the dock?"

"What do you mean my.... speech? He stood in a moist shaft of breath, exuding through every pore the appetising smells of roast meats and sizzling gravies. Startled, he saw where they had halted and stepped adroitly out of the sultry up rush of odorous air through the iron grating of a downstairs restaurant.

"Ma and me were killing ourselves laughing all last night listening to you from the bottom of the stairs and you up in your room giving out with 'My Lords' this and 'My Lords' that! It's a wonder the whole street didn't gather round the house to get an earful. Were you rehearsing in front of the wardrobe mirror or what?"

He walked on in a reddish haze of anger. On a sports field somewhere - in Saint Joseph's Orphanage where they went to play what Brian called 'the convicts' - he had been whacked on the elbow with a hurley stick by Spud Murphy. Once again ash on the bone and the sickening outspreading of pain.

"And having made us half-deaf with all that stuff about having no hopes that you could anchor your character in the mind of the court, and a lot of other twaddle like that, what did you do when you finally got there but turn yourself into a laughing stock of the town. I've never been so embarrassed in my whole life."

"Oh weren't you? Well, all I can say to you is - "

"Ah, shut up! You've said far too much already for your own good. Imagine - "I was just wandering around, sir!" Real stupid that was! And the other gem, " I was thinking of something else at the time!" After *The Herald* and, *The Mail* come out tonight those'll be catch phrases all over the city. Comedians on the Royal and the Queens and the Olympia will be using them every night now for the next few years. They'll be in all the pantos at Christmas. Christ, only a real flaming idiot would, have said those things in public. But come to think of it some of what you say in private is not much better. Look at all that stuff you were going on with a few weeks back, after you'd brought home that Bernard Shaw play from the library, about you being a Master of Reality! Listening to you anyone would get the impression you were a person with his feet planted firmly on the ground as you faced up with courage to all the harsh facts of life. But I see now that you know as much about reality as a little bird's feather drifting about on the wind. For that's all you do, drift from one foolish dream to another. And if what you say is anything to go by, some of the things you have in your head are the sort a child of twelve would be thinking it was high time to grow out of it. No wonder Ma's wearing out her beads praying for you for she's nearly in the grave worrying about what's going to become of you. I've looked up to you all my life, do you know that? But after that variety show in the courts - never again! No wonder Brian and Dev were so keen to get away from us and to think how friendly and how amusing and how kind they were before! I felt they were ashamed to know me just because I'm your sister. Why did you have to go and make such a fool of yourself? When you said, "I was thinking of something else at the time," I thought one of the reporters would have to be carried out he was in such a fit of laughing. You could see the Justice fighting hard to keep his face straight and covering up by pretending to be angry and banging his little hammer into his papers. Oh great Christ, I'll never be able to live this disgrace down. People'll be pointing me out and saying: "Don't you know who she is? She's the sister of that idiot who was in all the papers!" Oh my God! But there's one consolation isn't there? After what Brian and Dev will have told the rest of the school they'll crucify you with jeers and jibes when you get back there. And I'm glad! Real glad!"

She sprung away from him and went dodging through the traffic in a loose, loping run, head down, her long hair tossing on her shoulders. Let her go! He strode on tight with the urge to sink his fist into something, someone, anything - but preferably either Brian or Dev.

What was a sister anyway but an accident of birth you had to live in the same house with and tolerate, and coax and avoid and talk to and survive even though you knew in your heart she would never end up as your friend! Rather would she remain what she always was, an over-familiar alien who sat in judgement on your every action and peered without compassion into the depths of your soul, misunderstanding' and misinterpreting everything she thought she saw there. Surely he couldn't have sounded as foolish as she said? It was difficult through the drifting haze of his anger to envisage clearly the scene in the courtroom. He listened again to the responses he gave to the Justice. "I was just wandering around." Well, what else was he doing but that? "I was thinking of something else at the time," That was the truth he had sworn to tell and he told it exactly as it happened. Of course it wasn't brilliant! It wasn't Wolfe Tone or Robert Emmett. Yet if only he hadn't had the bad luck to drop his speech on the floor of the dock he might have been able to sneak a look at it and shoot off an arresting phrase or two that would make the pressman look up. As it was the Justice had seemed to be trying the case expressly for their benefit. But nothing even the Justice had said, apart from the witticisms, surpassed in style and expression the ringing phrases, the balanced sentences, the subtle rhythms he had included in his speech. What he had written was better than anything spoken in that courtroom during both of the hearings. God, suppose the person in the dock after him found the speech and actually used it! If a character such as Conlin, in the dock on a charge of petty larceny or obstruction were to blast off with; "I wish to offer my own few poor words relative to the slanderous charge that has been levelled against me by the blind forces of the law" or "All I crave now from this seat of injustice is the charity of its silence," there would be laughter in court indeed. But where now could he himself look for the charity of silence? Round the next corner was the college where, just as you'd expect, life, the Mad Axeman was of course waiting for him, whistling tunelessly as he worked to put a good edge on his grim instrument.

In the distance, passing along by the church, he saw McClery flanked by Brian and Dev, striding along as if through knee-high gorse, the skirts of his black, scabbing-it-on-the-clergy raincoat flapping about him like a persistent crow. His stomach muscles tightened. The ordeal he had gone through in the courts would be nothing compared to what was before him now! "Ma and me were killing ourselves laughing!" If his own family could do that to him before the trial what was he about to be let in for now by Franco, McClery, the two lousy informers, without which no Irish scene is ever complete, and the rest of the school as well? And of course Kathleen wasn't completely wrong about him. If only he hadn't been so unutterably stupid to be so out of touch with reality as to allow himself to act out a ridiculous daydream he would never have landed in a mess like this.

He couldn't even attain the faint satisfaction of picturing what she looked like, the plump girl he had been trailing down the quays having first seen her as he leaned on the green balustrade of Capel Street bridge admiring the delicate iron arc of the Half-Penny Bridge farther down the river. As she came past she gave him an expressionless stare which she held until to continue doing so any longer would have meant her having to turn round on her hips and stare back at him. Surely, he thrilled as he began to slouch after her, that was what Brian meant by the 'Come-on' sign by girls that let you know they were dead on. Each time she paused he couldn't decide whether she was waiting for him to overtake her or was displaying a genuine interest in what was on show in the various windows whose yellow light bathed maddeningly over her thick feminine figure which was precisely what his whole body ached to do. Whenever she stopped he went to the shop window nearest him and pretended an interest in what he found there, now and then shading his eyes with his palm against the yellow glare of the lights from within, while he mimed the excitement of discovery he had been impressed by in a magazine advertisement which carried a striking charcoal drawing of Christopher Columbus catching his first sight of America. It was an advertisement for canned soup - "A Whole new World of Taste!" Reliving those moments as he trudged on towards the college he smiled at how useful the Columbus act had been for it enabled him to retreat a few astounded paces from each window and scan the horizon to discover where was his as yet unexplored America and what was she doing? The various windows of that evening glided through his mind. He had shaded his eyes before gilded monstrances, gleaming chalices, wrought iron crosses, and other objects used in church ritual. A few paces on he repeated his performance before sunglasses, binoculars, magnifying glasses, microscopes, spectacle frames of different shapes and materials, and a framed letter from his Holiness the Pope to the incumbent optician - he had to use both palms in shading his eyes to check if the letter was indeed from the present pope and if his handwriting was of a kind that would satisfy Franco's high standards of legibility. Further on he did his eye-shading act before false noses, gaudy coloured balloons, party hats, itching powder, stink bombs and other jolly novelties. Moving on quickly to where he looked in at wash-hand basins, baths, tentacled shower units, an amazing variety of lavatory pans including one in what looked like green marble. Who would want one like that - some national hero? At yet another window he was doing his astonished act for a couple of minutes before he realised he was standing before a generous, brilliantly-lit display of ladies underwear and drawing the attention of the inevitable passers-by who in Dublin never let anything pass without having a good gawk at it. All that of course was before he reached the antiquarian bookshop that specialised also in old newspapers and prints. As the central display in its grimy window it had a colour print of the scene in the General Post Office shortly before the end of the siege. In the left foreground, James Connolly lay wounded on a stretcher dictating notes to a kneeling volunteer. Above him, revolver in hand, stood Padraig Pearse, in profile as usual, his brother Willies with folded arms beside him and Tom Clarke behind the both of them glaring defiance over their shoulders. The picture rang with gunshots and crackling flames. In the central background James Plunkett, a volunteer on a table, played water from a hose on the burning ceiling. At the windows the out-numbered volunteers continued to pour a defiant fire on the encroaching, unseen enemy Several figures lay prone on the ground - one receiving the last rites from a priest - while others sagged in frozen attitudes of death or mortal wounding. He had no need to pretend an interest in that picture for with his first glance it drew him into the heart of its desperate agony of heroic sacrifice. "It was really terrible but glorious at the end, lads," Mr Dodd had once confessed when led adroitly into a digression from the intricacies of the genitive case in Irish, "Every man there felt death standing at his elbow, yet we all fought with the gaiety and delight usually associated with victory. That was one of the few occasions when I knew Padraig Pearse to be truly happy. He had what I can only describe as a beatific smile on his face. God rest them all! They died that we here and the rest of the country might live, not only free but Gaelic as well, not only Gaelic but free as well!"

If only he hadn't halted at that particular window to be drawn into the restless drama of that blasted picture! There before him were the heroic men of Ireland fighting to the bitter end for him and all the rest of his generation while he, the beneficiary of their blood sacrifice, could find nothing better to do with his life than neglect his studies, refuse to think seriously about his future, drown his mind in futile dreams and trail unknown girls from one shop window to the next like a slavering dog sniffing after a bitch. In a fury of self-disgust he dodged round the next corner, hoping to God she would not follow him, - and went stamping through the streets cursing the ignoble, shallow thing he had allowed himself to become since the cravings of lust had awakened in his flesh. On and on he walked, forcing himself to look long and deep into that cesspool of sin, his soul. What he discerned there, writhing in the depths, appalled him and left him with the uneasy feeling that if he didn't take steps to amend his life pretty soon he might turn out to be a really contemptible character - like Brian. At length a stitch in his side slowed him down and he discovered he was in Hanover Street from which almost at once he swung into Erne Street and began to head south in what he felt was the general direction of home. And then, roused from his reverie by a murmur as of a great wind on the sea, he saw he had come in amongst a large crowd who, as if his surprised gaze at that moment impelled them into violent action, broke into shouts and screams and began struggling with whoever was in front of them, their faces vivid with the extremes of hatred and anger you see mostly only on the faces of characters in old silent films. Two or three of the crowd reeled, backwards as if from an explosion and fell to the ground in front of him leaving a brief gap in the heaving mass through which he glimpsed a body of policemen rushing forward wielding their batons. He heard the sickening sound of hard wood meeting flesh and bone, and sighing his despair at the old familiar noises of political strife he thrust his hands in his trouser pockets and began calmly to stroll around the heaving groups of struggling figures, seeking a way out, the cold, clinical Eyes-and-Ears of the World observing all, recording all. Round the dizzying confusion he strolled and came into a clearing of immense calm. For a brief moment he moved in the still centre of a hurricane piloting his battered airmail plane with its burden of world-startling messages on a narrow orbit untouched by the passions of the storm. And went out the other side bearing his still centre of calm with him until his path was abruptly blocked by a huge man hopping from one foot to the other, waving a large black bottle and shouting: "Why don't you bloody guards go home? Call yourselves Irishmen when you're only doing what England tell you! But I'm not afraid of yous! Be Jesus I'm not!"

As he made to go round the dancing effusion of the hurricane the man dropped the bottle and with a howl of fear came rushing past him, shielding his skull with his clutching palms. "I'm sorry for what I said" he shrieked, "O Sacred Heart of Jesus protect me now!"

Assailed by an access of shame at the arrant cowardice of the man he bent and retrieved the bottle from the ground. With an absurd sense of choosing to be a hero, of performing an act of selfless sacrifice, he stepped into the breach, into the living picture of the last hours in the General Post Office where as Padraig Pearse he stood in profile, revolver in hand, his struggling comrades all around him. Was it really true Pearse had a cast in his eye? How could you make a national hero of a man who looked like that? He stood a moment holding the bottle, the neck pointing to the ground, thinking about Gilmore's slanderous remark. And then slowly, deliberately, in violent rejection of what Gilmore had said fired his last scornful round against the slander and his own astounded better judgement! As usual, life showed up almost before the bottle crashed into the window, its axe coming down on his shoulder as the bony hand of Guard Flaherty: "Got you me bucko!"

How embarrassingly stupid it had all been! A Japanese would have committed Hara-kiri, oh several times over! And with nothing at all served by the fatuous act, neither the Glory of God nor the Honour of Ireland. Except of course that if it hadn't been for those two nights in the Bridewell he might not have been able to force himself to make a decision about what he should do with his life.

He entered the dreaded college and dashed up the broad staircase in a desperate charge, Captain Bolton, Eastern Command Irish Army, way out there ahead of his men in a heroically hopeless assault on a machine-gun post entrenched on the summit of a bleak mountain - possibly known on the map as Mount McClery. On the second landing he paused, panting, and slapped the flat of his hand against the slimy green wall. Jesus Christ, would he never shake free of these overpowering, childish dreams! Would he never learn anything from the things that happened to him, from the very condition of his life, out there in the real world? He went on again slowly, gritting his teeth in preparation for the howl of derision that must surely await him in the classroom. How could people be so cruel to their own kind? Because they sense their victim is different? McClery's favourite way of showing his derision was to emit a kind of whispering nasal snigger when someone in class came to the end of a faltering answer to one of his questions, or - as in his own case - when they put forward a new interpretation of well-known facts. At those times McClery lounged sideways in his chair, his chin resting on his palm, his eyes bright and scornful peering out from under his bushy eyebrows. In a somewhat similar way both Brian and Dev expressed their contempt and derision of others by whispers and high-keyed laughs from behind their hands and they too favoured a comfortable, sitting position to do that. He remembered their scoffing laughter as he came past them, sitting on the steps, to scrutinise the exam results pinned up in the hall where to his surprise he learned he had come top of the class. Gilmore had got exactly the same treatment the day he came past carrying for the first time the brief case with which he had replaced his over-the-shoulder schoolbag. But come to think of it, as he had learned from his holidays in the country and from his wanderings about in the city, there were very many people in Ireland just like that. In twos and threes they sat in gleeful or derisive judgement on their neighbour usually from some vantage point like a window, a ditch, or a flight of steps, sniggering and whispering and laughing when their chosen victim came past.

He reached the door of the classroom. Now for it! Oh damn that bloody picture of the siege in the G.P.O.! Damn Padraig Pearse standing in profile with his revolver! Damn Doddier with his weepy-weepy account of the last hours of the battle which when you took a long, cool look at it wasn't one of the great military encounters of world history. Damn Franco and the other brothers with their continual exhortation to work for the glory of God and the honour of Ireland! If he hadn't been fool enough to listen to all their twaddle and believe in it he wouldn't be in this present rotten mess, sweating like a pig outside Fennelly's factory trembling at the knees, wanting badly to go to the lavatory. And what did the so-called sacrifices of 1916 and the years that followed mean to him anyway? Life in two crumbling rooms and a damp-walled kitchen, his mother forced to go out to work up to ten hours a day in the stuffy offices of a canned meat firm - or as Flora Gilmore might put it, exploited everyday by a God-and-Money worshipping daily communicant. And never enough to eat and never anything really snappy to wear even for the usual Yahoos to scoff at. Yet even in spite of all that, suppose you felt impelled to do something good, not just for yourself but for Ireland, who would you be sacrificing yourself for anyway? Just people like Kathleen, Brian, Dev, McClery, Franco, the crowd who laughed at you in the courtroom and the thousands all over the country lurking behind window curtains, peering out of the plush interiors of motor cars, hiding behind ditches and stone walls, squatting on steps whispering and scoffing and sneering to their hearts content. Not bloody likely as whatdoyoucallher said in Pygmalion! To hell with the hero game. And as for the army what would life really be like if he got his commission? For one thing he would probably be shunted out of Dublin and stationed in some one-cinema town like Athlone where everything drops dead at six, except the public houses, and nothing circulates at night on its dreary streets except stray cats and discarded fish-and-chip wrappers. And of course the Mad Axeman. Nor would there be any heroic charging up hillsides or other film-hero stuff. Instead only marches at the head of a gang of foul-mouthed, ignorant bog-men through the moist mists and depressing drizzles of mountain tops which are interesting and exciting only if you're reading about them in the writings of Synge. First time out he'd probably get pneumonia. Worst of all, he would lose forever the freedom to wander through his beloved city streets. And as for the chance of seeing any action in the army who was Ireland likely to fight in the foreseeable future? It would hardly take on Great Britain to resolve the question of the six counties or embark on a mad crusade to bring Russia back into the arms of the church, a crusade no doubt in which life with its usual axe would be waiting for him, the wily smile of Ivan the Terrible on its face. Oh yes, his intuition had been right earlier! The day of his trial was certainly sorting out all his ideas, all his values!

Bracing himself for the inevitable howl of derision, he turned the handle of the door and went into the classroom, into a furtive hush that continued after the click of the door behind him, broken by no hoots of contempt, no sneers of scorn. Most of the fellows were crowded round the street-side window from which at the noise of his entrance only a few of them turned their wrapt attention. McDermott bobbed him a curt nod - "Oh, it's you, Bolton" - and resumed with the rest his intent scrutiny of whatever was going on out in the square. Seated on top of a desk, well apart from the rest, Gilmore shook hands solemnly with himself and smiled at him.

"Congratulations, old outlaw! Pleased to hear you cheated the gallows, Pearse. I must tell my sister all about it next time they let me visit her." "Thanks...! he said, embarrassed by his surprise that in all his years in the college he had never learned Gilmore's first name. No one in his hearing had ever addressed Gilmore by anything other than his surname; and when the roll was being called, as soon as he answered his own name, he invariably flopped back into one of his dreams while Franco creaked on through the rest of the names on the register. Gilmore nodded towards the intent group at the window.

"They never show that kind of interest to anything

McClery has to say, do they?"

He looked across at the group and wondered what they were attending to with their furtive, crouching air of someone peering through a forbidden keyhole. Shrugging his shoulders he came back to his own preoccupations and went to his desk at the back of the room where on raising the lid he was relieved to see his history textbook was still where he left it last time he was in class. He sat down at the desk, only then discovering how tired he was, and rested, his head in his hands. At once fragments of the day's events began to jostle past in hushed disorder. Sour Belly's face rose clear and immediate from the muttering confusion and smiled, warmly at him. He felt the muscles of his face respond to the smile as gradually, with a sense of pleased surprise, it began to dawn on him that he had met tokens of real, genuine friendship that day and that they had come from Gilmore, the woman in the courtroom, and the Justice himself. All he had had from the rest was annoyance, scorn and hurt. Yet in spite of that he had come through in one piece, bearing with him so much that he would need to ponder on in the days ahead. But more immediately, he felt he was now ready to allow his wary friendliness towards Gilmore to develop into something warmer, something more trusting in which they could exchange confidences, kick ideas around. His heart lightened. Who could tell, maybe at last his luck was beginning to change. After all, if the dreaded Justice could smile at him, anything could happen. Maybe in time even the Mad Axeman himself would come around to smiling at him as well. At the very least his name might no longer stand at the head of the list of the Axeman's favourite targets! And eventually, with a little more luck, the Axeman might even find it in his heart to forgive him for deserting that marvellous girl on the night of the mad bells in the old dark house.

"Look! There! It's come round again!" a voice called from the midst of the group at the window,

"See!" McDermott cried, "Coming round by the pub on the corner, the horse and cab!"

Voices chimed and clamoured in a criss-cross of excitement. "Is it Conlin's cab, Brian?"

"I think so."

"It doesn't look like it to me," Dev said.

"Take a closer look," Brian urged, "The same long whip. The same hat and coat."

"Even if it's not Conlin," someone's voice suggested, "It could be the same woman inside."

"And not on her own, I bet you!"

"Yes, and using a different cab to put the cops off the scent."

"And what a scent those women use! Jesus!"

"Knock you down!"

"Down to where?"

"Anyway, what's the difference if it's not the same cab?" Brian asked, "It's obvious it's the same racket."

"Using the square for a change!"

"And in the middle of the day as well. What nerve!"

"Yeah, and what lucky customers!"

"You're right Brian," McDermott said in a hushed voice,"Look the blinds are down!"

"And what else I wonder?"

"An' we've only *Poyning's Law* to look forward to!"

"Can't you imagine what's going on that cab now?" Brian said, almost with a sob, "Sweet Jesus!"

Pearse turned away from them in response to a timid knock far back in his mind. No, he would resist what was there for this was not just another life-wasting daydream, another opium den of stupefying fantasy. His heart knew it for what it was, an instance of the kind, of rare, creative vision poets are blessed with, after which nothing in life is ever quite the same again. And the vision came in dressed as he knew it would be, in red ermine, wearing a white wig, its cobra-green eyes winking slyly into his. Oh, no doubt about it at all now! His mother must write to Uncle Sam for money and still more money. He would need every cent she could gather to enable him to pursue his studies, to sweat his brains out over his books all day, every day, from morning till night for only then would he fling out into the street for a brief respite and a breath of air. And it would take years, years of a sacrifice of time and energy only a true hero could endure. But he could and he would do it! He longed, for it to be night on the streets of the city through which he would wander again observing the splendours and the miseries of his time, above all the secrets and the sins he would need fully to comprehend in order with compassion and humour to sit in judgement on them one day as Chief Justice of Ireland.

THE GREEN IN DUBLIN

"Is there another cup of tea on that pot?" Fleming asked. Musso Moran reached across the blotched sheets of the Evening Herald they had spread last night as a table cover and caressed his horny hand over the blue enamel teapot. Under the vibrating shadow of his arm Fleming saw the headline "De Valera on Economic..." end abruptly in the brown star-shaped mass of a tea stain.

"Ah, you'd be better off without this," Moran mumbled his meaty lips around the glowing speck of a cigarette butt, "The drop that's left in it must be as cold now as a nun's - er - nose." Sniggering moistly round the waggling cigarette he shrugged to his feet and slouched across the constricting room to the curtained window where the soft, rain-laced light from the hills haloed the angry stubble on his blunt red head striking random points of fire from his overnight sprout of beard. Fleming, his eyes aching for the ease of sleep, watched him in a faint fret of disgust. God, was it possible that in the early hours of the night, crouched beside that repellent figure under the huge bronze hoofs of the statue, his heart fluttering in his mouth like a linnet in a paper bag, there had swept over him with the force of an unseen hand pushing him off-balance, a disconcerting wave of warm, tender love for his rough, uncouth comrade-in-arms? What a horrifying experience! He chafed in the helpless dismay he had come to know so well as a child when his stepfather succeeded in playing yet another mean trick on him, leaving him bitter and confused. How terrible to recall that he had longed to cup his hands round the broad, red cheeks and kiss the face of that raucous-voiced, pig-ignorant, filthy-tongued guttie scratching his crotch over there by the window! It was anxiety that made him feel like that. He looked away sighing in quiet disgust. Moran was so typical of those fellows from the sprawling slums of the city who joined the movement more out of blind spite against the government, the hatred of the have-nots, than for love of Ireland and the undying ideal of the republic. But you had to work with the men who were there whatever they were like and make the best of it. For the Cause! The raw presence of the fellow in the room made him think of squat barrels standing sour and empty on the quayside, of interlaced muscles of stout rope slithering over the cobbles to the dumpy brewery tugs sputtering on the high Liffey tide. From the moment he first saw him, something about Moran had suggested Guinness's to him, though he knew perfectly well he was an electrician employed by the E.S.B. That was the reason the Commandant had chosen him as technical expert on the job.

"Ah well," Moran stirred the tip of his little finger in his nostril, "It won't be long now as the farmer said when he sat down on the blade of the scythe."

"Less o' that sort o! talk," Fleming growled at him out of the side of his mouth, "The job we're on is no joking matter at all."

The mention of the imminent event caught his breath and tightened in his throat as if he had a metal ring down there. Since last night the walls of the room seemed to have pressed in closer to where he sat at the table, shivering slightly in the morning chill. He stared at the pale peeling wallpaper and tried not to brood on the heavy odour of grease and stale bacon which reposed like a foul memory on the still, heavy air of the place. His student acquaintance - who knew him simply as O'Connor - had winked broadly in the pub when he slipped him the folded pound note, the hire of the room for the night, "A top-front room in Leeson Street," the student giggled into his cream-crested pint, "is as near as you'll ever get to heaven in Dublin. Unless, paradoxically, you want the privacy of the room to try a more earthy way of getting there." He hoped the student hadn't noticed the blush flaring on his cheeks for, almost from the very moment the job was assigned to him, lewd images, unwanted, uninvited, had begun to prance through his mind. Not since he had attended that frightening week-end retreat with the Passionist Fathers when he was fourteen were women so lurid and compelling in his sweaty dreams. Which made that impulse of passionate yearning for Moran last night all the more inexplicable and shocking. It was no wonder he had hurried up to the canal, more for reassurance than for lust, as soon as they climbed back out over the railings of the park. He eyed the bulk of the immense iron-frame bed in the corner. Only for Moran he could have taken the woman up to the room last night.

The moonlit canal bank scraggy with litter looked unspeakably sordid and was uncomfortably damp as well. But Moran had said: "I don't mind keepin' an eye out for you here but I'm damn sure I'm not goin' to hang around outside the house in the freezin' cold while you're upstairs enjoyin' yourself with her. My God, sure the two of yous might just forget I was there and leave me out in the street all night."

"Look out!" Moran chuckled peering out of the window, "Take my advice Miss an' turn back now or before you know it you'll be wettin' your drawers!"

How close would the girl be to the Green when it happened? Fleming wondered about that with the cool detachment he enjoyed showing off to the kids in the school when working out some complex maths problem on the board. He glanced at his wrist-watch. Yes, it was getting near the time. A girl walking from there at an average rate would arrive at the end of the street facing the Green just about when the mine would go off. He smiled slyly as he reached under the table and fetched up his small leather suitcase. Springing the catches he reached his hand inside and touched lightly over the contents, coils of wire, a spare detonator, a sheaf of exercise books he hadn't marked yet, a box of cartridges, a boxed deck of cards, the rosary beads his mother had given him for his Confirmation, his Webley 0.45 service revolver, the comforting shape of a bottle of Tullamore whiskey round which his fingers closed. He drew it carefully out from among the exercise books and placed it on top of the other objects, the lid of the case resting lightly on it.

"Volunteer Moran," he called out in his brisk, classroom voice, "Take those two glasses from the table and wash them in the bathroom down the corridor."

Moran looked across at him in surprise and began to rub his heavy chin with his dirt-grained hand as if remembering an occasion when he had been struck there. Fleming realised that this was the first time since the job began that he had called Moran by his official army title. Enjoying Moran's look of bewilderment, as if the horny hand was caressing it into his face, he said: "Look smart there man, it's twenty- five past seven."

In a delicate blur Moran's hand moved from his face to his waistcoat pocket. "I don't think my father's oul ticker'd agree with you there," he said. A heavy gold watch hopped on his palm, "By this timepiece here, as I told you last night, your watch is five minutes fast. Look at the weight of that! Solid gold! An' two quid is all my father paid for it. To a fella who took it off a dead German on the Somme. The fella said it didn't go for a whole week from the very second he plugged the Jerry between the eyes, sort of in protest for what he done. Course it hasn't lost a tick since, an' it's never wrong."

Fleming treated him to the long slow hiss of a man about to lose patience. "Look, are you going to wash those glasses or not?"

Moran held his angry stare and he found himself counting - seven, eight, nine - waiting for the damn fellow's eyelids to flicker. Leaning forward slightly as if pressing his weight against Fleming's exasperated look Moran suddenly whipped a greyish handkerchief from his pocket and draped it over his forearm. He clicked the rims of the two glasses between his thumb and forefinger and went slouching out of the room in a parody of a tired, overworked waiter. "Comin' up, sir!" he called over his shoulder. Fleming's gums ached from gritting his teeth. Beads of sweat itched under the thin wispy hair on his broad skull. He got to his feet, took a firm grip on the back of the greasy kitchen chair and pushed hard to control the tremors undulating through his limbs. Nothing must go wrong today, please God! His first exercise of command in the field must be a success in every way. That's why he was packed with unreasoning anxieties - and other wild feelings!

The Commandant who liked him and wanted to promote him further in the movement had set his heart on his doing a perfect job, he knew. He heard Moran rasp open the bathroom door and almost at once a strong jet of water began to slosh at full cock into the basin. Above the noise of the water he made out a groaning lilt as if anguish itself had found a voice to sing with.

"We're off to Dub-a-lin in the green, in the green, Where the hel-e-mets glitter in the sun..." Fleming rushed to the door and peered round the jamb.

"Quiet down there. Shh!" he called as loudly as he dared. Moran's stubbly head appeared from out of the bathroom.

"Come again?"

Fleming swallowed down the bizarre impression that the head had thrust straight out of the solid wall. "Quiet" he whispered and placed his finger firmly on his lips in a gesture that never failed in the school for Brother O'Meara.

"Oh aye! I get it" Moran said in a loud raw voice like that of a workman Fleming heard once behind an altar at which he was praying. "Mum's the word! As the girl said when she found out she was pregnant."

With deliberate, blank-eyed slowness he began to draw his head back into the bathroom which Fleming had to insist to himself was not straight back into the solid wall again. As the blue orb of his near eye vanished from view a whistling as of a tram trolley began to vibrate through Fleming's head. Slowly the other blue orb followed the first until only the palish rim of Moran's big ear was visible. Then to Fleming's intense annoyance the hairy-cored ear moved slowly outwards again and steadied as if it were some strange implement Moran was using to study him with. In a pulse of panic he called: "Cut it out, Moran!" The big ear wiggled and withdrew.

"Bloody comedian they foisted on me" he muttered to himself, "Let's see how funny he'll turn out to be if anything goes wrong!" He listened for untoward sounds in the rambling house which he knew was let out in rooms to students from U.C.D. and Civil Servants in the lower grades. Somewhere music was playing so faintly it was like a moment of past joy the mind sought in vain to recapture.

Moran tramped back down the corridor and marched in past Fleming who listened a moment longer in the whirring silence before following him back into the room. A glance at his watch showed it was just a few minutes short of the hour. Deftly be slipped the bottle out of the suitcase and sloshed a generous measure of whiskey into each of the glasses.

"Be Janey, now you're talkin'" Moran showed a long grin of irregular teeth. "If this is what your Volunteer

Moran wash this, wash that, was all about, why didn't you say so? Sure for a glass o' whiskey I'd even wash myself."

Fleming raised his forearm and squinted at the seconds hand on his watch racing his heart round its narrow circle.

"I give you a toast" he said.

"Sure you're five minutes too early."

"A toast" he splashed some of his whiskey in his agitation, "The Irish Republic!"

"Oh aye, I'll drink to that! The good oul workers' republic!"

Fleming hardly tasted the whiskey against his bitter urge to sneer: "God help us from the likes of you if that ever came to pass." His ears tingled. Imperceptibly, he bent away from the window watching the panes, wondering would they shatter when the explosion came - now! A heavy silence flowed in from the street where as he listened a car parked close by revved up and roared past the window in the direction of the Green. He listened to it drive rapidly away from the ensuing, blank, inexplicable silence.

"Jesus, it couldn't have failed! Just couldn't!" he blurted at Moran who began to move towards the window. "Watch out for flying glass!" he warned him. From the street arose the damp slap of striding feet, the piercing off-key whistling of "Stormy Weather."

"Your watch is fast, that's all," Moran said his eyes glinting at the bottle of whiskey, "We've even time to drink another toast. If you like I'll propose it this time."

"I don't want another." Fleming caressed the back of his neck with his moist palm. Moran's eyes raked over him so knowingly he feared his trembling was becoming obvious.

"Help yourself," he said looking away from the beady stare.

"Begorrah sez Joe, I don't mind if I do" Moran quoted from a song he'd heard an old Nineteen-Sixteen man sing at a Ceilidhe. He was relieved when Moran turned his back on him though he knew it was to hide from him the amount of whiskey he was sloshing into the glass. Moran drank and smacked his lips in the noisy way he probably assaulted everything in life. The seconds crawled through him like the onset of an illness.

"God, what could have gone wrong?" he broke out in dismay.

"Aye, it's past the time on my father's oul ticker as well."

"Could it have been the rain?"

"No fear! The thing was too well insulated for that."

"Jesus! You don't think one of the gardeners found it?"

"If they did we'd have heard them. Sailin' in a deafenin' bang over the bloody roof. I rigged that thing so sensitive a pigeon couldn't fart within a yard of it without every window within a mile bein' blown in."

"All right then, Volunteer Moran" he drew himself up as if on parade, "Explain to me please why your mine failed to explode!"

"Why has it become *my* mine all of a sudden?" Moran fell into the crouch he'd seen him adopt once after an exercise near Lough Dan when sparring with another volunteer. "Don't forget the fella in charge of the operation is *you*!"

"But you wired it up!"

"I can vouch for my side of it" Moran swayed red-faced from side to side, as if dodging flying fists, "The timin' device an' the detonators is perfect, all the connections slap on. But I can't give you a written guarantee for the explosives themselves. Them Northerners! I'm never happy with stuff brought in by strangers."

"They're our own people" Fleming glared at him, "Here we are running God knows what risks to destroy an arrogant relic of English rule in our capital city and you start talking about our comrades in northern command as strangers! Stop that! There are no strangers among the few of us who are still active in the country." He touched his temples in the span of his thumb and forefinger.

"All right. Let's think this thing out rationally" he said, "Don't panic!"

"Who's p - "

"We've got to think of all the possibilities, all the eventualities" his hard fingers ruffled the skin on his forehead, "Yes! Yes! I have it! That's what we'll do. All right, Volunteer Moran, get your coat. We're withdrawing from this position."

He went to the bed from the end rail of which he tugged his own raincoat, a lovat-green belted garment with military style shoulder tabs. Moran came towards him wearing a sour expression, lurching left and right into his hairy grey-tweed ulster.

"I don't feel safe goin' around with you in that green coat" he said, "With that coat on an' your Trilby pulled down well over your eyes you're the spittin' image of Hollywood's idea of an I.R.A. man. If you ask me it's a dead giveaway to the C.I.D."

"Nobody's canvassing your opinion, Volunteer Moran. Just make sure we don't leave any stuff here behind us."

"An' where are we off to? Or are you keepin' that a military secret from the lower ranks?"

"We're goin' to ring the Commandant, what do you think?"

"The Commandant?" Moran raised both hands and scratched his stubby fingers into his red spiky hair, "Sure doesn't the Commandant know bloody well the thing hasn't gone off? If it had, it'd've blasted him and half the city out of their dreams. Or whatever."

Fleming glared tight-mouthed down at his companion who to his annoyance stared fascinated at his Adam's apple. Curbing an impulse to swallow he adopted the deliberately clear tone suitable for speaking to backward children or congenital idiots.

"Unless we ring the Commandant how can he be sure we placed the mine in position in the first place? There was always the possibility we might have got pinched carrying the stuff in over the railings to the statue. Isn't it just possible he might think that?"

"Come to think of it, yeah!" Moran nodded dawning realisation, "Or even that we got cold feet on the way down from here and dumped the mine somewhere else. In the canal maybe. Or the mots' lavo."

"Let's go then" Fleming drew the belt of his raincoat tight on the fluttering anxiety in his midriff, "We'll ring him from the nearest box, the one opposite the Shelbourne. He's always at the shop first thing to catch the early morning cigarette and newspaper trade."

In silence they descended the three flights of stairs to the street door and began to walk towards the Green keeping well in by the houses. As they turned the corner Fleming felt the ominous silence of the park rush like a dumb shout through his head. Any minute the damn thing might go up and who then would be suddenly wet? Or worse! To no avail he tried to swallow down the dry wad of anxiety in the back of his throat. That would no doubt come out as an excited tremor or even a stutter when he spoke to the Commandant who would of course think it was due to guilt for having bungled the job. So Moran mustn't be present in the phone booth to witness his discomfiture. His over-anxiety, his sudden and disconcerting lack of confidence were due he felt sure to the horror of those untoward feelings for Moran which had swept over him last night. It was they that had driven him to the canal - and further anxious guilt. "Moran, I want you to keep an eye..." he said turning to find he was walking towards Hume Street on his own. He saw Moran back on the corner of Leeson Street looking about him like one lost in a strange city. He hurried back, the stitch in his side piercing as a raw wound.

"What the hell's come over you, Volunteer Moran?" he panted, "You can't just do what you like, you know. You'll follow orders and stick close to me. Is that clear?"

Moran thrust his arm out at full length and spun his

extended index finger round as if boring a hole with it, "You should have been the first to see. I hadn't noticed until we came down to the corner. It's then it began to dawn on me."

"What did?" Fleming's eye raked over the green silence of the park.

"You bein' a teacher I thought you'd have been the first to notice."

"Jesus, man! Notice what?"

"The schools! Sure there's crowds of schools all round this place."

"Two or three I believe! Sure any fool knows that."

"Yeah but does any fool know that the Green'll be open at half-eight and from then until nearly nine it'll be full of poor little kids traipsin' past that statue?"

"Snap out of it Volunteer Moran" Fleming stamped his foot hard on the pavement, but the distressing trembling remained in his leg. "We're here to carry out orders not to speculate on hypothetical consequences. Let's get on to the Commandant. He's in overall command of the operation. He'll decide an' tell us what to do."

"Aye, but the poor kids" Moran stared morosely across at the stark green presence of the park, "That's a thunderin' powerful mine. An' awful sensitive."

Fleming swung his suitcase across to his left hand and caught hold of the lapel of Moran's overcoat. "What's the matter with you? Are you going soft?" he hissed between his teeth whose faint chattering he was afraid might be audible to his companion.

"Hey, let go of me, you!" Moran tugged free, "That's me good coat you were pullin' there. I paid Montague Burton thirty-five hard-earned balloons for that!

"Sorry! Sorry!" Fleming sighed, "But for God's sake let's get in touch with the Commandant. He'll be as much concerned for the children as anyone." He was about to add: "He doesn't have to teach the little bastards," but felt that might give Moran the wrong impression.

"O.K. then," Moran glowered from side to side, "Let's hear what he has to say!"

Moran fell into step beside him as he hurried back towards Hume Street and crossed to the telephone kiosk. He swung the door open, dropped his suitcase on the stone floor and began to scrabble for coppers in his raincoat pockets. So that Moran couldn't follow him in he kept his back to the door. Finding to his surprise no money in the pockets he unbuttoned his raincoat and plunged his hands into the pockets of his suit and - his bewilderment growing - into his trousers pockets as well. "Jesus!" he exclaimed backing out to join Moran, "That bloody bitch! Should be locked up, so she should. The likes of her shouldn't be allowed to walk around among decent people."

"What's up?" Moran's head twitched round to a sudden rustling in the nearby shrubbery of the park. Two blackbirds rose twittering in fear. "Why aren't you makin' the call?" he turned back to Fleming.

"Because I've nothing to make it with. I haven't got a half-penny on me, not even the tram-fare to the school. That thieving bitch must've gone through all my pockets last night without my feeling a thing." He plunged his hand again into his pockets, searching desperately.

"You must have been feelin' somethin' else or you'd have noticed" Moran sniggered. He laid his forehead against the window frame of the kiosk and shook with laughter. "Yous holy guys are a real laugh, yous really are! You shudda seen the grey, peaky look on your dial last night when on our way out you went trottin' into Clarendon Street chapel to have your confession heard. You'd think you were goin' to be shot at dawn. Or earlier! An' the good drinkin' time you wasted urgin' me to confess too. Tried to make it an order, so you did. "Think of it" sez you "as an essential part of the job, a sensible spiritual precaution just in case the worst happens." By that I thought you meant that by the time we'd assembled the mine in that room, the pubs'd be all shut. An' later on, no sooner had we put the mine in position than you went dashin' off like a madman, looking for a brasser. It amazes me how a fella like you, waist-deep in prayer books and rosary beads, knew exactly where to find a big fat whore in the dead middle of the night. I've lived all my life in this town, but I'd no idea until I tagged after you what a hive of industry the banks of the canal are in the small wee hours. Or the night-work hours as I heard an ex-soldier I work with call them once."

"Bloody bitch!" Fleming fumed, "She even took a sheaf of letters I had in my inside pocket. From a girl down the country I know. Nice respectable girl. They were on a kind of creaky paper so she probably thought it was money. Everything she took! Volunteer Moran, stop sniggering there and let me have two coppers for the phone."

"Right you be, sor." Moran brushed his forehead in a mock salute and still chuckling to himself began to search through his pockets. After the first few casual gropings his forehead crinkled in concern. He plunged from side to side rooting deep into his pockets. Something jingled. Fleming's heart lifted.

"'S'only keys" Moran told him, "'S'matter a fact, this is all I have." He opened his hand to reveal a pound note screwed up on his palm.

"Oh my God, what'll we do now?" Fleming heard his voice tremble. His legs jerked spasmodically, flapping the skirts of his raincoat. He brought the face of his wristwatch close to his eyes and tried to understand its message. "Moran, there's nothing else for it. We've got to get change for that pound somewhere."

"What, at this hour?"

"I know! But there must be someone who'll change it for us. Think, man! Think!" He looked about him, his eyes sheering away from the park. "Hey" he recalled, "Down there! Isn't there a fellow that sells papers down there on the corner of Grafton Street? Yes, there is. I've seen him."

"Well let's go then!" Moran began to hurry away.

"Wait! Wait!" Fleming opened the door of the kiosk and retrieved his suitcase. He placed it on the ground while he fumbled into the task of buttoning his raincoat.

"Ah, come on" Moran swayed from side to side in impatience, "Sure you can button that on the trot."

"Wait! I'm not going to go dashing along there with

my coat flapping all over the place. We've got to be as inconspicuous as possible. If we attract any sort of attention to ourselves people may notice and be able to give descriptions later."

Walking as fast as he dared he held his head down as they passed a few early morning pedestrians trudging to work. They crossed to the corner of Grafton Street where a news-vendor was kneeling on the damp greasy pavement tugging sheafs of morning newspapers from a coarse sack.

"Try and not let this old fellow get a good look at us," Fleming whispered to Moran as they drew near, "If anyone gets killed today it could turn out to be a swinging job. If he looks up, turn away and start talking about the chances of getting a job on the building sites in Tallaght. Something like that."

He turned up the collar of his raincoat. A swinging job! The phrase had sprung unbidden to his lips. God, if the thing went off and some kid got killed it could turn out to be just that. He ruffled his shoulders inside the tight overcoat.

"Slip me that pound note" he whispered to Moran.

"It's *my* money!" Moran, aggrieved, shrugged his back at him.

"I know that! Come on, slip it to me!" He tapped the side of his hand on Moran's wrist.

"It's my money an' I'll get the change" Moran swung away from him and came round to where he bent over the news-vendor, a grey shrivelled elderly man in a flat tweed cap and a rumpled fawn raincoat.

"Give's an Independent there" Moran drawled, "A few coppers in the change." The pound note fluttered down and came to rest almost under the nose of the man who picked it up and tossed it casually into the air.

"Are you mad? A pound first thing in the mornin'?"

Moran threw an exasperated glance at Fleming who jerked his head down between the wings of his coat collar.

"Go on" he urged. Moran hovered over the news-vendor his hand lingering about his waist as if lazily scratching his stomach through his overcoat. "Dig into your oul bookie's bag there and jingle up a bit o' change. God, man you wouldn't be wantin' me not to see the racin' results from Newmarket that I missed last night an' me with me shirt an' all on an oul stanker in the last race."

"Take an Independent an' pay next time you're passin'."

Fleming caught Moran's exasperated glance and nodded him on to further efforts.

"Look we gotta have those coppers" Moran looked about as if searching for a convincing reason in the shop windows, "Gotta have them, because, because me an' my pal need to visit the Gents over there. Real bad. Jasus, we're sufferin' agonies so we need the coppers worser than we need the paper." He bent down, retrieved the pound note from the ground and waved under the man's nose, "Look, I'll leave this note with you an' I'll pick up the change on me way back from work. Just give's a few pennies an' we'll be on our way."

The man's gnarled hand twitched away from the pound note. "What's the game?" he whined through a yellow rake of teeth, "Is that a dud note you're tryin' to get rid of? It was all about yous in the paper a few weeks back." He scrambled to his feet, "Is there a Bobby about? Jasus, I'll get the two o' yous lagged, so I will. Police! Police!"

Fleming flung away from the shouting and bustled along the west side of the park hugging the doorways and shopfronts. Above the pounding of Moran's feet behind him he heard the irate calling of the news-vendor, "Get yous six months so I will! Why don't yous work for a livin' instead o' passin' out dud money on decent people?" The pavement brown and slimey from the earlier rain flowed beneath his hurrying feet. Sour with hatred he stamped into its scurrying surface the pale face of that raucous guttie Flanagan who sat in the end desk on the left in the front row of his class. No wonder he always associated Moran with Guinness's for Flanagan's father was a brewery drayman and the boy himself had the lardy stockiness, the red-headed rawness, the luridly offensive mannerisms of his maddening subordinate. At school, Moran had probably been like that terrible kid, delighting, like him, in spitting in other children's faces in the playground and jabbing them in the behind with the needle of his compass whenever they reached over the top of their desks to borrow a rubber or a ruler.

Thank God though Moran had never found out the nickname Flanagan had fastened on him, the low Dublinism for a gob of phlegm. What a name to be known by - the Gollier! Jesus, when class began today Flanagan would be the first he'd examine in the Irish homework and when he'd fail to decline some second declension noun, then by God, there'd be hair an' skin flying. Six of the best on each hand with a brisk scelp of the leather across the backs of the legs for good measure. Flanagan's for it, he gritted his teeth on the acid urge of his anger.

"Hey! Hey! Slow down." He heard Moran pant hoarsely behind him.

He swung round and shook his fist under Moran's nose. "You made a right haimes of that, didn't you? I told you to let me handle it! Ordered you! What're we going to do now without change I ask you?"

Moran shrank away from him almost to his knees in a maddening parody of terrified amazement. Moist, strangled cries dribbled from his mouth. His hands waved about warding off unimaginable horrors.

"Stop acting the bloody fool!" Fleming hated the shriek of exasperation he heard in his own voice.

"You were shaking your great big knuckly fist at me" Moran whispered his eyes round and grey-blank as riverbed stones.

"Of course I was" Fleming shouted. "I had every right to" he almost succeeded in quietening his tones.

"An' while you were doin' that your other hand was in the pocket of your Hollywood gunman's raincoat."

"What the hell do you mean?"

"Nothin' much" Moran straightened up with a mocking toothy grin, "It's just I was wonderin' what you'd done with your little attache case?"

"Oh Christ!" Fleming's legs sagged in a spongy morass, "I must have left it out of my hand that time I was buttoning my overcoat back there. It was all your fault hurrying me like that! You should have noticed what I was doing."

"I should've noticed?" Moran coughed a guffaw, "That's a bloody good one. Anyway what's all the fuss for? It's not important anyway. You'll just have to write off the few coils o' wire an' the bottle o' whiskey as casualties in the fight for Irish freedom."

"Yes, you fool, an' the exercise books with the name o' the school and the class and the teacher on them. And my forty-five."

"Ah be the holy mackerel" Moran's head swung from side to side, a grotesque red metronome, "Do you mean to tell me that all the time we've been on the job you've been carryin' your gun around in an *attaché* case? Were you scared a bit o' dust might get on it?"

"That's enough o' that, Volunteer Moran" he was afraid that if he tried to stamp his foot angrily he wouldn't be able to lift it back off the ground. "If I didn't want it bulging under my coat that's my business. But one thing must be clear even to you. I must get that case back. Your orders are now to cover my rear. If that paper-seller sends a Bobby after us make sure it's *you* he chases."

"But look at the time! Moran wagged his huge watch at him, "Think o' the poor kids!"

"I am! I am!" he instantly regretted his desperate overemphasis which he knew would carry no conviction for Moran. "This'll only take a few minutes. God man, you wouldn't want me to have to face a court of enquiry over this would you?"

"No! No! Of course not!" Moran over-emphasised. Getting even, damn him.

Fleming swung away on his undependable legs, crossing as swiftly as he dared to the park side and clumped on under the welcome shadow of the overhanging trees forcing speed and confidence back into his stride. The rumour wasn't true that he'd been picked for the job only because Rielly had fallen sick at the last moment. He was chosen because the Commandant liked him, knew him to be cool in a crisis. On the far corner the news vendor sat on his tarpaulin, his head hidden behind an outspread newspaper. God, how would tomorrow's headline read? Rounding the corner of the Green his heart leaped to see in the distance the tiny nut-brown oblong of his suitcase on the ground outside the telephone kiosk. "God is good" he muttered quickening his pace to outstrip a compact little man in a suit of hairy grey plus-fours walking with a lithe springy step some few yards ahead of him. Warm, intimate sounds floated back to him and he wondered was the idiot talking to himself until he saw he was accompanied by a squat Kerry Blue dog sniffing along the park railings beside him. "That's a good little dog you are, Paddy Boy" he heard, "Sure isn't it great to be out first thing in the mornin', the whole city to ourselves. No wonder you're waggin' your little tail, God bless it."

"Oh Christ what now?" Fleming muttered striding with all his might to come up with the man whose newly-soled shoes flashed like yellow insults at him. As slowly he drew abreast the dog bounced about under his feet as if it had springs hidden in its paws. Fleming strode on past the man, the stitch in his side hurting like an opened wound, his head tucked hard on his tense neck behind the wings of his collar. He nodded his head forward to the man's "Great mornin', what?" and panted on through a reddish haze in which the case and the telephone box began to twitch to and fro in a crazy dance. Passing one of the side gates of the park he winced his head down again. The Green beside him yawned open, vast and vulnerable as the rugged hillside beyond Lough Dan where they had trained under the Commandant for the job. Each of the three mines they detonated had slapped the breath from his body and jolted through him as if a heavy door slammed shut in the vastness of his heart. Glancing down he saw the dog bouncing in a shower of red spots near his pounding feet, its alert head thrust forward towards the case. "Get to hell!" he panted and moved sideways to force the dog to fall behind. He recoiled from the blue snout curling back in a chattering snarl of long yellow teeth. "Good dog! Good Paddy Boy" he mimicked the man's accent. A young woman came round the corner ahead of him walking in a brisk confident stride that would surely bring her abreast of the telephone box before he had time to reach it. "Jesus!" he panted and broke into a trot that brought the dog yapping at his heels. He pounded on and in a lurching swoop gathered the suitcase from the ground and fumbled into the telephone box. The woman passed without a sideways glance. He took the receiver from its cradle and tried to remember the trick a fellow in a pub had described by which you could make a call without having to insert any coins in the box. How did he say it was done? Something moved in the mirror above the receiver, the reflection of the man in the grey plus-fours staring suspiciously in at him. He saw he had a long face, grey and sharp as a knife blade.

"Oh my God I'm heartily sorry" he laughed airily into the receiver as if in conversation with a friend "For having offended Thee," he nodded "And I detest my sins above every other evil because they displease Thee, my God who for Thy infinite goodness art so deserving of all my love." He pretended to listen to the reply, nodding agreement, "and I firmly resolve by Thy holy grace" he laughed. The image passed from the mirror and leaning forward he laid his forehead against the cool glass of the instruction chart. Jesus, if I come out of this I really will amend my life. Suddenly he belched. A sour whiff of whiskey came up his throat turning him vaguely sick. He had to take a grip on himself. After all, he was supposed to be in command! His heart leaped in alarm as the door rasped open behind him.

"'S'only me" Moran sniggered. He curled his arm round in front of Fleming and held up two pennies. "That was great gas, you and the dog. Like a picture I saw once at the Luxer. Fella bein' chased half-way across Russia be wolves."

Fleming was already dialling the Commandant's number.

"Hey" Moran jabbed him with his elbow, "Aren't you goin' to ask me where I got the coppers?"

"Where?" In his ear the twin blurts of the call signal went on and on.

"Off an oul Judy down there. Told her I was startin' a job after bein' unemployed for two years an' that I was late an' hadn't got any tram-fare. Had her practically in tears."

Fleming danced his fingers on the pay box. "Come on! Come on!" he urged.

"When he replies" Moran said, "tell him to get word to the C.I.D. that the park's not to open. That's the best thing."

"We'll leave all the decisions to him!" He felt he hadn't the energy to outstare Moran and looked away, "Great Christ! Why doesn't he pick up the phone and answer?" The twin pulses stabbed through his head.

"Maybe he's not there," Moran said in a quiet sneer, "Didn't open the shop today in an act of supreme sacrifice for oul Ireland."

"Moran, that's not a nice thing to say!" he reflected a moment, "But in a way you could be right. He could be on his way down here with some o' the boys to find out what's gone wrong. Keep your eye out for a black V8."

He shook the receiver again. "Come on! Come on!" A nerve in the corner of his eye began to flicker as if a hole were being bored through from inside. Fascinated, he gazed at it pulsing in the mirror.

"Bugger this!" Moran shouted in his ear and wrenched the receiver roughly from his grasp.

"What are you doing, Moran?" he drew back from Moran's thrusting elbow.

"I'm countin' the Commandant out, that's what I'm doin'. It's nearly eight o'clock so you and me is strictly on our own. If anythin's goin' to be done about those kids it's we who've got to do it, not the bloody Commandant who doesn't even know how to keep his lines of communication open. What price this Von Clausewitz guy you and he are always chattin' about?"

"We'll obey orders" Fleming said with an effort that left him tired. A languor stole over him like that day on the mountain when after being buffeted by explosions and the strong wind he sank deep into the heather and slept. His heavy eyelids drooped. The elusive air in the box was warm and heavy with the sickening proximity of Moran's body.

"You just snooze there" Moran murmured at him twirling the dial on the telephone, "There's no time left to give orders or to take them either. Hello!" he spoke into the receiver.

"Who are you talking to?" Fleming pushed wearily against his weariness.

"Hello? Now listen carefully. There's a huge landmine under the statue of the King in the centre of Stephen's Green. It was set to go off at half-seven but somethin's gone wrong. Get in touch with the C.I.D. and tell them the park is not to open. Y' got that?"

Fleming leaned against him, shaking his arm. "Who are you talking to?"

"Sh!" Moran placed his hand over the mouthpiece, "I'm ringin' the exchange. Hello" he spoke into the phone, "Of course this is a genuine call. Sure who else would plant a bomb except the fellows who always plant them? Jasus, who'd be pullin' a hoax at this time o' the mornin'? Look, I wouldn't be runnin' the risk o' makin' this call only there's goin' to be droves o' kids comin' through the Green to school from about half-eight to nine an' I want to make bloody sure nothin' happens to them. Now, don't take that line Mack, there's too much at stake. I sound like a fella named Paddy Quinlan, do I? Well, would you believe Paddy Quinlan? You wouldn't? So why the hell did you mention him at all? For God's sake think o' the kids. Have you ever seen what one o' them mines can do?"

"Oh for God's sake" Fleming cried slamming his hand on the receiver rest.

"Jasus what did you do that for?" howled Moran, "I nearly had him."

"He was only keeping you in conversation while his other pals traced the call. He won't send the C.I.D. but the police, only it won't be to close the Green. He'll send them to catch us for usin' the phone to try to commit a nuisance. That'd be just wonderful wouldn't it? The two of us arrested for a stupidity like that with no chance of getting in touch with the Commandant or having someone dismantle the mine. And then when they found the mine and knew they had the man who planted it, what sort of sentence do you think we'd get?"

He thrust at Moran with his shoulder bundling him out into the street. Moran's leg, trailing behind him, brought the suitcase out at his feet.

"That bloody think again" he complained.

"Now look here, Moran," Fleming said picking up the case, "We've done all we can. In circumstances like these our duty is quite clear. We take evasive action. We've no right to risk the movement's reputation for being able to strike and get clean away."

"Who's bloody struck?"

A cold clang of church bells broke on the air.

"Eight o' clock" Moran whispered at him accusingly.

"There's no sign of the V.8. anywhere. Come on, let's go."

Moran lounged against the kiosk regarding him with his pale, red-rimmed eyes.

"That's an order, Volunteer Moran! Failure to obey may involve you in most serious consequences."

"Nine miles up!" Moran sneered, "It's the consequences to the kids that concerns me. You're so busy playing the good soldier, obeyin' orders, suckin' up to the Commandant that you forget what we're really fightin' for - those poor kids and their future. An' what'll that be for some o' them if the bloody mine goes off?"

Fleming heard the clink of metal from the huge gates just round the corner.

"The gardener" Moran said, "I'm goin' to stop 'im openin' up. You can do what you like - follow your orders, say your prayers, run home to your mammie, or chase up to the canal after another oul brasser. It's all one to me. I'm goin' to protect the kids. That should be your business. For the only reason they put you over me is because you're a teacher and they thought - at the least the Commandant thought - you'd be great at givin' orders. But givin' orders is not everythin'. You've never been in action before and that's what counts!"

Fleming, his cheekbones stinging hot, fought down his urge to vault the heavy black chains bounding the road and break into a mad run away from the place. The Commandant's orders had been most explicit; after the explosion, wait in the room until a quarter to nine and then take the tram to work. If anything goes wrong earlier get to a phone at once. Above all, don't get caught. And here was Moran risking just that. He licked his dry lips, how would it look for him at the court of enquiry if Moran got himself arrested? He followed on behind Moran at a discreet distance, peering at him covertly from between the wings of his upturned collar waiting for the right moment to reassert his authority. There was no mistake about it, Flanagan in the school had the same boastful, lounging walk as Moran, the same shrugging contempt for everyone and everything. "Flemmin the Gollier" must have been chalked on the lavatory wall for weeks before he discovered it and instantly recognised Flanagan's slovenly scrawl. Even though the Superior himself had given Flanagan the larruping of a lifetime, hands, legs, backside and all, the damage had been done. Everywhere he went that dreadful nickname was whispered behind his back. And the Superior hadn't forgotten it either. One day much later he said: "A terrible child, that Flanagan. No brains! No manners! No abilities. And I don't give much for his spelling either."

He saw Moran lounge over to the huge iron gate and bend to speak to the gardener, a grey elderly man in a dark limp uniform crouching to the lock. He would give him this last chance.

"Don't open up, Mack! There's a landmine under the King's statue. Keep everyone out. Keep away from it yourself. Ring the C.I.D."

"There's a landmine...!" the man looked around him nodding to an appreciative invisible audience, "Maybe

I'd better go back to bed. I've got Greta Garbo herself tucked up there warmin' my hot water bottle for me." He vented a scornful laugh and grated the key in the lock.

Moran took hold of the bars. "Honest, Mack, I'm not coddin'. Just leave the gate an' go round by the Lousy Acre an' take a look. It's a big black thing over near the hind legs o' the horse."

"I've seen you somewhere before, haven't I?" the gardener squinted through the bars, "You're wan o' them bowsies from the university over there, aren't you? A landmine! So that's what's on the menu for today, is it?" He began to tug the gate open.

"You dodderin' oul daisy" Moran shouted at him, "You rotten oul sight! If anythin' happens to those kids, be Jasus, I'll blow your stupid head off your shoulders, so I will."

Fleming could keep his feet still no longer. "I'm ordering you to come on away from there, Moran!" he shouted and swung round into the roadway, into the barrier of the terrifying bulk of a policeman falling it seemed straight down on him. A grey ghost flitted beside him - a strangely familiar young man in hairy plus-fours. Above the whirring in his ears he heard the intense barking of a dog. Jesus I've got to get away he realised a regretted second too late and yelped as the policeman's fingers closed like a metal trap round his wrist.

"That's the case there in his hand" the young man was saying, "It was outside the telephone box and he took it with him into the box pretending to make a call."

"I'll be takin' charge o' that" said the policeman in a lilting Cork accent, wrenching the suitcase from his grasp.

"So now we'll be after takin' a little stroll down to the station to see what all this is about."

The man with the dog grinned blank-eyed behind his glasses. The dog bounced round his feet, its tail bobbing like an obscene thumb. The policeman had black hairs in his gaping nostrils and smelled of cold water and Sunlight soap. Fleming gathered all his strength and made to wrench out of his grasp. His body was tugged hard against the hairy blue overcoat of the Guard. A hard edge jolted pain into the nape of his neck.

"Keep still me boyo" the policeman said to him, "or the contents o' your case an' your head with them'll be spillin' together over the path. What's in the case anyway? Some thin' heavy in there be the feel of it."

Beyond the blur of his pain he heard Moran's voice shouting. Focussing hard he made out: "You blunderin' bogman! Ye turnip- headed eedjit! Like all Bobbies you're as thick as a mule."

Straightening up on the tether of the policeman's arm he saw Moran weave from side to side in his boxer's crouch.

"The fella you want is me not him" Moran said, "Know what? I planted a landmine in the Green last night and it's failed to go off. It's in there now - tickin' away. So come on, you stupid country mug, an' get the gardener to keep the place closed before someone gets hurt by it."

"Tink you're smart, don't you?" the policeman mocked, "You're not goin' to git your frind away from me dat way." He tightened his grip on Fleming's wrist, "An' keep still you, you bostoon you, or I'll give you a belt o' me baton so I will God dammit."

"Look Mack," Moran came forward, the tips of his fingers joined, "Don't act as green as you're cabbage-lookin', just go into the park an' take a dekko at what's under the big statue there. Please! I'm beggin' you! Please!"

The policeman's lip curled back in a sneer. "De only place I'm goin' to is the station. An' if you're not careful you'll be comin' with me. A landmine!" he scoffed, "Ho! Ho! You'll have to do better than dat, young fella, much better than dat."

"Oh will I?" Moran sprang back weaving about on tiptoe, opening in deft delicate flutterings the buttons of his overcoat. He brushed aside the skirts of his jacket and reached his hand in towards the waistband of his trousers from which he drew a Parabellum pistol. He waved its long bluish snout at the policeman.

"Have to do much better will I? Will this shaggin'-well do you, then? All right Monkey-face, get that dopey gardener to keep the gates closed."

The policeman's face grew grave. He released his grip on Fleming's wrist as if it had dropped clean out of his mind. Fleming heard the suitcase thud to the ground.

"Now you just behave yourself, young fella," the guard said in a hoarse voice as if clearing his throat. "Just let me have dat ting from your hand there an' we'll go together an' investigate that other matter." He sneaked a long cautious step towards Moran, his red hand stealing almost imperceptibly towards the pocket of his greatcoat.

"Keep back" Moran's weight weaved slowly from one foot to the other, "You look a mug! For God's sake don't act like one."

The guard, as if falling down, gave a quick lurch to one side and hurled his bulky form in a flying tackle at Moran. The awful voice of the gun roared through Flemming as if one side of his head had slammed into the other. He howled at the horror of the policeman hanging forever in the air, his greatcoat linked to the barrel of Moran's pistol by a thin thread of angry orange. "Great Christ!" he cried as the huge blue form staggered on past Moran and clanked against the railings where the helmet jammed tight between the bars. He continued to stare into the dark, yellow-lipped mouth of the helmet though he knew the man was falling through the air away from it like a bundled blue blanket. When he heard the muffled thud he looked down and saw the grey face, the grinning mouth, the pulsing of brilliant red blood. "Oh God!" he moaned hearing again the shot jolt through his head and knowing he would go on hearing it all his life. Where was the grey figure in plus-fours running to he wondered and broke into a run after him. A hand clutching his elbow and turned him in another direction. He ran past a brown blur of buildings and then a grey blur of buildings with patches of green flashing now and then near the ground. He became aware that Moran was bobbing beside him thrusting something at him. He reached out his hand marvelling at the tremendous din their feet were making in the tall street.

"Your bloody case" Moran panted at him, "It'll get us

both hanged yet!" He grasped the brown oblong floating into his vision trailing unnameable terror. Moran laid a hand on Fleming's arm to steady himself and, without pausing in his headlong run, cast a look behind.

"Slow down! Slow down! Walk! There's nobody followin' us."

Fleming raised his head from the panting agony of the grey hurrying pavement and saw they were trudging up a quiet incline into Adelaide Road, He pressed the suitcase hard against the pain in his side.

"Walk normal" Moran whispered, gasping for breath, "Let on we're just a couple o' the unemployed out for a day's airin' on the banks of the canal."

Fleming ducked his head between the wings of his overcoat collar but the few people he saw sauntering down the road displayed no interest in them. Maybe the noise of the shot had not carried so far. Or maybe those in the street had put it down to something other than the report of a gun. Moran nudged the suitcase with his elbow guiding him towards the slimy sheen of the canal at the farther end of a street of dark, leafy trees and quiet, railed gardens. They moved on, meeting no one, and came out on the ragged unkempt bank. In the shadow of a grey mottled wall Fleming paused and regarded Moran.

"That was a terrible thing you did! And there was no need!"

"Jasus, what did you want me to do?" Moran kicked at a stone, "Stand there an' let that thick bogman take my gun offa me? Nothin' doin'! Only last Easter I paid Derry Hughes three bloody hard-earned pounds ten for that parabellum."

"You know what I meant" Fleming tried to gesture and flopped his hand to his side. "We're destroyed anyway. The fellow with the dog saw us. The gardener saw us. Even the paper-seller saw us. Wait till the C.I.D. get talking to them. No place will be safe for us. And what'll the Commandant say? Oh my God, what'll the Commandant say?" He heard the sob of despair in his voice and pitied it.

"O.K." Moran scratched his crotch, "Maybe we banjaxed it. But look here, I couldn't let you be arrested by...."

Fleming felt the shot jolt once again through his head like a door slamming shut deep within him, twitching the ground beneath his feet.

"It went off!" Moran jigged with joy, "Good Jay, it went off!"

"Do you mean...?"

"Jasus, man, you're not deaf are you? The timin' device must've been wrong. I'm convinced more than ever I should have used my father's oul ticker. We done it though! We pulled off the job! Congratulations!"

They began to trudge along the bank towards the railway bridge.

"Thank God" Moran's face looked disgustingly happy, "And the kids is safe now. That's a real big weight off my mind."

NO CAKES FOR DANNY BOY

Since the death of their mother two years before, Paddy looked after the shop for an hour before school every morning while Annie cycled round to the fruit-and-vegetable market to see, as she said, if there was anything of interest on offer. But he could never understand why she had to go there when all she ever brought back was an occasional dozen of apples or a soggy hand of over-ripe bananas. Most evenings after tea he came down from their flat, only a few streets away, to enable her to go to devotions in Merchants' Quay or sometimes even to the pictures, or on a long, window-gazing wander past the shops in Henry Street, after which strange men would sometimes pause outside the shop window gazing earnestly at the open boxes of aniseed balls, money lumps, Peggy's Leg and jelly beans as if they would find there the answer to the pent yearnings of their hearts. Though in the mornings he was kept fairly busy, there was little to do in the evenings except turn the greyish pages of the *Evening Mail* looking for interesting news items about airships and planes, or the latest daring depredations of the Chinese bandits or the current phase of the gang war in Chicago where

Scarface Al seemed to be putting practically everybody on the spot. The newspapers told also, usually in over-large black type, of something called THE DEPRESSION which was the reason, Annie said, so few customers came to the shop, but he could never manage to read further than the headlines in those items. Anyway, he was quite glad business was less than brisk for if customers were popping into the shop every minute he would have less time to talk to Jack Grace who came in every evening accompanied by his dog, Danny Boy, to make his modest purchase and swap limp, greasy copies of *Thrilling Detective*, *The Black Mask*, and *The Wide World*. And indeed it was when he was reading a long series in *The Wide World* about the terrible crime wave in Thompson County, Illinois, that he realised how foolish and childish were the stories he used to enjoy in *The Boys Magazine* and *The Wizard*, and he began to thrill to the idea that maybe he had lost interest in them because he might already have one foot planted firmly inside the dangerous threshold of adult life where, if you knew where to look in the world, you could meet gangsters and bandits and other interesting people of a kind who most definitely never came into the shop to buy a pint of milk or a loaf of bread or even - vain hope - to stage a holdup with a squat, black automatic pistol or a businesslike forty-five.

Jack Grace had had a forty-five during the Troubles and had shown him a photograph in which he pointed the round black mouth of the pistol at some target to the left of the astonished eye of the camera. He knew from what other customers said that Jack was the last but one of an old Dublin family of cab drivers. His grandfather, they said, had eight cabs, three mourning coaches, and two shooting brakes for use at election meetings, but round about the time of the fall of Parnell, which they never explained, which left you to speculate that it might have been from off a horse, the old man had taken to drink with the result that little besides his incurable thirst had descended to Jack s father. There were now only two shabby cabs left, each with a drooping horse to stagger headlong before it on the way to and from the several city cemeteries. Jack went to these depressing places dressed in the remnants of the uniform he had worn in what he called the Civil War, a faded green overcoat, fastened with a single reluctant brass button, greenish cavalryman trousers with the yellow of the inside leg turning an infected purple, and - as if in an all-forgiving gesture to a still earlier phase of history - British Army puttees and black hob-nailed boots. He walked with a tired swagger holding his head to one side, it seemed to conceal the violent cast in his left eye which he nursed as if it were a favourite wound. Whenever he entered the shop of an evening he brought with him the desperate air of great disasters on the battle-field, of broken troops reeling along the road of retreat, of bemused survivors looking around them for comrades they would never see again. Danny Boy, ever sniffing at his heels, did little to banish these impressions which never failed to thrill Paddy. The dog was an awkward accommodation between setter and Airedale born, it would appear, solely to slink along behind his master, bearing the memory of bloody last stands in the brown desperation of his eyes.

Paddy's liking for this odd pair was a sore point with Annie. "Don't let me catch you talkin' to that fella when I come in of an evenin'" she said, "I'm surprised at you, a Christian Brother boy, gettin' friendly with an ignorant fella like that an' lettin' that big ass of a dog sniff all around behind the counter and do God knows what under the window for maybe that's why the kids aren't buyin' the sweets any more." Paddy shrugged off all the dull arguments she would saw away with for how could a girl be expected to understand that Jack and he shared in a dangerous and thrilling world where long black sedans roared through sky-scrapered streets taking rats for rides, a world where grim-jawed men in dark overcoats, white silk scarves and grey fedoras who said: "Jeez!" and "Holy cow!" and "Oh yeah?" worked their way in the light-spattered rain through perilous alleyways, blue-nosed gats in their hands, to rub out some shyster for muscling in on their rackets. But for all his seeming unconcern, his heart filled with dread each time she spoke about Jack because any fool could see she was bound in the end to find out about his own racket with the stale cakes.

Every morning when Mr Cahill brought in his sweet, steaming board of bread Paddy was careful to order more rock cakes than he knew by experience would be sold. When they were as hard in texture as in name, instead of returning them to the baker's man who would allow for them, he would hide them behind the cardboard stand-up display for H.P. sauce and give them to Jack for Danny Boy's supper.

"An' now, Paddy oul son, is there any oul, stale cakes knockin' around for this oul man here?" Jack would say when they had finished chatting and swapping magazines and hold up a large stained sweet-tin part-filled with warm milk. Paddy would drop sometimes as many as four stale rock cakes into the milk and grandly gesture away any suggestion of payment. "Sure they were goin' to be thrun out anyway," he would lie and Jack's head would nod even lower in mute acknowledgement of the fiction.

He had grown so used to this evening routine that he heard the first rustlings of Annie's sharp-eyed suspicions without blushing all over and giving himself away on the spot as he dreaded might happen. He was standing on the street corner in the raw morning wind nodding his head sleepily at each brief pause in Annie's daily litany of warnings and recommendations.

"Be sure to open the side-door as well an' let the fresh air blow the damp smells out of the shop. Don't forget to give a good stir to last night's milk otherwise you'll he givin' away all the cream an' that louser from the corporation'll fine us again for deficiency of fats. If the rat's been at the bread again, hide the loaves he's gnawed behind the others so that the customers don't get a gawk at them." He watched her lift a white tentacle of leg demurely over the crank of her upstairs-model bicycle and grope for the pedal on the far side. He prayed that when he was big like her the mole on his cheek wouldn't sprout a cluster of wiry, black hairs as hers did.

"An' by the way" she said, skipping the bicycle into motion, "Keep a tight eye on that oul gurrier Cahill. I've a feelin' he's diddlin' us over the stale cake returns. I don't think he's allowed us anythin' for them."

He watched her waver her way down the quay towards Capel Street, too dismayed to make reply, her parting words spreading through him like a stain. How he hated to earn her disapproval! Not content with painting his future as black as possible - starving in the gutter or running thirty miles after a crow on the last day to snatch a crust away from it were two favourite envisaged ends - she would conjure up the image of his dead mother weeping for his misdeeds even through the unutterable joy of being in the presence of God himself, who would bend down to seek the source of her sorrow and shake his head sadly when he heard. He sighed and walked round to the quay to unlock the shop where he breathed in the odours of stale bread, riverside rot and the large yellow round of mousetrap cheese on the marble slab. His dread of what she would say when she learned the truth about the cake returns increased as he pictured her in a screaming quarrel with Mr Cahill whose reactions at being wrongly accused could not even be guessed at. He served the few customers who clumped in for their milk and bread and cigarettes and realised almost as he was doing it that he had given one of them sixpence too much in the change. God, wait till she got round to the stock-taking as well! His attention veered constantly to the cobblestoned road along the river, dreading the oncoming clip-clop of Mr Cahill's horse and the decision he would have to take when the baker's rounds-man arrived. The van came outside without his noticing its arrival, at the very moment he was putting on the kettle for Annie's tea, watching the living blue gas flame and wondering what colour the flames of the fires of hell were, a detail none of the brothers in their endless talks on the nether regions had ever supplied. "On the green banks of Shannon when Sheila was nigh" he heard Mr Cahill sing in the street in tones that reminded him of a missioner he once heard pleading with a dead-silent congregation to take pity on the passion of our Lord so soon to be betrayed in the garden and handed over to be scourged, mocked, and crucified. He came out into the shop and saw the usual dozen rock cakes on top of the board of sweet steaming loaves, turnovers, and pans.

"We'll have to cut down on the rock cakes" he said to Mr Gahill and found himself listening to the sounds from outside, the whirr and crash of a distant tram, a voice calling forlornly near the bridge - but nowhere the lonely barking of a dog. Suddenly he felt miserable.

"No! No! Let the rock cakes stand" he told Mr Cahill who was preparing to protest but who now smiled and licked his shiny pencil stub. He wrote in the order and sauntered out towards his van, singing: "He died at my feet on a cold winters day/And I played a lament for my poor dog Tray!"

To his surprise, Jack with Danny Boy at his heels arrived soon after on one of his rare morning visits to the shop. Paddy looked at them marvelling that they could see him and yet remain completely unaware of what he was suffering and still would suffer in the near future for their sake. "Here! Here Danny Boy!" he called coming round the counter to play with the capering dog while Jack picked up two or three issues of *The Herald* and *The Mail* which Annie always kept on the side counter to read with her morning cup of tea.

"Mind, Paddy, if I take a dekko at who's runnin' in the last race today?" He held the newspaper as if about to put it behind his back and read down the deaths column with his twisted left eye. "Let's see" he mumbled, "Doyle, at his residence in Charlotte Street, mourned by his wife an' - ah, no family - funeral from Saint Andrew's Westland Row to Mount Jerome. Ah, but it's not until tomorrow. This looks better, an' it's for this mornin'; McIntyre, Ranelagh Road, mourned by wife, son, daughters, parents, relatives, numerous friends, the staff of T & G Martin's. From Rathmines Church to Glasnevin. That's more like it. Give's a packet o' Woddiers there Paddy. Pay you this evenin' after the plantin'. An' I may have with me a copy of a great new magazine called *Underworld* that a fella's promised me. All about organised crime an' killin's an' shootin's an' so forth."

Paddy eased a short length of stick from a bundle of firewood and flung it far down the quay for Danny Boy to fetch. He came round the counter to where the packets of the different brands of cigarettes were stacked, on a glass shelf suspended on chains in the window. As he reached for a large packet of Woodbines he heard the squeal of brakes and an abrupt, irate shout following which Danny Boy slunk past the shop window, his long tail trailing like a discouraged snake along the pavement.

"Jasus, Paddy, did you see that?" Jack stood at the door pointing the rumpled newspaper down the quay. "A bloody taxi-man nearly ran over the poor oul dog. Oh the rotten bastards! Hung they should be! Hung, yis, all of them! Not content with takin' the bite outa me mouth they're tryin' to kill poor oul Danny Boy on me as well. I'll get them for this! Rub them out, so I will."

Paddy withdrew from the open window shaking sticky jelly beans and pink marshmallows from his fingers. "That wasn't a taxi, Jack. It was one of them Rover sports cars."

"No! No! What else could it be but a taxi?" Jack champed his teeth together, "Sure the bloody taxi-men can't take a run up O'Connell Street without knockin' some poor oul wan down. Have you looked in the gutters lately? The whole town is lined with dead cats and dogs an' oul grannies."

Paddy smiled without finding that funny and tried to shrug off the eerie impression the strange remarks were making on him.

"Just you wait an' see" with his straight eye Jack followed the swoop and plunge of a red-billed seabird, "there'll soon be nothin' on the streets but taxis - no trams, single-decker buses, bread vans, coal floats, Guinness's drays, not even asses and carts. But of course the people they're dead nuts on, that they're really out to get, that they really want to bump off, are the cabmen. Yeah, all over town they're musclin' in on our territory. They've taken over the weddin's already. The cabmen can't get a look in any longer. An' you'd think that would have started in Ballsbridge or Rathgar or Terenure or some other o' the swanky places in the town. But no! They get married in the Coombe in taxis now. An' in Cabra, Kimmage, an' Drimnagh as well. They've even started to horn in on funerals. At the moment there's just one or two o' them, out in front an' a few more bringin' up the rear. But they're there! An' can you imagine anythin' worse than a funeral made up completely of taxis? Sure it's enough to have the corpse get up outa the coffin an' walk off in disgust."

Paddy burst out laughing and grew silent under Jack's long distant look.

"You're too young to understand how serious this is"

he warned, "When a country loses respect for its dead anythin' can happen - to the livin'! An' them taxi-men have no respect for nothin' at all. They turn funerals into a sort of Phoenix Park Grand Prix in slow motion. You can see by the leer on their faces that they're just dyin' to jam their foot down on the accelerator and plant the poor bugger before he even knows he's dead."

Danny Boy came in from the street in a slinking swagger that was a close imitation of his master's walk and sat down on the step beside Jack's unravelling puttees, pointing his moist snout desperately at the increasing morning traffic.

"It's not funny, so it isn't" Jack mused, "The dead appreciate the way the cabmen carry them on their last journey. We turn up with properly solemn faces. The mournin'-coach men wear top hats and white gloves an' carry long fancy whips. An' you never see any of the old school like me father, without their shiny-black, hard hats. When we leave the church we go once round the diggins where the deceased lived, pausin' a sad minute outside his house, an' then off we go to wherever it is, Glasnevin, Jerome, or the Grange at a nice respectable trot that drags out the journey as long as possible and gives the mourners time to think their thoughts about the deceased - how good he was an' how much did he leave? - an' sort of get used to the idea of him bein' dead which gradually eases them into the nice friendly mood they're in by the time they drop in for a pint of porter or a ball o' malt in the Cross Guns or wherever after the ceremony. In a way it's a great big family party. Most o' the cabmen are related an' as a matter of fact so are the horses with the result that the corpse has the

The Hero Game and Other Dublin Stories

advantage o' bein' buried by as wide a circle of friends an' relations as possible. Lord, what feelin's have taxi-men? You see them roarin' away from the cemeteries as if they couldn't get away from the poor fella quick enough." He lapsed into a black mood during which Paddy served a few customers and didn't dare to break in on his private gloom.

"Yes" Jack said as if to himself "They're takin' us over a little bit more every day. An' do you know what's goin' to happen to the cabmen in the end? They'll go the way of the Dion O'Bannion gang. Rubbed out by the rotten wops who were probably all taxi-men at heart!" He raised his hand aloft and brought it down sharply as if pulling a chain. Paddy was glad Annie was not present to see that gesture. Some such excuse as that is all she would need to plant her foot firmly down and order him to refuse to hold any conversation with Jack beyond what was necessary in the way of business which of course you always had to encourage.

"Anyway" Jack replaced the newspaper on the counter, "it's time for me to be givin' the oul horse a rub down an' settin' off to pay my respects to the late Mr McIntyre. Come on, Danny Boy oul son. An' keep a sharp eye out for the taxi-men. They've got you in their sights! They've got us all in their sights, God help us."

Paddy watched the slinking swaggers, one behind the other as they set off down the quay. He busied himself with his Latin grammar - when would you ever say "to be about to be loved?" - until Annie returned from the market. "Nothin' at all goin' there this mornin' for love or money" she told him and in the long account which followed of all that happened there - less than nothing in Paddy's estimation - she seemed to have forgotten completely the matter of the stale cake returns. He set off for school with an easy mind but later when he came back after tea to allow her to go to devotions he saw to his dismay that she had the baker's book open on the table in the back-room and was conducting elaborate calculations on a large sheet of writing paper already as crowded as a Snakes-and-Ladders board.

"I've just made a small pot o' tea" she said. "Pour yourself out a cup while I go on with this mystery story here. It's so complicated I may have to get you to use that thing you're learnin' - Algebra - to get some idea of the right answer!"

She worked for a few more minutes before she sat back and said; "Yes, I'll have to miss mass in the mornin', holy day an' all that it is, an' have it out with that oul rogue Cahill over the way he's been cheatin' us out of our returns. He's made no allowances at all for months and months."

Paddy looked down into his tea-cup where a large black tea-stem was engaged in the desperate pursuit of a smaller one which was being drawn in narrowing circles towards the centre and ultimate capture.

"There's no note here in his book of any rock cake returns an' I know my eyes aren't deceivin' me for I've often seen three or four of them there behind the H.P. sauce show-card ready to go back in the mornin'. Just wait'll I face that oul bester with this when he comes in singin' about his oul dog Tray."

"There must be some mistake." Paddy ventured a phrase which had had felicitous results in a film he had seen recently at the Phoenix. He saw that the larger tea-stem lay atop of its fellow in the cup.

"Divil a mistake'." Annie said, "If oul Cahill doesn't cough up the money he's been robbin' us of I'll have to write a strong letter to his boss. Maybe even call in the police!"

Paddy sneaked out a sigh. The truth would have to be told. The only problem remaining was how big a lie would Annie accept in its company. He launched into a rapid Hail Mary for inspiration.

"Stop mumblin' to yourself there Paddy an' get out your pen. Why should we give that barefaced oul bester a chance anyway? We'll write a letter of complaint about him to Peter Kennedy himself."

Paddy took a strong swig out of his cup in the manner of a *Black Mask* character in a speakeasy waiting for the showdown. One of the tea-stems caught the back of his throat.

"Annie" he spluttered, tears in his eyes, "It's not Mr Cahill's fault. I couldn't see a poor dog go without his supper so I've been givin' them stale cakes to Jack Grace for his dog, Danny Boy."

"Ah you right fool!" Annie's shout was terrible, "Do you mean to tell me that you've been lettin' that fella take you in as he does the rest of the neighbourhood? Sure he goes round all the shops bummin' cakes for that unsightly, smelly animal. Mrs Moran tells me he pestered her so much she had to threaten to call in the guards. An' Mr Mack beyond says that if they ever come near his shop again he'll lift that dog over the Liffey wall with a runnin' kick!"

He felt his jaw tremble and recognised with alarm the full stinging feeling round the rims of his eyes. Annie musn't see him cry, he determined, and ran out into the shop as if he had heard a customer enter. He picked up a breadknife from the marble slab and gave the yellow block of butter sitting on top of it an unthinking stab. How rotten of Jack to regard him as just another foolish shopkeeper to be preyed upon! Tears sparse and bitter, fell on his cheeks. The damn louser, too mean to feed Danny Boy himself he resorted to lies and trickery to get others to do it for him. Not that he'd have minded feeding the dog! It was the way Jack had tricked him that hurt. Annie came behind him, her voice surprisingly gentle.

"Never mind, Paddy dear. He may be the first you found out was cheatin' you but take it from me there'll be plenty of others who'll try it on as well. Just keep in mind that everyone out there is just dyin' for the chance to diddle you and you won't go far wrong. Sure the whole world is packed out with chancers, diddlers and besters. The cheek o' that fella goin' around in his cavalryman's trousers anyway. Sure he was never let near a horse in the Civil War. He spent most of his time in the army on guard outside Oriel House where terrible things were happenin' inside to the unfortunate prisoners, women and girls amongst them."

She went off to church and Paddy attended the shop, his mind revolving around the inevitable encounter with Jack, in which he was angry, bitter and scornful by turns. However, when Jack came in a short while later he was surprised to find himself strangely detached from his own feelings. He chatted about stories they'd both read in their magazines as if nothing were the matter at all and he even went as far as to let Jack have a *Thrilling Detective* he had picked up on a stall the previous day on his way from school and had not yet had time to read as he had been kept busy trying to figure out what the big racketeer, Caesar was up to in Gaul. At last Jack swaggered over to the bread counter the can of warm milk dangling from his hand.

"And now, Paddy oul son, is there any stale cakes knockin' round this evenin' for this oul nuisance here?"

Danny Boy's snakey tail wagged the rest of him to and fro in a whimper of brown desperation, his snout nudging the dangling milk can.

"I have no stale cakes" Paddy said, his voice sinking to a hoarse half-whisper, "I don't expect to have any ever again. They tell me they're not bakin' them any more. Even for people!"

Jack attempted the impossible task of bringing both of his eyes to focus on the boy at the same time. His head wavered over the counter. Several spots of milk appeared on the floor beneath the can. At last abandoning the attempt he shook his head sadly.

"Ah, I see the taxi-men have even got to you! I never thought that could happen. Never! Come on, Danny Boy oul comrade, there's no sense in stickin' around where we're not wanted."

Paddy found he was trembling and near to tears.

In the days that followed the sight of the two of them moving in their waltzing swagger along the quay would make him think again of the violence of the trembling which had seized on him - as if an invisible hand was shaking him. It had been like an illness which left him weak and wary lest it should recur. At one of the Thursday school football matches the baying of a dog in the Furry Glen brought back a shadow of the distressing trembling and put him off his stride with no one before him but the other team's goalkeeper dancing about shouting for help between the posts. Another afternoon when he and Kevin Curran were going to the Mary Street Cinema to see *Little Caesar* for the fifth time they passed a horse and cab stationed outside Madigan's pub and all through the film Paddy had to fight against the distracting idea that any minute Jack was going to appear on the screen and greet Edward G. with "Jeez" or "Holy cow!" or "Sufferin' Christ!" Not long after that he saw him come out of a corner shop in Smithfield. He had a sweet-can of milk in his hand and a bundle wrapped in an old *Independent* under his arm. Paddy checked his pace lest Danny Boy would see him and somehow draw his master's attention to him. The dog however seemed wrapped in his own dark thoughts and slunk along the street, his nose almost touching the rain-damp pavement. "An' I told them again and again," Jack's voice reached to where he lurked in a smelly tenement doorway, "Again and again I told them, but they just laughed. They can't get it into their heads that the taxi-men is out to get them. But you know it's true, don't you, Danny Boy?" Paddy slipped with relief down a dark lane spongy with scattered rubbish, sickening with the odour of decaying vegetables.

On his way to school about a month later he saw a throng still and somehow ominous gathered at the mouth of the lane where he knew Jack and his father stabled their horses. He wondered what it might portend. It was too early in the day, in the week even, for a family row to have overflowed into the street with the usual shouts, screams, interesting variations on popular obscenities and maybe even a piece of furniture hurtling out like the hammer of fate through an explosively shattering window. Then he saw a policeman moving through the crowd, open notebook in hand. The crowd remained numbed and still staring before them out of large, pale faces. Some of the women stood with their bibs held up to their mouths as if they were praying or holding back cries of fright. He moved towards them impelled by a secret joy of foreboding.

"Now you, missis, you live in the lane, don't you?" The policeman paused in his ponderous progress before a wisp of a woman whose grey hair was tortured tight in steel curlers. "Did you hear anythin', Ma'm?"

"Only the same as Mrs Hyland there, sor. The shoutin'! As if he was pleadin' with someone not to do it."

"I see" the policeman tapped his chin with the edge of his notebook, "Did you not hear him shout: "Danny Boy, stop him from doin' it?" as this other lady here tells us she heard?

"Nossor, 'clare to me God, nothin' like that."

One of the buttons on the guard's coat touched cold against Paddy's cheek as he turned to question another woman.

"You're the one who seems to have heard most, Mrs...?"

"Callan, sor." The large woman snuggled her shawl closer about her as if to stop herself from shivering, "Ah sure don't I know poor Jack since oul God's time.

A decenter fella you wouldn't come across in a month o' Sundays, but things was so bad with him lately he hadn't a hae'penny to bless himself with. Ah, the poor fella starvin' he was most o' the time. Sure anythin' he earned he had to spend on the oul horse to keep it from fallin' dead with hunger on the way to Glasnevin or Mount Jerome. He used to go round all the shops in the diggins scroungin' stale cakes, lettin' on they was for that useless oul creature his dog. But sure they were as much for himself as for the animal. Some kids squintin' in at them through a crack in the stable door saw them both feedin' themselves outa the same tin an' he talkin' to the dog like to a human bein' an the dog lookin' up an' they swear, noddin' agreement to what he was sayin'. That shows he was not quite right in the head, you know. Sure he used to stop people in the street an' say the taxi-men was out to drive him off the road an' leave him without a roof over his head."

"That's all very interestin' Missis" the policeman chewed over the evidence, "We know he was a little strange. An' we know too that he was in there alone with the dog last night so it was nobody but himself he was shoutin' at. Still, all that doesn't seem quite enough to explain why the poor bugger hung himself."

"They say it was with a piece o' flex off the electric light" Mrs Callan said.

"Ah no!" The policeman hesitated a moment, "Well if you must know it was with a noose made out of one of his puttees tied to a rope. The thing stretched under his weight such as it was an' he was just a few inches off the ground when he died. Bloody bad luck!"

Paddy thrust roughly out of the crowd, his heart hammering the breath out of his trembling body. His jaw kicked like the leg of a rabbit he had once seen caught in a steel trap when on a day out with the school in County Wicklow. He ran down the quays and burst into the shop.

"Annie! Annie!" was all he managed to say before he collapsed onto a butter box and broke into frightened tears. Annie fondled him in her usual clumsy way running the woollen sleeve of her cardigan across his eyes and squeezing his ears and by degrees drew the whole story from him. When he came to the essential point she cried out: "O sweet Jesus have mercy!" and hid her face a moment in the apron she had on. She went off at once and brewed a pot of tea calling to him, "No, you don't go to school today. You're too upset." Soon she brought him a cup of tea which he drank sitting on the butter box watching the customers come into the shop with large, staring eyes and cries of: "God between us an' all harm, did you hear what that fella down the lane done?" and "Sacred heart of Jesus have mercy on him!" and other remarks that he was glad to hear for they were all prayers for Jack whom he was beginning with dread to realise he had misjudged terribly and in a way had foully betrayed. "But I didn't know he was starving did I?" he told his spreading guilt which remained coldly unconvinced and went on creeping like all-consuming lava through his mind. The man from the upstairs flat came in with his milk-jug and laughed when he heard the hushed remarks of the other customers.

"Ah, dat's a real good wan! He earned his livin' from funerals an' now it'll be someone else's turn to make a few bob outa him. That is if anyone at all will bother to go to his funeral. Suicide puts people off. An' you know what that means, don't you? - unconsecrated ground, God between us an' all harm."

Annie came round to collect Paddy's cup and laid the cool flat of her hand against his forehead.

"You're burnin' so you are!" she complained, "Ah, you better go on home and get into bed. I'll close up for an hour as soon as I can an' come around to see that you're all right."

He took himself home, climbed wearily into bed and laid his hot, throbbing forehead on the cool pillow. Was he ill? While he struggled towards an answer through a hot confusion of painfully flickering shapes and irritating voices he fell asleep. He woke up several times to find Annie sitting by his bed, her face grave and very narrow as if since he saw her last it had been squeezed by some sort of press. He struggled to bring out a question about that but when he got to "What...?" he forgot what it was and fell asleep again. A fat man in a black coat and large grey waistcoat held his wrist and placed a thin glass rod under his tongue warning him not to bite, that it wasn't sugar barley. The times he woke up after that it was mostly their neighbour Mrs McCall who was sitting by his bed and then the hot grey chattering in his head grew silent and he felt cool and light and wide awake.

"What was the matter with me?" he asked Annie when she came in late that evening.

"The doctor wasn't really certain. A kind of feverish chill he said. I told you, you shouldn't have gone out without your cap."

"What day is it?"

"Sure what do you care what day it is."

"I mean how many days is it since...?"

"Since what? Oh since you got sick? Just a few days. Now you just start gettin' better an' put that other thing right outa your head."

That was all very well for her to say but how could you put out of your head what seemed part of your very brain, the part that kept you supplied with things to think of and what you thought about when you were lying there was how mean and rotten you had been to Jack. "They tell me they're not bakin' rock cakes any more. Not even for people!" Had he really said something like that to a man who was starving to death? The lava of guilt crept on through his mind, burning there the conviction that he had done something for which he would never be forgiven, not even after about a couple of million years in Purgatory. Yet surely even now there must be some way of making reparation to Jack? If only he could find what that way was! "A couple o' lousy rock cakes might have saved his life" was the regret that came back again and again. In a vague sort of way it was like something you'd read in the *Black Mask* where the gang boss - Big Louie or Dino, or the Duke - details one of his men to rub out his best friend whom they have discovered to be double-crossing them. Yet how could Jack be accused of pulling a double-cross? He was ashamed, that's all. Anyone could understand that. How could he have come right out and said the cakes were as much for him as for the dog?

He sat up in bed as if the word had been shouted in

his ear. The dog! What was happening to Danny Boy during all this time? Who was feeding him, making sure he had a warm place to sleep at night, taking him out for a walk, throwing sticks for him to fetch? Certainly not Jack's father whom he knew couldn't stand the sight of Danny Boy. He once saw him kick the dog out of his path. And if he wasn't taking care of him it was clear nobody was. Indeed somebody might have already taken him - tied with strong ropes and muzzled - to the dogs' home where Kevin Curran said he had seen a big jar of colourless liquid which they poured out on a pad and held over the dog's snout to put him to sleep - forever. Tears fell on the pillow between the pale blur of his hands. One of the nuns in the first school he had attended had read a story of a faithful dog who couldn't be found after his master's death and later was discovered pining away on top of his grave - the whole class fell silent. Nothing like that was going to happen to Danny Boy. Tomorrow he would find the dog and beg Annie to let him take care of it. That was how he would make amends to Jack. And if Annie didn't agree, as was most likely, then there was nothing for it but for him and Danny Boy to set out into the country together far from schools and shops and cakes and taxis, where Danny Boy would catch hares and rabbits for their food and he would build a hut of twigs and leaves just like Robinson Crusoe. He clenched his fists as the resolve surged into his mind. Tomorrow would make everything right with Jack! Tomorrow!

Next day Annie made him accompany her to the shop and she kept him there all day while she ran into the back room every chance she had to see how he was feeling. "I'm all right now. Really I am!" he told her wishing he had the courage to bring up the matter of Danny Boy. That would come later, the important thing was to find the dog first. When it grew dark Annie said: "I've arranged with Mrs McCall to give you a nice bowl of warm soup, so you go on back an' when you've got that into you, curl up before the fire until I come home." He left the shop saying he would do that and headed towards the lane where the stable was situated. His incisive pace slackened when he came to the mouth of the narrow space between two shabby warehouses where a flickering gas jet in a glass case at the top of a thin iron standard cowered away from the shapeless hulk of darkness that marked the farther end of the lane. Holding his breath because of the sickening odours rising from the ground he went past the ineffectual light and on into the thickening darkness somewhere in the midst of which he hoped to find the high double-gate of the stable with its low door let into the bottom of the section on the left. At least that's how he remembered it from seeing it once in daylight. But surely it would be locked now? Didn't the police when they were involved in a case place a seal on door locks? The lane seemed much longer than he thought it was, interminable even. At length, he paused a moment wishing with all his heart he could leave that darkness which smelled of rancid grease and rotted cabbage and do what Annie said, curl up before a blazing fire. Already he had come a long way and hadn't that shown how willing he was to make amends? Hadn't he walked the length of that dark lane against the fear of his heart which rose trembling afresh at every step he took into that suffocating darkness? Surely there was no need to do any more, Jack would understand that he had tried his best. Gritting his teeth he went on. He would just touch the little wicket gate, which surely would be locked, and then come away. Tomorrow, in the light of day, he would return and find Danny Boy. Yes, that was the best plan. Jack would approve of that.

His wary foot knocked gently against the gate and he felt to the left for the handle of the door. His fingers curled round its metallic coldness and as if coming alive to his touch it pulled heavily on his arm drawing him with some force into the stable. He paused in the stifling atmosphere of the place breathing in stale warm air on which he smelled sour bran and damp straw and horse - what had happened to the horse? and old clothes and dog and - death! Why hadn't he thought of that before? Somewhere in here Jack had hanged himself, his putties knotted together and tied round a rafter, his body hanging down stretching nearer and nearer the ground which in the end was only an inch or two below his frantic feet cycling to his end. His eyes pressed into the frightening gloom. Where had it happened? He listened and seemed to hear the creak of the rafters high above the weight of the suspended body. Or was the creaking lower down? Was he really hearing it or just imagining the sound? He listened in the terrible dark. Yes, there was something in there, creaking, scratching, moving. Great God what was it? A baleful bundle of solid darkness was scampering towards him, coming up right out of the terrifying depths of his own mind it seemed. A smothered growl of hatred hurled towards him at which he dashed out through the door, knocking his cap off, and ran towards the frail refuge of the caged light. The baleful darkness came after him in a mad muttering of paws on the cobblestones. A bestial snarl that held a whole universe of hatred sought to swallow his sanity. Jesus save me! As he came under the street lamp he felt a gust of warm breath on his calves and immediately after the sharp lash of a dog's teeth on his bare flesh. He squealed his fright and ran towards a huge crate of yellow light, a tram passing the mouth of a street which led to the quays. He ran on hearing behind him Danny Boy rend the air with his hoarse stacatto barks which swung suddenly into a despairing howl of inconsolable sorrow.

He burst into the shop sobbing. Annie who was sweeping up uttered a faint shriek and made him sit at the table in the back room where she patted at him with fingers, knuckles, elbows. When he calmed down he blurted out what had happened and showed her the frightful wound on his calf which now that he had a chance to look at it seemed hardly anything at all. Was it even a scratch?

"Jesus, Mary and Joseph" Annie exclaimed - it had to be something really serious for her to invoke all the members of the holy family together - "Come to Jervis Street 'ospital, quick! That oul dog is maybe gone mad an' as sure as anythin' you'll get claustrophobia unless somethin' is done right away about that bite."

"But it's hardly anythin', Annie."

"It doesn't have to be much to be dangerous. Don't you realise that if that dog is mad you'll go mad too? Foam at the mouth an' all! No! No! That wound's got to be pasteurised!"

She struggled into her creaky green mackintosh.

"When Guard Dillon drops into the back room for his

smoke in the mornin' I'll tell him all about that dog so I will."

"There's no need, Annie. The poor dog didn't mean any harm."

"Maybe not but Guard Dillon'll know what to do. He'll have that mangy animal destroyed so he will. First thing!"

"No, Annie. Not that! Please!"

"Destroyed, that's what it's goin' to be. It would've been a blessin' if he'd hung that smelly mongrel before he done himself in. Two of a kind they were. I could never understand what you saw in him. Two of a kind! That oul thing'll be put to sleep before tomorrow night."

His soul sickened in despair. Annie always got her way. He would never be able to make amends now. Never ever!

POPPY AND LILY

As the deep quiver of power hurled the huge tram onwards into Redmond's Hill, Pearse rose from his seat beneath the whirring trolley on the outside and came clattering down the spiral staircase, his school satchel bouncing like an urgent reminder not to be late on the steps behind him. He made a wild Tarzan dive for the tall, brass bar in the middle of the boarding step and clung there with his gloved hands as the steel ship plunged with a roar of thunder through the ambush of the dark straits where the silver windows alarmed with hurtling life opened up a murderous fire of fragmented reflections. Undaunted by the fierceness of the attack he clung manfully to his post his sure hand guiding the ship past Rabiotti's fish-and-chip shop into the safety of the wider waters of Wexford Street where already the cream and grey bulk of the Gorevan building came swaying and bouncing towards them. Just short of the stop he hung his leg over the blurred roadway and was off the shattered ship in a deft backwards drop. He was half-way towards Harcourt Street before the crump and whirr of the tram merged into the other sounds of the early morning.

Several, groups of the enemy wearing their moulting poppies and war medals were already in Harcourt

Street heading towards the centre of town to attend church services, loyalist celebrations and whatever else they did before the two-minute silence at eleven o'clock. He chose his fastest horse, the stout Roland on which he had so many times taken the good news to Aix, held the reins lightly in his hand, and began to gallop in the direction of the Green. As he went with an angry scuff of heels past one of the enemy groups he heard several girls shout "God bless the Prince of Way-ils". Shout away! Just wait till the students start to march and they would soon change their tune for those silly faggots! The medals, service stripes, and poppies worn on all sides of him called out foul insults to Ireland. Which would be avenged! Yes, before the day was much older! He tugged Roland round onto the south side of the Green, cast a cold eye on whateveritwas - at school Mr O'Maolain was always quoting a verse that began something like that - and galloped towards the crowds fanning out of University Church.

Don't say he was too late! They were already coming out of half-eight mass and he had promised Maurice Moran he'd be there no later than twenty-to-nine. It was all his mother's fault. As usual she was completely unreasonable in not letting him leave the house until a heavy shower of rain had passed over. Even had he been going to school what harm would a little rain have been compared with the cold wait outside the locked classroom where Huddie the Horror led the morning prayers working up the requisite amount of holy heat to enable him to lay into late comers with four of the best on each crumpling hand. Maurice suddenly appeared in the sloping driveway beside the church, his school cap clinging as best it could on the stout red spikes of his stubby hair.

"For Jasus sake" he whispered peevishly sidling up beside Pearse "do you want to give the feckin' game away gallopin' up the street like that? Sure any eedjit'd see it's not to school you're goin'. It's stickin' out a mile you're mitchin; so come on! Let on we're two holy boys just comin' outa mass an headin' for school through the Green."

Pearse swung his school satchel behind him, hooked his thumb under the sling of his sharpshooter's rifle, and fell into step beside the tough good-natured sergeant spitting oaths and tobacco juice as he led him from the safety of the dug-out into the grim hell of no-man's land. Together they crossed the bluish asphalt in a taut silence menaced by hostile watching eyes and the gun-sights of snipers hidden behind the railings in the trees. The path beyond the side-entrance to the park was deserted and Maurice unthawed enough to say: "I'm glad you didn't funk it though, seein' this is the first time you've ever mitched from school. Poppy day's not much gas when you're on your own as I found out last year."

Pearse directed a nonchalant stream of his own tobacco juice towards a "Please Keep Off the Grass" sign and keeping the excitement out of his voice asked: "When does the baton-chargin' an' the head-smashin' start?"

Maurice yawned, ran his fingers up under the edge of his cap and scratched abstractedly,

"Oh, sometime after eleven, I think." He spoke as if the whole expedition was already boring him, "Come on.

We gotta trance them schoolbags or Mr Dooley or some other rotten school attendance inspector'll cotton on to us."

They gave a quick glance round the near-deserted park and moved cautiously in among the bushes. Pearse dropped behind, keeping a wary eye out for skulking snipers, savages with bones through their noses, wild-beasts with razor-sharp claws which at any minute might come flying through the air. He lifted his feet higher than usual from the grasp of the deadly land-mines and quick-sands and quagmires with which the soggy place abounded. Once you started to be sucked under nothing could save you except maybe your brown scapulars which his mother told him had once saved someone she knew from drowning out in Sandymount.

"Here we are" said Maurice moving round a thick clump of spikey bushes that were still whispering from the rain shower which had made his mother keep him indoors.

"I always trance my bag here when I'm mitchin'" Maurice said, "It's a straight line with the haunted window in Iveagh House."

For the moment Pearse forgot they were in a dangerous French jungle somewhere near Paris in the middle of a war and stared across at the opaque grey glass of the window.

"I can't see the mark of the rosary beads on the glass" he told Maurice.

"No, as I said yesterday it's only on Holy Thursday it appears, the anniversary of the day - God bless us - when the black sinner snatched the rosary outa the girl's hand and tried to fling it out through the window."

A delicious shiver of fear wriggled down Pearse's back. There, just across the road, God had reached down from Heaven and revealed his awful power as he would again next Holy Thursday, and on that same day year after year for all ages to come. And even if the building itself fell down on that day you would still see the mark of the beads on the very air itself. Maybe that was what he really felt when they crossed the road, the all-seeing eye of God stern upon him because he was mitching from school and had already made up his mind to lie to his mother and teachers about it if ever he was found out. He felt vaguely ashamed of the lie he had made up, already waiting to be told. "There was this poor blind man who asked me to guide him to a street on the northside to visit his mother. Berkeley Road he called the place and I had great trouble finding it." Yet having to commit a sin by telling a lie was a necessary sacrifice you had to make for Ireland, because Maurice said that everyone who loved his country should be out on the streets to support the university students who would show all those rotten loyalists with their poppies and medals that Ireland was free now and wasn't going to put up with Union Jacks being waved all over the place and the British national anthem being sung on the streets. Following his friend's example he pushed the satchel under the rustling bush, exactly the sort of place where you'd expect to encounter a poisonous snake with dangerous darting fangs. Or worse! You had to be careful in case a stray cat had left his calling card there.

A moment later he crept out of the jungle behind Maurice sucking his wrist into which calmly he probed with his Bowie knife to make it easier to get at the venom of the cobra that had lashed out at him just as he was withdrawing his hand from the bush.

"What y'doin'?" Maurice asked him.

"Just suckin' an oul scratch that's hurtin' me."

"You'll see more than scratches before the day is out, when the students and the loyalists start fightin' and the Bobbies make their baton charges. Jasus, there'll be skin an' hair flyin'.' Saw it all last year." He yawned grandly.

Pearse skipped deftly into step beside him in the smart way he had seen the Fintan Lalor bandsmen do it when he followed their band in a torchlight procession, earlier in the year, to an election rally or protest or something like that. It surprised and disappointed him a little, that Maurice appeared to be bored with the whole business, which was strange for it was his companion's vividly acted descriptions of the fights on Armistice Day which had made him eager to see them for himself. He looked at him trudging by his side, his hair sticking out like red nails, his lips pursed and peevish, his hands thrust into the pockets of his ragged brown-tweed overcoat from where the thumbs curled out over the edges like hard hooks.

"Where are we headin' for now?" he asked.

"To get our lilies, of course. I hope you brought your penny."

"I've got fourpence."

"You have? Fourpence!"

Maurice instantly lost his bored expression. He fetched a skipping kick at an empty Gold Flake packet on the path and began an animated account of what gurr cake tastes like when it comes hot and steaming from the baker's van.

"It gets cold terrible quick in the shop window" he explained, "an' you can never be sure if it's really fresh or if an oul cat hasn't been lying on it to keep itself warm. But straight outa the van!" He smacked his lips loudly and nodded encouragingly at Pearse, "Bloody great so it is! Spiffin! Would you like me to keep an eye out for a baker's van after we buy the lilies?"

"Don't mind" Pearse began to realise that on a long trek through the cold, say to the South Pole with Captain Scott, there might be nothing more welcome than a warm thick slab of gurr cake. Especially if you ran out of whale meat and penguins.

They trudged into Earlsfort Terrace which to Pearse's great disappointment he saw to be almost completely empty.

"Don't worry," Maurice told him. "It's just that we're a bit early for the students and the lily-sellers." He looked about him and made a dash to the top of a nearby flight of steps where he danced about calling "I've got the secret plans." Pearse ran to him and wrestled with the spy on the edge of a skyscraper above the silent progress of toy traffic, striving with his hands round his friend's wrist to keep him from turning in his direction the hump of his thumb which he had already agreed with himself was the muzzle of a gun. Just as he poised to cast the spy to a splatting death far below the door behind him swung open like a tunnel to hell belching out a terrifying figure in a reddish uniform who danced mad into the air and swung an unsuccessful cuff at his head.

"Geralongoutadat!" the reddish figure shouted, "I'll have your effin heads offa yous, so I will."

They ran further up the road until, a little tired, they slowed down to a slinging walk which offered nothing more interesting than piles of litter in the gutter which was too wet and soggy to fan out like an exploding shell in a battle if you gave it a running kick.

"I said not to worry, didn't I?" Maurice said, "See, here's one of the lily-sellers now."

He led Pearse to a sour-faced, cold-nosed lady who stood outside the gate of the College her steel spectacles glinting dangerously in the fitful sunlight. She had amazing curls of greasy grey-brown hair escaping like terrified long-tailed insects from under the crushing rim of her helmet-hard hat. Suspended by picture cord from her frail shoulders was a flat cardboard tray containing a generous collection of green-white-and-orange paper Easter lilies. As he came close Pearse saw her eyes gleam red through her round spectacles.

"Give's two of your ha'penny lilies, please ma'am."

Pearse turned in surprise to his friend.

"They're a penny each." The lady spoke as if she was taking bites at the words. Maurice recoiled a long dramatic pace. His jaw drooped dismally as he heaved a heavy "Ah" of disappointment. He swayed in a boxer's crouch, his puckering forehead and twisting lips revealing an immense struggle going on inside him. A long sigh marked its end. He turned to Pearse.

"All right," he said, the click of a catch in his voice, "Since you were called after Padraig Pearse who gave his life for Ireland, you of all people won't mind making a sacrifice for our country. I know you won't object when I say we'll forget all about that nice hot, steamin' gurr cake we were plannin' on havin', an' pay a penny apiece for the lilies. Sure we can have our breakfast when we go home for our tea, can't we?"

Realising just in time what the game was Pearse hung his head and extracted a penny from his pocket dreading that a merry jingle from the other three coins would arouse the lady's suspicion. He handed it up to her and when she didn't take it he risked looking into her face which he saw was contorting into a web of wrinkles around her bared, jagged teeth.

"Aren't yous the good little boys" to his surprise he saw she was smiling, "Denyin' yourselves your cake for dear oul Ireland's sake."

She bent swiftly and pinned a lily on the lapel of his coat. Then she did the same for Maurice, waving away their proffered coins.

"Off with yous now" she said, "The baker should be callin' on Madden's down round the corner there any minute now,"

Maurice took a swift pace backwards and snapped his grimy hand to his forehead in a brisk military salute. "For the sake of dear oul Ireland" he said, nudging Pearse who was teasing the stinging point of the pin out of the skin on his chest where the lady had jabbed it in her impulse of generosity. They moved off down the street towards the corner where Maurice looked back and said: "We took in that bloody oul needle-nosed fool great, didn't we? Eh?" Chuckling he led the way across the road and into the next street where he gave a leap of joy and pointed towards a horse and long van drawn up before a shop.

"Jasus, look!" he exclaimed, "The oul cow was right. A baker's van. Look at the steam comin' out of it. God imagine what the gurr cake must be like. You're goin' to buy some now after savin' that penny aren't you."

"Yes" Pearse told him wondering why he felt rather unsure about it. "I suppose so."

"Leave it to me" Maurice said, "I know the oul eedjit in this dairy. I bought a hae'penny woodbine and a match here last time I was mitchin' up this way.

They passed the van-man on their way into the shop sniffing the warm comforting smell of fresh bread and cakes.

"What yous want?" The grey-haired shopkeeper had strange, sick-looking orange eyes and a pale face only slightly darker than his brilliant white shop-coat.

"Just give's two ha'penny slabs of Chester cake."

"Where'd you get the idea they're only a ha'penny?"

"That's all I pay where I come from" Maurice turned to show Pearse his bored yawn.

"Well go on back there" the shopkeeper glared, "I want the space your rotten feet is contaminatin'. Git!" He made to move towards the end of the counter where Pearse saw the thick handle of a yard-brush. He jingled two penny pieces on the counter.

"Two slabs o' Chester cake, please" he said.

The man took the handle of the brush in his hand and laid it with some regret against the counter. He took two slices of the thick brown cake and wrapped them in greaseproof paper.

"There yous are" he grinned sarcastically, "Have a good hearty breakfast for if yous go round town with them bloody Easter lilies in your coats it'll be the last one yous'll be havin'. You're wearin' them as a protest against people cele-bratin' Armistice Day aren't yous? Well, why shouldn't Irishmen celebrate it when Ireland sent more men to the war in proportion to her population than any other country in the world? Did yous know that? And more casualties we had too. Why shouldn't we remember men who died savin' us from the terrible Germans?"

"What about the terrible English who've been robbin' and murderin' us for seven hundred years?" Pearse asked and broke for the door as the man made a lurch towards the handle of the yard-brush. They ran to the far side of the street where Maurice thumbed his nose in the direction of the man, who regretfully turned from the door to follow a customer into the shop. Pearse handed one of the slabs of cake to Maurice who immediately fell to eating it with such eagerness he seemed to be pushing it solidly into his face. Walking along towards the Green again he saw a bunch of hae'penny peashooters in a newsagents window.

Instantly he recognised the uneasy feeling he'd been having; it was the nakedness of being without a weapon of any kind, for with his mother fussing around him earlier on account of the rain he had been unable to slip his steel catapult into his school satchel. He strolled into the shop and bought two ha'penny peashooters, one of which he handed to Maurice.

"What y' buy these for?"

"Oh I dunno! If we go back into the Green while we're waitin* for the students maybe we could get a bang at a bird or somethin'."

"Maybe we can feck some peas for them over there." Maurice nodded towards a greengrocer's stall just ahead of them, "Good stick, look! The oulfella who owns it is wearin' a lily too. You go up to him an' ask him the way to - let's see - Christ's Church. Let on we're Protestants. You know, like Wolfe Tone. Go on." He nudged the point of his shoulder into Pearse's back impelling him forward nearer the greengrocer who bent over the stall weighing out a stone of potatoes for a stout lady with a small dog like a piece of smelly moulting fur on the end of a yellow-leather lead. Swallowing his shyness and a moist mass of gurr cake, Pearse approached the man who nodded "Ta" to the lady with the dog. The man was about to ignore his stammered question when his eyes fell on the lily in his coat. He smiled, spoke a phrase in Irish which sounded as if he was sneezing inside his mouth and bent to listen to what he was asking him. Taking him by the shoulder he turned his back on the fruit-and-vegetable stall and in a ringing Cork accent gave the necessary directions. All the while Pearse's eyes hurt with the strain of keeping them from looking at Maurice who was a mysterious active blur at the edge of his vision. Fearing the man would turn to look he blurted out.

"An' when will the fightin' start? I mean, when will the students be ready to march?"

"Same thing" the man grinned, "In about an hour. If you're back from Christ's Church in time you'll be able to see them teach a lesson to the lousy gaugers and bowsies with their Mons medals and their mangy poppies and their God Save the Kings."

He thanked the man and walked as calmly as he could across to the main gates of the Green. Maurice overtook him as he was vaulting his horse over the iron chains in his wild cavalry attack on the grey fortress.

"That was a cinch, look! Maurice squeezed his pocket which assumed the shape of a sixpenny rubber ball. "You did that marvellous, kept his attention away while I got the ammunition."

Inside the gate Maurice divided the spoils with Pearse who immediately looked around for a suitable target. Finding none he began to walk with heavy deliberation along the empty street of the wild-west town, his heels kicking up tiny clouds of blue pebbles, his long barrelled colt resting beneath his right hand in his overcoat pocket ready for a quick draw as soon as Indian Jake or Two-Gun Slim appeared out of the hazy sunlight at the other end of the street. Without warning his cheek stung moistly making him jerk his head back with a sharp yelp. Already it was too late to blast a retaliatory shot at Maurice who was plunging away into the Lousy Acre in a horse's loping gallop, waving his flashing peashooter and shouting: "I just shot the villain! I just shot the villain!" Pearse burned with anger.

How dare Maurice picture him as the villain! He ran after him on a twisting trail that took him over the legs of several unemployed men, some sleeping, some propped up against trees reading the Racing Herald and round and again round unattended prams, which brought one nursemaid running from a gossip circle on the grass and another flushed from the arms of a messenger boy whose bicycle with its large delivery basket had been placed between them and the prying eyes of the world. Maurice's gallop slithered to a halt in a spray of mud. He loped closer to the messenger boy and burst out laughing!

"Hey, Screw Pimpler Murphy! The Rudolph Valentino of the Lousy Acre, be Jasus!"

Pearse seeing his chance, kicked the rudder of his triplane and swerved in for the kill, the daring Red Baron himself roaring out of the sun, a stream of moist tracers flying from the muzzle of his Spandau synchronised with the spin of the blades of the propeller. As he zoomed past he saw over the edge of the cockpit the dismayed face of his adversary going down in flames. He ran out of the acre and along the path to the duckpond. Maurice, stocky and strong, was a better wrestler and boxer than he was and as he had never beaten him at anything before he wondered what he would do to avenge the stream of peas in his face. Not that he was afraid! Steering his battleship along the margin of the pond he released salvos of shells which fell among the enemy who wagged their tails and quacking with alarm moved out of range towards the middle of the pond. He was about to open fire on another enemy flotilla when he noticed Maurice strolling by his side as if he had forgotten all about being burned to a cinder in his wrecked Spad.

"The oul fella in the shop" Maurice said, "How long did he say it would be before the students got started?"

"'Bout an hour."

"They were earlier last year. Hey, let's go over an' finish our gurr cake sittin' under the statue."

All the way across the neat central area of the park with its pond, public seats and green twopenny hire chairs, Pearse sneered at the English King sitting up there on his horse. Looking up at the statue he sniffed the gunpowder of vague battlefields and once again felt the power of the horse on which the King sat. Its plunging strength flowed into his restless legs, his shoulders and his neck driving him in a noble prancing gallop around the statue at which he aimed his musket to discover how well he shot from the saddle. To his delight several shots got home. He sat down beside Maurice who was absorbed in reading a crumpled copy of *The Adventure* laid across his knees while his busy fingers extracted peas from the crumby remains of his gurr cake. Still, it was strange that the statue was still standing because he remembered the huge bang the morning King Billy was blown off his pedestal in Dame Street. Maybe even now there was a bomb hidden somewhere under the base of the statue all set to explode at eleven o'clock when the rotten loyalists were keeping their two-minutes silence. He saw the white face of the clock attached to the bomb, the coils of copper wire, the grey sticks of dynamite. The clock thudded in his chest, the spring ever tightening, driving the minute hand closer to the black notch on the dial when the horse and rider would rise in a huge bang high into the air and go crashing into the pond or maybe even through the window of Iveagh House - which God forbid! It wasn't eleven o'clock yet was it? He looked up at the statue and wondered would he have time to get in another shot before the end came. Nobby McTavish, the sharpshooter of the gallant highlanders would never give a second thought to whether a bomb was going to go off near him or not. In this week's *Adventure* he had fought off a whole group of German saboteurs, or whatever they were called, with shells exploding all round him. And the enemy were moving in on him now. There, on the left, a glint of medals, the hated helmet of the enemy. Nobby McTavish would go down fighting to the last. The hand of the clock raced round towards the fateful black mark. He aimed his Lee Enfield. Held his breath. Fired.

With a dry noise like the beat of a side-drum the pea bounced off the crown of a bowler hat and Pearse felt a wild release of joy as if a real bullet had ripped through the enemy's head. "Jitterin' ass!" Maurice exclaimed and rose warily to his feet. All the while the man under the hat remained as still as the statue above them. Pearse saw he was dressed like his Uncle Tommy, the printer, in a black overcoat with velvet collar, striped trousers, worn down but clean black boots. The man turned slowly and looked directly at him. He felt the horse within him rear in the air, wild to escape in a mad gallop round the far side of the statue. To his surprise the man seemed older than most of those he had seen that morning wearing poppies and medals. The pale skin on his face looked so thin that Pearse was glad the pea had not hit it for surely it would have gone right through.

The man stepped back a pace and Pearse felt the clear blue eyes play over him in what he felt to be surprise or maybe even a sort of wonder. It was strange to stand there and feel he was a kind of object the man had never seen before, like a creature from some lost world. Without taking his eyes off the man he bent down and pulled up his stocking after which he wiped the boot of his other foot along the back of it. A sad smile spread out from the man's eyes, sweetening his thin mouth. He leaned forward as if about to say something, frowned in thought which brought his sad look back again. He turned slowly on his heel and walked away in the direction of Grafton Street.

"Gawnie Mack" gasped Maurice, "I never thought you'd have the guts to shoot at an oul fella's hard hat. An' you were real cool when it looked as if he was goin' to come over an' murder you."

Delighted with the praise Pearse leaned back nobly nonchalant like the King on the horse above them. Curling his lip he ran his eye disdainfully over the nothing-people walking through the park one of whom seemed to have her eye on him as she strode with alarming determination towards him. The sun glinted on her greying hair pulled back in a bun from her huge round face, raw and red, like some strange living vegetable. Her voluminous black shawl, a sort of portable shadow, had slipped back from her shoulders revealing her gleaming dealer's apron with the large flapless pockets just above her thighs. Pearse realised that Maurice had not seen her for he was staring after the man in the hard hat evidently waiting until he was a safe distance away to shout some insult or other after him.

"I saw yous" the woman yelled up at them as she came nearer, "A right pair of whore's melts yous are an' no mistake. Why couldn't yous leave poor oul Mr Dalton alone? Was he doin' yous any harm? Was he?"

"He was..." Maurice's voice trailed off into the noises of the park.

"He has no right" Pearse got around the lump in his throat and went on, "goin' around wearin' English medals an' an English poppy in Ireland."

"Shut your gob you cheeky pup you!" The woman was alarmingly close, "The size or you talkin' about rights! When your rotten fathers was sweatin' gettin' yous that poor man's only son was out in Flanders gettin' himself blown to bits to save us all from bein' trampled on an' worse be the terrible Germans. It's his son's medals he's wearin' this mornin' an' a red poppy in memory o' the blood he shed! An' that's some-thin' he has every right to do. But tell me what do yous two mean goin' around wearin' Easter lilies right smack in the middle o' November?"

A voice spoke in a sad lilt somewhere in his memory. He recalled the speaker at the meeting he had arrived at through following the Fintan Lawlor pipe band in that torchlight procession just before the Easter holidays.

"On the eleventh of November" he caught the speaker's tone and rhythm "We Republicans wear Easter lilies in honour of Wolfe Tone, the founder of the Irish Republic, because on that day he was condemned to death..."

The voice trailed away from him leaving him small, cold, and afraid under the angry eye of the raw-faced woman who was biting her lower lip like Sister Mary

Carmel waiting impatiently for the right answer.

"Yis, in Green Street Courthouse" Maurice said, "condemned to be hanged by the bloodthirsty English an' he a prisoner o' War, an Officer in the French Army."

"Yous cheeky little bastards" the woman shouted rolling the trailing ends of her shawl round her arms in a rapid stirring movement, "It's a good clatter in the gob the two of yous need."

As she flew forward like a giant bird of prey, Pearse leaped after Maurice round the far side of the statue and ran away as fast as he could.

"Just let me lay my hands on yous" the raucous voice called after them. He looked back and slowed down when he saw she couldn't move very fast. She stood, her face dark in the shadow of the statue, holding her hands tight under her huge bosom as if to keep herself from falling apart.

"Ah y'oul wigger" Maurice shouted at her, "D'you want to come up a lane, y'oul brasser you, we got the fourpence?" He launched into a derisive dance hopping from one foot to the other and making with his hands the motion of climbing a thick rope. "WiggerI Wigger!" he shouted in time to his jigging dance. The woman recoiled and glanced about her as if for help.

"We got the fourpence" Pearse shouted too wondering what the significance of the phrase was. He would ask Maurice about that later. The woman took a few steps towards them, shouted a half-hearted "Whore's gets" and turned away. He saw her hurry towards the gate, suddenly change direction and make towards one of the gardeners at that moment strolling out from the shadow of the trees.

"Dekko! The Gar'ner" Maurice warned. He plunged his hands in his pockets and went at a fast stroll towards the Leeson Street gate. Pearse fell into step beside him, but a quick glance behind him showed that the gardener was moving rapidly along an upper path, his stick moving with the rapid strokes of a savage canoe in pursuit of the daring explorers approaching the gate of a fabulous lost city.

"Jasus, he's bloody quick." Maurice hissed and broke into a run. Pearse caught up with him as he passed out through the gate and went on running beside him across the road into Earlfort Terrace.

To his breathless joy the road was thronged with students. In the noisy confusion of movement and counter movement he sensed the emergence of some kind of order. He saw that the young men and women were being organised into squads of twenty or thirty between each of which a leader and two assistants paced impatiently back and forth. A murmur like that of the sea at Dun Laoghaire pier rose from the crowd and as he walked along the pavement wondering where he should place himself when they moved off, a ragged cheer travelled along from the direction of the college. He joined in the cheer when he saw it was for the tricolour, the holy green-white-and-orange, being borne along towards the head of the crowd. His face felt dry and hot and in his limbs there was a kind of crackling feeling, as of electricity. The flag-bearer marched past him and clicked to a halt a few paces beyond the crowd almost every member of which, he saw with a warm thrill, was wearing an Easter Lily in his lapel. His hand moved to where his own lily lay on his breast like love.

A man whom he knew instantly to be the leader appeared at the head of the throng. He was a tall, long-faced man dressed in a high-crowned soft hat, a belted fawn raincoat, and brown laced-up boots. He carried a knobby blackthorn stick in his hand with which he cut impatiently at the pebbles on the road surface while listening to what two other men, standing to attention, were telling him. A runner came from the back of the throng and whispered in the tall man's ear. He listened with gaunt-eyed seriousness and then clicking his heels he raised his stick at arm's length in the air. Silence fell like a damp sack over the assembled company.

"Irishmen and Irishwomen" he began in the familiar sad lilt of the public speaker which made Pearse want to laugh and cry and cheer all at the same time. "Are we going to allow traitors and renegades to wave their Union Jacks and flaunt their service medals and Flanders poppies in the city where Wolfe Tone was condemned to death and the heroes of nineteen-sixteen taken out an' shot by the comrades-in-arms of those very renegades and traitors?"

A tearing "Nooo!" as from the lion house in the zoo growled out of the crowd.

"So let's get started" the man called to them, "We'll convince them it's Ireland they're in even if we have to beat that fact into them with one of these! He swung the blackthorn in the air and an assortment of objects rose like an instant forest above the crowd - hurley sticks, walking sticks, chair legs, pieces of packing cases, sweeping-brush handles, and at least three swords, one of them not rusty. Pearse doubted if his heart could contain so much joyful excitement. All it lacked was a running charge against the loyalists or the police to make the day perfect. An axe, the head narrow and shining rose to join the other weapons.

"When will all the biffin' an' the bangin' an' the wallopin' start?" he asked Maurice.

"Soon! Soon!" Maurice had lost his pose of boredom, "Maybe when we get to College Green. Or O'Connell Bridge maybe. Be Janey, it was better there last year than the big battle we saw in the picture last Saturday at the Camden."

The column started off at a brisk pace, crossed the road diagonally at Saint Vincent's Hospital and marched along past the chains at the margin of the pavement outside the Green. Pearse trotted on the pavement beside Maurice who had found a short broken-branch from one of the trees and was busy tearing the leaves away from it. Anxious lest he should lose sight of the leader Pearse bumped twice into bystanders staring at the passing column and once almost head-first into a lamp standard. The marching students wheeled past the Shelbourne Hotel fanning out to occupy the middle of the road where they forced a tram to clang to a stop. On they marched. A whistled refrain from the rear was taken up in words by those in the middle of the column so that by the time it reached the leader almost everyone was singing "*The Bold Fenian Men!*"

The words soared through Pearse, bringing him out into the road, bearing him along in a breathless wave of delight. "...Their green banners kissing the fresh morning air... stepping boldly together... freedom sits crowned on each proud spirit there..." He saw a crowd gathering at the corner of Dawson Street to watch the approaching procession. They were packed so tight on the park side that he was forced further into the road, where for a few ecstatic moments he paced step by step with the leader, stealing shy glances up at his gaunt, grim-lipped face and at the glorious green flag kissing the air above them. If only he had a blackthorn he would carry it like the leader tucked firmly under his arm, ready for action at a moment's notice.

"Close the ranks!" the leader called out suddenly and following his hard gaze Pearse saw a thick blue chain of policemen swing off the pavement to bar their passage down Grafton Street and South King Street. A shivering descended upon him, flaying over his knees which began to feel so frail they might snap in two. The singing stopped and above the whirring in his ears he heard the determined solid tramp of many feet approaching closer to the police, a line of heavy, dark faces scarred with black bars, the chinstraps of their steel-tipped helmets. Pearse felt himself borne forward by the rising excitement of the crowd, on and on, nearer to where the hands of the police played restlessly with the tops of their black cylindrical baton cases. Something exploded in his head. He stopped and clapped his hands to his ears, A shot had been fired, he realised and saw the yellow batons appear like huge fingers in the hands of the policemen now surging forward out of their tight line and swinging wildly all about them. Screams and cries arose on all sides and with a numb jolt of shock he knew that those other sounds, short and blunt, mixed in with them were batons and sticks and fists biffing, and banging, and walloping just as Maurice had acted it all out yesterday at school. But what terribly frightening sounds they were! He ran with the crowd back towards Dawson Street behind the leader who shouldn't have run away, who he saw was without his hat. The man held his blackthorn by its narrow end waving the thick knob round his head in the air. Pearse stayed behind him trying his best to keep up with him. Suddenly the man slid to a stop, raised his stick high and brought it down fiercely several times. Pearse heard the muffled thuds of the stick on flesh and bone. The leader leaped to one side and ran on leaving him face to face with the man from the park. One of the blows had caught him on the cheek breaking loose a fold of the frail flesh above the drooping moustache which was already stained with blood. Pearse felt as if he had run full tilt into a stone wall. He hung gasping in front of the man who had sunk on his knees and was feeling blindly on the pavement with his hand. "Oh Danny! Danny! Danny!" the man moaned while fresh drops of blood fell on the poppy and dripped from there to the row of medals beneath it. His hand still scrabbled on the ground seeking what his eyes could not see. Maurice grabbed Pearse by the arm and looked delightedly into his face. "This is feckin' marvellous, isn't it? Come on!" Pearse shook himself free and bent to retrieve from the gutter the bowler hat the man's hand was vainly seeking. Slipping his hand inside to tease out the heavy crease in the crown his fingers encountered a moist stickiness which he knew was blood. He stood in front of the man dusting the hat with his elbow.

"Mr Dalton," he said, "It's goin' to be all right now. Don't worry. Please don't worry. I have your hat."

STRAIGHTEN UP AND FLY RIGHT

Johnny, darling Johnny, her toddler of three in his new blue Guiney's jersey, tottered, teetered, tumbled from the top of the wall dividing their backyard from Callan's and fell heavy as Christ's cross down, down, down towards the fright of her heart. Celia shot out her arms to catch his dear flesh of her flesh and dreamed wide-eyed in the cold sweat of another time and gradually came to see she was lying on her bed upstairs in her room which was full of dull thuds, shiverings, scraping sounds, distant music, and the fading image and sweet child smell of her own little flaxen-haired darling. God, who'd ever have thought that in a twitch of time, overnight almost, that little darling would become the full-sized, leering replica of that empty charmer, his father, and that in much the same style he'd drive himself to ruin through his craving for drink and for pinching every woman's bottom in sight without any shame or discrimination at all until at last, just like his father, he too had scarpered and was gone far away from home, from all who tried to love and care for him with never a word sent back, not one, to say whether he was living or dead. Never a word that is until this morning, if you could call the suggestive remarks on that telegram word of how he was. And he wouldn't even have sent that, unwelcome and uncalled for as it was, if it hadn't been for the wedding. How had he come to know about it? Who had told him? Up in Belfast, it turned out he was, probably working in some bar or other, overcharging the British soldiers and the American technicians and pouring all the boss's profits down his throat on the quiet. And maybe Belfast was the best place for him for so long as he was there none of the neighbours could see her shame strutting up and down outside the shop and have to lower their knowing eyes as they sidled in past him for their potatoes, their coal, or their paraffin oil. How could he have done such a stupid thing to himself, ruining his chances with old Mr Mack who had no one to leave his money to and had taken him into his hardware shop where he treated him just like his own son? God knows there wasn't all that much to do there and Johnny should have had the know-how to hold his horses until the old gurrier kicked the bucket which could be at any minute seeing the state his heart was in, not to mention the risks the dirty old dog ran by taking into the back room of the shop the terrible women who came down the quays to offer themselves - all that haggling and screaming in the nights - to the sailors off the cross-channel boats and any others that could bring their cargoes in despite the war. But he could never use his noodle properly and with everything to gain, all it took was for drunken Jack Fitzachery to drive up in a taxi that Saturday afternoon and shout: "C'mon Johnny, spree of your life in Bray. All the boys is celebratin' Wagger's gettin' a treble on the dogs" and he walked straight out of the shop and into the taxi without even stopping to take his black apron off. Little Lily who'd been picking her scabby face at the door had seen it all - Johnny scooping out the till and sauntering out to the taxi with the customers all standing there shouting after him: "What about me three-inch wire nails?" "What about me pound o' plaster of Paris?" "Where's my yard o' sand?" And Mr Mack had looked a sort of sick green when he called in later to ask where Johnny was and, more important to him, what had happened to the contents of the till? Still, dirty old sight and all that he was, it was decent of him not to bring the police into it and to agree to let her pay back all the money in instalments, even though she only had his word for what he claimed was in the till at the time. About seventeen or eighteen pounds still to go, which he'd have to wait for now on account of the expenses of the wedding. But it was a blessing from God that it didn't end up in Number One Dublin District Court for then it would have been in all the papers and everyone would start remembering the big splash on the front page of the Herald, bottom left, the time his father walked off with four cases of brandy from the unloading on the quay. Cool as you like, he'd taken the hand-truck from the shop and wheeled it up the street to where the French ship was unloading its cargo quite convinced that they'd think he was one of the dockers. The bloody eedjit! Wasn't his red head with its shiny bald spot practically a landmark for miles around! Known to all and sundry - even it seemed to the French as well! It was from him that Johnny got the rotten drop, wherever he was now spreading his empty charm around, Australia, Timbuktu, or maybe just Liverpool. Not a whisper from him in all of seventeen years and he'd left the house so friendly that morning to go to a new job on a building site in Doneycaerney. "I'll bring back a few fresh Dublin Bay's for supper," were the last words she had heard from him. No, not quite, for after that hadn't he stuck his head round the door to say: "When you're at the market this morning, try and get a few new potatoes to go with the fish." And he winked - one of the kind that made you wish the wear and tear of the day was over and the two of you were sitting together real quiet after supper thinking of bed. Thank God Ronald didn't take after him in any way at all. A nice quiet boy, Ronald, a bit dreamy maybe, and in so many ways still a baby. But a real credit and comfort to his mother. How handsome he looked this morning standing up there at the altar, polished and shining like a real gentleman, and the whole congregation looking on and you could see they were all admiring him. She heard herself sigh in the gloom and listened to the thuds and creaking in the house, to the dance music from the trio or the gramophone scraping like something trapped between the floor and the ceiling below her, to the laughter of a girl so high-pitched and so far away it might be the scream of someone in affliction. She shivered. Ever since the terrible Germans had bombed the South Circular Road she often came out of sleep shivering like that and almost in tears, listening for the metallic growl of planes and for the cries of the wounded.

She threw off the light cover and sat up fully dressed in the bed, in her mouth the bitter taste of sleep, and what she realised was Alice her brand-new daughter-in-law. Switching on the bedside lamp, she blinked at the unfamiliar burden of coats and macs draped over the end rail of the bed and bundled on top of the chest of drawers and the dressing table. She cupped her chin in her palm and stared at a lone coat drooped over a chair near the window, trailing its skirts slack, heavy, and lifeless on the floor - just like Alice God help us! Of course Ronald losing his job, just three weeks before the wedding, was worry enough, but somehow that was not quite so unsettling as his marrying a girl with absolutely no go in her at all. And if anyone needed a girl with go it was Ronald. Not for the other thing of course, but to get behind him and give him a good push and knock all the dreamy notions out of his head. True, Alice came from a decent, hard-working family, her father in Dockerell's and she herself traipsing off every morning to Players factory in Glasnevin - and she'd have to keep on traipsing now, wouldn't she to make ends meet. But was there anything to her as a person? Take a good look at her and what do you see for God's sake? Nothing at all. Just nothing! She drooped about like a bunch of dried-up rhubarb, all the cares of the world brooding in her face. The very living image of death warmed up! Still, she wouldn't be human would she - and sometimes she looked almost that - if she didn't let herself go sometimes? Maybe she changed drastically when she went out dancing for wasn't it at a dance at Ringsend that Ronald first became interested in her and he after living practically next door to her all his life and never sparing her a second look before? And she couldn't just droop around at work, could she? In Players the girls moved their fingers like lightning, picking up handfuls of cigarettes, twenty a time, no more, no less, slipping them straight into the silver paper in their packets. And Ronald wasn't the only one to be interested in her either. There was Jemser Kelly too, wasn't there, and he one of the best lookers from here to Sandymount? An incident of a month or so ago unfolded before her with an urgent vividness that held her still. She had stepped from the back room down into the shop one night to get a packet of Sweet Afton for herself and there past the window went Ronald and Alice, arm in arm on their way to the Leggett's place. The instant they passed, Jemser shouldered his way out of the darkness of the lane opposite the house and stood under the gas lamp glaring after them, his lips curling away from his teeth in silent ugly words. Then he swung round and slapped the flat of his hand several times against the wall and slouched off like an angry ape in the direction of the quay. The way he hung about the place always eyeing Alice, always trying to get her alone, was surely one of the reasons why Ronald was in such a frantic hurry to get married. Though why any young man should he driven to such lengths just to make sure of Alice was something she would never understand - and all those other girls crazy about him! But to give the dreary girl her due, she hadn't let herself be put off when Ronald lost his job overnight but went on with the plans for the wedding as if nothing had happened. She mightn't be the sort of girl a man would break his neck hurrying home to, but at least she'd always be there when he arrived. Not like some people she could mention! Two at least!

The furniture in the bedroom creaked as if the floor had started to tilt. In a moment the dressing table, wardrobe, chairs and all would come toppling over. There were several muffled thuds and a distant screaming laugh which went on and on like a train hurrying across the Loop Line Bridge down the quay quelling its whistle as it came along the platform of Tara Street Station. Things must be getting out of hand down there, be going too far for even Barney to control. And he certainly could count on no help from Tim. Just like her own boys, her two brothers were as different as chalk and cheese. So long as the drink kept coming his way Tim would be content to sit up on the platform with Les Gormely's three-piece band and grin out at the crowd like the monkey he so closely resembled, God forgive her for thinking that of her own flesh and blood. But he really was like one! Still if he could keep his eyes open long enough he'd work his passage. "Just sit up there with the musicianers," she had told him, "and make sure the crowd keeps over to the side of the store where the benches are. See they don't throw their cigarette butts on the bundles of sticks, the coal, and the turf briquettes under the sacks along the other wall. And for heaven's sake keep them from the far end of the place where the tinned stuff is. They're here to dance at Ronald's wedding, not to spy on what his mother has still managed to keep in stock in spite of all the war shortages." She slipped off the bed and regarded her reflection in the uneven strip of mirror above the layered mound of coats on the dressing table. Sacred Hour, how grey she'd become since the war started, how wrinkled about the eyes! And her mouth looked as dry and brittle as wrapping paper. That's what worry does! It was all in her face. Worry over Johnny, over Ronald, over the sick turn business was taking. In a year or two, if Ronald and Alice made a grandmother of her, she'd really look the part. "Better start looking out a lace cap," she said aloud and stuck out her tongue at which she frowned and then saw herself frowning.

She came out on the landing into an atmosphere stale with cigarette smoke, spilled porter, and the dried sweat of many bodies. Couples were sitting on the stairs, their arms wound round each other. She wove her way carefully downstairs and paused in the hall to reassure herself about a group of young men whom up till then she had seen only from behind, sitting on the lower steps as she came down. They were in stained working clothes and had a dusty look about them.

"Friends of Alice's, of the Leggetts', are yous?" she asked smiling. One of them opened his mouth to speak making an indistinct "ye-r-nr" sound and was instantly interrupted by a dark, ferrety-eyed young man on the bottom step who sat with his stubby legs splayed out over the floor.

"It was on Ronald's account we came" he confided, almost in a whisper. "We're in the stores at Carter's you see, just dropped in straight from work."

Celia was touched. "Ah, from Carter's." So there were no hard feelings as you might say, "Are you being treated right?" she asked.

"Up till now" grinned the ferrety-eyed young man holding up an empty pint tumbler.

"Come into the back room," Celia invited, "There's plenty of everything there."

"Well -" the man hesitated "We're just in our working togs and we'd feel sort of ashamed to go in there. If that decent oul skin with the big soup-strainer moustache and the red tie you know, the fella who looked after us before, if he..."

"I'll send him out to you," said Celia passing through the open door into the back room where the noise and the heat pushed against her mind making her a little dizzy for a moment. She blinked to her left into the tiny kitchenette partitioned off from the rest of the spacious room. There was a blue hint of light in the gloom of the far corner. Her daughter Jeannie had obviously managed to remember to put a kettle on the gas glimmer so that she could have a good cup of strong tea when she awoke. Great! But just as obviously Tim hadn't managed to remember to stay on the platform with the band. "Soup-strainer moustache" hit him off to a 'T', but "decent oul skin" was a bit misplaced as they'd know if they had him knocking in at dinner time every day having worked up a ferocious appetite on his morning saunter to the labour exchange to meet his pals and quieten his fears that there might be a job going. As she advanced further in the sweaty hubbub of the room she looked to see what remained of the stock of drink on top of the sideboard which flanked the other partition wall of the kitchenette. She must have been asleep for hours. More than half the bottles had disappeared and there were only a few platefuls of sandwiches left. As far back as three weeks ago she had known the supplies wouldn't last out the evening. Mrs Leggett had said then: "But six dozen stout, a ham, and a leg of pork is all I can kick in with, for you must remember that I helped Alice and Ronald with the furniture for the room you've got for them across the road." That's always the way it was when you ran a business. Everyone thought you were made of money. But all was not lost, for from what she could see through the jostling crowd there was still plenty to eat on the huge table in the centre of the room. As yet no one had noticed her as she eased her way silently through the crowd towards the far corner of the room, towards the entrance to what Barney had christened 'the slope', the few paces of passage he had covered over in a corner of the yard so that she could walk directly from the back room into the stores and not have to go round the corner to the double gates in the next street. She kept to the left of the table, deliberately avoiding the fireplace where she knew the Leggett contingent were sitting over their stout and sandwiches. None of the young people in the crush appeared to recognise her. One young man stared glassy-eyed at her as she pressed past, crumbs from his sausage roll showering down into the V-gap between his jacket and his doubly mottled tie. She paused near the slope and saw that Alice was sitting at the fire with her mother and several friends. Droopy as usual she sat driving furrows with the toes of her black patent-leather shoes into the drift of white turf ash which had begun to gather on the margin of the hearth. She spoke with heavy gestures of her left hand poised in mid-air, the light striking soft gleams from her new wedding ring. Well at least new to her if not to Kelly's pawn shop. Celia sighed and went up the slope. More kick in a radish!

Advancing towards her down the centre of the store came the source of much of the shiverings, thuds, and screaming laughs which had reached her upstairs. She recoiled a little from the unwelcome scene and the noise accompanying it which drove a passage of pain through her head. Ronald's best man Nagginer Doyle arms linked with Paddy Dukes and Ed Carlin came prancing towards her. Each of them had his trousers rolled up to the knees which were hidden beneath the hems of the frilly pinafores they were wearing. They were bellowing: "Roll me yover in the clover! Roll me yover, lay me down..." Clicking her teeth in disgust she snapped her head away from the sight of them. "Muck! Pure muck, that's all they are!" She saw Ronald standing with Barney and a young man she felt she ought to recognise but didn't. Barney and the young man, paying no attention to the prancing trio, were in earnest conversation. Barney punched his fist into his palm to reinforce some point he was making. Ronald stood slightly apart from them, a wistful smile on his face.

"God what a night he picks to go all dreamy" she thought and scrutinised the guests on the benches along the wall to discover who or what he might be looking at. Her eyes met those of Jeannie who sprang to her feet snatching Franny Agnew's hand from her bosom. "C'm over here!" Celia beckoned at which both Barney and Ronald turned to greet her. "See if that water in the kettle's boiled yet," she said to Jeannie, jabbing with the flat of her hand on her shoulder as she slunk past. "Ronald" she said with a smile, "Some friends of yours from Carter's is out in the hall. Bring them out a few bottles of stout. Four! I see your uncle Tim's otherwise engaged." Tim was on the makeshift platform holding hands with Minnie Stacey a girl from the far end of the street, young enough to be his daughter which seeing the terror he was in his youth, which apparently was still continuing, she could quite easily be.

Ronald frowned, "Fellas from Carter's?"

"Yes. I thought it nice of them to call round. In spite of

what happened it shows you still have friends there."

"I don't want them here poking their noses in. Sneerin'!"

"Now go on. They mean well. It's a nice gesture of them to come."

A roar of acclamation rose from the guests in the store at the end of the trio's performance. She brought her hands to her ears and so didn't hear whatever it was Ronald said, but that didn't matter for he turned away to weave through the grinning throng in the back room, crouching his head deep into the collar of his jacket as several young men in turn slapped him on the back. Celia turned to Barney.

"Was I asleep for long?"

"'Bout an hour-an'-a-half."

"And how did Ronald get on?"

Barney patted his free hand on her shoulder. "Now give over worryin' about Ronald. The hooley's goin' over great an' he's enjoyin' himself. In his own quiet way that is. 'Course Nagginer and Co 'ave been tryin' to inveigle 'm into takin' a drink, but there's nothin' doin' on that score. So you can quit worryin'. There's no danger of 'im breakin' his pledge. By the way, recognise this character here we were talkin' to?"

Celia shook her head and looked at the young man, chatting to granny Agnew, who under her frowning scrutiny dipped the point of his chin to the knot of his tie and shuffled his feet on the floor.

"Mad Maizie's boy" Barney said nodding his eyebrows above the glass he raised for a quick sip, "Back from the

R.A.F. on leave he is."

"I would have known him in a pot of stirabout," said Celia. "Even though livin' over there in England changes them, doesn't it? Gives them a sort of yellow Protestant look."

"It gives his ideas that look anyway," frowned Barney. "Course he's a bit screw-ways in the head and not just because he's his mother's son, but on account of 'im bein' shot down twice in the Battle of Britain. Know what he said? "Yous remained neutral even after the Germans bombed yous," sez 'e, "but that's because it was only the oul Synagogue in the South Circular they clobbered. If they'd have pranged the Bishop's Palace in Drumcondra," sez 'e "an' ruffled a hair of the miniature God Almighty that lives there yous'd have been in the war overnight." Terrible thing to say."

"Disgustin'" said Celia, "England's a terrible pagan country so it is. The missioner in City Quay was dead right when he preached that the punishment of God is fallin' on them today, God between us and all harm. A modem Sodom and Goodmorrow he said it was bein' destroyed by fire from the sky."

A tearing shout from the hall quivered through her. Ronald' voice, high and tearful in anger. "Lousy scroungers! Chancers!" she made out above the screams of girls and a scuffled confusion of rushing feet. She surged in the wake of the crowd through the noisy back room, heard the hall door slam to, saw it wince open again as she drew near.

"Gangway! Gangway there!" Barney shouted forcing a way for her through the throng, his glass held aloft, the contents tossing darkly under the hall light. They reached the street where she saw Ronald his fists clenched angrily, darting his head from side to side before the screen of darkness between them and the river.

"What was up?" she asked taking him by the arm which twitched angrily from her grasp.

"They weren't from Carter's at all," he panted "Just a gang of scroungers from Ringsend who heard about the party and crashed it for the free drinks."

A voice mocked out of the darkness "Yous'll all catch your death of cold there. Go on back in to your lousy party and drink some more of the money Ronnie got for leavin' Carter's van-load of tea outside that pub for his pals to knock off."

Ronald gave a broken howl, like an injured dog. He leaped forward, ran towards the voice, scraped to a white-angry stop, his arm stretched towards Barney who held him tight by the wrist.

"Let me at them."

"Let it lay," cautioned Barney his eye on the black helter-skelter of stout in the glass he held in his other hand.

Again a voice mocked from the darkness. "And how much o' the booze did Johnny help yous to buy with the few makes he fecked out a oul Mack's till?"

Ronald leaped to tug free of the restraining hand, his feet slithering on the icy surface of the road.

"Blast it!" swore Barney looking down at his damp trouser leg, "Whoa there! Whoa Ronald! You have me half drownded. Them gougers is not worth a drop of what you're after makin' me spill over myself."

"Yes, leave them be," pleaded Celia, "They're not worth spittin' on, son."

The yellow beam of car headlights carved capering shapes on the screen of the dark. They danced abruptly clear and solid against the mottled camouflage of a ship perched high on the Liffey tide.

"There's the gang o' lousers" shouted Ronald straining to shake free of his uncle.

"Now you see us, now you don't" called a laughing voice as the group scuffled out of sight. A derisive laugh hung in the brightening light until the car, flinging its brief roar down the street, swept along the length of the ship and droned away from the darkness.

"Well, that's the end o' that," stated Barney, "Let's be gettin' back into the warm."

Ronald stood rubbing his wrist and staring at the ground.

"C'mon son" said Celia taking his arm.

"I didn't leave that van out there on purpose," Ronald said aloud looking from her to Barney.

"Of course you didn't" Barney said holding up his glass against the light from a window on his left. "Sure everybody knows that. It wasn't your fault that you were delayed and had to go into that pub to ring up the place in Bray and find out would it still be open when you got there. Sure how were you to know a gang of black-marketeers must have been tailing you?"

"Sure we all know what happened," agreed Celia coming in front of him to press on him the comfort of her smile. "It wasn't your fault at all."

"Not everybody is as trustin' as you, ma" brooded Ronald, "I caught a few o' them in there givin' me funny looks. They should ask the boys in Carter's why I was really sacked. The oul geezer has had a down on me ever since I asked him for overtime for workin' late."

"Let it lay," urged Barney, "Them's not the sort of ideas to be entertainin' on your wedding night. Sure it's another set of ideas entirely that should be entertainin' you now, especially as it's gettin' late. Course, the overtime idea is very adjacent to the other situation as well." He leered in Ronald's face. Celia saw Ronald's eyes follow the glass Barney waved in his hand.

"It's a drop o' that, or somethin' stronger, I need to steady me up." Celia met his accusing eye. "It's not easy to keep the pledge, Ma. Especially on a night like this with everyone around you drinkin' Loch Erne dry. That lemon soda you laid in for me has put as much gas in me as there is in the gasometer up there."

Barney stepped backwards into the lane opposite and craned his neck at the giant cylinder bulked black against the crisp stars, "O be Janie, it's a bloody good job the Gerries didn't clock that. Just one big tearin' yellow flash there'd be an' that'd be the end of dear old dirty Dublin. There'd be no complaints in the Evenin' Mail from 'a Reader in Rathmines' about the gas pressure then. No, be the holy!"

"Come in an' I'll get you a nice strong cup of tea," invited Celia, "You've held out against the drink so long it'd be a cryin' shame to break your pledge now. An' besides, girls is very sensitive at a time like this. You wouldn't want to be goin' to your bride smellin' like Guinness's brewery, would you?"

"Johnny wouldn't have given a damn" said Ronald bitterly, "An' he'd have got away with it too."

"Well he didn't get away with the Mr Mack thing, did 'e? After two years they can still call out from the dark what they're thinkin' in their hearts about him all the time. You're not like Johnny at all an' you should go down on your two knees an' thank the livin' God that you haven't got the rotten drop in you that's in him. Don't remind me, don't remind me of that - criminal!"

Ronald walked silently by her side back to the open hallway where a young man propped against the wall gazing into the eyes of a pink-cheeked girl was crooning an accompaniment to the tenor whose voice pierced sweetly from the store through the hushed back room. "But it was not her beauty alone that won me!" The words pierced on through Celia.

"That's Fintan Armstrong," said Ronald suddenly brightening holding up his index finger. "I can't miss Ringsend's own Mario Lanza." He slipped away from her and began to weave through the throng towards the stores.

"Jeannie made the tea," Barney announced from the kitchenette, "C'mon Celia, have a Woodier and put your feet up for five minutes."

She went into the cramped room and closed the door behind her, an unease whose source she could not fathom gnawing at her mind. The shouting voices from the incident in the street were still with her; they rang through her throbbing impressions of tugging bodies, of scuffling feet, of Ronald's saying: "I caught a few o' them in there givin' me a funny look." She sighed. How awful to have that sort o' thing nagging at you on your wedding night! "Barney," she said wearily, "Sideboard bottom right, in behind the box o' mendin', a bottle o' the best."

"Oh very adjacent! Very adjacent indeed!" Barney went in a glide of dance steps to the sideboard and she smiled at his tired take-off of Noel Purcell as the pantomime Demon King. "And don't ration it," she encouraged as he took the bottle and two glasses deftly in one hand, "There's too many damn things on ration today. Peace of mind for instance. They'll be rationing the grace of God next."

"With a drop o' this," Barney laughed sloshing whiskey into the glasses, "you'll hear the angels singin' from here to Chapel-izod. You can't bate the hard tack."

"I hope they'll make out all right," Celia said taking her glass, "After all, at twenty-two he's only just a little more than a child and now he has a wife to support."

"Go on!" urged Barney, "Get this singin' through you. An' have a nice cup o' tea to follow." From his seat he reached behind the cups on the dresser and drew out a packet of Aspro which he placed at her elbow. "Maybe the Sunday mornin' standby'd help as well."

"Ah this terrible war," she insisted, "Who knows what turns and chances God has in store for us all!"

"Drink up and not another word out of you. Give oul John Power a chance to get a grip on you where it feels nicest." She caught the twinkle in his eye and laughed through the burden of her worry.

"Not another word till you can say a good one," smiled Barney.

She drank praying 'thank God for Barney' and saw him in his fresh young manhood on perhaps the only occasion she remembered when he lost his temper. She had rushed into the shop coughing with the smoke from down the quays, gunshots popping bleakly in her ears like the distant tuck of drums. Barney came down from the back room. He had his flared navy-blue suit on, spats and all, with a stiff white collar and a plain silver-grey tie. "There's holy murder down there," she told him, "The Customs House is on fire an' the Tans an' the boys are battlin' it out all over the place. Armoured cars an' all." Barney removed the cigarette holder from his lips. "Well the curse o' God on the whole bloody lot of them," he stamped, "What a time to start a battle an' me with a date in ten minutes in Abbey Street with a gorgeous piece o' leg from the chorus line in the Tivoli. An' both sides is supposed to be fightin' for the happiness of the people! Jasus, after this may none o' them ever have a day's luck!" She smiled at the memory. What a comfort he'd been to her when her husband left her. Every evening he came straight from his job in Brooks Thomas's to help her dress the stock for the following day, lifting sacks of potatoes with one hand as if they were no weight at all. And later, when his wife died, poor, laughing Ellen, he moved hack into his old room upstairs where he spent hours of an evening trying to get his parrot to talk, "Who'd ever have thought that the old joke on the Guinness's sailors would turn out to he true," he'd say, "One of them finally did "bring back a parrot. From a pet shop in Liverpool."

"I feel "better now," she said to him when she finished her tea, "I'd "better go now and see if Ronald is all right."

"Celia," said Barney quietly as he patted into place the greying wave above his temple in that way she realised, avoiding her eye, "It's goin' to he far harder than you think, but from now on you'll have to get used to the idea of not seeing how Ronald's getting on. He has someone else to do that for him now!" And he gazed earnestly into her eyes.

"Of course I'll get used to it," she said, "Sure I'm half used to it already." And she went, her heart fluttering uncomfortably, into the back room and almost bumped into Daisy Turner her neighbour from the square who stood fumbling in her handbag and tossing her thick dark hair out of her eyes.

"Ah, there y'are, Celia. I'm lookin' for me latch-key,"
"You're not off already, Daisy, are you?"

"Have to. He's on night work. Jeannie's ages upstairs gettin' me coat."

"Jeannie!" Celia felt a tingle of apprehension as if she were breaking out in spots. She went into the hall, "JEANNIE!" she called and waited, tapping impatiently with her fingernail on the banister until her daughter appeared in the shadowed area above the light, her dyed hair strangely dark, her bosom fuller and more widespread than Celia remembered it to be.

"I'm bringin' Mrs Turner's coat, Ma."

Celia shivered at the tremor in her voice. "See you bring You-know-who along with it too" she called and stood tapping the banister until Franny Agnew's long white nose thrust down into the light which cast shadows on either side of his frightened face. She watched them pick their way around the courting couples on the stairs. "I'm sure the boys's missin' you, you're such great company" she said smiling at Franny and holding hard to Jeannie's elbow. She watched the young man wriggle his way white-faced through the throng in the back room before she turned back to Jeannie. "A right rossie you're turnin' out to be," she accused her, "The very idea, bringin' men upstairs. An' I saw you out in the stores as well. I'll have you know that no daughter o' mine is goin' to allow herself to be mauled about and clawed at by men. It's ashamed of yourself you ought to be, distractin' me when I should be in there seein' if your brother is all right. Get into the kitchenette there and throw a tidyin' hand over it."

Jeannie stood where she was her bosom heaving, the heavy coat in her arms trailing on the floor. "Ma," she said, "There's somethin' you ought to know. An' don't blame me for it. It was Uncle Tim's fault. He let him in when you were havin' your tea on account of him bein' such a great friend o' Johnny's."

"Don't mention that fella's name in this house."

"But he was a great friend o' Johnny's, honest."

"Who was?"

"Jemser Kelly was. He's in there sittin' on the far side o' the fireplace. Very quiet though. Sort of keepin' out of sight."

"Sacred hour! Has Ronald seen him?"

Her friend, Daisy Turner, touched her arm. "Ah you got me coat I see. Thanks very much for askin' me to come. It was a lovely hooley!"

"Yes! Yes!" Celia replied distractedly, her eye raking the back room for Ronald.

"But what a great pity," Daisy said, "that Johnny couldn't've been here. Sure all the life went out of the street when he left. Who is there nowadays to spread a laugh around? An' that's what you were never short of when Johnny was here, a real good laugh! Heart an' soul o' the whole diggins, so he was."

"You can say that again," Celia said groaning to herself, "I've got to see to somethin'. Help Daisy on with her coat, Jeannie." She pressed into the hot murmurous throng towards a cracked voice shouting in the distance, her arms tingling with the memory of Johnny falling through her dream. What damn right had that fella to be so close to her when that bitter knot in her breast, that hard fist of impatience and resentment, was clenched so hard against him? All very well for Daisy to say that the life had gone out of the street, but what about the untold misery that had come into the home? A real good laugh! I ask you! That quick, ripping laugh of Johnny's brought nothing but dread, for there was no telling what new outrageous idea already festering in his mind had given rise to it. Even when helpless in drink, in the state when most men are fit only to be bunged into bed and forgotten for twenty-four hours, there was still a cutting edge to Johnny which made a body lose all concern and patience. "They don't baby you no-how" a flabby-mouthed young man belched at her as she passed. "Disgustin'!" she clenched her teeth jogging her upper plate. Yes, let's face it, just like Johnny. There was the night when with one of his good-old ripping laughs he had crashed against the street-door and fallen flat into the hall. She rushed to him mistaking his laugh for a cry of pain, fearing he was hurt. He raised his flushed, slobbering face to her, his eyes full of shifty glitter. "He meets his Afflicted Mother" he mouthed, even in the helplessness of drink ready, willing and only too well able to repeat the old joke that mocked the Stations of the Cross. Just as well he stayed in Belfast and didn't dare show his dark grinning face at the wedding. But he had sent that outrageous telegram which Nagginer Doyle had read out without batting an eyelid: "Wish I could be with you tonight Ronald. I'm sure it's nice down there." That bad drop from his father!

She reached the slope and peered into the store where to the wailing agony of the trio on the platform and the cracked shouting of Nagginer Doyle, couples whirled about in one of the new disgraceful dances in which the young men flung their partners away from them and hauled them back again, pranced a few steps with the girls clutched tightly to them and then launched into their flinging and hauling all over again. "Wearing a bird of paradise" shouted Nagginer above the din of the whirling dancers among whom she failed to discover Ronald. She turned and to her surprise there he was just left of the fireplace sitting on the arm of the broken-springed chair in which Marcie Kelly, a good customer from down the street, was installed, her arms folded tightly under her bosom as if to prevent her from sinking deeper into the chair. In spite of the sweet tea she had drunk, the bitter taste returned at the sight of Alice sitting as downcast and mousey as ever on the far side of the fire, furrowing away with her pointed toe at the growing wedge of white ash. "There's more life in a bunch of scallions," she thought edging her way closer to Ronald who mused, chin on palm, listening to what Marcie was saying. "A gorgeous pome. Be Kippilin it was. In another of them books me husband had, Lord rest him. All about the 'If's' that make a man of you. Like if you can walk about with kings and not be so common as to try to touch them for somethin'. Or if you can run a mile when you have an odd minute to spare then you'll get everything you want in the world and grow up to be a man into the bargain."

"Must be a nice thing," Ronald's chin waggled in his palm.

Celia nodded an empty smile across the fire to Mrs Leggett and ran her eyes over the people present among whom to her relief she failed to spot Jemser Kelly. "Must be with the gang in the store" she concluded and heard Nagginer's ringing tenor repeat: "Yes! Yes! You're nobody's sweetheart nowwww!" There was a cheer and the stamping and scuffing of feet. Barney was beside her, comforting her with a gentle hug, "Old Mrs Boucher'd like a word with you," he smiled, "She's just over here by the slope."

"I'm comin'" she said and bent her head close to Ronald. "You're not dancin' with Alice at all at all. Don't you think you ought to?"

"She's O.K. there chattin' with her ma," Ronald said out of the side of his mouth. "Leave well-enough alone, eh?" He inclined his head sideways towards Marcie who sat moistening her lips, impatient for his attention.

"An' another pome, wan be Service," Celia heard her say as she turned reluctantly away. "*The Shootin' o' Dan*

McGrew. 'Bout the woman known as Lou who kissed him and pinched his poke."

"His what?" Celia gritted her teeth at the mocking tone in Ronald's voice. She heard them both laugh. "Oh you're gettin' as bad as your brother Johnny," said Marcie.

Some of the group that had been dancing in the store came into the back room, one or two of the young men attempting in short brisk runs to slide down the gentle incline of the slope.

"Plenty to eat and drink on the table," she told them smiling against her impulse to recoil from their brashness, their sweaty animalism, the crashing din they raised in performing the simplest action. "It's gettin' late so make the best of it."

"An' Ronnie's gettin' impatient" laughed a young man she knew slightly. He clapped his hands above his head and jigged up and down on his toes. "Straighten up and fly right. Yeah!" he chanted, "Da-Da-Daddie, don't yo' blow yo' top'."

She reached Mrs Boucher wishing it would all soon come to an end. From the depths of her chair, Mrs Boucher peered at her through folds of wrinkles that looked as if they had been grained with coal dust. "Ah, Celia'." croaked the old lady, "You must be very happy in yourself tonight!"

"I am! I am!" she nodded speaking up so that the old lady would hear. Nagginer Doyle appeared at the mouth of the slope, threw a shrewd raking glance into the room, and withdrew as silently as he had come.

"An' Ronald looks so well. An' a lovely girl. A decent

hard-working family."

"Yes! Yes!" She bobbed her head to the distant croaking and squirmed in the unease of the shrewd look she had seen. She knew that look so well for Nagginer was a bosom friend, a boozin' friend you could say, of Johnny's. Two of a kind. He was up to no good. Because he was so like Johnny was why Ronald had asked him to be best man.

"A pity though," croaked Mrs Boucher's tiny voice through the din, "that Johnny couldn't be here to share the occasion. Poor Johnny was a boy I always had a great gra' for. No real harm in him at all. So good-hearted he was. So well-meaning. Like his father!"

"Ah yes," said Celia softening with an effort the bitter edge of her tone, "The life went out of the street when he left."

"You never spoke a truer word!" The old woman's mouth wobbled all to one side and there was a moist hissing echo to her laboured croak. Celia heaved a sigh, God is this what's in store for me? Just a few more years and... this? The noise, the stuffy heat, the weighty burden of the years to come pressed down on her. With a start, she realised that without her noticing, Nagginer had come back into the room accompanied by Paddy Jukes and Ed Carlin. The light found a sharp gleam on Nagginer's pink, downy cheek as he and his two companions pressed in around Ronald. They hid him from sight, the lines of their bodies hard and rigid as if with difficulty they were holding something down, something dangerous and explosive. "'Scuse me." She went towards them and heard Ronald say; "Oh no! Not another glass of that bloody lemon soda."

"You're not afraid of havin' to get up durin' the night, are you?" laughed Nagginer.

Celia brushed past Ed Carlin and saw Ronald lolling lazily beside the dark cleft of Marcie Kelly's bosom, a glass of colourless liquid in his hand.

"I wouldn't drink that if I was you!" she snapped at him.

"Sure isn't it all you'll let me drink, Ma? Just bloody gassy, fizzy nothin' since you persuaded me to take the pledge?"

"Is it?" She glared at Nagginer. "Are you quite sure me bucko that there's only lemon soda in that?"

"Sure what else would there be?" Nagginer fixed on her a look of round-eyed innocence.

"You're not foolin' me one bit, Nagginer Doyle. What's in that glass or do I have to drink it myself to find out?"

Nagginer looked away with a hurt sigh. "Was only a gag! No harm meant. The boys an' me, we thought it'd be a bit o' gas seein' the night it is an' the way Ronnie's been on the wagon for, for years it seems, to get him a bit merry. So we just laced his lemon soda with a little drop o' first-shot whiskey."

"A right crowd o' lousers yous are" she spat at them and Nagginer crouched, slit-eyed, as from an anticipated blow.

"But there was no harm meant," he protested.

"No harm is it? First-shot whiskey can turn the quietest man alive into a gibberin' maniac. Is this what yous planned for my Ronald on his weddin' night? To have him foolish and footless, not knowin' where he is or what he's doin'."

"That'd be real awkward in the circumstances!" A lurid grin flashed across Nagginer's face and was instantly succeeded by a pensive, contrite look which he directed earnestly at her.

"Sorry, Mrs Ginochy. As I said, no harm meant. But this is a real good hooley, the best we've been to isn't it boys? And you know how it is, you get up to all sorts of divilment without thinkin'. An' that lemon soda trick was really harmless. Sure there was a night when Johnny an' me..."

"Don't mention that fella's name in this house" she snapped "That fella, he's... he's...'" There was something more she felt she wanted to say but whatever it was - and for a second she almost had the words ready - she couldn't get it in the right order on her tongue. "God, what's happening?" she wondered at the swaying room behind the black-mouthed bulk of Nagginer's head. The rank warm air stilled in her mouth from which she thrust it in a wrenching sigh encountering as she did so a throbbing ache deep within her which traced the tired frame of her body in a curious and incomplete form. Tired I am, tired in spite o' the rest I've had. She felt small, a child almost, as Ronald loomed beside her startling her with how tall he had grown without her even noticing.

"Ma, who'n the hell let him in?"

She blinked in the direction of his curt nod and saw Jemser Kelly stretched on the floor at the foot of the sofa, his oily head reclined lazily against the new stain on the wallpaper, his eyes quiet, closed almost.

"Oh God!" she said, "It was that eedjit of an uncle of yours. Tim!"

"I'll ram my boot up him, so I will!"

Her mouth fell open at the unexpected crudity of his expression. A curl rippled along his upper lip, a shadowed line ran from the whorl of his nostril across his face below his red cheek to where it thickened and merged into his golden sideburn. Her heart sank. Why had she never noticed the resemblance before? It was as if another face was impressing itself on his from within, moulding his features to its own bitterly familiar lines. Two other faces in fact.

"Just let on you haven't noticed" she said through the tug of her weariness. "Anyway it's late, very late. "Why not get someone to give him a drink? Or better still, why not bring the evenin' to a close?"

"What, now? Y'mad, Ma? Sure I'm only startin' to enjoy meself. Give 'im a drink? Hey, Nagginer, lads, let's go over an' say how-do to Jemser."

"Yeah, right y'be," drawled Nagginer, "Rub it in with the good old 'Long time, no she!" Eh, Ronnie?"

When they turned away the edgy noises in the room rushed hotly in on her again like when you wake on a long train journey, the carriage over-hot and stuffy, your mouth full of dry bitter fluff, and the engine beating away, beating away, as it had been all through your fitful sleep. To her relief there was Barney making towards her, a sad smile on his lips.

"Sort of guessed what was goin' on there, Celia."

"Barney I had a sort of queer turn. Felt suddenly over-tired. And why do they keep on and on talkin' about Johnny? God, can't they forget him, just for one night?"

"Mrs Boucher is still wantin' to chat with you."

"Ho! It does me no good bein' with her. Seein' her so old."

"There's none of us gettin' any younger," Barney smiled.

"I realised that when I was chattin' with her. Bein' with her sort of rubs it in."

"Here," said Barney proffering a cigarette, "You'll find this very adjacent for the oul nerves. An' don't be afraid to inhale."

She eased her head back on her shoulders and squinted through the blue sting of the smoke at the group surrounding Jemser who had risen to his feet. His crimped hair, brown as the river after rain, rose above them catching tiny scattered points of silver from the light bulb just above his head. She knew from the fussy toss of Nagginer's hands that it was he who was doing most of the talking especially as every other second he gave himself a soft pat on the back of his greasy poll. There was a smile on Ronald's lips when he turned his head aside to find a vacant spot on the floor to tip his cigarette ash. And even though Ed Carlin began to laugh his loud ass's hee-haw and had to rest his head helplessly a moment on Ronald's shoulder, there was a curious stillness about the group which set them apart from the deep droning voice of the room. Jemser's white forehead surged briefly into the light. His collar must be too tight, she surmised, from the strained look on his face. Still they looked friendly enough together and thank

God for that because no matter how good a party is any unpleasantness at the end makes people look back on the whole evening as a disaster.

"Things look all right over there," Barney murmured in her ear and held his hand in front of her so that she could see he had the two fingers next to his thumb tightly crossed.

"Yes," she said and immediately pursed her lips as Nagginer followed by Ed Carlin swung away leaving Ronald in an untidy lounging stance between her and Jemser, his whole weight resting on one leg, his arm drooping limply at his side. "We'll liven up the party again and hurry back in," she heard Nagginer pant as he brushed past, his narrow eyes glittering. "Eh, Ed, isn't Ronnie a caution though? Cool as you like. How's your oul whistle, Jemser?" Ed Carlin grinning like a monkey stuck a finger in each ear. "Any minute now - Bang!" They laughed their way to the slope where Nagginer skipped into a dance step. "Take it out, here's me mother!" he bawled vanishing into the store. What possessed her boys to regard such a creature as their friend? Muck is all he was. Muck! Ronald made a swift, deft movement. She saw him hold Jemser firmly by the wrist insisting him gently backwards to the vacant end of the sofa. Jemser thumped heavily on the seat and dropped something from his hand which made a ringing tinkle on the floor. Several guests in the vicinity looked to their feet and moved gingerly aside. An empty glass rolled before her in a pool of light, rocked to and fro, and then lay still its twinkling mouth gaping open towards her like a dead fish.

"Ronald!" she called across the dead silence of the

room: "How could you do such a thing?" He looked calmly back at her the hateful curl rippling along his lip. In so many ways she couldn't explain, he was and he wasn't the young man who had stood at the altar that morning making his quiet responses. When he kissed Alice she had wanted to burst out laughing at her ridiculous conviction that at one and the same time he was a handsome bridegroom, a fluffy bundle of baby smells burping his wind, a spiky-haired schoolboy scuffing off to school a slice of bread in his hand, a pimply brilliantined youth dancing into the kitchen and dropping the two-shilling pieces of his first week's wages among the cups and saucers on the tea table. She could find none of those earlier Ronalds in him now. Instead two other and more upsetting personalities suggested themselves in and around him as if they were almost visible ghosts passing back and forth through his body at will. And all through the silence he held his heavy eye on her, but somewhat abstractedly as if he had passed having any interest in her.

"How could I do what, Ma?" he asked at last as if he had just heard her question.

"Give that terrible drink to that poor chap!" Behind him Jemser frowned desperately before him and appeared almost to know where he was.

"As Nagginer said - was just a gag. For a bit of a laugh, Ronald said offhandedly, "Nagginer tried to slip it to me, I slipped it to Jemser. It's all in the game. Better him than me. After all he came in lookin' for a drink an' a bit o' gas like everyone else, didn't he?"

"Not a very nice game for you to have a hand in. I never saw you do anything like that before. And tonight of all nights!"

"Well I did it, Ma!" The catch of sadness in his voice squeezed at her heart. "And I suppose there's more things I'll do in my life that you won't like, but that's just too bad, isn't it? I have to go my own way now. I made my bed an' I'll have to lie in it whichever way I can, no matter who does or who doesn't like the way I do it." He shrugged his shoulders at her and began to move through the crowd towards the slope. Passing Alice he bent - he had almost gone past she saw - and kissed her lightly on the cheek. "An' how's Mrs Ginochy?" Alice's face creased in tight lines which came to a point in her tiny smile.

"Me Mammie says it's gettin' late, Ronnie." She bent her head and fluttered her eyelashes.

"Late? Sure there's hours o' dancin' in it yet." He swaggered across to the mouth of the slope where he leaned his shoulder lazily against the wall, his hand groping for his trouser pocket.

"And after that," thought Celia, "he'll go all dreamy again." The confusion he raised in her made her restless. She had an impulse to go to the kitchenette and start tidying up after Jeannie's tidying up. Was she still there? Ronald laughed rocking his shoulder against the wall. From the store she heard Nagginer's shouted song. "I can't give you anything but ba-ba-ba-ba-babies, the only things Woolworth's doesn't sell - babies!"

"Muck!" she spat. Behind her came a thump heavier than the other sounds beating in the house like the din and clatter of a Guinness's boat being loaded on the quay. A still heavier thump followed by a tearing howl threw a pause of silence into the room and drove the jaw-champing guests back from the table. A gasping tinkle struck on the air and she knew someone had trodden on the glass which she realised had been tucked somewhere in the back of her mind waiting to be picked up. Then round the edge of the vacated table Jemser Kelly came in sight, crawling for the fireplace like a broken-backed animal - crawling for Alice! For the first time that evening, Mrs Leggett exerted herself. She creaked out of the sunken valley of her chair and leaned forward, pulled forward it seemed by the weight of her enormous bosom. "Go away you!" she shrieked pushing with the flat of her hands at Jemser's head. Celia sought the relief of movement. "Barney! Barney!" she called going round the end of the table, throwing an anxious eye at Ronald on the way. She stopped, her heart pounding. Ronald still lounged against the wall, his chin resting on his shoulder, a sharp, malicious grin sickening his face. Celia panted in amazement, looking from him to Alice who had drawn her legs as far as she could under her and was fluttering her hands in the air. Barney and Mad Maizie's son came beside her. "What's goin! on?" asked Barney. She could hardly focus on him. "Ronald... Ronald..." she said and felt herself drown in wordless dismay. Jemser's howl slammed through her with the terror of the bombs that had come screaming down from the black skies. All about her she could feel everyone strain against whatever it was that was preventing them from doing anything. "Jasus! Jasus!" howled Jemser his contorted face a greasy, livid red. "Jasus, how could you let it happen?" Alice cowered deeper in her chair evading the aimless sweep of his hand. "Keep 'm offa me!" she wailed. Far away, in the shadowed dismay of Celia's soul, Ronald giggled and called: "Nagginer! Eh, Nagginer! Come an' get a load o' this!" Jemser beat with his fists on the floor. "Oh Alice darlin'! Darlin' Alice!" He retched as if he were about to be sick. "Oh, Alice, how could you do it? Down the, down the lane that night you said I was the first. And God, I knew I was the first. You said there'd never be anyone else." A laugh shrieked from one of the girls at the fire. "Oh Alice," Jemser drooled in the breathless, graveyard silence, "Your lovely soft, swellin' breasts, your lovely big warm thighs, your..."

"Shut up, you bloody bugger," Ronald shouted and rushed forward swinging a kick which, missing Jemser's head, caused him to lose balance so that he floundered sideways into a group of girls who immediately raised a tearing scream.

"Don't Ronald, please!" Celia called, choked by the fear leaping in the back of her throat. Barney went calmly forward and staggered a little under the impact of Ronald's fresh rush at Jemser. For ever and ever it seemed they struggled together like men testing how slow they could move. "I'll be dug outa him!" Ronald kept on shouting and then Nagginer and Ed Carlin flashed past and began to drag the fallen man out of the room. Ronald wrenched free and landed a kick somewhere on Jemser's body - "You rotten louser!" - which raised the shrieking all around to an even higher pitch. Nagginer's fingers were lost in Jemser's hair. Above all the other noises came his long despairing howl. "Alice! Alice!" Then they were in the hall, Ronald leaping through the doorway after them. She heard further shouts and thuds until a ringing silence followed the thunderous slamming of the street door. Ronald flushed and panting appeared in the room. "Bloody bastard, insultin' my wife, muckin' up my hooley!" Nagginer came in a few moments later, dusting his hands, his face oily with joy. "Eh, Ronnie," he laughed, "Wait'll the corporation men come round to sweep the street in the morning and find that all coiled up among the cabbage leaves in the lane!"

Celia's bosom heaved desperately. "You can't leave'm lying out there. A neighbour's child. No matter what, you should treat him like a Christian."

"We'll go one better," Ronald sniggered. "Treat him like Christ so we will. Bloody well crucify'm! Did you hear what he was insinuatin'?"

Celia instantly looked at Alice and sensed that everyone in the room was doing likewise. Alice had sunk back in her chair her fists knotted under her bosom which trembled and shook with the despairing cry which broke from her. "Mammie! Mammie!" she wailed struggling to her feet. She thrust the palms of her hands hard against her face and made smothered wailings into them.

Barney, breathing hard, whispered in Celia's ear. "I'll go out an' take care o' Jemser. You get that wan upstairs. Out o' harm's way."

"Come on," Celia said going to Alice, "I'll take you upstairs. You'll be wantin' to powder your nose."

Deftly she manoeuvred the girl out of the room passing Ronald on the way. He stared cool-eyed at them, as if at strangers.

"Will yous make way please," Celia said to the couples entwined on the stairs. She surmised that they had probably noticed nothing outside the throbbing of their own passion.

"Has the bride had more to drink than is good for her?" Mike Mallen grinned up at her through the yellow haze of his girlfriend's hair.

"Mind your own business. Or better still, mind your own business somewhere else than on my stairs."

The slack weight of Alice and of her own tiredness ebbed strength from the marrow of her bones. She was bathed in sweat when she reached the landing and opened the bedroom door to help Alice onto the bed. She slammed the door shut not caring whether or not Mrs Legett was behind them. Beneath her feet the floor heaved slightly like the deck of the Royal Iris on a pleasure trip round the bay one Sunday with him who had obviously taken to the idea of travelling by steamer and left her to face all this and so much else all alone. Alice took the corner of the pillow case in her mouth and wailed a low, wet dribble.

"What'll I do? Oh God, what'll I do now?"

"You'll forget all about it," Celia told her, "And hope to Christ that others will as well. Though I doubt it."

"That madman shouldn't 've been let in to my weddin'."

"Well he was and that's that. The main thing is that Ronald shouldn't 've given him that drink. Whatever possessed him to do that? Not like him at all."

Alice burst into tears. "What'll everyone be thinkin' of me now?"

"Sure it's not everyone you have to worry about, is it?

The one to consider is Ronald. What a terrible thing for him to have to hear - on his weddin' night an' all! An' I after doin' everythin' to make sure nothin'd go wrong with the evenin'. Oh you young people'."

"I didn't do what that fella said. I didn't, honest to God, I swear I didn't!"

"Whether you did or you didn't is not important now. But everyone down there heard him an' those who didn't have been told - with variations! And Ronald heard him. That's the terrible part of it. How could you have done that to him?"

"Oh God," Alice wept bitterly, "An' I was all right up to that minute. That was long before I met Ronald at that dance. An' I was just keepin' quiet, not drinkin', not dancin' or anything, exactly as Ronald told me. Because of my condition. But it's bringin' on me sickness again now so it is!"

"What sickness? What condition?"

"All this upset won't affect the baby, will it?"

Celia turned away and went to the wicker armchair which creaked under the burden of her years, of the hopelessness of anything ever working out right. So the Ginochy's had done it again! Another nine days' wonder, only this time for a change a nine months' wonder or whatever months were left. And God, the misery of the days ahead standing among mounds of damp cabbages and potatoes in the clayey air of the shop, parrying off the hard stares of the customers and trying not to notice the smiles wisping across contemptuous lips. "Is Alice near her time now, Mrs Ginochy, ma'am?" "I'm sure Ronald finds it a real comfort to have Tim for company every day traipsin' off to the labour exchange. Nothin' like havin' an old hand with you." "An' how's Johnny gettin' on - in America, isn't it?" "An' do you never have a word at all at all from that man o' yours? Must be gone donkey's years now. Surely he must have written. Even a comic postcard? I'd have the police on him, I would. Keepin' quiet he is because he's married again if you ask me. You could have 'm for bigamy." That's what it would be like.

That's what it was partly like already, day in, day out, with one remark or question mostly about Johnny in every one. What are they all tryin' to do to me, she worried, land me in an early grave?

She sensed the furtive touch of Alice's eyes on her. "So that's why yous were in such a forked-lightnin' hurry to get married," she said to her, "How far gone are you?"

"Four months. But it's Ronald's child so it is, I swear by all that's holy it is, so I do."

"After "the pipes, the pipes are callin" downstairs you may have your work cut out to convince'm that there's no doubt about that."

Alice sunk her raw wet face in the greying pillow and began to cry again. The bedstead rocked and clanged to the drumming of her feet.

"Does your mother know?" Celia asked struggling to her feet.

"Yis! Yis! I had me row with her two months ago."

"Right then. I'll send her up to you. If she can waddle her way up the stairs."

She came down and found Mrs Leggett sitting on the

bottom step looking somewhat anxious but full of defiance as if anticipating trouble.

"Ah, Mrs Leggett, a right pair we reared!"

Mrs Leggett made a spitting sound and taking hold of the bannisters she hauled and urged herself to her feet.

"You'll say nothing against my girl so you won't. She comes of a good respectable family. There's never been a finger o' scandal stuck in our eye. But whereas your Ronald...!"

"I'm saying nothin' against Alice. I don't have to. Annie Kelly's boy has done it for me." Celia instantly regretted the swoon of pain in the other woman's eyes. "God, what are we sayin' to each other, Imelda?" She stretched her hand out and gave a comforting pat on the other woman's shoulder. "What we should he doin' is givin' some little thought to the child that's goin' to he born. How are they goin' to manage at all at all? I can't help them much on account o' the terrible state business is in. I think you ought to go upstairs an' quieten her down. Then when she's a bit better they should go home. You an' I can talk about it all later. Tomorrow."

Mrs Leggett was frowning. Celia wondered at the covert look she cast at the couples on the stairs.

"But surely Celia, you know there's not all that much need to worry about them. Ronald still has the you-know-what."

Celia smoothed her palm where on her forehead the pain was most intense. "I must be wool-gathering tonight, Imelda. What are we talkin' about?"

"Surely you know quite well?" the other woman

nudged her painfully in the ribs, "What them fellas gave Ronald for leavin' the van o' tea for them outside the pub. They were bloody generous Alice says."

Celia brushed past her as if she had not heard. All the way to the kitchenette, to the bottle of whiskey in the bottom of the sideboard, she kept the other woman's words at arm's length, humming "Run Rabbit, Run" to herself and relishing the tune which beat on and on and might even drive the dread of what she had heard completely away. As she hummed her heart pounded, it seemed in every part of her body, particularly her head. Jeannie had done a fairly good job of tidying the room and had even remembered to put a kettle on the glimmer. She tried to hum in tune to its hoarse subdued whistle and didn't stop even when her aim in pouring out the whiskey was so bad some of the spirits splashed on the top of the sideboard and dripped with the rapid beat of her heart to the floor. She drank most of the generous double she managed to pour out. "Please God it won't get known" she prayed and waited stiff against the edge of the sideboard for old John Power to do what he was paid for. She stared at the kettle and tried not to think of anything at all, just to contemplate the roundness, the squatness, the metalness of the chipped iron and merge the hurt of her mind into its calm, sleepy hum. Pain still throbbed in her heart which grew used to it and gradually came to accept it. Sure what else was there ever in this family but pain, worry, and weariness, she thought and felt the whiskey was drawing a thick enough skin over her hurt to allow her soon to venture out into the back room. She found an open packet of Players and smoked one slowly, lighting it from the glimmer.

Everything was much quieter now. Only three or four guests stood eating by the table, more not to let the opportunity pass than because they were really enjoying it. Barney came towards her with a smile. "What are they all sayin' about it?" she asked him.

"Just that Jemser was ravin' mad with the drink," he nodded reassuringly, "An' Mad Maisie's lad has come up with a good one that has most o' the crowd laughin'. "A desperate case o' wish fulfillment" he called it."

"I'm goin' to get Ronald to bring this fiasco to a sudden end. I suppose he's in the stores with the Nagginer gang?"

"Oh aye," Barney replied in a hurried, subdued murmur which another time would have sent a shiver of alarm through her. But thanks be to God an' John Power it hasn't, she thought. I may even get through the evenin' yet. She went up the slope where on a chair just inside the store she discovered Jeannie and Franny Agnew locked in each other's arms.

"Jeannie, love," she said quietly, "You've had enough of that to last you a half-dozen lifetimes." Jeannie fluttered red-faced to her feet and stood tugging her dress back down into place over her hips. "Watch out," Celia said dryly, "Or you'll get like your new sister-in-law in a way that's goin' to make itself obvious to all before very much more water gets the chance to flow under Butt Bridge below." Jeannie, perplexed, nibbled the ball of her thumb in a gesture that peeled away her grown-up glow, her high-heeled poise revealing a tired little girl, somewhat frightened of life and her mother, longing to be tucked in for the night. She patted the girl's cheek. "Don't you do anythin' outrageous. Let me have it to say that I reared at least one of yous all right." She smiled a sigh. "Run into the kitchenette, there's a good girl, an' see what the chances are of a cup o' good strong tea, the national standby." Jeannie flashed her a puzzled smile and dashed away. "Not you!" Celia pressed her extended finger into Franny's midriff holding him still. "Fond o' my little girl, are you?"

"Yis! Yis!" Franny nodded his head like a toy mechanical clown.

"Well don't get too fond of her too soon. Y'know exactly what I mean, don't you? The birds and the bees but especially people?"

"Yis!" Franny began to brood over the chair he had been sitting on.

"Just remember that. Not too fond, too soon. Or they'll be diggin' bits o' you outa the path from here to Glasnevin."

She advanced farther into the store. The dancers had vacated the floor leaving it free for a lone couple who waltzed in a slow, tight circle in the shaded part of the room. The band had left and so also had Tim, presumably with the girl young enough to be his daughter. Or who was his daughter. The dirty sight! She felt the bitter taste of him on her tongue, between her teeth. The only person left on the makeshift stage was Nagginer who sat staring at the whirling disc on the gramophone his head in his hands. "Lovely lady, I'm fallin' madly in love with you," he moaned between his palms. Around the walls, the young guests lounged, some even on the floor, tired, silent, and for the most part the worse for drink. But so long as they were quiet! No one seemed to be paying any heed to the dancing couple who, as she looked at them, came in a slow whirl out into the light, their inclined bodies thrust hard against each other, their faces so close they might be joined in a long swooping kiss.

"Ronald!" she exclaimed in surprise. They danced past her. Ronald surged his strong body closer still to his partner whose knuckles gleamed white on his hunched shoulder. They made another dipping whirl and she saw that the girl he was holding so close was Alice*s younger sister, Mary. She called "Ronald!" going towards them and skipping back out of the way as they swooped at her in a wheeling curve. Suddenly she felt small and crumpled and old as Mrs Boucher. On her back, on her trembling legs she felt the stab of the many draughts from the broken, wired-over windows. Through the shield of the whiskey the loneliness of the cold shivered into her. "Ronald!" she called dreading the jerk of a sob in her voice.

"Ma?" He had stopped dancing and was looking into her with cold, draughty eyes, his face hard against Mary's which she knew would bear the red weal of his strong, thrusting cheek-bone for a little while after.

"Alice," she said through the cold bitterness gathered in her mouth, "Alice is wantin' to go home. Now!"

"Oh, is she?" He released Mary so slowly their bodies appeared to peel reluctantly apart. "Well, Mary," he said, his brow almost touching hers, "All good things must come to an end. For the time being anyway. But never mind, we're all the one family now."

He turned on his heel and went past Celia as if she was

not there. She raised her hand to his retreating form, and let it fall wearily to her side. What was the point of saying anything now? Something in her expression must have revealed to him that she had learned about Alice. If not indeed about the theft of the van. Tonight when the last shouted song of the last homebound guest had ceased to afflict the air, that's what would come in its full force out of the silent darkness to harass her. This wasn't just a matter of Mr Mack's which at the time seemed a small fortune. How she had fretted when it became obvious that Johnny had left home and Mr Mack was muttering into his moustache about the police. At present black market prices the tea in that van was worth thousands of pounds. No wonder the police had made Ronald sweat blood the day they had him in the little room in the station. But if the truth ever came out it would be the Army Tribunal he'd be up against. Up in Arbour Hill it was they tried all the black market cases doling out five-year sentences as if they were just pinches of snuff at a wake. "Oh God" she sighed, "Anything I'd say to him now would be bound to be wrong. And I wanted this day to be just perfect for him. But then it was an entirely different boy I was frettin' over. My own dear Ronald. Not that fella!"

Biddie Mason, all in pink, gave her a funny look as she passed her on the way to the back room. She knew her lips were moving but God knows what sort of expression was on her face. Hardly thinking of what she was doing, she followed Biddie and stood by Marcie Kelly's chair feeling she wanted to confide something to her old friend yet unable to think what it was. Ronald's ringing laugh reached her from the hall. Most of the people in the room began to throng around the door.

"Well if it isn't the young Mrs Ginochy," Ronald was calling up the stairs. "The brand-new Mrs Ginochy! Eh, which of yous is helpin' which down the stairs? Ah, you can let her go, Mrs Leggett. She'll be quite safe with me. I won't lay a finger on her, honest! What are you lookin' so disappointed for, Alice?"

The crowd roared their approval. Nagginer rushed in from the store. "What's goin' on?" He took in the situation. "Jasus! It's zero hour! Eddie! Mickser! Gunner-eye! C'mon!"

He dashed to the rear of the crowd, lowered his greasy head, and began to worm his way through to the hall. Ed Carlin and several other young men clattered and slid down the slope.

"Nagginer's got it all planned," she heard one of them say as they passed. "Just wait'll they get into bed and begin..."

Celia started in alarm, but absently as if it were someone else who was fretting in concern for Ronald. All the objects in the room stood starkly apart from each other. The endless tiredness taking its toll. And the worry too, not to mention the whiskey. Oh yes, no sleep tonight at all, the bedroom restless with scurrying figures shouting, singing, dancing, fighting. And driving away vanloads of tea. And scooping money from tills. And sticking their heads round the door for a final, mocking wink. She was amazed that a body so small, so frail as hers could contain such an infinity of weariness, could be such a dead weight.

The crowd loud with shouts and snatches of song had flowed out into the dark street. She came and stood outside the hall door, her eyes aching for another glimpse of Ronald. With his arm tight around Alice, he stood on the steps of the house opposite in which they had their room. "Speech! Speech!" clamoured the crowd. Ronald held up his free hand and kept it aloft even when the street grew quiet.

"Eh, do you hear that, Celia?" whispered Barney surprising her by looming abruptly out of the darkness. "A funny sound."

"Shh!" She held her eyes on Ronald.

"My friends...!" he said in Roosevelt's ringing drawl as if about to launch into a long speech. He pushed the door open with his free hand and swung Alice feet first into the house. The door slammed on the mock boo's and groans of the throng. Nagginer began to shout: "For he's a jolly good fellow" and the crowd immediately took up the song, roaring through the choruses and breaking off for a rousing cheer when a light came on in the first-floor room. While they sang, Ronald appeared at the window, grinned down at them, and drew down the blind.

"Eh, Ronnie," called Nagginer, "You can do that all right now, but just you wait till the mornin'." The crowd cheered and someone amongst them began to play on a mouthorgan. "Straighten up and fly right!" pranced Nagginer, almost in tune to the music, and several couples started to jitterbug, slithering awkwardly over the cobblestones.

"Don't mind the noise that lot's makin' an' just listen," Barney pleaded in Celia's ear. She closed her eyes and listened, striving not to hear the clamour of the crowd.

A slow, an infinitely slow rising-and-falling moan beat heavily in the depths of the sky.

"What is it, Barney? A boat comin' in at this hour?"

"No, not a boat. Planes. Lots o' them. Listen to them comin' nearer'."

She did so and felt the beating moan in her head, scratching, probing, screwing deeper into her, growing into the threatening growl she heard the night the bombs came down on the South Circular Road. A scream of delight from the throng drew her eyes to the window of Ronald's room. The sash had been raised without disturbing the blind. Several objects came into view beneath it, empty tin cans, an old tea caddy, a white enamel chamber-pot, all linked together with yellow orange-box rope.

Ronald's laughing voice came to her. "Thought you'd catch us out, eh Nagginer?" His pyjamaed arm shook the clattering objects over the crowd this way and that and then let them fall. Those beneath the window leaped away in screaming delight as the objects banged and clattered on the pavement. A loud cheer rang out, faltered, and faded into the air which had now begun to tremble in a deep, metallic growl. A clamour rose. "Planes! Planes! D'you hear?"

"Shurrup! Shurrup'." shouted Nagginer," An' stop playin' that bloody mouthorgan so as I can hear better. Eh? D'you hear that 'arrh! arrh!'? The bloody Jerries is back, the Nasties! Oh the lousers! Just like them to creep up on us like that when we weren't lookin'."

The growling roar loudened, bored into Celia's eardrums, trembled through the weariness of her limbs, beat in her bowels. About her the houses, the pavements shook under the gigantic vibrating noise from the sky, the moans of the damned in hell.

"Jesus, Mary, and Joseph!" exclaimed Barney, "There must be hundreds of them up there. Thousands! Oh God forgive me! I've lived a terrible life, really. Oh God have mercy!"

The clattering boom of the bombers hammered down splintering echoes from the cobblestones. A girl screamed briefly.

"If they hit the gasometer," said Barney, "it won't be very adjacent at all, will it? All of us gone in one big yellow flash!"

Ed Carlin snapped his head back and went into a swaggering dance, sparring up at the sky. "Well c'mon if you're comin', Adolph. Drop your bloody bombs, I dare you!"

"Ah, shurrup, you" said Nagginer, "If they were goin' to let us have it, they'd've started long ago. I don't think it's us they're after at all. Listen!"

The booming roar began slowly to shift away from them, northwards.

"Christ, how's that for nerve?" said Nagginer, "They're only usin' the lights o' Dublin to rendezvous by, comin' in from all sides, meetin' here an' off again with them."

"Ah thank God for your quick head, Nagginer," said Barney, "It's only Liverpool and not us."

"If it was Liverpool they'd he flyin' out to sea but this gang is goin' straight up north - overland. Can't you hear them?"

Celia's heart hammered to the roar in the sky. "What do you mean, north?"

"Belfast, where else?" said Nagginer, "Aye, that's the target for tonight! The Orangemen're going to get it in the neck. They'll need to wrap their sashes tight about them tonight."

"Belfast?" Celia repeated, "Belfast?" Suddenly she could no longer keep back the flood beating, vibrating, booming within her.

She shook her fist at the sky and screamed through her tears. "God blast the whole bloody lot o' yous! God, Oh God, is there no rest for a body anywhere in this terrible world?"

DISCIPLINE

Love sweet and tender went pouring on and on suffusing his being in a silver trilling of delight that lifted him through an immensity of still air high over lush green plains rolling towards a low tawny horizon, incredibly distant, immeasurably wide, from which, as he soared nearer, there began to rise a scratching, a scraping, a scribble of noises that brought him abruptly back down to the depressingly grey ordinariness of the morning hour of meditation. Yet another apologetic cough from behind made him aware that the whole dark line of head-bent novices had paused and was growing impatient for him to come out of whatever it was, the joy of the Lord or an ambush by Satan or maybe just the cuff of his trouser leg caught in a briar by the side of the path. He began to walk forward again listening in fresh wonder to the noises in the garden - the trilling of the bird in the beech tree that had drawn him so completely into that immense distracting vision, the casual hum of insects among the trim flower beds, the random whisper of wind in the elms and - with what a disconcerting wrench at his heart! - the whistling thump of a good old Dublin tram, number six, seven or eight, passing the mouth of the avenue below on its singing way towards the city where lived his father and mother whose faces were today even more indistinct and dim than ever before. How long now since his father had said: "Well, John, there's one good thing to be said for the place, if ever you change your mind, you know, discover you've no vocation, remember there's always a tram handy!" He lengthened his stride to close the gap between himself and the three novices in front - what an enormous bottom Flynn had and wiggly! - and tried to get back to the seven dolours of the Blessed Virgin, the subject of the morning's meditation. What had he been thinking about when that birdsong lifted him into the spacious heart of that overwhelming dream? Something about the sweet pain of a sword going through the heart of a mother every time she thinks about her absent son. But the restless flame of the idea was quenched and he wondered was that because they were about to go for the first swim of the summer? Since yesterday when it was announced a hushed restlessness had spread through the halls and corridors of the place. He tried again but got no further than an awareness of the flow of warm air over his hands and face which was a bit like the sweet warmth you felt flow at you out of girls standing close to you downstairs in a crowded tram. How unutterably wonderful it must be to be even closer! How sweet! How tender! Panic scampered through him. "God forgive me!" he prayed in his heart and in desperation drew on his vivid image of the discipline on the top of the dressing table where he had laid it that morning, its strong leather thongs hanging over the edge and swaying in the draught from under the door as if restless to be put to use once more. The flesh of his back prickled alive in excited anticipation. Tonight the thongs would have their turn again as he continued his stern relentless battle against the lusts of the flesh. With the light lift of a sigh he recalled the first time he had seen a discipline, in the assembly hall where he sat with the other novices shortly after their arrival at the college listening to an address by the Director. "Whenever your family comes to visit you" the old man said, his eye exploring something of absorbing, even comic, interest on the ceiling behind their heads, "try as far as you can to avoid any physical contact. If you can avoid it don't even shake hands. Of course there's no need to be abrupt or rude. You must show some tact. But I don't have to tell you that under no circumstances must you allow any of them to embrace you. This is to apply even to your mother. Yes, your own dear old Irish mother at whose side you first learned to say the rosary! Keep your eyes humbly on the ground all the time she is with you for as you know in your heart - where Satan lodges - you cannot look into the eye of another human being, no matter who that person is, without there being some hint, some element, some danger of sin. Oh yes, the devil lurks even in the most innocent-seeming glance. And so you must be eternally vigilant, for he is, make no mistake about that! - to defeat his works and pomps." He had listened in some astonishment but in firm agreement to the Director who spoke with his hands hidden in the sleeves of his soutane, winding his watch or scratching his wrists or maybe even feeling his own pulse. Was there no sure armour one could don against the onrushes, the ambushes of evil? Even as he fretted about that, a wicker basket was brought in by a stooping brother with a face like a dried out dishcloth and set down in front of the Director who bent the pink, hairless orb of his head over it and drew forth an object which he held aloft by the handle from which an unravelling plait of leather thongs hung down over his trembling blue-veined hand. "The devil strives to capture our souls through the temptations of the flesh" he said in the sort of tone you might use for discussing the weather with a casual acquaintance, "And with very good chances of success as we all know, don't we? In our order this implement here in my hand is one of the means we use to discipline the flesh and make it less susceptible to the pleadings of the devil. Don't be afraid to use it on yourselves - like this," he flicked the discipline gently on either side of his body, "The person who'll feel the most pain will be Old Nick." He sniggered quietly to himself as if sharing the joke with someone inside himself. Many of the novices present started to snigger along with him when they realised that he wasn't just clearing catarrh from his head.

He was almost walking on Flynn's heels - they delayed so long in front of him - and slowed back to the discreet distance they had been enjoined to keep from each other when meditating in the garden. To his surprise he was assailed by an impish impulse to giggle aloud at the sight of the three leading novices, their eyes solemnly on the ground as if searching for the sixpence Dingo claimed he had lost yesterday through a hole in his pocket. There was something comic in their slow mincing walk - like conspirators in a Disney cartoon in the dedicated way they steadfastly refused to look at the fresh green of the grass, brilliant with a lush life of its own, on either side of the path. Or at the amazing skyward heave of the solid trees all about them. It was like coming upon grown men secretly met to play some silly child's game like Blind man's buff with your eyes open. "Oh God!" he groaned causing Flynn to pause in his stride and incline his head sideways hopefully to hear more. And of greater interest. This would never do, this selfish indulgence in the sort of ideas he would have to discuss in confession later with Father Paul. But in the meantime, tonight in point of fact, he would make up for those lapses and drive this skittish restlessness, this giggling mockery, this offending Adam, out of him. Like he had his wild surge of lust in that amazing session last week when for a terrifying moment he feared his arm would grow too tired to go on flogging his flesh and leave him defenceless, completely at the mercy of the persistent memory of the big, soft-bosomed girl he had almost bumped into as she stepped right in his path - into his arms almost - out of a shop doorway during the walk the Deputy had led them on last Sunday. Her candid eyes had thrust invitingly into his and he had almost swooned in the joyful mystery - God, the blasphemy! - of their dark depths. As he was on the point of doing again. With the cunning of a seasoned chess master he moved quickly to the forefront of his mind an image of the Blessed Virgin, her heart pierced by the seven swords of sorrow as she sat beneath the cross holding in her arms her own beloved son, his divine body pitifully torn by the offending cruelty of the nails, the thorns and the spear. Because of his special devotion to her, it was she who would come to his aid as she had undoubtedly last week when his arm tired and his flesh, lustful as ever, defied the thongs. He yearned to share in the pristine purity of she who came forth as the morning rising, fair as the moon, bright as the sun, terrible as an army set in battle array.

A bell chimed within the college building summoning them in from the garden. As soon as he reached the end of the path he swung into his strong stride and overtook the three novices who had been ahead of him. At the door he checked an impulse to shoulder Jack Ryan out of his way. Instead he slipped quickly around and ahead of him grinning into his face in triumph as he passed. He hurried down the corridor which echoed with the clear sharp sounds of summer so different from the damp scufflings of winter when a chair could not be moved without its legs growling sullenly along the floor and right through your distracted thoughts. As he began to change out of his soutane to dress into his street clothes, the flesh on his back awakened in a delicate criss-cross of itchings. Naked except for the bathing trunks he slipped on he distinguished with nice precision the length and soreness of each of the stripes he had laid on his back last night, swinging the discipline under each arm in turn until his offending flesh from shoulders to buttocks had received its due measure of mortifying chastisement. The pattern of that chastisement was so clear in his mind there was no need to twist round his head to examine the result in the mirror on the dressing table. Anyway, his long face with the sharp high cheekbones jutting like sills below his long almond shaped eyes, the hair black as a raven's wing always revived the fear that someone in the place might have learned the offending name the kids along Sundrive Road used to call after him as he passed by on his way to school - "the Chinese!" And later when he went by in his long black winter raincoat - "Jasus, will yous just look at Doctor Fu Manchu!"

All in all last night had been a good session. First he

had flogged out of his system his most persistent memory, a pair of long shapely legs in flesh-coloured stockings thrusting straight at him from within a low-slung sports car he had passed outside the Shelbourne a few weeks before he entered the college. It took a little longer to banish the lure of the swelling naked breasts - the size and shape of melons - of the assistant in the shop on the corner who revealed them to him as she bent loose-bloused over the till making him wait a burning eternity for his change from the small Players he had nipped in to buy while Dingo kept nix at the door. But in spite of all his zeal, the thrust of the inviting dark eyes, though they had retreated before the flail of the discipline, found other means of getting in under his guard. So last night once again, close on daybreak he had shouldered frenziedly into clammy wakefullness from a warm enfolding dream more vivid than usual in which he was on the point of being drawn down by strong white limbs to drown in the swooning depths of those tender candid eyes. "God, doesn't the devil ever give up?" he said aloud to the discipline on the dressing table, "Doesn't the bloody fella ever take a day off? Or go on strike now and again just like everybody else?" He finished dressing quickly, knelt a moment thinking a devout prayer to the Blessed Virgin, and then went out to join his colleagues lining up noisily in the corridor.

Walking in pairs the novices wound in a casual crocodile down the avenue towards the sea which though not yet in sight was already with them in the tang of salt on the soft breeze. Exulting in his superior height John looked down along the line of bobbing black hats towards the cloud-crowded sky and felt his spirit chafe like a restless horse pawing the ground in a narrow field.

"Who's trail boss this mornin', pardner?" he asked Dingo whose hat was perched lightly as a girl's on his black pear-like head as he sidled along as if seeking an opportunity to slip past the ever-advancing obstruction of his ample stomach, "The Dep'ty as usual, Slim ole pardner," Dingo said abstractedly as if his heart wasn't really in the game of carrying on their conversation in the lingo of cowboys in the exciting action stories to be read in such magazines as *Wild West* and *Aces High*, copies of which O'Toole smuggled in from a bookshop in Blackrock.

"Sure a sloo of hombres ridin' the trail to the ole swimmin' hole today. Y'd never think we had so many cow-punchers in the ole ranch-house, would you? How many you reckon we got on this range, Kid?"

"Quien sabe, amigo" Dingo said digging his fist into the back of Keogh, a fellow Kerryman, to attract his attention. He at once launched into a bitter diatribe against the tackling rule which had been the cause of Kivane being sent off at a crucial point in yesterday's violent friendly match between Kerry and Carlow at Croke Park.

"Gut that ref, so I would." Dingo grew red in the face, "Yeah, gut the divil, that's what I'd do. Robbed us of the game so he did, bad cess to him!"

Only half-listening to Dingo's remarks John yawned and screwed his neck around in his narrow collar which he was certain now his mother had bought one size at least too small. He allowed himself to hear snatches of conversation from the couple behind and found that they too were discussing the match. Lonely and isolated above the bobbing hats he sighed his incomprehension of the childishness of his companions.

What was interesting or exciting in one man's pitting himself against another for the brief possession of a football when the pounding excitement of real life lay in pitting your whole self against the wily strategies of the devil and fending off all his attacks for the salvation of your soul? It was gratifying to know that the Director was well aware of the wiliness of those strategies, of the power of those attacks, for even though he knew the result of yesterday's game before tea-time he had kept it back until just after evening devotions. Shuley and Stapleton, the most slippery duo in the place, had hung about outside his study from which the yelping howl of the commentator was heard each time the door was opened yet they failed to learn the result before he himself chose to announce it. And he was quite right to do so. The withholding of the result was part of the general punishment meted out following the fight that had erupted with screams and scufflings outside the refectory door one evening early last week between one faction supporting Callaghan for the vacant captaincy of the hurling team and another favouring Lynam who must have been the cause of it all for the whisper was he'd been packed off home in disgrace. He marvelled at the cool detached manner in which the Director had handled the affair, using the occasion to engage the whole college in exhilarating spiritual exercises. It filled him with pride to belong to an order which never lost sight of the things that really mattered in life. In a way they were like an army being trained in discipline, dedication, and devotion for the struggle on the vast front of the nation's classrooms where they would mould the minds of the young into a form that later would produce alert, concerned, Catholic men, the future hope of Ireland. And like an army, the sense of comradeship he felt all around him was a comfort in times of trial. Especially at night when the beasts lurking in your flesh awoke and came shambling through the livid darkness towards you, their faces gleaming obscenely with the beauty of girls. At times like that it was good to know that you were remembered in someone's prayers, that restless in your lone cubicle where nothing stirred but the whispered obscenities of the devil you were not utterly alone. Others in the college were facing the same evil at exactly the same time praying that, in spite of the overwhelming onset of temptation, you hold on so that they too would have the strength to endure as well.

"An' what about the lousers" he heard Dingo say, "that lep up for the ball with their knees stuck out to give you a jolt in the you-know? Oh man dear, gut them all I would, gut them all!"

He would remember Dingo in his prayers tonight. He would remember them all, especially those his mind had mocked at however briefly in the garden. How proud he was to belong to the college! What a marvellous gift of grace he had received to be called by God to serve in the order! He felt so proud he thought it must be showing as an intense light shining on his face.

His heart gave a sharp hitch of joy at his first glimpse of the sea. And instantly he felt dejected. Had he not declared himself to be proud? Had he not actually revelled in the emotion? And was not pride, as Father Paul was in constant pains to remind him in the confessional, the most besetting sin of all? Pride of any kind was to be shunned, pride in your intellectual prowess, pride in your body, pride in your possessions. With infinite patience Father Paul repeatedly pointed out to him that pride in little things led to pride in greater things until the mind was lulled and lured from the narrow path of truth by a distorted image of itself, swollen like a bag of foul wind in intellectual pride. There was the bolt to shut the gates of heaven in your face! There was the very sin of Lucifer himself! He shuddered. "You've got the divil's own pride" Father Paul chuckled through the grating of the confession box the last time he had confessed his sins to him. At his side he heard Dingo muttering away about the match mostly to himself for Keogh seemed to have lost interest in it. Listening to his friend he wondered if his arch lack of interest in football was yet another manifestation of his pride. Otherwise how could he explain the superior smile he reserved for Dingo whenever he talked about the game and the shallow pity he felt for him because he could be upset by something so trivial as the result of a football match. On sports afternoon he himself played without haste or passion as if performing a mechanical exercise, completely indifferent to the end result. He sucked in his cheeks running his mind over whatever he could manage to remember of Dingo's remarks about the tackling rule.

"That ref was an idiot" he said, earning a startled glance from Dingo. "What he should have done was give Carlow a free kick and not do anything as drastic as sending Kivane off the field."

"Jakers, John" approved Dingo, "If even you can see that then the injustice of the thing should he as plain as a pikestaff to everyone else. Yeah, sure was a no-good hombre that ref. I could keel him myself, personal!"

"Yeah!" John agreed following the frantic spindly flight of a dragonfly, a sort of famished, acetic angel of the insect world, which he surmised must have come from the marshy wastelands past which they were walking on their way towards the iron railway bridge where the Dep'ty stood his broad-brimmed hat tilted over his right eye in the rakish cowboy manner that had earned him his nickname from Dingo.

"Take it easy now" the Dep'ty warned in his bleak Belfast twang as they drew near the bridge, "I want no mad rushin' up the steps here. No wild jumpin' up and down on the top to test whether it'll bear your weight. It may not, you know! An' when you come down on the far side keep together on the top of the wall and stay as far away as you can from any - er - people who may be on the rocks down there."

John crossed the bridge with Dingo and climbed up onto the spine of the wall stretching long and white between the railway lines gleaming to a point towards Blackrock and the sea on the other side, crowding green across the bay in gentle waves which broke cool and white along the curt lip of toffee-brown sand directly below them. After they had walked a short distance the Dep'ty ordered them down on the flagstones sloping to the lapping water. John climbed down behind Dingo his restless feet slithering on the stones, his flesh yearning for the cool caress of the sea with the same kind of eager excitement he guessed was also gripping his companions most of whom were shouting and shrieking and giggling in rough horseplay with some among them, for no apparent reason, breaking into high pulsing laughs behind which he sensed a taut, indefinable fear.

"Hey, Slim ole pardner" Dingo said to him, "Are you on for a race? Last one in pays for the pictures next time we can bunk into that cinema in Blackrock. Are you game?"

"Sure Dingo ole dogie!" And he burst out laughing when he saw that Dingo had already undone his shoes, socks and his collar which he shot together into an untidy heap on the rocks. In a flurry of deft movements he too undressed and when he leaped out on the warm lip of sand he saw in a quick glance that he had beaten not only Dingo but all the rest of his fellow-novices as well. He flurried out from the narrow strip of strand and felt the cold grasp of the water rise higher and higher up his body until with an exulting cry he plunged head first into the gentle waves. The thick greenness thrust soft against his eyeballs as he pressed into the depths of the tender challenging eyes of the soft-bosomed girl stepping out of the shop. God, not even here was there escape from the toils of the tempter, but the beauty of the girl ceased almost at once to lure him as the stripes on his back awoke and manifested themselves to his mind as a haphazard pattern of main roads on a map of pain. His left side bore the greater complexity of criss-crossing lines along which the water probed with sharp slate-edged fingers. He wondered would the salt make them even redder than they had appeared a few nights ago when he had twisted round to examine them in the stark light of his reading lamp. He broke the surface and treading water squinted through beads of light at the thin grey line of Pigeon House Road across the bay and the stiff red chimney stack thrusting up from the bulk of the electricity works. As he turned over on his back to face the shore a memory stirred somewhere in the ebbing and flowing of the restless depths but failed to reach the surface of his mind. For something was terribly wrong! The whole foreshore rang with silence and immobility. The figures on the flagstones and at the rim of the water rested immobile as frail wax statues. The still silence pressed down on him like guilt. For a wild deranged second he almost believed that while he had been swimming his brief burst of joy under the sea some dread fixity had fallen on the world and he was the only one in it endowed with life and movement. How still they stood, all staring his way! "Jesus, no!" he implored and flopped sideways under the waves. His frantic hands explored his trunks which he found were sitting properly on his body with no telltale holes front or back or embarrassing wisps of hair struggling out of the leg holes or over the elastic sagging at the waist. When he came to the surface again the scene was flickered with movement like in the cinema at Blackrock following some failure in the projection room. The reason was not far to seek. As he swam back towards the shore he heard the Dep'ty's angry voice ordering everyone into the water. "Yes O'Toole" he was saying, "I know it's cold. And I've got further news for you boy. It's wringin' wet as well."

He swam on towards Dingo who stood at the edge teasing his toes into the water.

"What was up?" he asked Dingo when he reached him.

Dingo freed a coil of seaweed from his legs with his

pudgy fingers and idly stirred the surface with it.

"For God's sake, Dingo, what were you all staring at?"

The green coil unravelled from Dingo's fingers and plopped on the surface like a brief burst of rain.

"They always said you were a bit of a show-off" Dingo said as if each individual word bore a bitter taste, "But I never believed that. At least not until now."

Avoiding John's eyes he plunged away brusquely into the water. His stomach made abrupt contact with bottom and rising to his feet he floundered away red-faced muttering to himself. "Gut the half o' them I would. An' not just the refs."

John stood looking after Dingo the streaks of pain across his back reawakening, raw and urgent, in the harsh touch of the sun. Most of the novices were now either swimming or standing taking a breather in the gentle heave of the incoming tide. They had found their voices again but there was a breathless curbed quality in their calls and giggles. A little to his left O'Toole lifted out of the water and turning his back to him began to blow his nose between his thumb and forefinger. The sunlight gleamed on the drops of seawater studding the broad white back and dripping copiously from his tight red curls. Watching O'Toole he became aware that as his own back dried in the sun the quality of the pain again changed subtly. It felt now as if hot wax had been laid in a complex pattern over it. How surprisingly hot the sun was! If O'Toole went on standing there with his back to it his pale skin would turn painfully red in no time at all. And the other fellows standing there, allowing that fierce heat to play on their backs, they would know all about it tonight. All at once he had a sense of something yielding inside him as if his spirit had tripped over some obtruding fact which should have been obvious to him earlier. He felt as if everything within the envelope of his skin had shifted subtly from its accustomed place. In growing alarm he darted his glance from one pale body to another. A cold aloneness began to spread from a numb centre near his heart, moved trembling along his limbs and into the bones of his face. The back of every novice turned to him gleamed in the sun as smooth and unmarked as a sheet of plain white writing paper. That was why they had stood silent on the rocks staring out at him. His was the only back to bear the clear, obvious marks of the discipline. The dirty, lousy hypocrites! None of them until now had ever hinted or joked or revealed even indirectly that they weren't using the discipline on themselves as the Director had urged them to. Or if they had it would appear they had done so merely to scratch some idle itch. Yet hadn't some of them even boasted of the pains they inflicted on their bodies? "But I even heard them disciplining themselves," he whispered to himself, "O'Toole and Hamilton in the rooms on either side of mine, I heard them, actually heard them, stroke after stroke!" The Dep'ty slithered down past him and squatting on the flagstones began to call the bathers in from the sea, wisps of tobacco smoke escaping from his mouth. "Hurry on there! Don't stay in long the first day. And I've things to do, so don't delay me." Turning, he gave John a friendly nod. "It kept up fine, thank God." John nodded and began carefully and modestly to dress, his fingers thick and blunt. With averted eyes, Dingo came and carried his crumpled bundle of clothes to where Blennerhasset and Keogh were dressing all three silent and grim as if brooding over some great wrong. How he dreaded the walk back to the college and the long evening stretching ahead! A haze of imminent sleep poured into his head which became a heavy burden he had continually to remember to raise. Once when he raised it he saw that the group were clambering up on the wall and beginning the dreaded return walk. To his surprise the Dep'ty joined him on the far side of the bridge and launched into an absorbing account of the origins of some of the families mentioned in the *Annals of Ulster*. That led him on to local history anecdotes which he illustrated by singing snatches of songs in a kind of strangled wheeze. When one of these drew a laugh from John he saw a look of quiet relief come into the Dep'ty's eyes. Him he would remember in his prayers.

But when the Dep'ty left him part way through the garden he realised again how alone he was, moving as in a still pool of silence around which his companions flitted like dark figures in a nightmare, their faces studiously averted, their bodies stiff and taut as if they would scamper away should he try to speak to them. In the refectory at tea not even Dingo urged him to pass the bread-plate which lay untouched on the table in front of him all through the meal. Why should they shun him, he raged, simply because his body showed he was disciplining himself in the manner that had been enjoined on them all? What wrong had he done them? Surely they knew as well as he that the flesh was the fiend's fifth column through which the soul could be delivered to eternal damnation? Did none of them fear the scourging flames, the shrieking demons, the despairing agony at being bereft forever of the sight of God? Of course they did, but unlike him they had persuaded themselves that somehow or other God would slip them the grace through which they would be saved with the minimum of effort on their part. Especially the effort of wielding the discipline against the urging lusts of the flesh. A joy of pride came into him. Let them all go! Let them do as they wished which could be nothing for all he cared. He would continue as before only with more zeal, more zing, more power to his elbow!

Later, when he escaped to his room he switched on the reading-lamp and slumped on the edge of the iron-framed bed wearily leaning back his head against the wall. A dull, throbbing started deep in his skull and kept on steadily for some little time until it ceased abruptly only to begin again after a short pause at a shallower depth it seemed and in a slightly slower rhythm. His heart leaped on a heavy thud which appeared to shake the wall, and he scrambled breathless from the bed. What was Hamilton next door up to? He laid his ear lightly against the wall and listened. The dull throbbing was louder only it was not just a throbbing, it was a steady rhythm of beating. No, not just of beating - of flogging! Was Hamilton using the discipline on himself? It sounded like it! He removed the drinking glass from next the cruet on the tin tray beside his bed and advanced on the area where he had heard the rhythmic beats. Placing the mouth of the glass flush with the wall he slid his ear against the thin base and listened, "...renounce the bloody divil an' all his feckin' works and pomps" he heard Hamilton say so close to his ear he almost dropped the glass. The hammering of his heart was so high in his chest he could for the moment hardly

The Hero Game and Other Dublin Stories

distinguish it from the sounds beating in the next room. Hamilton's foot crashed noisily against the skirting hoard as he made an abrupt movement. "The bloody scourgin' at the feckin' pillar!" Hamilton's voice rang out and was succeeded by a burst of noise as if a machine gun was being fired at the wall. "Thy holy will be done, Oh Lard!" Hamilton's voice said as the flailing rhythm continued in impulses of sound bearing an oddly metallic core. The quality of the sound changed with a slight hitch to a sharper, lighter, less metallic, more wooden tone it seemed. His realisation of what was happening next door startled the glass out of his grasp so that it disappeared up into the shadows of the upper section of the wall, bounced softly down on the bedspread and flashed outwards towards the floor. He dived and caught it, rolling on his throbbing back and spluttering: "Holy hell!" He lay panting on the cold linoleum at the far side of the narrow room nursing the glass to his chest. He couldn't have been mistaken in what he heard. It wasn't Hamilton's frail flesh that had rung under the scourge of the thongs. Something else had done that. From his knowledge of how each room was furnished he knew that Hamilton had been swinging the discipline first into the bedspread, next against the iron bedstead, and lastly onto the top of the dressing table. "Christ, the lousy hypocrite!" he breathed as he clambered to his feet. Hamilton always had a large Latin missal with him at mass at the sight of which Dingo, exasperated, had once asked: "Are you scabbin' it on the priests, Hammo?" What a crowd of hypocrites! For the past year he had been scourging himself religiously - his own mind wasn't beginning to mock him was it? - while the rest of them agitated the lavender-scented night air with their scourging of bed posts, dressing tables, bedspreads, chairs, the floor and God knows what else. Was it Saint Theresa who said that having lived her life in a religious community she realised why Christ had chosen to live his out in the world, among sinners? Anyway, it was some saint like that. But never mind, he soothed his forehead with the glass, virtue is its own reward and certainly the Director's injunction had enabled him to grow in mastery over the frailty of his flesh. That was true, but did the Director himself ever use the discipline on the frailty of his own flesh? Maybe he was down there now in his room sitting on his fat bum, a glass of Power's whiskey at his elbow, a long thick cigar in his beefy fingers laughing at all the idiots beating or pretending to beat themselves all over the building while he ran his juicy eye over the naked pin-ups in full colour and vivid detail spotlighted on the walls.

No! He mustn't think those evil thoughts. No, that was unworthy of him! He thrust out his hand to ward such thoughts off and heard the glass clink against the wall beside him, the one separating him from O'Toole's room. Turning the glass in his hand he fitted the mouth against the wall and crouched to listen. He moved along the wall until he heard a movement quite close to where he was. How strange that he should be eavesdropping on O'Toole of all people, the very fellow who had been sitting in the same classroom with him the day the recruiting sergeant sidled in through the door to talk about the challenge and the joy and the glory of the religious life and to discover if anyone there felt he had a vocation from Almighty God to follow it. A stirring broke out in the room, as if some heavy piece of furniture was being moved about, and to his amazement the voice of the Director came down the slim tunnel of the glass. "You must be a man, O'Too-il. You've been shown the way today haven't you? Come on now, boy, lay into yourself there. Flog the devil outta you. Come on, it's not so terrible once you get started. Just like diving into the sea."

There followed a heart-emptying sigh and a whimper such as a hurt dog might make. "Ah but it stings so it does. It stings bloody awful." He pictured O'Toole on his knees cringing away from the Director, the last person you'd expect to find in a novice's room at that hour. He wished the Director would speak again for there was something a little strange about the tone, the accent in which he spoke. "Come on now O'Too-il, let's see some elbow grease there, boy." What was strange was the manner in which he pronounced O'Toole's name for the only person he ever heard pronounce it as O'Too-il was the novice himself. "Be a man so you must. Let's see you swing that discipline" said who else but O'Toole - how crazy! - talking to himself in the Director's voice. There was a scurrying movement and an angry snarl. "So I'm to bloody well swing it am I?" O'Toole cried, "If you'd ever done it you wouldn't say that, you'd know how awful it stings and that's a fact." The furniture moving sound came again followed by a brief silence. "Think of our Blessed Saviour" said O'Toole in the Director's voice, "Think of how he endured the scourging at the pillar for our sake and never a whimper out of him. So come on now, offer your pain up for the Holy Father's intention." A brisk clatter of staccato slappings rushed down the stem of the glass, "Oh be the holy elephant!" O'Toole whined. "Oh me poor back! Ah, Jasus look what you made me do! You made me nick the pimple on me arse, so you did! Up to me ankles I'll be in a minute in me own blood. Oh be the hokey!"

John flopped heavily on the floor and spun the glass angrily along the shiny linoleum to where it knocked into a chair leg without breaking and began to twinkle in a wild elipse round its weighted bottom. He pressed his knuckles against his temples. "My God, what have you brought me to? I never thought I'd spend my days with such a gang of snivelling hypocrites! Looking down on us you can see can't you that I'm the only person in the college who sincerely suffers for your sake, who selflessly offers up his agonies that your holy will be done!" His voice booming back at him from the walls of the narrow room seemed to be echoing in some building of vaster dimensions, some high-domed temple maybe or an assembly hall. Behind his closed lids there came stalking from the shadows a noble figure in white who with grand gestures asserted wordlessly something he immediately knew to be proud and despicable. He caught his breath as he recognised the familiar image of the temple which always sprang to mind when he read with unflagging fascination the parable of the Pharisee and the Publican. In the story he always felt himself to be the humble Publican sitting in the shadows seeking the right words to pray while the shallow-souled Pharisee proclaimed to God that he was not like other men who without exception were evildoers. God, how dreadful that you can be stricken so blind by pride! For truly he wasn't the humble Publican at all but the rotten Pharisee whose hypocrisy exceeded all bounds. A whitewashed tomb in fact! He sighed, watching the glass winking right, winking left turning from Publican to Pharisee from Pharisee to Publican. Oh how true that the bloody devil never took a day off, or an evening off, or even a second off! He never slept on the job which was made all the more easy for him by fools like him who let their stupid vanity lead them into the deadly sin of pride. It almost made him puke to think of how he had allowed himself to be tricked into defiling the image of that most god-fearing of men, the gentle Director. Grave and reflective, he eased himself to his feet, ignoring the thuds and groans coming in on both sides through the walls. Let others in the college do as they pleased. Their thoughts and actions were between them and God and no one else had a right to pass judgement or to sneer at them no matter what they did. Or did not do. Quickly he undressed and stood naked in the room. He approached the dressing table on which the discipline rested, the thongs hanging down over the brass handle of the drawer. Taking it in his hands he drew the thongs slowly through his fingers willing himself into that stern detached frame of mind in which he began the necessary task of humbling the spirit that had so exulted in its pride. In some ways the spirit was more dangerous than the flesh. He bent suddenly and swung hard at his body. He flogged until there was no longer any force behind the blows. He fell into bed mumbling abstractedly his private prayers in a thickening flow of fog which rose it seemed straight out of the pillow on which he rested his head. The fog fell away into oblivion until, towards dawn, he walked in dread of what lay ahead of him, along a narrow peninsula lush with brilliant grass, heading towards a yellow spearhead of sand where the land gave place to the sea. On his left moving rapidly in the same direction came Dingo and O'Toole both of them naked except for the black-bordered straw boaters each of them wore jauntily tilted over his right eye. O'Toole was directly behind Dingo, so tight against him they walked like some obscene double-legged beast. Their skin smelling faintly of old socks in a drawer, was of a scabby green horn the surface of which scurried with light - or was it with insects? On they pranced towards a swoon-eyed girl with large white breasts who lay facing them on the sand her thick thighs sunk in the soft foam of the greenish sea. His soul ached to plunge full length into the balm of the waters, to lose itself in the never-resting sea towards which his legs refused to move no matter how hard he strained and yearned to impel them, no matter how desperately he wished to move himself towards the wavering margin of hissing foam in which the girl lay. O'Toole rested his sharp chin on Dingo's shoulder and soundlessly drooled shameless suggestions to her at which she gleamed an evil smile and placing a hand on each breast squeezed until blood began to trickle out between her dirty fingers. Dingo giggled in glee and reaching out a horny hand he beckoned her to him. She began to draw up out of the water her body below the waist a huge malformed bone streaked with grey cracks emerging from an envelope of heaving tissue and raw flesh from which drops of blood splashed bright into the sea. With a cry he wrenched out of sleep.

The hard greenish light of the dream gleamed behind all the morning's tasks and played over his brief meditation in the garden where he grew light-headed in his efforts to prevent himself from reliving its horror which fringed and tinged with its hue all the familiar sights of the morning. At one point he whispered: "Let this chalice pass from me" and wondered numbly was there any means more immediate than the grace of God by which the mind might be scoured out like a soiled utensil until it was clean and fresh for use once again. The morning seemed endless until at last he was able to seek the relief of movement in joining his companions filing out of the gate behind the Dep'ty and down the long avenue to the sea. He saw he had paired off with Doyle, a fellow he had never been able to sustain a conversation with because of his gusts of bad breath and his maddening habit of continually blinking his raw-rimmed blue eyes. "Excuse me" he murmured to him and stepped out on the roadway to seek a place further down the line.

"How are things, Jackie?" a familiar voice asked him and O'Toole took him by the arm and drew him up on the pavement where a straggling group had not yet settled into ordered pairings.

"Sure mighty white of you, li'l dogie, to treat a maverick like this" he said and from O'Tool's startled expression realised he had spoken as he would to Dingo. His cheeks burned. "I love swimming, don't you?" he said to O'Toole in his confusion, "At the school I was at we only went swimming once a week in the summer and that was only to the public baths."

"Why'n the hell are you telling all this to me?" O'Toole glared at him, "Sure didn't we both go to the same bloody school?"

"Oh, of course we did," He grew more confused, "I'm sorry. It's just I wasn't thinking,"

"And a bloody pity we didn't stay there instead of coming to this dump. Where did you get that "mighty white of you, li'l dogie" and so on? No! Don't tell me. Let me tell you. Life in this joint's getting you down too, isn't it Jackie?"

John simulated an interest in the traffic fussing past them towards the junction of Rock Road, hoping O'Toole would think the noise had prevented him from hearing what he said. The repetition of his familiar boyhood name disturbed him. His mother's voice spoke it close to his ear and his anguished heart had a sudden startled revelation of the immensity of his loneliness.

"O Jesus Christ" O'Toole said, "You're getting like the bloody rest of them. Say anything personal or significant in any way and yous all start to clam up. It's like living in bloody Russia as Father Paul was tellin' us, where they're all supposed to spy on each other."

"Life here's not getting me down at all. But if it's posing problems for you why don't you take them to the man you've just mentioned, to Father Paul and stop speculating about other people?"

"Why should I go and chat to Father Paul? It's not him who's thinking of packing his attaché case and scramming out of here, is it? Of course it isn't. It's you, Jackie! I've been noticing you on and off for weeks now and you're showing the same signs that Maguire and Lynam did before they took it on the lam down to the tram-stop. You know, laughing to yourself when you think no-one is watching, wandering all the time in your thoughts and coming out with strange expressions, but most of all goin' to town with the scourging at the pillar act to convince yourself that you're a terribly holy fellow who's in exactly the right place for a holy fellow to be. Maguire was like that and so was Lynam. And look what happened! They both packed it in practically on the spur of the moment. That big scrap last week wasn't on account of the captaincy of the hurling team at all. Lynam made the mistake of telling Callaghan he was thinking of taking a run-out powder and Callier went off and blabbed to the Director. They had Lynam in and practically gave him the third degree, laid all kinds of pressures on him, sort of spiritual hose-pipe to force him to stay, making out it might be hard to get a job after leaving the order and hinting that he might be falling into the sin of intellectual pride. Even said it would break his poor old Irish mother's heart if he left. But Lynam stuck to his guns. So you see he wasn't expelled as the rumour has it. He jumped aboard the number eight tram all by himself and laughed all the way back home to his tea. And remember Maguire? Now you see him! Now you don't. He just vanished - overnight!"

"What makes you think I care a damn for any of that?" He longed to rip off his collar to relieve the pressure of the stud which bored into the back of his neck like a steel finger. "As I've said before, if you're having problems go an' talk with Father Paul. It's nothing to be ashamed of. We all get doubts sometimes."

"Oh so you admit you have some?" O'Toole squinted a smile at the sky, "God, there's hope for old Ireland yet."

"What do you mean?"

"Just the way Lynam used to talk, as if everyone had big problems except him. You may not go the distance either."

John inserted his finger under the rim of his collar and eased the pressure of the stud on the hard knob of bone at the base of his neck. He was surprised to find his burning flesh cool to the touch of his finger.

"Don't compare me with him," he said, "The whole place could see Lynam was in trouble for the minute he came here."

"We're all in trouble." O'Toole thrust the flat of his hand against the back of the novice in front of him. "Go and listen to someone else's confession" he pushed the fellow well beyond arm's length. "And when I say trouble, it's trouble I mean, Jackie. Look at the gang we've decided to spend our lives among! We're in a kind of limbo in an order that's neither laity nor clergy. If we were priests we'd have the satisfaction of saying mass or of hearing confessions which, when you come to think of it must be great gas. Imagine the marvellous questions you could put to women! And Jasus, look at what you'd hear then! All the details of what goes on out there in what the Director calls the world! For they'd have no option but to tell the truth - the whole lovely truth! You know, it mightn't be too bad in the order if we had permission to get married."

"I'm not interested in any of that."

"Like hell you're not. An' Lynam wasn't either! And look at where he is now - at home, free to do what he likes. To whoever he likes. And look at what's in store for us - a lifetime of holy endeavour. And bloody boredom! After all, what are we in the long run but cut-price teachers scabbing the job on married men who have families to support."

"You mustn't talk like that."

"They hooked you and me, Jackie, when we knew no better!" There was an alarming gulp of sadness in O'Toole's voice. "What the hell do school-kids know about the real things of life except what they pick up in dirty stories or figure out from what they read on lavatory walls? When they got us to join a celibate order did any of us really know what we were doing? Screw that gang in front, does anyone among them know what it's really like to have a nice piece of skirt in your arms?"

"Look, you'll have to cut out that kind of talk." Sweat eased out of his body into the tangle of stripes on his back. He saw that the novice in front had slowed down again, his head turned sideways the better to hear their conversation.

"I found out what it's like during the holidays just before I came here" O'Toole's voice boomed in the hushed air, "Among the sand dunes out near Skerries. She was a friend of my sister's. They tell you that you ought to feel guilty about it, but there's no need to feel like that at all. I wised up on that real quick. It's not like what they say at all. Dirty, I mean. It's nice. And sort of happy."

John thrust his face so close to his that for a moment he was sickened by the yellow—crested pimples lurking just below the carbolic smelling surface of O'Toole's pinkish skin. "So that's where all this talk is leading to, is it? You're planning for the day when just like the other two you're going to leave the order as well. Only the impression you'd like to leave behind is that you left to get married, that no matter how hard you tried, and you did try hard, you just can't live without women. But no one can blame you for that, can they? And after all you're just changing one sort of order for another - holy orders for holy matrimony. That sounds good but it's not true is it? The truth is that you haven't the guts to stay here and mortify the lazy old lard that covers you. Yeah, pardner, you're aimin' to vamoose outta this one-horse outfit because last night you nicked the pimple on your arse, by gor. Yeah, what doth it profit an hombre to save his immortal soul if in the process he has to nick the pimple on his arse and wade up to his ankles in his own blood?"

O'Toole's thick lips gasped apart. He sagged sideways, his eyes darting unfocussed glances as if seeking desperately in his mind for something whose loss was panicking him. One of the pair behind shouted for them to hurry on. O'Toole's strong shoulders winced as if under a great weight.

"How could you know that?" he whispered. "Oh that's real vile that is! To spy like that on a fella! But it changes nothing. It makes you even more like Lynam than I thought. I'm convinced now you won't go the distance. And you'll be bloody good riddance, won't you?"

O'Toole bent his head and charged between the couple in front and went straight on beyond them bringing chaos to the sedate order of the winding line of novices.

"Wait, damn you" he called after O'Toole, "Don't you dare say that about me." He shouldered his way through the protesting line on fire with the impulse to smash his fists into O'Toole's mouth. Angry voices rose all round him. He felt someone's fingers pluck at his arm. A roll of thunder ahead told him that the head of the line had reached the iron railway bridge and was stamping up the steps. He saw O'Toole dart out into the roadway and make a dash for the bridge, and the protection of the Dep'ty. He made to follow and bumped into Keogh who staggered out into the gutter from where, rubbing his shoulder, he leered up at him. "Can't wait to get to the sea and do your show-off act again, can you?" He bent his head and slipped past Keogh without looking at him. In the tumult of voices in his wake he heard the tones of offended dignity, of protest, of contempt.

"Hey there, John Burke" the Dep'ty said approaching him from the shadow of the thunderous bridge. "What's got into you man? You came through that line like a knife through butter. Fall in orderly now like the rest of them."

He climbed up the steps in the company of some fellows he couldn't remember having seen before. He paused on the top where he felt the sea breeze whip against his forehead soothing his anger. As he came down and climbed up on the wall he found to his surprise that the Dep'ty was immediately behind him pacing him step by step so close it seemed he must tread on his heels. "That's my dream out" he breathed in wonder to himself and climbed down on the rocks where the Dep'ty squatted close beside him rolling a cigarette.

"I was watching you back there" the Dep'ty said as if talking to himself. "You came through that line with a complete disregard of everyone and everything. Such egotism! Such pride!"

"It wasn't pride. I was mad at a fellow."

"Who hurt your pride?"

"No." He avoided the hard glint of the Dep'ty's gaze.

"Are you quite sure?"

"He was saying I won't be able to stick it here. That I'll leave the order."

"And were you too proud to admit that you might?"

"I won't leave." His heart sank at the unwelcome lack of conviction he discovered in himself.

"Well, we might have a chat about that when we go hack. But tell me, had the fellow's remark anything to do with what happened yesterday?"

"Yesterday? What do you mean?" Bland-faced he pretended he didn't know what the Dep'ty meant. And almost believed that himself.

"Going my own quiet way about the place I heard several remarks about you and I had to put some of your colleagues right. They were saying you were nothing but a big show-off like Lynam. Remember how Lynam used to stand up in the middle of the chapel when we would all be leaving after mass, staring at the tabernacle as if he and he alone had a special relationship with the Lord? Anyway, I put your colleagues right about a simple physical fact."

"What fact?"

"Place the flat of your hand on your forehead, man."

Wonderingly John did what he was bade. His skin felt taut and tender, stinging to his touch.

"See" the Dep'ty said, "It's only your second day in the sea air and already your skin's turning as red as a beetroot. It's hypersensitive. Why, you can't scratch yourself without cutting deep grooves in yourself."

"That's not the whole truth!" He fought his growing dismay, "I followed the Director's injunction to the letter. I wasn't afraid to humble, to hurt, even humiliate my flesh. Not like them! Not like them!"

"Pride!" the Dep'ty's chuckle mocked him, "The divil's own pride! I'm sure Father Paul is going to have his hands full of moral problems by the end of the week. That hypersensitive skin of yours seems to have started something, but whether it's for good or evil I'll leave the professional theologians to decide."

"I don't understand."

"Well have a look around you. And remember that most people's skins are not as sensitive as yours and so it takes twice as much effort on their part to achieve the visible results the lot of us saw yesterday on your back." As the Dep'ty moved away humming what sounded like *After Aughrim's Great Disaster*, he looked around at his companions who were undressing with more studied self-consciousness than usual. Directly before him Blennerhasset slowly tugged his shirt forward over his matted head revealing a sparse scribble of pinkish marks over the lower curve of his pallid back. "Who's the show-off now" he muttered clenching and opening his fists as he looked from one bare back to the other being bared to the sun, some lightly shadowed with red, others with clear scarlet patterns, and one standing out from the rest with marks heavily scored into it as if with a sharp tool. "I don't give a curse what he said about hypersensitive skin" he breathed to himself, "They were doing shag-all to mortify the flesh until they saw my back yesterday. And do they call that disciplining themselves? Just wait till tonight. I'll show them. Just wait, I'll show them, by God!"

His eyes moved from one scored, wealed back to another until, feeling faint and slightly sick, he listened again to the insistent voice in his head asserting what he now felt too weak to deny, that a blind sense of pride was driving him to show them all he could scourge his flesh more than anyone else in the place had the courage to. He sat still, crouched, it felt, round a quivering core of nauseous disgust, dreading it would grow worse and make him faint or even vomit there on the rocks. But surely, before yesterday, when no one had seen his back, he couldn't have been scourging himself purely out of pride! It had been simply the need to protect himself from the burning lusts of the flesh which before he entered the order had seduced him almost nightly into lone orgies that spread a contamination as from a running abscess over his soul. His nausea gradually succeeded to a nagging sense of unease. The novices were splashing in the sea in a din of scream-like laughs and pulsing giggles. His eyes continued to explore their backs seeking the message the scarlet marks were trying to convey to him. Had they disciplined themselves as he had, out of a sincere desire to curb the dumb cries of the brute flesh, or had they done it in a fierce spirit of competition as if it was just another game, like football, the only activity about which any of them seemed to be enthusiastic. But even if the struggle against the urges of the flesh was just a game to them could their act be considered wrong in any way since its result, the curbing of sinful desires, was a good in itself? And wasn't there a hierarchy, a league of virtuous achievement even in heaven itself? Wearied by the complexity of the problem he looked away and saw that the nearer reaches of the rocks, usually deserted at that time, were occupied here and there by bathers of both sexes unnoticed by him until now so absorbed had he been in watching his fellows. Obviously the overwhelming onset of the summer had drawn to the seaside many who through luck or chance were free at that time of day. All round the air trembled with the hum and whirr of unsuspected insect life drawn by the clamorous heat of the sun from the rock clefts, the fields, the nearby marsh.

In the corner of his eye a slight movement drew his gaze and turning slightly he saw a large loose object, a white towel, flutter to the ground from the beautifully formed body of a tall, slim girl in a bright-red bathing suit who, as a sweet pang in his heart acknowledged her dear, mortal beauty, raised her hands above her head to coax her thick shining wealth of chestnut hair into a white bathing cap. She gazed about her, evidently unaware of his breathless scrutiny, totally absorbed in the task her long, white, ring-less fingers were accomplishing with dainty, strangely delighting gestures. Her gentle fingers paused in momentary difficulty and he longed to rise and go to her aid to mould that mass of softy shining hair under the rim of her cap. He continued to watch, yearning to comprehend the mystery of her otherness. What does it mean to speak in a high, light voice, musical as a wild bird's? To carry in the heart always the awesome knowledge that within the body whose sensations make up so much of your consciousness another life could start in an instant of ecstasy, and develop, and grow heavier, and press forward to be born, two hearts heating in an intimacy than which no relationship in life can ever he closer? And how aware would you be of the thrust and swell, the languid weight of rounded breasts? And how different the urging, the sweet torment, of the insistent flesh as it presents itself to women, the yearning passion to receive, to absorb, to contain rather than madly to press forth and give? He dared not move lest some untoward gesture disturb the vision of the vivid girl, living and breathing in the uniqueness of her own separate self, the beauty of her firm young body impressed on the world that without it would be so much the poorer, disappointingly ordinary, infinitely empty. To his great relief and wonder nothing stirred in him either to defile her image with lustful thoughts or to urge him to banish her from his sight as a temptation to sin. Deep in his heart he breathed a prayer that her life be happy and joyful, safe from disillusion and above all from ugliness. In a moment she lowered her arms and looked across at him. Her eyes moved warmly over his face as if on the point of recognising him as someone she knew. And on to his black clothes. She looked away quickly, a little shocked and even sad he thought.

"Howdy, Pardner." Dingo's voice called him back to the bleak world of the order. "Mighty sore I shot my fool mouth off yesterday. Hope you don't bear no grudge for it against this poor ole cowpuncher."

"No Dingo" he laughed in relief and amusement at his friend who stood ankle-deep in the hissing tide, the taut orb of his stomach bulging above the tight elasticated rim of his sloppy swimming trunks.

"Ain't you gonna pollute the ole water hole today?"

"I'm coming in now."

"Dig your spurs in then. Last one in the water's an Orangeman."

Dingo turned his face to the sea presenting the round hulk of his back from which John recoiled with a gasp of dismay. The ridged flesh on Dingo's well-padded back bore an erratic pattern of bluish stripes and raw weals that stretched from below his shoulders way down to his waist and probably even lower still, the area above his left hip bearing several thin red threads fringed with black where the flesh had cracked and bled. Flexing for his dive, already knee-deep in the tide, Dingo looked round and gave him a long wily smile.

"Beat you on the draw there, old cow poke," he said.

"God Dingo, how could you have done that to yourself?" his voice croaked on a sob and he knew his friend had not heard because of the prodigious crash of water which accompanied his explosive, belly-flopping dive. John bowed into himself, rocking slightly, his arms folded taut around his body. The image of Dingo's abused back throbbed as a wound behind his mind where something fundamental, some solid support or ground had dropped out of place like a stair rung giving way beneath urgent feet. The impact of that moment of yielding hovered like a ringing in the ears that follows a sharp noise. Even if you granted that the motive behind Dingo's action hadn't been just to be quicker on the draw, but rather to discipline his flesh and assert the mastery of his spirit over it, surely the abuse he had perpetrated on his body, made in the image of God, was obviously wrong? It was even more than that. It was evil. The conviction that this was true did not need to be reasoned out. It lay deep within him beyond debate, beyond faith even, in the very marrow of his bones. Yes, an insult to the glory of God, wrong with a wrongness for which there could be no justification anywhere by anyone. A stealthy guilt for which he feared there might never be a remedy assailed him, a chafing sense of having soiled his spirit, of having led others through his wilful pride to soil theirs. Yet he was not in sin. He had done nothing that had not been enjoined on him by his spiritual advisors. His head throbbed dully. Could there ever be a solution to this moral dilemma? He grew aware that the girl in the red bathing costume was watching him from where she waded waist-deep in the sea, a steady look of what appeared to be concern, on her long beautiful face. How wrong it would be if she or anyone else were to hurt or wound that fair flesh of hers, that flesh he longed as in a dream to draw close to, that flesh he knew had been created solely to be caressed and comforted and protected from all the ills and all the ugliness, and all the pain of the world. Her glance brushed lightly over his and shyly she averted her eyes, diving sideways to swim away from him parallel to the shore. He melted with tenderness behind which he sensed the imminent outbreak of a vast forest fire of desire, one brief flame of which would burn away all the dilemmas of right and wrong that were plaguing him. But was that right? God there was so much heart searching, so much mind probing to be done he would never get to the end of it all! So he must begin NOW!

He stood up to begin the task and looked across the bay at the massed electricity works his father once told him was called the Pigeon House. The thin red chimney stack ascending out of it was trying to tell him something and as he continued to squint his eyes across at it the memory which half stirred in him yesterday at last shook free and rose to the surface. It was of a day shortly before he came to the Provincialate when on one of his last, long keep-fit walks about the city he tramped the length of East Wall Road and came out onto the quays. Among the little group waiting for the ferry to row them across to the South Wall he saw Joe Daly, an ex-British naval officer he had come to know quite well while on holiday in his cousin's house at Salthill. When they saw each other, Joe, his face unaccountably bright with excitement, reached forward and took him by the arm.

"God, it's lucky we met" he said, "Look lad, this is a chance that'll never come again. Life herself is waiting for you to take her. Look! There!"

Joe pointed across the river where to his astonishment he saw an old-world sailing ship preparing to set out on her voyage. The intent movements of the crew rippled like muscles all over the white superstructure; some of the sailors were high up in the rigging, black squiggles against the sky.

"A windjammer!" Joe exclaimed, "Do you realise how few of them are left in the world? This one's going out on the evening tide and they're short of a few hands. There you are, lad. Life is yours for the taking!"

John shrank from the overwhelming immediacy of the challenge, from the brisk reality of the tall intimidating ship. He told Joe that arrangements were now being concluded for him to enter the religious life, that his mother that very day had laid out hard-earned money on two sets of clothes for him.

"Ah shag that!" Joe said, "Where's your spirit of adventure lad? Life herself is waiting for you over there and no prayer-books, no rosary beads, no long boring sermons from clergymen can ever give you anything remotely like what she has to offer."

"I have a vocation" he muttered.

"And there she is! Stretch out your arms and take her!"

He stretched out his arm realising with a crazy pang of regret that the ship and the opportunity were long gone. That same evening, probably as he sat down to tea, she had sailed down the Liffey, the white bosoms of her sails rounded out taut before the wind from the west, the rays of the sun coaxing red flames and gold fire from the masts and rigging. Joe had said she was going all the way round South America and then north to Seattle and after that maybe to Australia. A lust for action sprang restlessly into his legs. Where was the ship now? Oh God, where? Craft like that travel so slowly at the mercy of the whims of wind. Had she rounded Cape Horn yet and started the voyage north past Conception and Valparaiso and Lima and all those other South American ports whose names he couldn't remember? Were he able through some miracle to board a plane today he could be on the Pacific Coast before the week was out watching for the high white bosoms driving north towards him before the wind. "Christ, I've got to find that ship!" he exclaimed and scrabbled up the flagstones to clamber to the top of the wall. But where, where was the ship to be found?

He ran along the top of the wall towards the railway bridge frantic lest he never find it. Shouts rose along the shore below him. Was that Dingo's voice calling "Come back, range-rider"? He couldn't be sure, but there was no doubt about that other voice though, rising almost to a scream - The Dep'ty's. "Have you taken leave of your senses? Come back! Come back! Come back John Burke this instant!" But he padded on away from that instant and all the others that belonged to the past, his jacket flapping about him like wild sails in a storm. He clattered up the iron staircase of the bridge and pounded across to the other side. Hearing him running there his mother put the kettle on the gas and turned to lay another place at the table for tea. I've got to find it, he yearned and ran on finding it strange and mad and marvellous that he should be doing just that, chuckling to himself as the shrieking voices began to grow dim behind. But what was all this crazy stuff in his head about finding a ship? He allowed himself to know at last what he was really doing on the joyous spur of the moment. He was taking it on the lam like Maguire and Lynam before him. His heart gave a bound of joy as he raced for the number eight tram to rush him whirring towards the soft bosom, the deep dark eyes, the long slender thrusting legs of the impatient, lustful city and the immortal beauty of mortal girls.

THE WINDOW

Evening again! Frances sighed her acceptance of the mellow light dappling with a hint of early summer on the draining board she was scrubbing down for the third time since tea. She could not dawdle much longer in the tight kitchen for the more she toiled there the closer it came to wearing the fiercely scoured look of the kitchens in Saint Agatha's convent where she had spent six years as a boarder. She dried her hands with careful labour, rubbing the rough towel heavily over one finger after another, squeezing her wedding ring hard when she came to it. How loose it lay on her finger! Could you lose weight from your hands as well? My face is his memorial she thought, holding the reflection of her solemn grey eyes in the mirror on the opposite wall. The charity of the mellow light could not fully deny the shadowy weals smudging from her cheekbones to her sharp chin nor change back the shocked white of her hair to the rich chestnut he had caressed so often. Slowly as one divesting herself of hope she took off her pink apron and hung it behind the door. She set it swinging with a curt pat of her hand and went into the lounge where the click of her heels on the polished boards struck back at her sharply from the walls as if resounding in a much larger room devoid of furniture or life. She took a copy of the *Evening Press* from the coffee table, turned to *Letters to the Editor* and settled herself in an easy chair by the window, opening out the newspaper on her lap. It's evening again, she sighed.

The first of the evening strollers passed, a tall, middle-aged man erect in a blue suit, his head bared and steady in the air as if listening for something. Who knows, a whisper of hope, maybe. Shyly she peered through the curtains as he crossed from her side of the road towards the tobacconist's outside the gates of the park. As he reached the shop a group of young police cadets coming the other way, from the Garda Depot, passed him, their country accents ringing out like desperate cries of defiance in a half-forgotten tongue. The cadets, red-faced and stiff, tramped past on the far side and quickly were gone from view. The courting couples would not begin coming past until a little later. Idly, her glance followed the number nine bus whirring past with hardly a soul aboard to the terminus round the corner and moved back to rest on the sleek black car purring to a discreet stop outside the house. The near door of the long car opened and a pair of shapely legs in expensive flesh-coloured nylon stockings emerged and remained still, one ankle curled over the other, while the woman whose head was hidden by the roof of the car reached her long arm for something on the back seat. The legs moved further out and the woman, tall and elegant, eased herself onto the pavement slamming the car door casually behind her as if quitting herself of a toy that bored her. In a brisk determined stride she crossed the pavement towards the garden gate. Frances's eyes moved hungrily over the arrogant swing of the chinchilla coat, the tight lines of the blue silk dress clinging to the vaguely familiar figure, the steely beauty of the face beneath the fierce backward sweep of the corn-yellow hair. She rose to her feet with a cry of surprise. It was Nora! Dear Nora was coming to see her. She hurried from the room anticipating the rare pleasure of the bell filling the dark hallway with its cascade of silver joy. The ring drilled its joy through her and she paused in her stride to relish it fully before flinging the door wide.

"Nora! Darling! How marvellous to see you!"

She held out her arms to gather to herself the warmth of the years of their close companionship in the convent, the breathless intimacy of their love for each other whispered under the tender shade of the huge oak in the field above the chapel, the firm comradeship of their life together in the flat they shared in Baggot Street until shortly after the time when they each became engaged - coincidentally, as they were delighted to discover, on the very same evening. Before she could grasp what was happening Nora had sidled briskly past her outstretched arms and was standing fumbling with her silver-clasped handbag in the hall. She turned and grasped Nora's hands gazing at her through a welcome haze of tears,

"Nora, you haven't changed a bit!"

She looked away in a pang of envy from the unlined beauty of her friend's face and gestured her into the lounge.

"Sit down! Sit down, dear! Oh it's grand to see you again," Her hand flickered towards the light switch and dropped quickly to her side. Turning as she spoke the short, disjointed phrase that came into her mind she slewed her chair round so that her back was to the mellow glow of the window. She realised she was taking in none of the conventional phrases Nora was lobbing back at her at intervals like polite requests for attention.

"Oh! It's been ages, ages!" she said, not listening to the murmured replies and comments clinging desperately to the sweet welter of memories that had come flooding into the house with Nora. Somewhere behind them moved the shadow of Joseph. She could almost feel his dear breath on her cheek again. But the sight of Nora settling back on the faded couch in the hated familiarity of her room - she had aged about the eyes, her famed hair was dyed - hearing the cold beat of footsteps going past the house, she lay back with a long sigh feeling the warmth and excitement of the past slipping like water through her greedy fingers. The past was dead. Nothing would ever come back from there. Hope lay on neither side of the dark pool of numb anguish that was always the present.

"Oh Nora!" she said looking at the carpet, "If you only knew!" Tears eased out of her eyes like guilty secrets.

"As I said a moment ago, I heard only recently," Nora said fumbling with the clasps of her bag, "It was a terrible shock. And he so young too. Younger even than Paddy."

"Thirty-eight! Just thirty-eight, a year older than me."

Nora made a sympathetic cluck into the gaping bag and drew out a silver cigarette case. "The heart, wasn't it? By the way, still not smoking?"

She nodded, swallowing the lump in her throat.

"He used to get this breathlessness, you know" she began slowly as if thinking her way into a complex problem of extreme consequence. "He first noticed it in the office when he had to take files upstairs. One evening when we went for a walk in the park, only as far as the Gough monument, he got into a terrible state like a man with a severe attack of what looked like asthma and I had to get a cab to take him home. Of course, neither of us knew what it was, for he was a terror about doctors ever since - you know - the time we lost the baby."

"I never knew that!" Nora jerked her unlit cigarette awkwardly from her lips.

"Ah yes. I was in a nursing home, one of the best and most expensive, and Joseph always claims that when they handed the baby to him to hold for a minute, it was quite all right. A lovely little boy! And even hair. Soft black hair. But then the doctor said he wasn't happy about its breathing and gave it an injection."

"Oh good Christ!" Nora said in her old forthright manner.

"Anyway, that's why Joseph wouldn't go next nor near them even after his asthma - for that's what we thought it was - got worse especially at night. He kept on trying different bottles for it, the cures and the tonics you see advertised and even ones specially made up by the chemists themselves. And then one day going upstairs with an armful of files at the office he collapsed. By the time they got him to Saint Vincent's he was dead."

In the silence Frances saw the motifs in the carpet

shift about restlessly like the terrible events of that day - Frank Naylor, Joseph's boss, standing trembling in the hall like a man with the ague, grey buildings falling past the window of the hurtling car, a heavily rouged woman laughing on the edge of the pavement as they went round Trinity College wall, Joseph with a coy smile on his grey lips stretched in a narrow bed. At a slight sound she glanced up and saw Nora grimacing a yawn to its close and remembering her friend could never stand being in a stuffy room for long she sprang up and said:

"Let me get you a cup of tea!"

"No thanks, Frankie girl, sure I can only stay a brief minute. Even less! You know the sort of rush we live in, Paddy and me. I'd have been in to see you before but you know what it is with him, something always coming up to make terrible demands on your time."

"Ah yes!" she nodded her head, "Still I suppose you can't complain when you see how well he's done for himself. Who'd ever have thought when he came round frozen from his digs where his landlady let the fire burn down after seven o'clock, that one day he'd end up owning McSwiney's." She peered in covert envy at her friend's expensively fashionable clothes.

"Of course" Nora's face creased more than it used in a smile, "I wouldn't say no to a nip of the hard stuff if you have a drop handy in the place."

Frances winced at the guilt she felt flushing her cheeks. "To tell the truth, Nora," and she felt it best to do so for her friend could always read her thoughts, "I'm afraid it wouldn't be really safe for me to have it in the house. Joseph and I were such home birds. After we married we sort of dropped out of things simply because we never felt the need to see other people. Socially that is. We lost touch with our friends and so the evenings here for me are terribly long, interminable, eternities you might say of - nothing. And when I was cleaning out the cupboard a few weeks after he died I came across this bottle of Jameson's whiskey he'd had since the previous Christmas. Just to pass the time, to deaden the loneliness a bit, I sat down with a drink and do you know, the bottle didn't last two days. I was so frightened, I haven't touched a drop since." Her spirit sighed in a silent eventless limbo all through the long yawn of silence which grew between them.

"And - er - how are you managing?" Nora asked, easing her long white hand out of her sleeve until her watch sneaked into view on her slender wrist.

"I've got this temporary job with Tolka Assurance. Between you and me it's, well - terrible. I'm jammed into a little cubicle with no windows and not a soul speaks to me from the time I go in until I come out again. Company, just common or garden, passing-the-time-of-day company, that's what I miss, I sometimes wish I could get a job in one of the big shops where I'd be meeting people all day long. It wouldn't matter a damn what we'd talk about. It'd take me out of myself and God knows that's what I need most of all now I think."

"I'm afraid Paddy's laying off staff."

Frances blushed again and turned away to find an ashtray. "Oh I didn't mean McSwiney's Nora. Please don't think that!"

"I know you didn't" Nora said easily, "I was just pointing out that business in general doesn't seem to be too bright at the moment. There's not much doing anywhere."

Frances saw her move her cigarette from her mouth, the gold wristwatch gleaming in the amber light from the window. She should have opened the window a few minutes ago when Nora yawned. She rose and as she undid the catch she saw that the lovers were moving towards the park, the couple immediately outside the window held their heads bent, the smoke from their cigarettes flowing back over their shoulders like blue wispy scarves. "Do you ever see any of the old crowd now?" she asked coming back from the window.

"None at all. Sure, I live in a completely different world now." Nora's head shook shortly from side to side with the dint of all she had to contend with.

"I was hoping only the other day I'd run into some of the old crowd. Remember Mary Hyland, and Jennie Yeats - dear mad Jennie - and Patsy Sheerin? Any idea what happened to them, where they might be?"

"Not a clue!" Nora began to light a fresh cigarette with the glowing butt of the other. "When I smoke this I'll have to go" she said in her old forthright way.

"That's a pity" Frances sighed, "You know, when I was thinking of the old crowd I wondered would there be any chance of us all getting together for a night out."

In the silence she heard the urgent ticking of Nora's watch.

"Of course" she continued when the silence yawned into every corner of the room, "I suppose you're too busy to come out of an evening."

"Me? Oh indeed I am. And sick of it all." She pursed her lips and flicked ash from her dress, "Of course though I knew Paddy was go-ahead when I married him, I'd no idea he'd be anything like he is today. You just can't imagine the mad rush it is from morning till night. Do you know, he never makes a decision without first consulting me? There I am at home scolding the impossible servants so as to have everything just right for another of his interminable dinner-parties when right in the middle of it all he comes on the phone with; "How do you think Danish kitchen furniture would go next season?" or "Do you think there's any future in false hair for men?" Then before he rings off he tells me three extra people are coming - upsetting all the previous planning you see - manufacturers from Manchester maybe or - like we had last week - some fellows with a new line in jam all the way from Bulgaria." She stubbed her long cigarette in the ashtray and stood up. "Oh Frankie" she sighed, smoothing her dress round her ample hips with her palms, "How marvellous it would be if you and me were to have a day out together! Ah, how bloody marvellous!"

Frances nodded, touched by the girlish wistfulness of the warm voice.

"Just like old times it would be" Nora mused a distant look in her wide eyes. "Coffee in Roberts', a window shop in Grafton Street with a long wander around Switzer's, a few drinks in Davy Byrnes, a MacLiammoir show maybe, but definitely dinner in Jammet's. Ah, that'd be the day with all the time in the world for a good old gossip about all the people we knew.

And about that weirdest thing of all - life! But it can't be done, girl, it just can't be done. I'm a slave, or even worse," she smiled sadly, "You could say a victim sacrificed on the altar of my husband's social and commercial success."

"It was a nice thought just the same," Frances wondered about the undertone of bitterness or was it even contempt in her last remark, "And it was very good of you to come see me, very good indeed and you so busy."

"Oh not at all, Frankie. Sure, I'm only sorry I didn't hear at the time. It was only recently, a few weeks ago in fact, that someone chanced to remark that it was such a pity about poor Joseph and I asked: "Joseph who?" And that's how I heard the news."

Frances leaned forward and kissed her on the cheek. "Sure I understand, dear."

Nora gathered up her bag and went out into the dim hallway her hand faltering towards the catch on the door-lock.

"No let me" Frances said not remembering and switching on the light. She came in front of Nora who flashed her a smile which slowly wilted and died on her face. Her hand rose to her gaping mouth on which her smile came back as if at the touch of her fingers.

"In spite of it all, Frankie," she said "You're looking quite well."

"No I'm not. Lost my girlish laughter and much, much more besides."

"Still, you just have to look on the bright side." Her hand moved as if to pat her cheek and fell quickly to her side.

"It was lovely seeing you." She went out of the door and into the porch where she paused over her interlaced fingers as if trying to recall something.

"By the way" she said looking down at her gleaming, spotless shoes, "You might he able to do something for me."

"Yes, dear. Of course, what is it?"

"Well, I don't quite know how to put this" Nora fumbled her cigarette case out of her bag, "Don't get me wrong, Paddy's a wonderful man, you know, a truly wonderful man. Only with him it's business, business all the time, even...! And of course you daren't have any friends in except the ones he chooses. He's terribly jealous, you see. Of everything. You'd be astounded at the trivial things that make him jealous." She paused, tossed her beautifully kept head back with a brave smile and sighed. "So the point is you get very lonely for - well - just for conversation. And then all of a sudden there was this man and one day when coming out of a hotel not a thousand miles from here what did we do but walk slap-bang into a pal of Paddy's,"

Nora is still sixteen, she thought, sour with dismay. She felt the dumb appeal in Nora's eyes before they narrowed over the task of lighting her cigarette.

"I hoped this fellow hadn't really noticed or at least would think so little of it to say nothing to Paddy, and time passed, and everything seemed to be all right. And then, just last week, Paddy came out with it. He'd been to the doctor again with his stomach upset and he looked awful. He caught me right off-guard as we were coming down in the lift from the Dress Department. "Who's that man you were with?" I didn't know what to say. "It was Joseph Smith" I said."

"What? You said what?"

"Oh I know!" Nora shook her head in acknowledgement of her fault, "But it was out before I knew what I was going to say. Oh, I felt awful when I realised I'd mentioned poor Joseph."

"Had you heard about him at that time?"

"Of course not," Nora said quickly, "And I kept wondering afterwards why I said it until I remembered that Joseph and you lived more or less just around the corner from the hotel I'd been in with the - man. You know, just having a quiet drink in the bar."

Nora's cigarette left her hand in a comet of sparks as she reached out and drew Frances to her, leaning her scented head against the point of her shoulder.

"Oh I felt awful, Frankie. Awful, really! You do forgive me, don't you dear?"

Her forehead pressed into Frances's shoulder as if no time had intervened since they were schoolgirls exchanging confidences and confessions under the cool green umbrella of the oak tree in the field above the chapel.

"Of course I do, Nora!" Her hand moved and hesitated above her friend's head which was so clean, so well-cared for, smelling so freshly expensive even the caress of the evening breeze seemed an affront.

"You couldn't help it" she soothed, "As you say, it slipped out before you knew what you were saying."

"Oh thank you, dear. Thank you. I knew in my heart you'd understand." Nora hugged her warmly to her and she felt the old sweet flow of sympathy and fond indulgence her friend could always awake in her. How incredibly long since such feelings had touched her spirit!

"And then Paddy asked me," Nora hesitated and looked steadily into her eyes, "what I was seeing Joseph for. All this time we were in the lift - going down! I had to think very quick indeed so I said I had invited him for a drink in the lunch-hour at that hotel - you know - to ask some advice for a girl I knew who was moving to Northern Ireland and wanted to know the most painless way of exporting her furniture and her car."

"Lucky you thought of that." Frances murmured discovering to her surprise that under the scar of the past there still lurked a tweak of guilt for the lies Nora had told with intense sincerity to Sister Charles. "It was only out of politeness we spoke to those boys. They were German tourists asking the way to Drogheda where they wanted to have a look at Oliver Plunkett's head in the church there."

"With Paddy you always have to think like lightning," Nora smiled over the lies of the present, running her hand softly through Frances's hair, "God, Frances you were always so dependable, so obliging, so terribly good to me. 'Bye, dear!" Her lips brushed lightly over Frances's cheek. She smiled and went down the garden path towards the gate pausing there reflectively as if there was something still on her mind.

"Goodbye dear, nice of you to have called," Frances said from the porch her hands clasped over her stomach.

Nora did not seem to have heard. She stood silent, her hand on the top of the gate, sparkling with rings, moving the creaky iron frame to and fro as if testing for ease of movement. "By the way," she said, enunciating each word with desperate clarity, "Just in case Paddy should drop in one evening - you know what he's like when he gets an idea into his head - would you mind saying that you knew Joseph was helping me with some customs problem?"

Frances swallowed down her dismay.

"All right, Nora!"

"You're a brick, always were honey!"

The car door slammed and the long sleek vehicle hissed away in the direction of the park. Frances watched the baleful winking of the tail-light as it paused a moment and pulsed round the corner out of sight. She went into the house and on through the lounge to the window. Life had ebbed from the evening light and a range of black clouds immensely high in the sky were slowly spreading a grey pallor over the street. Any moment now the evening lamps would awaken into globes of light at the top of their slim columns and there would be the immensity of two whole hours before her final cup of cocoa, two arrowroot biscuits, and the loneliness of her bed. On the opposite pavement two lovers paced towards the dark privacy of the park, the young man with a raincoat folded carefully over his arm, the girl smoking a cigarette in quick puffs. They did not speak to each other as they moved onward, an urgency in the lines of their bodies their slow pace appeared to contradict. Frances found her face was wet with tears.

James Manning

"I'll always tell lies for you," she sobbed "But couldn't you have left my dear dead man out of it? How could you think of my Joseph as Just another alibi?"

A CASE OF CONSCIENCE

The woman Dinnie was assisting down the slope out of Westland Row Station stumbled again and jarred the heel of her shoe against his shin. The new hot centre of pain jolted his attention from the relentless throbbing in his feet, the tearing aches in the muscles of his arms and back.

"Oh I do declare, Mr Russell," the woman spoke in a high Keener's wail, "I'm after goin' and doin' it agin, amn't I? What'll you be thinkin' o' me at all I wonder!"

"Nothin' at all," said Dinnie forcing his good-old-skin's laugh, "Sure comin' back from a holy pilgrimage isn't the very best time to start thinkin' about a woman's legs."

The woman hopped on her good leg and trilled an excited laugh in his ear. She placed her free hand against the wall to steady herself while Dinnie tugged her other arm tighter over his shoulder.

"You're a caution, Mr Russell. "We'd've been lost on the pilgrimage without you there to keep our spirits up with the odd oul laugh."

"It's Father McGurk who'll be havin' the laugh if he comes down and finds us like this. He'll say it's very early in the day for a man an' a woman to be clingin' together on the slippery slope."

The woman's laughter drew her closer into the support of his arm. Her soft, cushioned body shook against his hip. For the first time in three days Dinnie allowed himself cautiously to think of his wife. That was quite in order now for the period of prayer, fasting, and spiritual meditation was over - all but the shouting anyway - and there was nothing wrong in recognising the return of the crawling itch of desire, the wordless yearning for the warm enfolding of firm, white limbs. He had missed his regular Saturday night but later in the evening, when he got through totting up the accounts, there would be time to take care of that. As a sort of fringe benefit the annual pilgrimage always provided two Saturday nights in the same week. Above him he heard the heavy clanking of the train leaving the station. Great fragments of hissing sound bounced with a metallic ring from the soot-streaked walls and scattered in acrid tremblings through the air. Dinnie closed his eyes against the buffeting of the noises and followed the lurch of the train out onto the bridge until the storm of clanking and puffing fell to a quiet rhythm which faded into the individual morning stirrings from the street below.

"That sounded like the divil's partin' shot," he joked to the woman. "All right then, ma'am. Let's see if we can't waltz the rest of the way down. One, two, three!"

By dint of hopping and tugging they came down to the level of the station entrance and emerged into the street where Dinnie freed his stiffening arm to hail a taxi.

"You've been so good, Mr Russell," said the woman whom he still held close to him trying, but not too hard, not to notice the glow of pleasure his act of assisting her was affording his body as well as his soul.

"'S'all in the day's work, Missis - I didn't catch your name."

"Cannon. Mrs Eileen Cannon."

"Well, Eileen Allanah, it really was a great pleasure to be of some assistance to you. Will there be anyone in the house when you get home?"

"Me eldest daughter, just turned fourteen'll be there to give me a hand. She's just left school an' I don't know what to put her to. All the crosses you have to bear in this world!"

"Send her to a commercial college. Knock all the silly ideas out of her head. Businessmen is always on the lookout for well-trained girls from respectable families, good-livin' girls, honest, and trustworthy."

A taxi drew up at the kerb. The driver threw a shrewd glance at them and leaned nonchalantly through the window to snap open the rear door. As Dinnie helped her to her seat the woman called out an address in Kimmage West. He made one of the lightning calculations of which he was justly proud and slipped three half-crowns into the taxi driver's limp hand.

"Now you shouldn't have done that, Mr Russell," the woman said with a warm smile, "It's too kind you are! Sure you poor man, you must be half-dead and you practically carryin' me since this time yesterday when I knocked me oul varicose vein against that stone on the mountain."

"Never mind about me, Allanah. Sure I was only doin' what I was there for, helpin' me fella pilgrims. An' wasn't the whole thing great value? Pains, aches, bare feet, no sleep, fastin' an' all. Father McOurk was right when he said we made the divil gnash his teeth good an' proper this year. An' did you hear what he said after that, on the railway station before we left? Says he, since they're the divil's teeth we're talkin' about, you can bet your bottom dollar they're false."

They laughed looking in each others' eyes, and whatever the woman began to say about Father McGurk was lost in the revving of the taxi which nosed out into the stream of traffic with her leaning obliquely out of the window, clutching the bottom of the frame with her hand on which Dinnie noticed two rather expensive diamond rings which hadn't been there yesterday. Slipped them on in the train no doubt. She waved and he realised that all the time on the pilgrimage he had been thinking of her as a somewhat older woman. He was surprised to see that like himself she was only in her early forties. Framed in her shining brownish hair, her pert face held a mute appeal which half-formed a question in his mind. He waved back wondering where in Kimmage West was the road on which she lived. Who could tell, it might even be close enough to his retail branch out there for her to be one of his customers, which she wouldn't realise as he had said nothing that would help her to connect his name with the Cash-value Stores. His body still remembered her soft contours. A nice woman, he adjudged, good-living, the kind who wouldn't run up a huge bill and take her custom somewhere else without paying it. His body insisted a faint yearning for her. Luck might have it that she'd stroll into that branch next week when he was out there doing the monthly stocktaking to ensure that after sales, wages, overheads, breakages, lifting, and bad debts had all been taken into account he still got his clear twelve-per-cent out of it. She was completely different from his wife. He couldn't imagine her meeting him when he came home tired in the evening with a string of wailing complaints about nothing at all and going around screaming her head off at the children wearing that same old tattered apron that he bought her five years ago. It would be nice to meet that woman again, have a few laughs for a change, look into her warm eyes and hear that breathless voice in his ear. He sighed. The divil's parting shot was not what he heard in the station, it was what was happening now in the yearning of his body. That would have to stop. There could never be anything like that between them for as soon as you started chasing women in Dublin the whole town found out about it and that sort of thing never did your business any good. It became somewhat harder to get credit.

"Is it yourself I see there?" a voice called.

Father McGurk in the company of three young women was bustling towards him from the station entrance.

"Hello, Father! Ladies!"

"The hero of the hour himself! I was hoping for another word with you Mr Russell before you left. I wanted to thank you on behalf of us all for the wonderful help you gave on the pilgrimage. Rarely have we seen such selfless devotion. Isn't that right, ladies?"

The women, surprisingly fresh and smart after all they had been through spoke all at once, their voices light, silvery, and - why not? - exciting!

"Last year," the priest went on, "the organisation was atrocious, but this year thanks to you, everything was wonderful. I'm sorry though that you had to stand all the way back in the draughty corridor of the train."

"Sure I had to," Dinnie dared a wicked grin, "What would you have thought of me if I'd travelled all the way back with one of these charming ladies sittin' on me knee?"

Father McGurk struggled with a whining laugh which broke from him in dry spurts. A flutter of delicate movements passed over the women, one of whom, a heavy red-cheeked woman in her early thirties, rubbed her palms vigorously on her thighs. She had such perfectly-formed breasts that Dinnie instantly recalled a conversation he had overheard between McArdle and Nolan, two of his travellers in the loft at the stores. It was about real dairies and false bottle tops and it had taken him some time to grasp that they were swapping notes on how to tell whether you were looking at the natural contours of a woman's bosom or merely a highly-padded brassiere. Still driving out his good-old-skin's laugh he thumbed his eye over the girl's breasts which looked soft and richly authentic. He licked his lips and found them dry and envious. The grocery trade dealt in necessities, but brassieres were items that were in constant demand by the entire female population for the age of thirteen or fourteen up. And the margin of profit in the rag trade even for a wholesaler couldn't be less than fifteen-per-cent and might even go up to twenty-five. He wondered what those things cost and what the competition was like in that business.

"There's no mistake about it," said Father McGurk, "the life and soul of the pilgrimage you were, Mr Russell."

To indicate that his coming remark was to he taken seriously Dinnie frowned truculently. "All I say is thanks be to God that everything worked out so well. It's the best pilgrimage I've been on since that one during the war when practically everythin' went wrong, includin' the train runnin' out of fuel an' strandin' us in the back of beyond in the divil's own rainstorm. That was a real stinger. You felt that every new cross you had to bear was doin' your poor oul soul no end of good."

A taxi whispered to a halt at the kerb.

"Can I drop you off at your warehouse?" the priest asked.

"No thanks, Father. I always walk it after a pilgrimage. It sort of breaks me in gently to the shocks of business life."

Father McGurk bundled the girls into the taxi. As it began to fuss into line in the stream of traffic he thrust his head out of the window. He wore a solemn expression as if the serious note Dinnie had introduced into the brief conversation still echoed in him.

"I'll be dropping down to see you about that other matter one evening, Mr Russell. Is there any special night you're out?"

"I'm always home," Dinnie called across at him,

"workin' on me accounts. You know, tryin' to keep me nose above water."

Removing his steward's arm-band he stood for a moment gazing after the taxi. Then he crossed into Pearse Street and headed west towards his place of business. The morning air, crisp and salt-tanged was as light and fresh as the persistent wind on the bare mountain which had blown into the dark, cob-webbed corners of his soul. Despite their raw points of pain his feet sparkled along the pavement as he went into his firm, sturdy stride, hissing *Hail Glorious Saint Patrick* between his teeth in a heavy march tempo. He always enjoyed to the full this insulated hiatus between the rigors of the annual pilgrimage and the daily struggle to make ends meet. He strode on deigning to look at the windows of the grocery stores on either side of the street. He would be plunged all too soon into the heat of the struggle where a lightning glance at any given window would tell how well or how ill his competitors were faring against him. The hunger pangs prowling through his insides and yearning in his mouth were imbued with an angry life of their own that it was exciting to face and control. He hissed the melody of his happiness between his teeth. But the greatest joy he carried feather-footed with him was the certitude that the burdens he had been carrying half-acknowledged for years, the shadowy pressures on his soul whose source he had dodged round in equivocal, general statements fortunately never probed into in previous confessions, particularly the dread (though secretly exciting) guilt of the black market sugar deals of last spring, had all been raised miraculously from his spirit and scattered to the rinsing winds of the bleak mountain. Father

McGurk whom he had never confessed to before had been so reasonable, so surprisingly realistic about it all that while he was murmuring his absolution, Dinnie had great difficulty in refraining from blurting out: "God, Father, what a bloody great businessman is lost in you!"

That was when it was all over. But there had been many moments of terror in the cold, constricted confessional when the priest eased into his soul with amazingly shrewd questions and waited in bland silence as he blundered towards the answers. Most of which thankfully he reached in time. Significant parts of some he hadn't remembered till afterwards though that was all right for at the time of confessing his intention had been good. He was contrite, and encouraged by Father McGurk's gentle voice he had striven sincerely to tell the whole truth. But then again who can say what the truth really is? Some questions were so tangled up with so many, complicated, half-forgotten details that had he persisted in trying to unravel them all for the priest he might have confused the poor man and given him the unfortunate impression that he was dealing with a soft-minded, over-scrupulous, half-wit. Yet all things considered it was a good and as complete a general confession as even the Pope himself could have been expected to make under the circumstances. He was certain of that in his heart. Which in the future would be more vigilant and not so easily induced to sin. The priest's bald spot had loomed like a miniature moon through the mesh of the confessional screen and Dinnie's heart turned over in sympathy at the sight of him bowed under the weight of the sins of the world. Striding on down the street he listened to what he had retained of the priest's words and strove to recapture the magical moment of the first lift of relief in his soul. "Ah, yes, no doubt about it, the war years were most trying on us all," - thankfully the priest's voice was reassuringly gentle - "particularly for you with the worry of having to bring up eight children, no nine - imagine me forgetting Bernadette and the fun we had that day after the christening - and of course the responsibility of running both a wholesale and a retail business at one and the same time. The peculiar economic circumstances brought on by the war exposed you to more moral stresses and temptations in a few years than the average man meets in a lifetime. It was contrary to the moral law, of course, for you to deny goods that were justly theirs to your wholesale customers and to sell those same goods at special prices in your retail stores. And, of course, it was wrong too to sell sugar on the black market. Since the commodity was on ration - it still is in fact - it must be clear to you that as a result of your act, some people somewhere had to go without their just supplies. Business of this nature places the soul in great moral danger. And did you ever stop to consider the trouble it might get you into with the State? Or the distress it might cause your family if you were found out? Or the deleterious effect it might have on your business reputation? I am sure - indeed I know - you are sincerely sorry for all this and good though that is in itself, it does not resolve you of the grave moral responsibility of having to make just restitution. But the problem here is how are you going to do that? Since all this happened during the five or six years of the war shortages, and since you haven't the records nor, I imagine, the time to delve into individual cases, the best way to ease your conscience, the right way to make a general sort of restitution would be for you to donate a generous sum to a deserving charity. You might think about that. And I'll drop around one evening and maybe we can put our heads together on it. And now, the Act of Contrition..."

Dinnie plodded on, his head set firmly back on his sturdy shoulders, his firm lips moving through the cleansing words of the prayer and then he closed his eyes briefly to feel on his forehead, through his crisp hair, the play of the fresh morning breeze which brought back the exhilaration of the open mountain and the stark joy of striving upwards into the misted heights towards the balm of God's forgiving grace. Gradually, of themselves, his eyes turned to the windows of the shops so that to frustrate their eager probing he raised his gaze to the signboards repeating to himself the names and numbers, left and right, as he passed down the street. There weren't many grocery stores, he noted, but none of the few he encountered had ever appeared on his books for anything, not even for a bad debt to be placed in the capable hands of Stubbs and Company. A slight ripple of annoyance puckered the surface of his calm joy. After three days of soul-scouring, of selfless commitment to the rigors of the pilgrimage, the familiar urgent current running along his nerves was a strangely fresh and reassuring feeling, rather like a friendly wave welcoming him back to the hectic world of everyday events. But he would have to keep a firm grip on himself. In his quiet persuasive way Father McGurk had convinced him that his predominant passion was anger. "So far as salvation is concerned, anger is a real bad debt" he chuckled through the grille. If only he had a man like him out travelling for him! He quickened his pace, framing a remark he would make with a wry grin to his present team of travellers, something to the effect that though they might not he exactly lying down on the job, there were enough lost business opportunities in Pearse Street to suggest that they weren't in a mad gallop to keep ahead of their competitors. The broad wedge of his face reddened by the sun glared at him from a shop window and he grinned at catching himself out. There was no sense in playing games any longer. He was tingling with excitement to be plunged into the heave and hurry of business and there was no profit in pretending he wasn't. At that instant he was passing a bookshop in one window of which he saw the portrait of a portly man like a publican wearing a coal-heaver's sweeping-brush moustache. He recognised him as one of the leaders of the 1916 Rising, but though he had often seen pictures and accounts of those men in newspapers he had never been sufficiently interested to relate their names to their faces. "What the hell are we celebratin' now?" he wondered and saw that the portrait was wreathed round with grey, paperbound copies of a book entitled *Labour in Irish History.* He vented a derisive chuckle and passed on thinking about his employees and speculating uneasily on how his affairs had been conducted in his absence. "Labour!" he chuckled to keep his spirits up, "If there's one thing you won't find in the Irish or their history, it's labour. Sure the most of them never heard of it. Or if they did, it's always something done by somebody else. Never by them."

He was still chuckling as he waited at the mouth of Townsend Street to allow past a stream of motor traffic and a horse-drawn dray which clattered away with the heart-clutching echo of Castlebar on a fair-day morning. He stared after it his stomach rumbling. The drab figure on the driving seat might have been old Dan Russell himself driving back from the disaster of another fair to his failing farm and his silent, blank-eyed children. "No idea of business!" Dinnie shuddered, "Taken in by everyone. If you've a soft heart take a job with the Government or the Vincent de Paul where you can give away someone else's money." He thrust down the snarling hunger prowling impatiently within him and made to step out on the road. A blurred object skipped past almost catching his hip. "'Zactly like you!" sang a familiar voice and he saw Willie Nolan, one of his store hands, tearing away from him on a racing bicycle devoid of mudguards, his head low over the handlebars, his grey-flannelled buttocks writhing from side to side in the air like what he'd rather not think about. A whip of anger lashed through him. "Well damn the atrocious cheek of him anyway," he muttered, glancing at his watch. "Half-an-hour late for work! God, imagine how injured he'd be, imagine the bad name he'd give me, if I docked that from his wages!" Clenching his strong teeth, he forced down the hot uprush of his anger. "When the cat's away, I suppose... he joked, yearning back his mood of detached calm. He crossed the street, his eye on Nolan weaving in broad, waltzing swerves round buses and cars from one of which a fist appeared and shook in the wake of his grey writhing buttocks. He gave a derisive chuckle. Why should he allow an idiot like that to rush him into the sin of anger and rob him so soon of the spiritual fruits to gain which he had endured so much pain, discomfort and hunger on the pilgrimage? "There goes the whole history of Irish labour," he grinned after the weaving figure, "Half-blind to what's goin' on around it, and anywhere else except where it should be to earn the money it's paid."

He strode up Fleet Street, the ache of a fixed grin on his face, heading westward, parallel to the river, a route on which he had several substantial accounts. Some of the freshness, the sparkle of promise, had drained from the morning and his feet began to ache again as if blisters were rising on those points of his skin where his bare feet had come into abrupt contact with the sharp stones of the mountain. Farrington's, a business whose account with him averaged a hundred-and-fifteen a week, loomed up on his left and he looked hungrily into the window at last acknowledging the anxiety he had held in abeyance since leaving the station. His strong teeth clicked together in a grunt of vexation. The back, right-hand section of the display space in the window was stacked high with white-and-gold family-size packets of Corn Kracknels. Not one packet of Wheateens, his own line, was to be seen even on the shelves in the interior of the store! He plodded on dodging the stab of Farrington's eye which yearned out at what he must have thought was a prospective customer. "Probably one of his girls sweet on Noonan's traveller ordered all that junk when Farrington was out," he hoped, "Just a lucky shot, that's all. An' the best o' luck to them all if she gets pregnant." But the next shop and three others after it had each a lavish display of Noonan's lurid line and when he reached Capel Street his aching feet could hardly carry him on any further for every grocery store window bore its miniature skyscraper of white-and-gold packets, each with its golden picture of its golden product bordered with the brand name in jazzy golden letters. "God, Noonan must've had a fantastic week last week," he breathed incredulously, "Maybe I shouldn't have gone! How's he managin' it? Givin' away a blonde free with every dozen packets?"

As he turned into Mary's Abbey the wind came at him from the east flicking a vicious sting in its tail. He went past a carter sitting on the front of his cart below an emerald pyramid of cabbages, drinking steaming tea from a blue-rimmed Delft mug and biting avidly into a doorstep-thick slice of black-crusted bread. Hunger reared up and roared within him. He could neither eat nor drink until after twelve o'clock, but never mind his hunger now, never mind the festering pain in the soles of his feet. The important thing was somehow to light a fire, a rocket under his travellers, something to get them to burst into action and ram his Wheateens into every shop in the city. He came in sight of his warehouse and paused on the opposite pavement, squaring his sturdy shoulders, gathering his flagging energies for the day ahead. "Well this is it," he gritted his teeth, "Seconds out of the ring! Time!" As he crossed to the stores he remembered Father McGurk's sermon and dedicated all the thoughts and actions of his working day to God. "A great idea! Maybe He can make a better fist of it than me. For look at the useless gang I have workin' for me! Irish labour, I ask you!"

His warm possessive pride in his warehouse, a concrete, two-storied structure, suffered an affront when he saw what the street urchins had been up to over the week-end. They had returned to their old game of shying mud, cabbage stumps, and horse manure at the sign over the broad open entrance to the building. And from the clutter of filth concentrated on and near the 'O's of WHOLESALE GROCER it was clear that these had once again served as bulls' eyes. Dinnie clicked his teeth in disgust, "A bloody good hiding is what they need," he affirmed and plodded into the drive bearing with him the grim solace that later on Nolan would be out there on the top of a ladder with a scrubbing brush and a bucket of warm water - no, cold water. He came into the body of the stores, a huge square of unrelieved grey concrete with a gallery, reached by two separate staircases, running round the four sides overlooking a large area in the middle on which pale light filtered down through the wire mesh covering two large sections of frosted glass set into the roof. In a shaft of light from the windows stood his dark-blue Ford van around which were grouped cardboard boxes and wooden crates containing the orders collected late on Friday and on Saturday morning. It was with some surprise that he saw his four travellers writing price changes into their notebooks at the broad deal counter which ran for several yards parallel to the right-hand wall. They looked up at him with set intent faces. Kinahane, his Manager, came from behind the van, a docket in his hand, and stood silent before him, the expression on his face wary and questioning.

"Wus a good pilgrimage," Dinnie nodded to him, "And what's MacArdle, Egan, and the other two still here for? They should he out on the road even if it's only to have a gawk at the Kracknels Noonan is stickin' in everywhere."

"Wright rang up Saturday. Jam's goin' up sometime this

week. Seein' the place upstairs is packed out with it I told the lads to wait until you came in to see if we're goin' to push it as usual or play it down."

"God, Jack, can't you take a simple decision like that by yourself yet? What'll yous be askin' me to do next? Hold yous out? O.K.," he called to the travellers, "As of now we've no jam, or not more than a dozen each to special customers. But hold on a minute, I want a word with yous before you go."

He turned and appraised Kinahane from under his eyelids.

"Everythin' all right when I was away?"

"Yis! Didn't get finished here until after three on Saturday. There was a bit of a nark on."

"There'd be a bigger nark if they'd no work to come to. An' was everyone in on time in the mornin' on Friday? Saturday? Today?"

"Oh yis!"

Dinnie smiled benignly at him and went towards his fawn store coat which hung from a nail in the wall behind the counter. The barefaced lies they came out with, people you had every right to trust. But then as Father McGurk said in his sermon Christ moved in a world of deceit and betrayal, and in the end all men discover that they can depend on no one but the Almighty. He pulled on his coat and leaned on the counter looking from one to the other of his travellers.

"I don't know what you fellas are doin' on the road at all," he said keeping his tones casual, "Look at those boxes of orders over there, not two quids worth in any of them!"

"Was hard goin' last week" Fegan shook his mousey face at him, "Specially Friday an' Saturday. There wasn't a penny stirrin'."

"I'll tell you what was stirrin'" Dinnie brought the flat of his hand down on the counter, "Noonan's men were stirrin'! Corn Kracknels is bulgin' out the windows of every shop in town. What's the matter with yous all? Can't yous move me Wheateens for me?"

MacArdle pinched the end of his thin nose. "It's very hard to get them in at the price we're askin'. They tell us Kracknels is sixpence cheaper, gives a better margin o' profit, an' the public likes them because you can eat them with cold milk. Unless you put scalding hot milk on Wheateens, they say, they cut the kids' mouths they're so sharp and crispy-like."

"God, you ought to be workin' for Noonan," Dinnie shook his head, "It wasn't you by any chance that spread the rumour that I got the agency for the Wheateens because no one else in the trade would touch them on account of them bein' laid up in a warehouse on the docks since the end o' the war an' were all stale?"

"Of course not," MacArdle's sharp nose stood white in his darkening face.

"The price is the trouble," Fry said in his usual gulping way. "After all, sixpence cheaper makes a lot of difference."

"I wouldn't care if they were ten bob cheaper," Dinnie's face grew hot as the words hurled out of him, "Wheateens is a better product. Do you know what I get on them? Threepence a dozen! An' out of that I have to pay your wages, your commissions, the overheads, the breakages, the bad debts and God knows what else."

He paused and rooted in his trousers' pocket for his handkerchief. Was his face hot because he was angry? Or was it because he was telling a blatant lie? He was back in a familiar situation, burning with unbidden anger, taut with unbearable tensions almost to the point of snapping in two. He pushed the feeling aside. How simple, how fresh, how clear as the morning light everything had been on the mountain and in the confessional with Father McGurk! He blew his nose rocking his head from side to side. It wasn't really a lie. It was the sort of half-truth you had to tell in business, otherwise you wouldn't last a day. And besides, what right had his travellers to know exactly what his profit was? Anyway, the things you said in business were all just part of the game. You couldn't start applying what Father McGurk called the moral law to them. Whatever that meant. He reflected a bitter moment on his profit margin of a shilling a dozen on the Wheateens. "All right," he sighed, suffering a pang as if some essential, vital part of himself was being torn raw and screaming from his soul, "Knock fourpence a dozen off the Wheateens. We'll sell them at a loss just to be shut of the bloody things. An' if you think it'll help, drop the word that jam's goin' up. They can have three dozen pots o' jam for every case of Wheateens. But no dice if they don't bite. An' somethin' else. I jotted down a list of items this mornin' that you really need to get your backs into."

He drew a crumpled note from his inside pocket and in its squiggly writing recalled the swaying panel in the corridor of the train on which he had laid it to write out the list. Why did he keep on remembering the pilgrimage? The thing was over wasn't it? He was back to business as usual.

"Have a look at this and flog them at the new prices on the list. An' take out fresh samples with you. But hurry up. Half the day's gone an' we've nothin' to show for it yet."

A voice sang from the gallery. "Zactly like you!"

"What's Nolan doin' upstairs?" he asked Kinahane.

"He's with the apprentice sortin' out the empties that have to go back today."

"Don't call him the apprentice. Say Malachy. Do you want the public to think we've people here only learnin' the business?"

He cast a smouldering glance at Kinahane bent over the boxes of orders and plodded down towards the office at the far end of the counter. Ginnie Lawlor, his secretary, her face like a pale pear, looked up warily from the morning mail strewn across the office table.

"Wus a good pilgrimage," Dinnie told her, wondering why it was that even she with whom he could crack an occasional borderline joke failed to give him a smile of greeting, but like everyone else in the place regarded him with an intent and wary expression.

"What was Saturday like?" he enquired.

"No better than last week. I haven't got all the figures out yet but so far they're low."

"This just can't go on," Dinnie shook his head, "All the stuff standin' up an' nothin' movin' out. God, an' only a few years ago in the war they'd go down on their knees for an extra hundred cigarettes to be put on their orders. I can see no way out of this. Business can't go on gettin' worse an' worse. There'll just have to he another war, that's all, or we'll all be ruined."

"By the way, all Friday evening and Saturday Mr Fennell was on the phone." Ginnie "bent her head expectantly.

"That's all right," Dinnie exclaimed whirling round towards the door.

"He wouldn't believe you were on a pilgrimage an' kept on sayin' he's laid his hands on some more of the you-know."

He pulled the door tight behind him but the clatter in his ears failed to obliterate her closing words: "Four tons!" Assuming the wrapt expression of being engaged in an urgent task he fussed past Kinahane and took the stone steps to the loft in a brisk run. Up there in a shaded alcove formed by soaring stacks of crated jars of jam he paused safe from the curious eyes of his employees. A sense of violent motion possessed him as if he were still in the corridor of the train swaying to retain his balance and throbbing to the metallic beat of the urgent wheels beneath him. A hard anxious weight turned over in his insides, trailing strands of the tingling excitement he felt at eleven o'clock on Saturday nights as he drew his wife's firm body to him. He moved from the alcove as in a laboured dream and went to the wall of the loft from which he stared down beyond the van, and the stooping figures almost directly below him, to the area near the farther wall where snow-white sacks of flour rose in a soft mound beside the firmer, darker contours of sacks of Egyptian rice. In the middle of a similar mass, crowned with cardboard boxes, he had hidden the last consignment Fennell had sent his way. It was there only two days before Agnew took it out in the van, four or five sacks at a time, hidden beneath the regular deliveries. With Kinahane acting as look-out, Agnew drew up at the trade entrance of several hotels in the quiet hour just after tea. But it wasn't just a ton-and-a-half Fennell was offering now. It was four. Four whole tons of sugar! He allowed the word to trickle into his mind and the hard lump in his insides turned over again. He pushed away from the wall and went deeper into the loft where tiers of Wheateens in their brown cube-shaped cases cut him off from the overhead light. They towered brooding above him. Suppose, even after reducing the price, penny by agonising penny, he was stuck with that huge mountain of stock? Suppose even now that Fennell, thinking he had cold feet, was ringing up other likely prospects? Noonan even? He drew out his handkerchief and dried his moist palms by rubbing it into a ball between them. Certainly there was a risk in selling sugar on the black market but it wasn't as if the stuff was stolen. Didn't Father McGurk say something about the laws of the state being different to the moral law? Fennell was to be trusted and though he couldn't ask him straight out where the sugar was coming from he could make a shrewd guess. Some jam or chocolate manufacturer, or maybe even a sugar wholesaler with a surplus acquired by greasing the right palm. Too scared though to send their own vans around selling the stuff in small lots. And look at the names on the boards of directors of those concerns! T.D.'s, the usual old I.R.A. men, Knights,

Freemasons, and inside the firms young, sharp-nosed college hoys who never sweated lifting a sack of sugar in their lives, walking around with that grinny, know-all look on their faces, safe in the snug jobs their fathers got for them by blowing up a bridge or a British army lorry or through fleecing the public in some twopenny-halfpenny business somewhere. If people like that could do it, why couldn't he? And anyway, what was the sense of slaving away in a business unless you were prepared to go the whole hog, prepared to grab the real big opportunity when it came along? You had to do it. It was your duty - to yourself, to your family, to your employees, to the very idea of business. Otherwise you ended up like old Dan Russell, staring at the wall and muttering to yourself. A shudder seized him and he felt cold. He needed a cup of thick, black coffee to clear his head. Could he afford to wait until midday? If only the pilgrimage could have taken place next week, next month even, anytime but when Fennell was on the prowl again! How unfortunate, just when he made such a good confession, got himself into such a perfect state of grace that he couldn't even lose his temper without feeling guilty, couldn't even contemplate an exciting business deal without getting tangled up in all sorts of confusing, restricting ideas about the moral law! Funny, he'd never come across anyone in business who had ever mentioned the moral law, although Father McGurk said it was businessmen more than others who had need to take daily account of it. The moral law, the feeling of holiness, the sense of being in a perfect state of grace, all that was wonderful on the mountain, but here with the unsold stock grinning down at you, it somehow seemed unreal, unnecessary, unnatural even.

He longed to do something - he had no idea what - which would make him feel more like his own true self. Then he might be able to see clearer and know what best to do!

He heard the phone ring and waited, his heart turning over, for Miss Lawlor to come out of the office and call for him. Voices floated up from the well, the scrape and tinkle of orders being handed to Agnew and slid into the body of the van. He listened and guessed it was a call Miss Lawlor could handle without consulting him. But while she was chattering down there, was Fennell on the phone trying to reach him and fuming at the pulsing engaged signal? Or was he ringing up someone else? Or had he already done so? "Oh God!" he breathed, "What will I do?" If only Father McGurk were there to sustain him, to bring back the joy, the clarity, the beautiful simplicity of the long talk in the quiet church on the mountain! He was not due to see Father McGurk for a few days, and then it would be to talk not about his problems but about the contribution he was to make to some deserving charity. "Christ, how much is he going to shake me for?" he worried, "With that hanging over me I need cash more than ever!" The tiered cubes of Wheateens seemed to have drawn closer to him, to have cut him off from the air as well as the light. He moved out from among them, bearing with him the sensation of being suffocated, of being hemmed in on all sides by shapes and forces that lay in a dead, depressing weight on his spirit. Wasn't there a prayer a man could say in times of stress and temptation? He couldn't remember. He turned down a corridor through the bulking blocks of goods and paused, only partly hearing the voices on the other side of the cases.

"Course it's true," that was Willy Nolan's voice, "Me father ought to know. He's been to meetin's where fellas who'd been there were talkin' all about it. An' he's got a lot o' books about it too. Full o' hard words."

Who was he talking to? he wondered and recalled what Kinahane had said about the apprentice. On tiptoe he moved closer trying to think of a prayer and holding his breath at such a good chance to listen in on his employees. You couldn't call them workers, not even their insurance cards did that. Lazy, lying, lightning-fingered the whole lot of them! You'd be mad to let the chance slip to overhear them for only in that way could you learn what was really going on in the stores. In his anxiety not to make noise he failed to hear what the apprentice said. He narrowed his eyes listening to Nolan's reply.

"Of course it's the workers' paradise. Me father says no-one could have got them to fight the Germans in the war if it wasn't."

"Sure aren't we well enough off here as we are? Am'nt I learnin' a business that'll teach me how to make lots o' money when I grow up?"

"Pis that! Your father paid in bags o' money for you so that oul Himmler can work you to death for three years for practically nothin'. Crack that whip! Do you know what they did to businessmen in Russia? Up against the wall they put them - Ping! That was in the revolution. Now the workers own all the means of production. An' the picture-houses. An' the dance-halls. An' the billiard saloons. An' the pubs! Two months' paid holidays they get every year down in the Crimenia where they live in the palaces where the Czars an' their cronies used to hang out. An' do you know who the workers' servants are down there? All the oul dukes, an' lords, an' factory owners, an' black marketeers. They keep them on the trot all the mornin' runnin' upstairs with their tea and their toast. Honest! Me father has it all in books. The workers are free. They aren't wage slaves like us. That's why they produce more. Did you know that the production of grain in Todjackstan went up by a hundred-and-fifty million poonds last year? Me father heard that from Radio Moscow, one-seven-three- four metres long-wave or thirty-one metres short-wave. An' it'll be the same here when we get the workers' revolution. All the wholesalers up against the wall - Ping! So perish all parashites!"

A speckle of red spots played before Dinnie's eyes, like missiles rushing in at him.

"Nolan!" he shouted, "Is this the way you're wastin' me time an' me money?"

"Is that you, sor?"

"What are you supposed to be doin'?"

"Sortin' out empties with Malachy."

"Is that cigarette smoke I'm smellin'?"

"Oh no, sor!"

Dinnie heard an abrupt, creaking movement.

"Look out there!" wailed the apprentice.

Dinnie heard the chiming gasp of breaking glass followed by the thud of a heavy object against the tier of containers almost directly above where he was standing.

"Oh good Jasus!" wailed Nolan, "Ah no God please don't let it happen!"

Dinnie looked up and saw a shuffling struggle between the topmost case of the stack and the one directly beneath it. As the tier steadied the case on the top danced about in a series of hops bouncing part of its base into his view. Its up-and-down movement ceased abruptly. It paused, poised, and then leaped sharp-shouldered and black against the blunt glare of the window in the roof. Dinnie cowered from the wind of its fall as it swept down and struck the edge of the gallery wall where it burst, showering packets of Wheateens and blizzards of their crisp contents into the body of the store. A shout shrieked from Kinahane. Rushing to the edge of the wall Dinnie saw that the broken case had burst like a bomb among the assembled crates of orders. His horrified eye leaped from detail to detail - burst packets of flour, crushed pots of jam, torn bags shedding buff flakes of meal, a lone bottle of ketchup shorn of its head, Wheateen crisps clinging to its bleeding sides. A long howl tore out of his angry heart.

"Nolan! Nolan! I'll cut the legs from under you!"

He rushed round the stacks and came into a sort of clearing where Nolan was hopping about on one foot clutching his shin.

"Oh I'm done for! Crippled for life! This'll cost an awful lot of compensation so it will."

He sucked in his breath wincing in unbearable pain, his blue eyes cold and solemn on Dinnie who felt his whole being a dancing flame or anger.

"Nolan! Nolan! You prancin' useless! You lazy layabout!"

He hung panting in the fire, his broad hands jerking open and shut, his lower teeth gleaming between his lips like a dangerously sharp wedge.

"He tripped, sor," said the apprentice who bent over an upturned case, picking up shards or earthenware and glass, "He jumped up so quick he tripped over the case, broke the jars and fell against the stack, was an accident."

"He shouldn't have been sittin'!" Dinnie shouted, "Nobody sits on his arse on time I'm payin' for! Get outa here, Nolan. Pick up your cards at the office. Clear out o' my sight before I hamstring you! Go on! Git!"

"Are you after sackin' me, sor?"

"What would you expect me to do? Pin a medal on you?"

"Why are you sackin'me?"

"Why?" A gust of hot anger whirled through Dinnie's head. "Why? For - for damage! For bein' late! For encouragin' people to tell lies to me about you! For..." His eyes raked over the floor. "There! Look at that! A stamped-out cigarette butt. There's another reason - for smokin'! An' for tryin' to turn me apprentice against me. Now are you going to get out of here before I lay my hand on you, for if I do there won't be that much of you left to be worth payin' compensation for."

Nolan released the leg he had been nursing and strolled towards the stair-head. He paused there and grinned down into the stores.

"Yous can all relax now. It didn't take him long to get this year's victim, did it? He's back to normal again. Ah, God bless old Saint Patrick an' his annual pilgrimage. It keeps the labour exchange busy."

"Get out before I cut the head o' you!" Dinnie raised his fist.

Nolan grinned back at him. He rested his hand on the stone stair-guard, squared his shoulders, and gleamed a blue look of contempt down his nose. "Es for you, me good man," his shrill voice was vaguely English, "Yew can taike yer penny-farthing job and stick it. Ah, yais! It's a far, far better thing I'm gonna do, than I have ever done. It's a far, far better labour exchange I'm gonna go to than I have ever known."

He minced down the stairs. Dinnie watched him, his breath rushing up his neck as if a blacksmith's bellows were busy within him, shaking him with every wheezing blast. The sensation of being in flight, of rushing headlong towards a point of thrilling impact, still sustained him. He moved under its impulse, following Nolan down the stairs.

"Don't wait for your cards, Nolan. We'll post them to you."

"Aye, an' dock the price o' the stamp outa me wages."

"A good idea. I'll put it into a fund I've just thought of startin' to save up for a whip to beat the slaves with!"

Nolan came past him in a wide, careful arc and began to dance down the drive waving one arm after the other wildly in the air. "I'm free! I'm free'. Mother, I'm free!"

Kinahane approached Dinnie. "Actually," he said, "when you look at it, there wasn't much damage. Just a few bob's worth."

"Are you tryin' to cover up for that louser again? Like you did this mornin' when you said he wasn't late? There's such a thing as loyalty, you know. An' trust!"

Kinahane blushed and turned away to his task.

"An' yous," Dinnie shouted at two of the travellers who were still there, "Does it take yous all day to pack a few lousy samples? Yous don't hang around like that Saturday when it comes to collectin' your wages. Now get out on the road and start shiftin' some o' that stock upstairs. Go on, get to it. Travellers is two a penny an' if yous can't shift the bloody things I'll get in fellas who can."

He leaned his back against the counter and sneaked out a long easy sigh. Though heavy with fatigue he felt more himself, and as a sort of bonus, light of heart as well, strangely relieved, even delighted. Nolan's shout reached him from the entrance.

"Join a union fellas or next year Saint Patrick'll get one of yous too. Like Flanagan last year. An' Mack the year before! Victims of the pilgrimage."

"But it's you this year," Dinnie laughed at him and pointed his index finger, "Ping!"

Among the debris on the floor he saw a bottle of liquid coffee, the neck broken off.

"Hey, save that bottle o' coffee, Jack. Waste not, want not. That's the real moral law. An' plug in the kettle while you're at it. I could do with a cup o' coffee this minute."

Miss Lawlor smiled from the door of the office.

"Mr Fennell's on the phone for you, sor."

"Comin' up," grinned Dinnie and strolled towards the office humming *Hail Glorious Saint Patrick* in quick-waltz tempo.

AGNES

Agnes raised her head from the cradle of her hot palms and listened again. Outside, round the cold shell of the tall building, the city stirred in its uneasy, neutral sleep scattering on the night wind the haphazard rustlings of its restlessness. Somewhere, in the direction of Rathgar, an urgent car moaned faintly through a change of gear. In the opposite direction, near Harcourt Street Station it seemed, a lone steam engine hissed its quiet exasperation at the muted gnashings of its wheels along an icy track. And here and there when the sounds from the station sighed to silence, surfacing through the darkness, nudging for notice, were humps and bumps of fragmented ripples, almost-sounds rising continually almost to the point of becoming distinct. They whispered of unspeakable acts agitating the night, of lewd shapes crawling crablike under covers and down dark slimy lanes and into foetid corners to escape the all-seeing eye of God who because He was divine and not just human like her would somehow have to find it in His mercy to forgive the vile trespasses of the world. And of Eddie.

There it was again, rising through the dark building towards her, an almost-sound, the soft nudging of blank eyes, of a firm body against the velvet of the silent dark.

Downstairs in the cold innards of the building, between the doctors' surgeries on the first floor and the pretentious, over-priced flats on the second, it was now clear that someone was fumbling his unsure way upwards. She knew it was Eddie from the tautening about her heart, from the tug on that delicate thread of awareness, so frequently of unbearable awareness, that had bound her brother to her practically from the moment of his birth. It had taken her until she was nearly twenty to become fully aware of it and even longer to learn to live with it - if she ever really could! How maddening at times to know that no matter how fierce the disagreements, how interminable the stretches of angry silence between them, the delicate thread linking heart to heart in secret sympathy never slackened for an instant, never threatened to snap. But it maddened her at times to feel she was at the beck and call of his mind, forced against her will to listen to his thoughts as if to water dripping in distant pools. There had been that incredible moment at her work in the Telephone Exchange when, fuming with anger with him shortly before he went to England, she had yielded suddenly to an overwhelming impulse to tap one of the operators on the shoulder, take the earphones in her hand, and listen in on a call pretending not to notice the moist gape of surprise on the girl's upturned face, Eddie's voice sprang alive in her ears sickening her with its cooey cockiness, its insistent insincerity. He was speaking to a girl who dribbled inane laughter too close to the mouthpiece. "But of course you can come out with me tonight, Nuala," his voice purred, "You know you can if you want to. And you always want to with me, don't you li'l darleen? Dees ees Funf speaking..." A harsh, abrupt sound reached her from the landing, an unsure foot scraping on the metal stair rods. Who else but Eddie raised noises like that? So she had been right, a little while ago, when listening to the lone footsteps coming along Rathmines Road from the direction of the city. Eddie's step had altered since he joined the R.A.F. but that semi-military stride punching bleak slaps through the silence still hinted at his old indecisiveness, his dreamy vagueness, his unimaginable thoughtlessness. "The obscene beast" she said aloud and listened to the soft dents her words made on the black wall of the night.

How long had she been sitting there in the dark alone? She discovered wedges of pain in her shoulder blades, niggling aches in the points of her elbows resting on her dressing table before the blind sheen of the mirror. Her fingers, even her wrists, still stung from the soda in the black Dirt-shifter soap she had used earlier to scrub out the flat. "What in God's holy name is possessin' you to start washin' out the place at this hour, girl?" her mother complained when at ten o'clock she could stand no longer the sense of being soiled and taking a bucket of warm water and a scrubbing brush in her hands she had knelt down to cleanse the scum of sin from the floors and skirting boards of their home. "You go to bed, Mamzie and just let me do what I have to" she said in her crisp, over-clear, international-call voice which she knew always intimidated her mother. Sitting in her aches before the mirror she became aware of the cold as well creeping up her legs like a hardening of icy cement. The last time she had heeded the clanging of the Town Hall clock, loud enough you would imagine to blot out Big Ben in London, she had counted four strokes which meant that for over two hours she'd been sitting in her bedroom dressed for some unfathomed reason in the lighter of her dressing gowns hardly noticing that she was shivering. Shock always affected her like that. Hours afterwards, even when dressed in her heaviest clothing, she would still find herself shivering with an icy cold that pierced to the heart. Yet, it was the grace of God that it was she and not Mamzie had come in first and as she always did had gone straight to the lavatory! She shuddered over that and pressed her fingers on her temples caressing them gradually upwards from her heavy eyebrows to the crisp rim of her hairline. She must look a sight by now, her cheeks raw and puffy, the strong blade of her nose devoid of the subtle softening of cosmetics, poking nakedly from her face in that unfortunate thrust which had earned her the nickname of Beaky Baggot in the Dominican Convent. No wonder her schooldays were so miserable! Even now, past her thirtieth birthday, the hurt of that name remained with her.

With a whispered hush the door of the flat sighed shut behind him. Instantly, as if the lights had been switched on in all the rooms, the whole place sprang to life in her mind. Over everything there still hung that intangible scum of defilement, the irk of insult, which no soap and water would ever be able to erase. Her heart trembled as if it would burst into tears. No matter how thoroughly she would wash and scour through all the long evenings of the bleak future their home would never be clean again. A snigger of filth would always lurk beneath every surface inaccessible, mocking, gleefully elusive. A hint of nausea at the back of her nose brought the incident swimming back to her. She saw herself come in from the landing, slip out of her heather tweed coat, and just as Mamzie would surely have done, walk urgently down the corridor and into the lavatory. There, hovering in the bowl like a pale obscene foetus was an unfurled rubber object like the one that had fallen from Frank Dawson's wallet one evening in the narrow vestibule of the Gate as he fumbled snuff-fingered for their theatre tickets. With a gasp, Frank had swooped to retrieve it from the floor while the crowd in the queue behind them scraped their feet and looked away with taut faces, especially the women. Uttering a squeak of anguish she pulled the chain on the floating obscenity and raced her onrush of nausea to the washbasin. A moment later she was in the corridor, reaching her hand blindly for support and wavering in through the wide-open door of Eddie's room. Shocking details hurled themselves at her, the eiderdown slipped partway to the floor, the blankets lying in a tight twist against the footboard, a lone dented pillow perched mutely on the white expanse of the under sheet. Wonderingly she moved into the room. On the cover near the head of the bed were minute coils of wiry black hair. As she moved closer to examine them two hairgrips irritated through the thin sole of her shoe. It was as if Eddie - dreamy indecisive Eddie - had rampaged through the flat scrawling obscenities on the walls. At first she thought it was a street girl he had brought in and it was only when she found a familiar blue kerchief crumpled in the corner of the settee that she knew it was Molly Rudd who had been in the flat with him. Even though he knew several really nice girls, there was a creature like Molly always tucked away in some hidden corner of his life. Kathleen, of course, he brought out into the open, at least during the period of their engagement whose doom she sensed the evening she went to answer a ring on the door dressed in her old tweed skirt, sweater, and dust-cap and found Molly there lighting up the dim landing with the synthetic brilliance of her heavy black hair, her large gleaming eyes and the oval silver brooch shining below the cleft of her bosom which, like her hips, bulged in an unbearable tension against the thin fabric of her red dress. Again she pictured the skin-like object hovering like a monstrous creature drowning like lost life just below the surface in the bowl. How low he must have sunk to have dared to do the act of sin in his own home! "I won't have you bringin' girls to this flat any more" Mamzie had screamed at him when she learned that his engagement to Kathleen had been broken off, "I was practically a second mother to Kathleen and tonight she cuts me dead on the street as if I was a total stranger. An' it's only now you tell me that it's been all off between you for weeks! No girls here any more! Not even if they come round just to borrow a book which you said is what that Molly whatevershecallsherself came round for. I wonder if that's really what she was after. Never again! No girls here!" Mamzie flapped the flat of her hand against the wall which still bore the smudged ghost of its imprint. But he had always been like that, sly, underhand, never telling you what was happening in his life until it was no longer possible to keep it a secret. Like the callous way he dropped the news that he was leaving home. "Mamzie!" he said that morning on the way out to work, "Can you leave my suit in to be cleaned today?"

Mamzie looked across at the blue pin-stripe suit drooped over the back of a chair, the trouser cuffs flat on the floor.

"Sure, there's not a brack on that suit, son."

"Have it cleaned just the same. I want to look real smart next week."

"You always look smart, son,"

"This is special. I'm going to England. I've arranged an appointment with an R.A.F. interview "board."

It had been just like a scene in one of the plays he was so fond of at the Abbey and the Gate, with him picking up his brief case and strolling offstage and Mamzie collapsing in a chair hardly able to get her breath.

It was several days after that before they found an opportunity to sit him down and get him to tell them all about it. "I have to go" he said. "Boscombe's made it crystal clear that unless we do our bit for Britain now, there'll be no work for us after the war. After all the firm came over here from England and there's still an awful lot of British money in it. Boscombe's only doing his job. He just wants us to make the world a better place to sell paper in. There's nothing to be surprised at in what he wants us to do. In spite of all Dev's gush about neutrality this sort of thing's happening all over the country. In one way or another thousands are being pushed into joining up."

"Oh he was always impossible!" she said standing up, her head throbbing as if all the restless sounds of the sleeping city were flitting about in there like bats. She went to the door and switched on the light. She blinked about her. Now that he was home at last what would she say to him? Her spirit shuddered in embarrassment from the words she would have to use. But never fear,

I'll say them she affirmed, tucking stray wisps of her hair under the elastic band of her hairnet. She went on tiptoe down the corridor, past Mamzie!s room, and into the lounge illumined now by the reading lamp on top of his bookshelves with their neat red-and-white and blue-and-white lines of paperbacks. Eddie was sprawled at the table, his cheek resting on his curled arm beside the pool of light thrown by the lamp. Pursing her lips she stretched out her hand to shake his shoulder but on an impulse so secretive she barely noticed it, bent instead to read what he had written in the neat square notebook which lay open in the shadow of his tousled hair. There were just a few scrawled lines.

"Rocked in the cradle of God's palm

We almost believe He cares.

O may we never wake

And slip His casual fingers."

It was a typical Eddie effort. A few faltering lines of what he probably thought was a poem, saying nothing much and leading nowhere. Like his life, she shivered.

"Hello Agnes."

His voice startled a gasp from her. He had not stirred but his clear blue eyes were open and for a toppling instant she had the impression of looking down on the fixed, impassive face of a dead man.

"God, you put the heart cross-ways in me" she said. "That makes two of us." He straightened up and looked in surprise at the notebook lying open at his elbow. He read the scrawled lines, grimaced, and tearing out the page he crumpled it in his fist and tossed it across the room towards the fireplace in which under its mound of grey ash a large log still held a faint red glow. She went round the table, picked up the ball of paper and made for the fireplace. He was forever doing things like that, scribbling odd lines, tossing wisps of paper all over the place without any thought for those who had to clear up after him. Like tonight! As she squinted in the glow from the log, lines she discovered on a similar wisp of paper after his last leave came back to her as they had several times during the early part of the winter when the moan of highflying aircraft invaded her sleep. He spoke them again in her mind:

"Weep Horseman, weep!

The Gods of air desert you

And still your restless hand;

Deep in your heart where

All your lost loves dream

A snag of shrapnel sleeps.

And dead over Dortmund

You sit in on eternity

As your lost five thousand horses

Pound the night."

What a strange mixture he was, all dreamy and vague but don't let that fool you for underneath it all - rotten to the core!

"You came in so late" she said to him, "it's a wonder you bothered to show your face at all." She placed a hand for support on the mantle-piece frightened of the fury that had begun to pound in her heart.

"Would've been home hours ago" the words yawned from the dark gash of his mouth, "But I couldn't get away from a fellow I knocked into on my way across town. A fellow you know quite well in fact. Frank Dawson!"

She fussed with the folds of her dressing gown and turning from him she took the china horse from the mantle-piece and blew at the minute specks of white ash gathered on its cool surface.

"Yes! I ran into Frank on my way back from seeing home - "she exulted at the catch in his voice " - someone I was out with. Hasn't changed a bit has Frank. Well, in looks anyway. And in spite of the paper shortage he's doing quite well in the printing game'

"How nice for him" she sneered down at the last few specks of ash.

"Anyway, we had the kind of evening we used to enjoy before all this." The casual wave of his hand encompassed the whole disrupting impact of the war. More even, the end of childhood, the death of innocence, the advent of perpetual anxiety. "We strolled across town to the Pillar, down Henry Street and on by North King Street to the quays. Had a few drinks in the Stag's Head, at least I did for Frank's on the waggon, hasn't had a drink for years. And we've been sitting down there in the cold on the push beams of the lock gates at Portobello gassing about this that the other, but mostly about you."

"You'd a damn cheek to discuss me with a man like him!" The phrase struck a discord in her ears and she wondered should it have been 'a man like you!'

"Why shouldn't I discuss you with Frank? He's a good old skin, absolutely crazy about you. If you were honest with yourself, you'd have to admit that you're not all that indifferent to him either."

"Bloody cheek of you both talking about me" she swept into the kitchen where perplexed at not being able to get her hand into the pocket of the dressing gown, she discovered her fingers were still curved tight round the little china horse. Surprised at the access of tenderness it raised in her she placed it gently on a shelf in the kitchen cabinet. Daddy's present to her on her twenty-first birthday. She regarded it wistfully as she sought in her pocket for her cigarettes. She lit the wavering blue flame of the gas ring under the kettle and brought the match to the tip of the cigarette. From its full gritty feel on her lips she knew it was one of the various American brands at present appearing in the shops. It tasted how her heart felt, harsh and bitter, Yet, beyond the wavering flame of her anger, wasn't there a heightened awareness, a warm sympathy, a yearning even for Frank Dawson? She drew deep on the cigarette. But what was the use of going into all that again? When she'd been with him, even during the times when he wasn't drinking and gambling, there had been always between them that inexplicable barrier, rather like a sheet of frosted glass through which her heart saw only a confused outline of its own feelings. And what were they really? She could never be sure. And it was that uncertainty, that frustration which drove her inexorably to humiliate and hurt him with a compulsive cruelty that afterwards left her shocked and frightened. None of the priests whose advice she sought at confession had ever been able to explain to her satisfaction what impulse compelled her to act like that. And more important, none of them had been able to make it go away. Once for a pulsing instant when she had seen into her mind, it seemed with the eyes of a stranger, she realised that she almost enjoyed her eagerness to twist his most innocent remarks into indications of meanness of character, of hints of insincerity, of proofs of animal lust. But she hadn't always been wrong, had she? Look at that time in the foyer of the Gate when that thing fell out of his wallet! That's what he meant by his continual hints that it would lead to no harm were they to go to bed together. How dare he make such a suggestion! She stubbed her cigarette hard into the surface of the ashtray.

"Could you make me a cup of coffee, Ag?"

She turned to find him lounging in the doorway his fingers busy about the knot of his tie as if dressing for breakfast.

"This is for a hot-water bottle for I'm shivering with cold," she urged on her anger, "And you've a helluva cheek to come home in the middle of the night - morning nearly - and expect me to wait hand and foot on you." She willed her anger to well up and overwhelm her. He would hear a thing or two then. By God he would.

"If it's so much trouble don't bother" he smiled, "You never know, I may be able to get something on the boat."

"The boat? What boat? What do you mean?" She blinked helplessly like at school when everyone around her snapped fingers and raised hands at questions she felt to be easy but which she could never find the answer to.

"Got to go back to work." With his palms he smoothed the thick, shiny wings of hair above his ears and yawned briefly.

"But you've got ten - eight - a whole week of your leave left."

"Little birdie says they want us back. Did you know the Yanks walked into it two days ago?"

Alvar Liddell's plush upholstered voice on the B.B.C. news. Something about raids deep into Germany during daylight, large numbers of Flying Fortresses shot down. On holiday last summer in Bundoran a crowd elbowed out of the hotel bar pointing skywards. "Flying Fortresses being ferried to England for the Yanks." Even at that great height, a dull silver against the blue, they bulked huge. Large numbers of those screaming down out of the air over Germany. And at night, Halifaxes, Blenheims, Lancasters. A dread of anticipation leaned forward in her and waited breathless.

"But they've no right to want you back so soon" she said uneasy at the gap of silence between them.

"Oh never mind that" he said advancing into the narrow room "That's another world. No concern of yours at all. What does concern you though, and it concerns me far more than you realise, is Frank Dawson."

She declined her head from him and watched the blue flame wavering under the kettle.

"You'll oblige me by not talking about that fellow."

He sat down in a chair at the end of the table in the

corner beneath the wall cupboard which still bore its faded blue cretonne curtain. Incredible that she once had to use a chair to climb into that cupboard, the secret room of her childhood where her dreams always waited for her. In there among her father's cold-cheeked golf clubs there was a fat smell of oil, sour wool and oranges. Through the chink in the curtains she had once watched Eddie march up and down the kitchen, a Woolworth's rifle on his shoulder, singing: "The Legion of the Lost they call us." The tiny room echoed with the shrill song from the past and her heart began to unclench its anger. Where does all the timeless joy vanish to when you grow up? An impalpable barrier like the one separating her from Frank Dawson sundered her from the tall sun-filled days of her childhood. Already she seemed to have lived - to have endured, rather - for half an eternity in the tense anxious world of always being grown-up.

"O.K." he said after a thoughtful pause, "If you won't talk about Frank let's have a little chat about the fellow you're going out with at the moment."

"That's my business if you don't mind."

"Also his wife's I believe," he said in a near whisper. "It's your usual sort of love affair, isn't it? All romantic gush and anguish and no future at all! Aunt Mamie told me all about it when I went to see her yesterday What's the snag with this latest beau? Is he married to someone who doesn't understand him? Or about to be married to someone who thinks she does? Or trying to get out of being married to someone who understands him only too well? Haven't you got an answer? Don't you ever get wise to what you're really doing with your life?"

She reached into the nearby shelf and took out the china horse. It was so wrong to leave it reclining in shadow in there when it really belonged on the mantlepiece in the lounge.

"Well, do you?" he insisted.

"Mind your own bloody business" she said running her finger over the arch of the horse's neck. When her father gave it to her at breakfast that morning he placed his hands gently on her shoulders and kissed her briefly on the lips. She recalled her thrill of amazement at how warm and young his lips felt.

"Whether you like it or not, what happens to you is my business, Ag," He leaned forward resting his elbows on his knees, spreading his hands, just like her father, "You must realise by now, you always get involved with men who can't possibly marry you. Even the single unattached fellows you fall for always have some major drawback - an incurable disease galloping them to the grave, expensive aged parents to support, a late vocation for the priesthood, some urgent date with destiny on the other side of the world. Remember the fellow you fell in love with in the very week he was booked on a plane to take him into the African jungles to dedicate his life to the medical missions? He's probably still there, dedicating. Men you could marry, men who'd marry you if you gave them half a chance, men like Frank Dawson for instance, you treat as if they were dirt under your feet. Time's passing old girl. All over the bloom of your youth. This kink of yours is getting too serious to be ignored by you any longer. Has it never occurred to you that something inside you is playing a very crafty game with you to have you end up as a vinegary old maid?"

"How dare you!" The china horse twirled from her hand before she knew of her intention to throw it. It spun in a flash of alarm under the ceiling light and struck against the far wall with a surprisingly metallic ring. What was there so strange about him she wondered as gradually she gained control of her shivering limbs? He had betrayed no movement whatsoever as the object whirled across the room straight towards him.

"Blast you!" she stamped her foot, "Look what you made me do!"

"Seems I hit a nerve there" he said softly "bending to retrieve the two pieces into which the ornament had broken, the noble head and the prancing body with part of the high arched neck. "What scares me about this thing of yours - pattern, call it what you will - is that it doesn't seem to cost you a thought. You just go on through the same routine, over and over, learning nothing for each disappointment. Oh yes, it scares the living daylights out of me all right! Over Germany, the sky alive with flying metal, the very rain looking as if it's on fire, and I'm in a cold sweat about what's going to happen to you. Unbelievable isn't it? What's going to become of you if you go on like this, I ask myself, and fume because I can do nothing about it. You don't want to turn out like those sour old maids you meet in practically every business or public office and big stores do you? Those efficient women with that resentful, unsatisfiable look in their eyes? Ag, for my sake as much as your own, save yourself. Go out with Frank again."

"I'll have nothing to do with him." What had possessed

her to throw her lovely china horse like that? Even if she succeeded in gluing it together again, the mark, the dark scar, would always show. As the shock of the evening would always shadow her face, maybe.

"Frank's a changed man. To hear him talking about you tonight you could see how crazy he is about you. Not like these other muffs, Frank would really take care of you, treat you like a queen."

"No he wouldn't" the horror in the lavatory bowl intimidated her "The first thing, the very first thing, he'd want to do would be to treat me in the same shameless, immoral way you treated Molly Rudd here this afternoon. In our very home! Is that what you want for your sister? Your friend to treat her like a whore? Or are you too rotten to really care?"

His calm eyes steadied and focussed on some speck of space short of hers. She had the impression of a face reflected in the windscreen of a car, steady and unmoved against the onrush of wind and rain and night. Like Frank Dawson's driving her home from the races at Fairyhouse. She saw him exhale a long furtive breath as he always did when bored and settle down to wait until the conversation shifted to some topic more amenable to his tastes. Hot bile burned in the back of her throat. For the sake of her outraged feelings couldn't he even pretend to feel shame!

"You had her here, hadn't you?" she said, "In defiance of Mamzie and all!"

His calm gaze hovered over the blind void between them. He remained immobile, hardly seeming to breathe, one strong hand folded over the other except when briefly he rubbed the ball of his thumb lightly over his right nostril. She knew this trick of old. He was waiting until this too, like all the other unpleasantnesses in his life, would go away.

"Don't try to brazen it out with me" she heard the echo of a shriek. "We both know you had her here."

"All right I had her here." Sighing he looked with shy kindness into her eyes just like her father used when coaxing her out of one of her sulky moods. "This is the last day of my leave and she was free from work only for the afternoon. What would you expect me to do? Spend the time at some silly film or walking her around in the dreary Dublin drizzle?"

"So you don't deny it"

"Jesus!" Suddenly he slapped himself on the forehead, "Here I am in the middle of a war and all you can do is go on at me like the District Attorney in some frightful B-picture." He mocked an American accent, "Which of your stoolies blabbed, kid? One of the snoopy old broads on the second floor?"

"The two of you yourselves told me." The burden of anguish toppled over into hot tears, raining down her face.

"What's the matter, Ag?" He moved swiftly towards her, his greyish concerned face darkening as he passed underneath the naked bulb. The swinging purposefulness of his movements, the abrupt shadowing of his face, the sense of a contaminating evil pressing close in on her brought her hands up to ward off the terrifying touch of his nearing fingers. She pounded up at the overwhelming bulk of him.

"Filth! Filth! Both of you! Our home! Damn you!"

She snapped her wrists from the hard clench of his fingers. "Don't defile me" she heard herself shriek. What if she was screaming? What if Mamzie and the whole sleeping city heard her?

"Keep your filthy hands off me!"

To her relief he sidled carefully away from her and stood near the door frowning, his eyes small and calculating. Tears rolled warm and sticky down her cheeks. She slipped awkward and exhausted into the basket chair next the window.

"You used to be so good-living" she accused him "All the times Mamzie and I watched you serving mass in Rathmines chapel. Like a little angel you were, so good, so innocent."

"Ag, what's behind all this?"

She dreaded he would begin to approach near her again.

"I'll tell you what's behind it!" she rushed the words fast between them "You and your rotten Molly turning our home into nothing better than a brothel, that's what's behind it. Sacred heart, the shock, the disgust of it all when I came in! I went into the lav and the first thing I saw was that rubber thing in the bowl! And when I staggered out of there I saw your room was open. It wasn't hard to guess what had been going on in there!"

"Oh no!" He bent his face into his joined hands as if kissing something held between them. "Oh lor, I'm sorry, Ag. So far as I know I flushed the thing. And I closed the door of my room. I wouldn't have had that happen to you for worlds."

She drew away from the warmth of his presence. Her head nodded over the immense dark of her tiredness, over a swirl of formless movements from which random voices called, voices from far off thin and wavering as if on an open plain. Mamzie's face swam towards her bearing a sour expression, fixed and hard like an image raised on a bronze medal. She was in the atmosphere of those shifting moments on the crumbling edge of sleep in which an intimate voice assured her that her father could never really have loved such a face. A voice spoke distinctly in her ear: "Agnes is a queen!"

"Agnes." She withdrew only slightly from his warm nearness as he knelt beside her chair, his eyes keen and pleading. Childhood hadn't passed at all she felt. He was on his knees again trying to coax her out of telling Daddy that he had hurt her.

"You probably don't believe this, Ag, but I'm really sorry. You know, deep down sorry."

"Suppose Mamzie had come in first?"

"Oh God! It doesn't hear thinking about," He shook his head on a long hiss of relief. "But I was certain the door of my room was closed. I admit it was all panic stations at the end, when I glanced at my watch and saw that it was nearly five. We scrambled like hell out of it, and the last thing I remember was closing my door. Or was it just my intention not to forget to close it?"

"God, I'm so cold!" She shivered remembering her anger and wondering where she had misplaced it.

"Water's coming up to the boil" he said, "If you'd like to

make a pot of coffee, I'll get a drop of the hard tack from my room. It'll do us both good. O.K.?"

She nodded relieved that he was again coaxing her out of telling on him, out of her resentment, out of the storm of anger that had exhausted her mind. She watched him go down the passage to his room moving so softly it was as if he made partings rather than sounds in the curtains of the air. His movements made that absurd impression on her because she was tired and because of that tiredness she couldn't feel anger about anything, not even about the broken horse. Later it would flare up again for what he had done to their home was unforgiveable. To think that every night of his leave after she did the washing up she went to his room and made his bed for him! She could never do that again. He was in that room now but she refused to think of the crumpled blankets and the lone pillow. Instead she listened to the sounds that came back to her from him, her mind moving from one to the next as if feeling its way through, a journey in the dark. Why was she so concerned all night with sounds, with listening for them, with hearing them?

When he was away, at work as he called it, what she and Mamzie did most of all was just listen. In his absence an unbearable silence reigned between the everyday sounds their voices and actions made in the flat, a silence in which she listened for his foot on the stairs or for other feet alien and unwelcome hurrying up through the building with that dreaded telegram. The silence hung over the hands of the clock which seemed hardly to move at all so that they had to be urged forward not so much by reading as by dozing over her book. She would never get through the three volumes of War and Peace she found on her dressing table the day he left for Liverpool. How fixed the routine of their lives had become since the war! Long meandering nothings of time, night journeys to nowhere, lit briefly by pointless gossip, indifferent meals, dreary housework, the news bulletins on the B.B.C. and the sneers and guffaws of Lord Haw-Haw from Hamburg telling what was really happening in the war. Mamzie spent nearly every evening by the meagre fire, her beads clicking against her rings, her head rising up from the depths of her prayers only when a voice from the radio told of the war in the air. "Our bombers are out in force again tonight."

She rose and tended to the kettle whose whistle became unbearable behind her. He returned as she was making the coffee in his favourite brown earthenware jug and he stood briefly beside her to pour a generous measure of whiskey into it. She sat across the table from him sipping her coffee, relishing secretly the dark warmth seeping into the rigid chill of her bones. Unnoticed the night had gone - it seemed in the brief moment she turned her head away - and morning was already pressing grey and damp against the uncurtained window. A seagull sweeping in over the sea, perhaps from imminent rain, sent through the chill air a despairing scream of protest against the burden of another day, another round of tasks and anxieties, of desires and appetites never to be satisfied.

"Yes!" he reflected into his coffee cup, "Lucky for me it was you and not Mamzie who came in first! God, how would she have taken it?"

In the pale light which brought the ceiling to life above the shadeless yellow bulb his face was grained with grey, like a well-thumbed eraser. That was the war and the bad food in England and of course his moral rottenness. She remained quite still, loath to disturb the warmth flowing comfortingly through her veins. Yet the calm gossipy mood that came over her impelled her to speak.

"Mamzie and I were debating last night whether to tell you about Molly or not," she said reflectively as if settling down for a long chat.

He raised his head and frowned over the rim of his cup. The seagull screamed again and she knew if she went to the window she would see a ragged grey curtain of mist unravelling along the vague humps of the hills.

"Tell me what?" he asked.

"But then again I said to her that Molly probably means nothing to you at all and so there wouldn't be any point in warning you." She yawned comfortably.

"What do you mean 'warning me'?"

"But if I was wrong and you were really fond of her then we felt you really ought to know."

"Oh for Christ's sake!" He pushed his chair roughly from the table and went to the window. Through the chill morning she heard a canal barge send its lazy thump-thump-thump the length of Rathmines Road. She pictured the long boat rising inside the box of the lock at Portobellow Harbour and saw Frank Dawson struggle for his life in the mad swirl of white waters. She would have to snatch a brief sleep before she went to work otherwise all day absurd stuff like that would be popping in and out of her head.

"Out with it'" he sounded as if swallowing as he spoke, "We both know you're dying to tell me. What dirty gossip have you dug up?"

"Would you call what your own mother heard and saw with her own eyes dirty gossip?"

"Mamzie?"

"After you went back last time she stayed late in the church one night praying for you. The front gate was locked so she had to come out the back way, into that laneway place. And there in a kind of niche in the wall of the church, in the very wall of the church mark you, was your precious Molly in the arms of an elderly grey-haired oul-fella in a camel-haired coat. Mamzie wouldn't have looked as she passed only she heard the oulfella call Molly by her name and of course she knew her famous laugh. Who could forget it?"

"Ha! Ha!" he mocked, his forehead resting against one of the windowpanes which grew misty arid grey as the lined skin on his face. How still he could remain at times!

"Then quite by chance" she said, eager to get it all out, "I heard all about her from another source. A girl in the telephone exchange whose brother plays the trumpet with the Shadows was talking one lunch-hour in Bewleys' about the real well-known characters he sees at all the dances. It turns out that Molly is one of them. She has a terrible name. Every other week-end the girl said, she's with one or other of the American technicians who come down from Belfast for the T-bone steaks, the fried eggs, and anything else they can buy here. Worst of all, the fellows in the Shadows call her the honey-pot from the way the black students are always swarming around her. And we all know don't we what those dressed-up savages are like and what they're after? While you were away there was a terrible case in the papers about one of them and a girl from Kimmage."

"So whether Molly means anything to me or not, I've got the dirty gossip anyway, haven't I? Thanks very much."

"What I saw with my own eyes is not gossip."

"I don't want to know. I just don't care."

"You must! You're my brother and you should know the truth about the girls you go around with especially the one you bring into your own home. Our home! From the very place where you're standing now I saw her coming up the road late one night with one of the students. At first I wondered why the fellow's face was always in shadow and then when they passed the jeweller's shop I saw him as large as life. She was traipsing home from the Adelaide or the Olympic or some other of those awful dancehalls with a dirty blackamoor."

She watched him covertly. An amused smile appeared on his lips. He stroked his chin, began to scratch it and raised his arms to study his watch.

"Yes, that's what I'll do" he said, "I'll shave on the boat. I'd better dump all my gear in my bag and git!"

"Do you have to go so early?" She tapped her spoon on the ridge of her saucer disappointed that he had heard all and made no comment.

"No point in hanging around here as the old lady on

the airstrip said in the Jack Warner joke. Yes!" he sighed brusquely "I'll mosey down to Paddy Winstanley's. He's off to work too. His father'll probably run us out to Dun Laoghaire in his Austin Seven."

As he came past her she said: "I know it wasn't nice for you to have to hear all that. I'm sorry I had to tell you, but it's only right that you should know the truth."

His leer bared his lower teeth which were white and sharp like dangerous creatures lying in ambush in his mouth.

"Don't try to fool yourself" he sneered into her face, "You loved every minute of it."

Turning her back abruptly on him she took the cups and saucers to the sink and began to wash them in the warm water remaining in the kettle. In the bowl their outlines hardened as if they were emerging newly carved from the frail coils of vapour rising off the water. Other objects around her, the room itself, manifested themselves in the strange exaggerated reality that comes with tiredness, lack of sleep, hours of anxious waiting. How was she going to get through the long day ahead? The voices of the telephonists clamoured in her ears: "Holding", "Trying to connect you", "Ringing", "Putting you through to directory enquiries", "No lines open to England at present." She must sleep! She dozed over the spoons, rubbing their bowls continually with her thumbs.

"I'm off" his voice came from behind her.

Surprised, she spun round to find him standing by the table his long fawn raincoat belted tightly around him, his old smudged fibre suitcase in his hand.

"So soon?" Hadn't she heard that phrase somewhere recently? Had she said it herself? Life she felt was ceasing to flow in her, she existed only in random disconnected instants of awareness. What was he waiting for, standing there a vague unease in his eyes.

"Would you like to wake Mamzie up?" His expression said he expected his request to be deferred and dented before being acceded to, "Tell her I have no option, that I have to go back to work today. Now! Please try to impress on her that I'm in a terrible hurry, that she's not to - you know - start crying and clinging on to me, not wanting to let me go. You will impress that on her, won't you?"

"Of course I will, dear" she said as warmly as she could. She drew her dressing gown tighter about her and looked away from the knowing glint in his eyes.

"But before I wake her up" she swallowed and paused a moment, "there's something you must know. You see I was so shocked and upset when I came home last night and found - you know - what I told you, I simply had to tell somebody. You can understand, can't you, a shock like that you can't keep to yourself. So I told Mamzie all about - you know - the rubber thing, the bed, Molly."

"Jesus! You lousy frustrated old maid! There was no need to involve Mamzie!"

"How do you know? You weren't here were you?" She cringed away from the sick grin of hatred on his face. Over his shoulder she saw the open door and went shuddering round him towards it, dreading the flail of his fists she knew so well from childhood.

"Where the hell are you going?"

"To wake up Mamzie to say goodbye to you."

"Jesus Christ don't be so bloody stupid! Don't you know what she'll be like if you wake her up now? It won't be goodbye at all. It'll be one flaming blitz of a row - tears, accusations, dire warnings, appeals to God and his sacred mother, hair coming out at the roots. The whole bloody pointless symphony in fact."

"But you can't go away without saying goodbye to your own mother." Her heart trembled in dread that such a wrong might be committed.

"Oh yes I can! And do you know why?"

She shrank into the passage away from him. He came slowly after her and paused just outside the door, the light from the lounge catching the leer of his grey face.

"It's probably never entered your bird brain that when I'm going away I want to be able to remember both of you at your best. The last thing I want to take with me is the memory of my mother sobbing and screaming about my damned soul just because I ducked out of the murderous madness I'm up to my ears in to try to corner a moment or two of human happiness for myself. No thanks, I don't want to remember her like that. It's quite enough, don't you agree, to have to remember you as you've been practically since the moment I came in this morning. My God, you really enjoyed destroying Molly, didn't you?"

She retreated before his raised voice and slowly he moved along the corridor after her, talking it seemed more to someone in his mind than to her.

"Neither of you have any conception of what my life is like out there, have you? When I'm home I never talk about it as much to escape from it as to spare you both from worrying over me. But maybe it's high time you heard a bit of the truth. You're shocked, or pretend to be shocked, at what went on between Molly and me in my room this afternoon. But I've news for you, that's mainly what's on my mind when I'm up there, driving down hell's alley - yes, the beauty of women, the joy of making love. Most of the time it's Molly I think about - so you see it helps to have a fresh memory or two to bring back - but what really matters is the pure womanness of the thing. It helps to comfort and distract me because the truth is every second I'm in the air I'm so frightened my legs feel like water and it takes me all my time not to vomit into my oxygen mask. That's why I press myself into a woman, into her arms, her lips, her breasts, her thighs. I drive myself to become lost in her so that memory and fantasy become the reality, and all the rest is a flaming, screaming nightmare I hope to wake up safe from - eventually."

She reached the lounge and he followed her in, his case knocking against the door jamb as he passed with the thud of a fist on flesh.

"I see from the curl of your lip" he said "that you probably think I should spend my time offering up prayers for my safety to - to - " his eyes gleamed " - to Mamzie's favourite Saint. Saint Jude or some other darky. And I might too if I were in some situation that had the feel of reality about it. But stuck up there behind the perspex, watching the artificial horizon and the air-speed indicator and the engine boost gauge and all the rest of it and trying like hell not to drive the ship into one of those great big bursting bags of metal emptying out all over the shop, how could any sane man regard that as reality? Even when the bombs go down I'm afraid I don't even spare a moment to breathe a prayer for the souls of those about to die. Instead, I hope with my whole heart that up to that last minute they've had the good sense and the courage to have grabbed on to every bit of joy, every bit of happiness, every bit of experience that told them they were alive. Mamzie and you stand in judgement on me for what I did as if you two are models of all that's good and I of all that's evil. Well maybe you are, but have either of you any idea of the extent of the real evil I'm part of? There are moonlit nights when I turn the ship for home and look down and am amazed all over again at how vast the world is. And how evil! For I know that far beyond the horizon of the flames, beyond the children burning in the cities I've helped to set on fire, the evil of which I'm part is running everywhere, in all directions, in all its forms and in a few new ones as well. And in spite of all that I'm glad I'm coming safe through the mission, glad I'm still alive and breathing. And it's on occasions like that sometimes I think of Ireland. And shudder! In the rest of the world the evil is in the open, it bears a face, wears a uniform, speaks in an unmistakeable voice! But here, as I've always known, it's so furtive, so mean, so petty, so needlessly and heedlessly cruel, it bulks so huge in my mind it dwarfs all the other evil elsewhere. You've given me a good sample of it this morning, haven't you? For some twisted reason of your own, you've saddened my vision of a girl I happen to be more than fond of, a girl who has been unselfishly kind to me in the way she knows best. And, worse maybe, you've made it impossible for me to remember either you or my mother with any sort of Christian charity."

In the silence she winced at the pain in her palms and unclenched her fists. Where was the old indecisiveness, the old inconclusiveness she was so used to and knew exactly how to deal with? Never in her life had she heard him speak like that before - at length, to some definite purpose, with a firmness she had never before associated with him. If only she was able to think in other than sporadic impulses she would examine whether she had really done the right thing in telling Mamzie about him and Molly, in shouting all those terrible things at him, in striking at him with her clenched fists! And as they both stood still in the unbroken silence she found herself listening again, listening to clusters of almost-sounds, to uneasy stirrings which she knew were outside her but moving in close in the ringing dark of her mind. And as clearly as if Eddie had roused himself from his reverie and spoken to her, all the uneasy stirrings joined and became his voice, faint, distant, yet closer than the core of her heart. "Pray for me, Agnes" he said, "This time I'm going to be killed." She started as from a nightmare and looked at him. She saw he was frowning over something that had moved in his mind and knew it was at the premonition of his death.

"Oh Eddie, forgive me!" she cried making forward to enfold him, her arms flung wide. Her thighs thudded against the suitcase he swung up between them.

"Get stuffed, you frustrated old maid."

The crudity of his phrase, his glare of hatred, held her still as he strode across the room towards the door. Breathless she hung there, pressing against the unyielding air. He opened the door and passed through into the corridor turning almost at once to look back into the lounge. She saw his eyes, tired and sad, move around the room, to the fireplace with its smouldering log; to Mamzie's favourite picture on the wall above it, *The Laughing Cavalier*; to his bookcase with the neat batches of books; to the faded pink settee in which the springs were now going; to the table at which he had sat hour after hour reading or writing inconclusive fragments into his notebook; to her eyes into which he stared as if wondering who she was.

"Bye, Ag!"

He smiled curtly and pushed the blank white face of the door between them. Great God, it couldn't end like this! He was going to his death and there was nothing she could do now to stop him. "No! No! He can't" she said aloud and hurried to her room where heedless of the tears streaming down her cheeks she dressed in her white blouse, grey two-piece, and black shoes. There was no need for him to go back at all. The city was full of men on leave from the British Forces who never returned. For that matter there were many Englishmen safe for years past in Dublin eking out a living until the war would end. There were even Germans living in safety there. The jeweller's shop in the light of whose window she had seen the black student's face was run by a man from Frankfurt. It was wrong, to have said all that to him about Molly and the student, but she was only thinking of his good. He would have to forgive her for that. She would earn that forgiveness by persuading him to stay at home. Even if he could find no work for the duration she would work her fingers to the bone for him. Mamzie would work for him too. Somehow they would manage, the important thing being that he shouldn't go away.

She smoothed away her tears with a damp face flannel and left the building sucking her finger where the pin of her scorpion brooch had caught in it as she dressed. She ran all the way down Castlewood Avenue before she saw him ahead of her walking steadily down Charleston Road, his suitcase swinging by his side. His head twitched at the patter of her feet and he turned to face her.

"Oh, Eddie, you can't go! Come home, dear. We'll look after you."

"Don't be ridiculous, Ag. Go back!"

"Please, Eddie" she called and made to move towards him. A faintness assailed her, a dapple of grey showerings, a ringing hum in her ears as of a menacing machine. Wavering, she reached for one of the bars in the railing of a garden, holding her face towards the crisp tap of his feet. The sickening greyness lifted and she saw him tall as a spear in the morning, striding into the distance as if he had forgotten who she was, as if all that bound them had died years ago and was no longer of any importance whatsoever. He drew near the corner of Kanelagh Road and in a few swinging steps would be out of sight, lost to her forever. A cry wrenched out of her.

"Eddie! Eddie! We love you Eddie! Don't go."

He paused on the corner and bent his head as if thinking out some problem.

"Everything'll be all right, Ag. You just go on home.

There's a good girl."

His voice carrying across the grey space between sounded harsh, hopeless even. He waved and was gone. She stood looking at the blank grey curve of pavement where he had stood reflecting. Her heart exulted. He was gone but of all who loved him she was the last to see him alive. A horror of joy engulfed her.

THE HARD COLD WORLD OF THE O'KENNEDY ACCOUNT

As Dessie eased into the station-wagon to retrieve the current issue of *The Economist* from the glove compartment - what did that headline mean about the depreciating value of the dollar? - his golf-bag manifested itself to him as an obscene, tubular life-form crouching ready to spring from the back seat where he had laid it earlier when he came out with Deirdre to drive to mass in Phibsboro. The interior of the car was as breathless and oppressive as a bake-oven and for a blurred moment, in which his fingers lost interest in the journal, it felt as if he were supporting the hard, rigid weight of the car-roof with his skull. Even when he withdrew and slumped over the bonnet drawing careful breaths, he still felt intimidated by the rumpled bulk of the bag and by - inevitably - the edgy memory of Deirdre's mousey presence in the car. His limbs took to trembling again but this time they felt strangely fragile as if his bones were turning into some such yielding substance as plasticine which as a child he loved to mould into the shapes of horses, dogs, elephants, all with that sweetish smell which made him feel sad. And no doubt it was the hint of Deirdre in the car - sweetish with a kind of sour after-whiff as of milk - that had set him trembling again after the ten minutes or so of peace he had found out in the open, waiting for her beside the grey, roughcast wall of the house. When would it come, he trembled, the disaster his crazy folly of last night had made inevitable? He must have been mad! On the eve of what could easily prove the most crucial encounter of his life, what impulse to self-destruction, what lurking hatred of himself - for what else could it be? - had driven him after so long, so peaceful, so welcome an interval to nudge her out of sleep and make silent, desperate love to her? Twelve months of planning, of shrewd manoeuvring had gone into wangling this appointment with O'Kennedy, twelve, for the most part, fruitless months of striving for even the briefest flash of significant eye-contact, of seeking to be inadvertently overheard in an unguarded moment by the great man, of compiling a repertoire of conversation openers for the day he would at last get his chance to speak face to face to the tycoon and make his play for the remunerative O'Kennedy account. His soul cringed at the memory of all those bleak evenings in the steely cheer of the bars in the United Services and in the Bankers Club where, with the cold skill of a dead-eyed gambler, he dealt out carefully garnered gossip and scandal and character assassinations and subtle dirty stories in his best carefree manner, flicking into the conversation now and then the unsuspected ace of power-fringed names some of which unfortunately dropped with a dull flop all over the expensive carpetings as he worked from one leeringly appreciative group to another, drawing ever nearer to the frustratingly closed circle of well-heeled cronies always crouched hard and grey as an impenetrable stone wall between him and the great man. All apparently to no avail until that morning early last week when at the crumbling graveside of yet another member of the seemingly numberless G.P.O. garrison - cut down by that old sniper Father Time in the prime of his senile decay - O'Kennedy at last acknowledged his existence and turned his raw, scored disaster of a face towards him to whisper behind his huge, gnarled hand; "Pardon me for buttin' in, young fella, but did I hear you aright when you were sayin' to your friend back there that most big advertisers in Ireland are a crowd of mugs because none of them is gettin' full coverage for their money?"

Dessie's heart soared with the third ragged volley over the grave of the dead volunteer - late managing director of Gaelectrics Inc. - "Name any big advertiser" he said holding the ire of O'Kennedy's piercing blue eye, "and I guarantee that with no bother at all, I could get him from fifteen to twenty per cent more coverage for his outlay."

O'Kennedy looked down at him as if he hated what he saw.

"Be God, you couldn't do that for any of my groups!"

"Oh yes, I could," Dessie smiled his tenderly nurtured sincerity and concern, "And incidentally - by the way it's Mr O'Kennedy isn't it? - by making the advertising content more effective I could give each advertisement at least another twenty per cent more pulling power. And that's what counts, isn't it?"

On the way back to where, on the face of it at least, the living outnumbered the dead, to the big sleek cars lurking like giant black beads outside the cemetery, O'Kennedy inclined his stark white head towards him over a moving wall of old cronies and sharp young executives, "Ah yes," he exclaimed, "That's where I've seen you before, young fella. The golf club! Be God, if you were out there next Sunday mornin' say eleven o'clock, maybe you and me might play a round o' golf that could turn out to be very, very interestin'."

Dessie smiled his imitation of Uriah Heep, realising as he did so that it needed a change of only one letter to turn golf into gold. Ideas for advertising slogans never missed their chance to pop into the mind. So why - Oh God tell me why? - with, the big fish munching at the bait and loving it, had he placed an explosive charge under the foundations of the project by turning - a shivering little boy in the shapeless dark - from the uncertainties of the impending day to the comfort however brief and shallow of Deirdre's hard pale thighs? And harder voice: "Well, if you must, I suppose you must! After all it's supposed to be your right isn't it?" But maybe God would be merciful. Maybe He would allow the intervening hours to sneak past without the inevitable whirlwind of shrieking complaints and bitter wounding sneers into which she flung herself with a kind of mechanical gusto the day following their making what some married couples, somewhere, maybe, could still call love. Already the storm signals were up and whipping in the wind. At breakfast after mass he looked up from the rash of cornflakes, spilled in his nervousness on the fresh tablecloth, to meet the grim champing of her sharp jaws, the blue squinting glare of her eyes. Oh please let this chalice pass! Surely God would not refuse to be merciful just this once and grant her the grace not to explode into her mad dance of vindictiveness, of twisted spite, and send him to O'Kennedy as limp as a dishcloth, his spirit bruised, his ideas scattered, his mood capable of inspiring an irresistible advertising campaign only for suicide! He would never learn what lurking guilt, what oblique twist of soul drove her to react to the gift of love as if she were a modern survival of the malignant hags, yellow-fanged and poison-eyed, who infest the misty, soggy wilderness of ancient Irish literature. She would have got on well with the one whose big act was to stand on one leg while she chants a death-spell over the Hound of Ulster. Alias Dessie Conlon. After their first year of marriage, whose brief moments of careless rapture were prearranged on the calendar with reference to Father D'Arcy's extremely helpful little booklet on Rhythm, he could never turn to her in desire without a despairing sigh for the lash of hate and outrage he would have to bear on the morrow. Once, about six years ago, he had prepared an ad for Raymor's Rings and was just about to send it off to call its direct black-and-white message from the chaste pages of the Capuchin Annual, when a final glance at it showed him he had balanced his display line of 'Marriages are made in heaven' with a bold subtitle in the body of the ad which announced: "And sure as Hell unmade in bed." He worried for days about having no recollection of blocking that out and pasting it onto the layout. None at all! And once again

The Hero Game and Other Dublin Stories

last night, his soul limp and subtly soiled, as his marriage took another step towards its unmaking, he floated away from her onto the verge of sleep trying vainly to recall where he had read the story of a shipwrecked man who keeps on hoping through hours of desperate darkness that the noise he hears ahead is of waves breaking on a welcome shore, but suddenly gives up his efforts to reach it, more to escape the continuous inane leapings of unrealised hope than to sink in surrender to an impulse of black despair. How immeasurably different this insipid life with Deirdre to the joy and fulfilment he had known with her it would be stark raving madness to think about today! No definitely not today of all days! It would really be the end to let all the patiently-contrived barriers down and start remembering Polly.

He roused to the slam of a door somewhere in the house. Deirdre was coming. Which made a change. His distorted image on the curve of the station-wagon fender was vaguely ellipsoidal, like a pear seen from underneath. He smiled - outside every striving thin guy is a prosperous fat man screaming to get in - and ran a shrewd eye over his dress and appearance. The ivy-green cravat peeping from the open collar of his green-and-orange check sports shirt was bound to have some subtle even subliminal effect, however small, on one who in his younger days had fought to make Ireland free. Or to put it another way had shot his way to fame and fortune under the green banner of the Gael. But the total effect of nonchalant confidence achieved by his suede golf jacket, his buff gabardine trousers and dull-brown brogues, was rather ruined by the perpetual criss-cross of wrinkles above his left eyebrow which gave to his features a tinge of anxiety that shone through even the gay mocking expression - so popular at the moment in women's magazine stories - he drew on his face whenever he realised he wasn't wearing it. And the reflection on the fender made darker than life the hard line running from the grim valley at the corner of his mouth to the fleshy crest surrounding the shadowy dimple in his chin. If only his whole ellipsoidal aspect suggested something other than a man perpetually on the point of springing to his feet in alarm. But you couldn't be in the advertising racket without its showing somewhere on you - and in you. Thankfully - maybe because it was Sunday - his ulcer was having a quiescent lie-on in its alkaline bed.

He winced as the front door crashed shut and at once moulded a look of saintly calm on the chinny image of himself on the car fender, listening in trepidation to her heels chipping like busy hammers on the path towards him, growing louder and louder into - silence. He looked up and saw she had passed between the rear of the car and the garage doors and was wavering on tip-toe looking out over the garden wall. He flipped his copy of the Economist over the lowered window of the car and waited.

"Ah yes!" she called in her railway-station announcer's voice to the startled pigeons hurtling up over the roof top, to Mrs Tankery's long white face which always appeared in the top left bedroom of the next house whenever the front door slammed, to an enviably distant heave of cloud, powdery as snow, drifting it seemed inch by inch along the blue expanse of the eastern skyline. "Ah yes! Give or take another few weeks and that house they're buildin' over there'll be peepin' over this bloody wall as well. Then there won't be any view left on any side of us at all. Comin' from a good home as I did I never thought I'd see the day when I'd be forced to live all hemmed in by corporation dog-boxes."

So that was what she was going to press into use as a running fuse to her inevitable explosion of hysteria - the house she was nagging him to buy! He should have guessed. She turned and marched towards him in her long stride, the padded shoulders, the abundance of buttons on her beige two-piece giving her an intimidating military look. Her hair ignited a whitish yellow by her latest hair-stylist, swept back from her high porcelain forehead in fussy curls and as she came near he could hear the soft slap of her long pendant ear-rings against the sides of her neck. He looked quickly away from her bright legs kicking out sharp as blades below her skirt. Polly! Polly, he regretted in spite of his resolution.

"You can see it now, can't you?" with a toss of her yellow head she indicated the barely-visible shell of the rising house. "They're gettin' on with it fast, aren't they? So now, be God, you'll have to do somethin' about it at long last, so you will! Otherwise, in no time at all there'll he droves o' kids clamberin' over that wall there, tramplin' all the rose bushes into the ground an' committin' nuisances behind the rockery."

"Don't worry" he chanced, "It won't turn out like that."

"Oh I know quite well it won't" she stood close, her armoured brassiere nudging into him so that he looked at her and got the full benefit of her hard stare as well, "We'll have taken action, won't we, long before that happens?"

He snapped the car door open for her and came around to his own side. In an oppressive silence - the air in the car felt too heavy to circulate - he began to drive through a hectic backward topple of familiar buildings down the long Cabra Road in erratic spasms and lapses of speed. A point on the back of his neck tensed in dread of a sudden blow from a malignant something lurking behind him until he remembered the golf bag on the back seat. But even then he dared not breathe easily for she remained so quiet beside him he feared she might have been raiding the drinks cabinet again to give her outburst a little more sting and carefree zing than usual. He heard her nails scrape over the surface of her silver cigarette case and as imperceptibly as he could he wound the window lower in anticipation of the hated clouds of her rancid tobacco smoke. She had never learned how to inhale. And several other fundamental things as well. He drove on through the quiet morning city in a blur of dread until as he wove through the hotch-potch of Ballybough to the wind-scoured sweep of Marino he felt her give a prim toss with her bottom and knew the attack was on. At times like this even the sound of her voice was as unbearable as the words she uttered with it.

"I know you too well by now, so I do, so don't bother denyin' that ever since we left the house you've been dreamin' up a whole batch o' new excuses not to buy that house I've set my heart on. I'd respect you much more if you came straight out and admitted that. Yes, an' agreed into the bargain that the real reason you won't decide on the Killiney property is not that it's

The Hero Game and Other Dublin Stories

too far out of town but that you're too bloody mean to buy it. You'd have to put down too much hard cash all at once and you know what it's like gettin' money out of you - don't you? - blood out of a stone!"

"That's not it at all!" he prodded hard on the accelerator and for a moment couldn't understand why the car took it into its head to run away with him, "You know quite well that from a business point of view it's not practicable for me to live so far out of town. Look at all the chasing about after business I have to do! Anyway, why let ourselves in for a five-thousand house in Killiney when we can have the place in Rathfarnham for three-and-a-half?"

"Oh listen to that will you'." she clicked her teeth, "You've just said it all! What did I tell you? Mean! Oh yes, mean!" She trilled a short brittle laugh, "Now you hear me for a change! I had greasy Jews all around me on the South Circular when I was growing up so I'm not going to move out to a place they're busy turnin' into a second Little Jerusalem. They move into all the nice, quiet, respectable places so they do and ruin them with their flashy, pushy, slimey ways. A gang of sly snobs the lot of them!"

"So I should be fifteen hundred pounds more bloody snobbish and move out to Killiney, should I?" The irony of his mimicking the Dublin Jewish accent didn't quite travel the whole length of the uncomprehending distance between them. He held his breath. Just keep it cool! Don't give her any excuse to argue, to contradict!

"Oh sneer away" she sneered, "But get this really straight. This little Christian family here is going to arrive at a momentous decision today for...." In an agitated cloud of tobacco smoke her outburst floundered into a spasm of coughing. He saw the manic look of desperation in her eyes and knew it wasn't there because she was fighting for breath.

"Deirdre" he pleaded, "For God's sake not today! This O'Kennedy thing is really big. It could be the making of us. Myers said if I land the account he'll make me a junior partner."

"And what'll I get out of that?" her cry struck his ear like broken glass, "Rathfarnham is it? Rathfarnham and the bloody Jews? You'd feel rightly at home among that crowd, so you would! You have an awful lot in common with them. For do you know what you are Dessie Conlon? A real, sly, mean oul Shylock that's what!"

"It needn't necessarily be Rathfarnham," he smoothed the nervous edges from his voice, "There are plenty of other nice places. And anyway, we really don't have to decide about it today, do we?"

"What you don't seem to understand" even though her voice was clear he could tell her teeth were clenched, "is that I really like that house in Killiney. And my mother is mad about it as well. So, I've got news for you. Today is the day you're goin' to decide about it, like it or lump it!"

"Be reasonable, Deirdre" he strained to hold the car to an even, legal speed, "How can I decide any important question like that with this O'Kennedy business on my mind? I could say 'yes' to Killiney just for a quiet life. But what would that be worth if I went back on my word afterwards?"

"Well, it'll be all off your mind by lunchtime, won't it?"

she said in her tuneless everyday voice, "And you'll have the peace and quiet of the drive from the club back to the hotel to mull the whole thing over in your mind. And that'll help you to come up with the right answer. And when you get it I'm sure you'll see that livin' out in Killiney won't be the great inconvenience you're tryin' to make out it is. But of course if you still think otherwise then we'll have the whole long afternoon to ourselves to go over all the alternatives, won't we?"

Though she leaned forward the easier for him to see her, he declined to look at the cold, sweet smile he knew she was wearing. "In that case" he said, "let's give it a rest for the moment and just relax and enjoy the drive."

"Just a little rest" she scratched lightly with her long pink nail on the back of his hand. furtively he sighed his almost incredulous relief at this unexpected reprieve. He decreased speed a little watching the blackish ribbon of road leap continuously towards the snout of the car where it split and shot frenziedly past on either side. The onrush of air through the side window cooled the lather of cold sweat sticky all over his face. His whole body was bathed in sweat he realised; he felt it even in the hollows behind his knees. What a cross to bear, this life with Deirdre! So offer it up! At least let God get something out of it! All for Thy sake O Lord! All for Thee! Yes, God was being merciful all right. For his mind was free to think of the impending encounter. How had he seen it as he tossed from dream to restless dream last night? He would stand at the clubhouse door in an attitude of obvious anxiety and expectation drying his palms with a handkerchief as big as the flags you saw the Germans surrender with in end-of-war newsreels. When the tycoon drove up in his big black Plymouth he would give him a quick wave and trot briskly like a small boy to the parking space to snap open the door of his car with a flutter of nervous smiles, a ducked bow, and some bright quip that was bound to occur to him at the time. Something really obsequious of course to show how fully he realised that O'Kennedy was indeed a great man, one of the nation's real rulers and benefactors, a man it was indeed a special privilege to speak to. But mixed in with all that would be a taut hovering anxiety, an eager impatience to get through all the social preliminaries and waste no further time in turning the game of golf into a brisk business conference. And then with these impressions clearly conveyed he would make a complete switch and adopt an elaborately casual throwaway manner with which he would chat as boringly as he dared on topics not even a tortuous mind as O'Kennedy's could remotely associate with business, the thrills of hunting to hounds for instance or neo-realism in the Italian cinema. That should throw O'Kennedy into some confusion and act as a counter to his well-known ploy of launching into long discussions on the virtues of different varieties of potato whenever he suspected the other party was most interested in talking business. It would be revealing to see how those tactics would work. If O'Kennedy could see that he was having no success in indulging his penchant for dangling those who wanted something from him over the slow fire of uncertainty, how long would it be before his native greed and cunning would break to the surface? Would he be talking business by the fourth hole? Or would it be the fourteenth? What did it matter how long it went on? The way to survive in the advertising world was to lean hard on your ulcer and hold out to the bitter end. And beyond if necessary. Even after the game, all would not be lost for he could dazzle O'Kennedy with the foolproof profitability of his ideas just as briefly as it took to down a parting drink in the clubhouse. And there would still be hope even on the following day when he rang up O'Kennedy to enquire about whatever aspect of his health was causing him anxiety for like every other businessman in the club he would be sure to dwell long and lovingly on his favourite complaint on the way round. Shrewd tactics! And they just might work. And God, how they stank to high heaven.

He smiled wryly at Polly still thinking in him, still passing judgement on his ideas and actions, eight years later on. The not-to-be denied memory of her living beauty flooded his mind like a release of light. If he were writing copy for the experience the main heading would be 'A Pang of Light', something like that. No wonder he loved driving. His subtle intercourse with the car, the vibrant purr of concentrated power insinuating through his hands and feet always evoked some memory of her, some heart-constricting instant from the past - at least from the better part of it before the bitterness took over and began to destroy everything. But none of that today! He stared fixedly ahead and found himself speculating about the unusual speed of the double-decker bus which he realised had been in front of him ever since he had turned into the Malahide Road. Driver probably behind in his schedule. Another poor anxious bastard sweating behind the wheel!

"Switch on the Light Programme, will you?" Deirdre always made a request as if protesting because it hadn't yet been granted. In a few moments the radio came on and a popular melody - he recognised *A Slow Boat to China* subtitled Deirdre's passion - gave an oversweet taste to the air flowing over his face as if violins were dripping treacly sound all over him and the woodwind puffing soft marshmallow into his mind. At the first opportunity he would make a note in the ideas book he always carried in his back pocket. There might be a chance to work in sound-and-taste combinations in the ads for some of O'Kennedy's products. 'Let your tongue hear the splash of Kencanned Herrings!'

The road curved slightly and they were speeding through the artisan anonymity of Coolock where a cluster of worshippers stood in bareheaded silence outside the high open doors of what he surmised was the parish church. To his surprise he suffered a sharp stab of nostalgia and - how absurd can you get? - began to wish he had not already attended mass. How wonderful it would be to leap back over the intervening years and stand in his callow innocence hearing mass once again in the midst of the People! The very word had the feel of another age, almost of life on another planet. It echoed straight back to the days when he made it a point to attend short twelve - the cabman's mass as his Uncle Dick called it - in High Street church which was just a short walk from his home, that beloved warren of untidy rooms above the bedding factory his father ran at just half-a-pace faster than the official receiver who finally overtook him the same week Czechoslovakia came under the Hitler hammer. Poor man! Drowned in a social system he never learned enough about to keep himself afloat. But in those days - he was seventeen or eighteen - what had the name Marx meant to anyone in the family apart from the crazy antics and brash wisecracks - loathed by his mother - of Harpo, Groucho, Chico, and Zeppo in *Horse Feathers* and *Animal Crackers* and *Duck Soup*? And so, on the steps of the church, cheek by unshaven jowl with both fervent believers and those he sensed had been driven forth to mass at the last minute by the threats, bickerings, and lamentations of wives and mothers, he felt a deep sense of fellowship, a quiet surge of strength, an almost overwhelming conviction that he was living the experience of consciously being part of the mystical body of Christ. How moving it was to stand there among his fellow-citizens, the salt of the Irish earth, and hear from within the church the silvery tinkle of bells announce that once again the miracle of the mass had been accomplished and that Christ was made flesh to shed the light of his glory over the quiet dignity of their lives. But gradually, it must have been after the factory had been closed down, certainly it was before he had begun to read Marx, not a little of the magic had started to fade from his romantic, almost religious concept of the People.

At first it was hard to admit the truth of his growing impression that the men praying bleary-eyed beside him were no better than senseless cattle chewing the cud of a ritual that, though it touched the fibres of their fears, made hardly any impression at all on their minds. They seemed singularly unaware of the reality of the great gifts which God through his holy church presented to them. Appearance alone was everything to them - the priest in his bright vestments murmuring in

Latin, the slumped figure on the cross, the pictures on the stations of the cross along the walls of the church. None of them by word or deed ever showed an awareness of the awful reality behind all that. Later, he found that Marx summed it all up when he said that religion was the opium of the people and truly where the people on the steps were concerned, Marx's dictum held all the *appearance* of truth. And, in essence, that point about appearance was the great revelation his reading of Das Kapital brought to him. Marx expressed the truth about the appearance of society. He was totally right if one discounted divine providence, the grace and the will of God, the reality of His presence in the Eucharist. But not for a moment did one dare to discount these awful truths. Marxism postulated the great 'as if.' If one left God out of the reckoning, then all that Marx said about the form, the structure, the dynamic of history and of society appeared to be irrefutably true. And since you had to live through your era of history in the woof and warp of society and wrest a living from it - aye that was the rub - what harm was there in taking a hard, shrewd look at the appearance of society through Marx's eyes so long as the truth of God was always alive and safe in your heart? If only Polly had made a real effort to understand that! If only she could have seen that his was a sincere and valid attitude she might not finally have become so unreasonable - so disastrously unreasonable so far as his life was concerned. "All that your famous attitude adds up to" she once said, "is the betrayal of Christ, of Marx, and of Dessie Conlon." But that wasn't true. Or if it was he just couldn't see it no matter how sincerely he tried. In a chafe of embarrassment he found himself remembering a Good Friday afternoon before he had stopped attending High Street in favour of the more fashionable and supposedly intellectual University Church on the Green. He stood on the steps waiting for the crucifix to be borne towards him, hoping that none of the New Theatre crowd or any of his Jewish friends were on the buses nosing noisily through the narrow street behind him. As the priest came in view bearing the image of the broken Christ for the people to kiss he had an excited sense of being both unpredictable and self-consciously dramatic. "I have betrayed you" he whispered to the proffered crucifix, but whether he meant Christ, or the People, or himself he wasn't sure, even now. Even now as the road ahead cleared of traffic and he overtook the blue double-decker bus. He looked up curiously at what he realised had been attracting his attention for some time, the soft outline of a man's head inclined against the back window of the upper deck as if listening to music. A head vaguely like Frank Comerford's. But of course it couldn't be Frank who at last account was in London infiltrating the Electrical Trades Union with some other dedicated comrades and making it a highly efficient instrument of Party Policy. No it wasn't Frank for if he were back in town then Polly would be there too. And Polly wasn't in Dublin. He would know immediately if she were. The air would somehow be sweeter and crisp and electric with excitement. "Can you light me a cigarette- er- dear" he broke away half-turning to Deirdre. God, what business had he to think of the past in the hard cold world of the O'Kennedy account? They were even driving through part of his empire. That light flashing away on the left was the sun striking reflections from the glass roof of one of the O'Kennedy packing plants. The fields on either side, as far as the eye could see, were planted thick with the produce which later would go into his cans, his jars, his plastic containers, his cellophane packets, "You can see these are not O'Kennedy crisps" was a line he might just manage to work into the conversation at the clubhouse bar as he proffered a saucer of the limp potato crisps invariably on the counter there.

Deirdre's nails scratched faintly on the surface of her cigarette case. Thankfully, the Light Programme was providing music whose charms appeared to be soothing the savage breast - small with an off-putting firmness like the red sponge balls of his childhood. But how he hated himself whenever he thought of her body, for God how he had come to loathe all its firm, unyielding contours. For the past few years he made love to her only in the dark - brusquely, mechanically - for when the bedside lamp used to be on it pained him to see her expression of long-suffering and faint disgust, her refusal to look at him, to hold his gaze lovingly in hers. Always her eyes turned away to look inward both savouring and loathing the advance of her own sensations as if they had nothing whatsoever to do with him and what they were engaged in. The character and development of the means of reproduction plays a determining role in every marriage. He grudged a grin at the channel of leftist jargon through which his thoughts about her flowed, the result of having thought about Frank Comerford. And Polly of course. Always Polly! But wasn't it inevitable that he should think of both of them together for wasn't it Frank who had introduced him to the world of the Left where he had met Polly? Yes, and it was Frank who had taken her away from him.

He inclined his head to the match Deirdre held in her cupped palm and felt mildly giddy from the blue effulgence of smoke and the staunchless streaming of the road and of time in the corner of his eye. It was not unlike the giddy sensation he had when Frank, whom he had not seen since they left school, met him by chance one evening in the bar of the Gaiety Theatre and launched without preamble into an attack on their former teachers. "A right crowd of latent homosexuals those Marist Fathers were! A crowd of bloody boyeurs!" Until that surprising moment he had had no idea how his old friend felt about the clergy and the education they had had under them. During the argument that ensued Frank said several times: "But you're only taking that reactionary line because you haven't read Marx!" Still, he smiled to himself, they had parted friends with Frank, almost as an afterthought, turning back to him and saying: "And by the way, if ever you want to see some real plays as a change from this load of intellectual cornflakes - it was a piece by Terence Rattigan - why don't you come along and see what we're doing in the New Theatre Group? I'll send you a list of our current productions. Drop in to a rehearsal if you like. Are you still at the old address, helping your old man to keep the corpse of capitalism warm?"

When he told Frank that the factory had been forced to close down and that he was now working in Myers and Taylors, he swayed away from him with an exaggerated gasp of horror. "Jasus! You mean you're mixed up with the pimps, parasites, and prostitutes in the advertising racket? O be God, you need to start reading Marx

- quick!"

Watching the onrush of the blackish road his nervous system, his very bones, remembered the horror of that period of his life, those months before the war with one disaster after another overtaking the family, almost daily it seemed, culminating in the death of his father, the selling up of his home, the hasty retreat with his brother Bob to a crumbling flat in Thomas Street from which he departed anxiously every morning to flounder through his only part-understood duties as general office boy and occasional copywriter in Myers and Taylor, in continual dread of making some irrevocable mistake that would cost him his job.

"Yes, that one's not bad either" he nodded in agreement towards the house Deirdre pointed to, realising as in a dream that for some time past she had been making comments on some of the houses on the way and he had been supplying appropriate retorts. It never failed to amaze him how, unless he went in fear and trembling of one of her emotional outbursts, only an infinitesimal part of his essential self was ever engaged by Deirdre. Sitting there beside him, helping out Helen O'Connell on *Tangerine* with her inimitable tinny hum, she was as distant from him as the vague inchoate person he had been in those early days in the advertising business. Before in fact he actually got down to reading Marx, which despite Frank's constant urging happened almost by chance. He still thought about the day he first held a copy of the Communist Manifesto in his hand as 'that Saturday'. He was waiting outside the Queens for a girl he'd made a date with the night before at a bottle party in the flat of one of the girls at the office, when he noticed across the road a new bookshop called Progressive Books outside which eventually he stood looking idly in at the titles in the window with an occasional glance back towards the Queens to see if his luck might still be in. The titles and dustcovers of the books almost without exception were dull and uninviting and he was about to move on to see what was featured round at the Royal when his eye caught the name Marx. The next time he ran into Frank he wouldn't feel such an ignorant fool! He entered the shop and spent what stretched into an absorbing hour dipping into one book after another his mind slowly catching fire with the sort of inevitable spontaneous combustion that starts the kind of conflagrations that burn down whole buildings, cities, civilisations. When he left the shop he had under his arm a thumb-smudged copy of *Capital, Book One*, a clean paper-edition of *Labour in Irish History*, two back issues of *International Literature*, several pamphlets on Dialectical Materialism and Marxist-Leninism and a crisp, freshly-printed copy of the mind-toppling *Communist Manifesto* itself. He hurried home almost at a run realising that he had at last some idea of the sort of experience Saul had on the road to Damascus, which is something that had always puzzled him at school. Easing the car along a straggling line of laughing men on a much later, much different road, the road through Balgriffin, he tried to recall the words he had used to describe to Frank the effect his reading had on him, "It was like being kicked in the head over and over - from inside!" Something like that. What a large corner of his heart - but not his soul, one must be eternally vigilant, not his soul - was still warm with the excitement of discovery, of revelation, of shocked realisation that came to him through his dedicated reading in the months that followed. Still somewhere in the house - no, in a cardboard box under the workbench in the garage out of Deirdre's scornful reach - were cherished copies of Left Book Club books with the intriguing Not For Sale To The Public - too dangerous? too daring? too incitive of revolution? - in heavy black type across the bottom of their red covers - *Man's Worldly Goods, These Poor Hands, Fallen Bastions, American Testament, We the People, The New Propaganda, Comrades and Citizens, Something Went Wrong, China Fights Back, Red Star Over China.* Ah, yes, *Red Star over Bessie,* for due to the influence of his leftist, Marxist reading he had come to accept that though he would never in thought or deed go against any of his fundamental Catholic beliefs, some shadowy part of him would always be red, holding aloft an exultant clenched fist like the men of the International Brigade in that compelling photograph in *Picture Post* at the end of the Spanish Civil War. He had wondered at the time what gave them that earnest, dedicated look and after Progressive Books he was beginning to understand.

He drew deep on his cigarette and for an absurd instant almost believed that the car was standing still while the streaming road and the flickering landscape hurtled towards him from straight out of the past. Where Polly was. And what of it if he were allowing himself to think of those other days? Weren't the insights about the form and pressure of society he had gained through his infatuation with the Left most relevant to the age of O'Kennedy? For beside the shrewd insights his reading gave him into the Class Struggle, the exploitation of the working classes by the rising bourgeoisie, the naked brutality of American capitalism, and the hope held out to humanity by the great Soviet experiment, its greatest value was the light it shed on the dynamics of Irish society. To his amazement he came to see that contrary to what he had been taught in school, the Anglo-Irish War, though it gave rise to the Citizen Army, the first Red Army in Europe, was in no sense a real revolutionary struggle. It was merely a desperate grasping for power undertaken in the guise of romantic nationalism - noble speeches at the courts martial, heroic deaths before the firing squad - by the petit bourgeoisie whose subsequent victory in no way extended the real freedom or enriched, materially or intellectually, the lives of the urban proletariat, the agricultural labourers and the small farmers who formed the bulk of their battalions. Recognising that the real power in the country lay with the church whose ability to control and direct the masses was evident on all sides, they were most careful to use their newly-won power only in the economic sphere where by joining up wherever possible with the old Ascendency class whose great, wealth in spite of all the shooting and the shouting, was more or less intact, they began to plant the seeds, however meagre, of their future industrial and commercial success. Not of course before they cut their fingers on their new toy, political power, and granted themselves the unearned luxury of a Civil War, that fierce moral, hair-splitting struggle which left the survivors scratching in the ruins for moneyed opportunities and jobs for the boys. When the smoke from the guns and the backroom cigars had cleared and the nation returned to business as usual, it became evident that though the two political parties into which the emerging class had split would remain divided forever by the bitterness of war, there was a remarkable degree of agreement between them on the sort of economic future they wanted for Ireland. A future of private property, state enterprises and raw capitalism. A future in which they could both with luck and opportunism, grow rich. Both parties united in the respect and the support and the tacit permission they granted the church to own rich properties and large tracts of land - Black Ireland as Polly called it - to control the minds of the next generation in the schools, to dictate to the nation at large on any question that broadly could be construed as moral. While it was clear that the church had need of material wealth to ensure that Christ's message be heard it was also obvious that the very possession of that wealth led it in some degree to identify itself with the economic interests of the new emerging class. A marriage fatal to both! Consequently you did not have to be a political genius to see that in those circumstances there could never be any essential radical change in Irish society, that real democratic socialism could never come to life there. Neither the Labour Party nor the trade unions could proceed far along the road towards true social justice without stubbing their toes against the accusation that they were attempting to lead the people to godless socialism. In any public confrontation on such issues, the church to make them bow down like primitives before a wooden idol, had only to click moral disapproval of their actions. Or if it came to bare knuckles, to threaten to withhold the sacraments as it did from the Irregulars at one stage during the Civil War. The bishops in Ireland could always swing their intimidating crosiers as effectively as any good faction fighter his trusty shillelagh. An ideal set-up for the O'Kennedys of this world - a whole society to exploit with the church standing by to ensure that the free-thinking intellectuals - the whole half-dozen or so of them - the workers, the agricultural workers and the small farmers could not interfere with the laying-up of treasure on earth for the chosen few, who largely had chosen themselves for the role. Ah, yes, a most valuable period in his life. His new insights into the true nature of society, into the social aspirations of the rising middle class, into the yearnings, the dreams and frustrations of the workers gave his advertising copy a new bite, a compelling blend of realism and fantasy that made for successful campaigns and climbing sales graphs. And unexpectedly exciting opportunities for more and more business. Like on the very day war broke out when Myers paid him the compliment of calling on him at the unfortunate flat in Thomas Street. "I suppose you heard the doddering old fool Chamberlain declaring war this morning?" was the first thing Myers said as if to get that trite subject out of the way, "What dreadful copy! God, in any given century how many men get the chance to declare war, to call their country to arms? Two or three. And he muffed it. All he did was produce a dull business letter. Any one of us here could have written better copy for the occasion, especially you, Dessie. And that's what I want to talk to you about, your work and prospects. I want you to become ideas and contact man in the agency. Taylor is not a hundred-per-cent for it, but throw in with me and we'll soon ease that old fool out of the firm. He's only a front anyway, not an idea in his head later than nineteen-ten. And there should be very interesting accounts to go after now. War always throws up the really gifted, enterprising businessmen."

And by working on the really enterprising businessmen who rose to the top - of the dunghill? - in the days that followed, he won with his persuasive ideas most of the really big accounts in town. Except one! He smiled to himself, but even O'Kennedy might have been coralled long since if it wasn't for Taylor's narrow-minded interference. "I find an unsavoury sexual suggestiveness in this new presentation the agency is preparing for Mr O'Kennedy. I'd have you both know" - Dessie and Myers exchanged glances - "that while I'm here this agency will not revert to such appeals, more especially as Mr O'Kennedy, who belongs to the same club as me, shares my own feelings about the sacredness and sanctity of human relations." Like his own father, Taylor too had no inkling of the profound changes taking place in Ireland in the confused aftermath of the British withdrawal. His outdated, deferential politeness of manner, his expensively acquired, English public-school lisp, his wide Ascendancy connections counted for a shrinking little in the poker-faced, Tammany-Hall reality of the new Ireland in which the rising class confined all their moral scruples to their religion thus keeping them well away from their business lives where the exploits and the exploitations of their champing greed, their peculiarly Irish meanness of mind and act, which would have brought a shudder to the soul of an unrepentant Scrooge, was beginning to lay up treasure in what passed with them for heaven - their bank accounts. Still, Taylor hung on until just after the war when Myers was at last able to buy him out.

"And it's not with great sorrow that I sever my connections with this establishment" he remembered Taylor swaying his champagne-blurred farewells at the office door, his folded copy of *The Times* tucked neatly under his thin arm. "A certain cold transatlantic amorality has crept into the way business is now sought out and transacted here" he said, "A cynical contempt for human dignity which is lost when man's dreams and desires are used as mere aids in the selling of goods. A lack of respect for truth itself in layout, illustrations and copy. An unsavoury tendency to go as far as you dare in Ireland with the base appeal of sex in advertising campaigns. And all this I blame principally on you Mr Conlon for as your responsibilities here have increased so has that despicable trait which I can only describe as a brash, clinical ruthlessness which now informs all the activities of the agency." A beatific smile spread over his face. "How's that for a parting piece of copy?"

Dessie shrugged off the memory of the look of contempt Taylor had laid on him after that. Which when you came to think about it was mild compared to the one Polly gave him the first evening he met her. That was when he made his way to a small trades hall to attend the first night of a New Theatre Group play, *Desire Under the Elms,* and Frank backstage took him by the elbow and said: "By the way I don't think you know..." the usual trite formula for many a man's encounter with the true meaning of his life. A good slogan. That too he would write down at the first opportunity for you never know where you might be able to work it in. But what his feelings were on meeting her - was it really love at first sight? Or just a shiver? - always remained like something forgotten in another room that he would recognise if only he could find the key to get back in there. What Polly felt however came right out in what she said: "Oh so you're the advertising genius Frank's always talking about. One of those fellows who waste their lives trying to turn the people's natural need for sex into a desire for goods they would largely be better off without." He winced, recalling the brutal way he asked: "And what do you do with your natural need for sex?" And was chastened by her girlish blush.

A month later, in a bedroom in a house in Raymoncf Street, following a party at which Frank sang the *Internationale* in Irish accompanied by Syd Friedman, who bellowed it in Yiddish, she had solemnly removed all her clothes as one performing a sacred immemorial rite, to stand shyly before him bathed in the yellow light of the street lamp streaming in through the dust-blotched window. He sank on his knees before her and rested his face against her soft flesh feeling the gentle orbs of her breasts cool on his forehead. "God, you and Frank are right" he said, "I'm nothing but a vicarious prostitute. I've no right to use something as beautiful as human love as a means of just selling things, of making bigger profits for greedy, grasping men." To think he had actually meant that at that moment! And that she believed it was more than his wonder at the great gift of her love; that it indicated the hope, of a permanent change in his outlook.

Hardly daring to breathe, almost oblivious of the shapes whirling past the car, he dropped all pretence of not wanting to think about her and began with cautious patience to coax back the carefree joy of the brief days of their happiness. When Bob was away youth-hostelling at week-ends, how wonderful it was to wake up and find Polly beside you whispering of the joy their love had brought her and of the hopes she had that the war now unleashed in Europe would before its end bring to Ireland a true workers' republic. The totality of her commitment frightened him though he loved to watch the light it brought to her eyes and the delicate lustre it caused to spread over her soft skin making him oblivious to what she was saying. Like when she got all worked up about the Dail deputy's wife who employed schoolgirls by the hour to make hair-clips in the filthy basement of a tenement property owned ultimately and torturously by the Church, and she lost him partway in his wrapt contemplation of the magic glow her denunciation brought to all her features, even to her long yellow hair. But in the dark he always listened, for her tremulous voice moved him as no music ever could. He sighed, recalling an evening when they lay in each others' arms in the mountain heather looking down on the erratic pattern of lights that was Dublin while she speculated on when the big moment might arrive for the Party. When he tried to suggest, as delicately as he could, it would never arrive at all, she refused to hear: "No! Ireland's neutrality is isolating her from the rest of the world and if the invasion of Britain takes place the safety valve of emigration will be switched off. Then the mounting tide of unemployment here will be bound to force the rotten ruling clique to abandon its stranglehold on the land and divide it up among those who need it. As you admit yourself they have been able to keep capitalism alive only by forcing out of the country twenty or thirty thousand workers a year who if they stayed at home unemployed would form the backbone of the battalions of the new Citizen Army."

Why did he always have to argue with her? Why did he always have to allow her to see his indulgent smile? Wasn't it enough just to be with her?

"Only I'm in love with you" she said as he sensed she had begun to realise there was no hope ever of turning him into a dedicated revolutionary, "I'm sure I'd find you a most despicable person. Probably more clearly than anyone else you see that what this country needs is a Marxist revolution and yet you give all your talents and all your energies to that unspeakable advertising firm."

He reminded her that not quite all his energies were spent in the service of advertising. "I love you and I love your dreams" was probably how he had put it, "But surely you must see that there is no future for Marxism in Ireland. Just as the Communist Party in Russia has indoctrinated its people against capitalism so has the Church in Ireland kept most of the people here from ever turning to socialism. I'm in the curious position of disagreeing with the practice of my Church while I believe totally in its doctrines. In much the same way I believe that Marxism appears to be true but I can't give myself to it because it leaves out of the reckoning any provision for the action on man and nature of the will of God. I suppose I'd define my attitude to life as something like this: I want to observe, to know, to understand, but not to be involved, at least not until I'm certain that what I might get involved with is both consistent with the will of God and certain to win. You may find that despicable, but to me it's a realistic attitude. For the reality of life is struggle. And I take reality seriously. That's why I don't just play at advertising. I'm a professional in every sense. On the other hand, what are Frank and you and the rest of our Leftist friends but deluded romantics playing at being revolutionaries, for you know as well as I do there's not a chance in hell of staging a communist revolution here. The whole place is jammed tight, packed solid - standing room only - with committed conservatives. Frank is always running down Fascism. But why doesn't he take the logical step and get involved in the war against it? And is Syd Friedman helping the revolution, or the Jews in the camps, by staying in Dublin to make a fortune out of the war, as you can see he has started to do. He's becoming one of my best accounts."

Thank God that even for those brief months their love proved stronger than their differences of outlook. That was the only time in his life when he stopped going regularly to confession for how could he truthfully say he was sorry for living in sin with Polly when every night he spent with her was a sacrament of joy? If only he could have persuaded her to marry him then! "I want to, Dessie" she said, "God knows I want to. But there's something in me, something I can't explain especially to myself - and it's not a doubt about our love - but whatever it is, it holds me back."

Deirdre's elbow probing into his ribs insisted him back to the present, to the staunchless yearning for Polly.

"Well is it?" She sounded more irritable than usual, so it was probably something quite trivial she wanted to know.

"Is it what?"

"You're always broodin' over business, aren't you? An' I suppose what that boils down to is plottin' and plannin' how to hold on to your money! Sure what else? What I was askin' was is that the place they found the manuscript of that dirty book?"

He realised they were driving past the demesne of Lord Talbot de Malahide.

"Oh, you mean Boswell's London Journal" he said, "Yes, the papers were found in - I think - a chest in the castle beyond the trees there. But who says it's a dirty book?"

"I know that game" she gave a mocking guffaw, "'to the pure all things are pure' is just a great excuse for reading filth."

She fumbled, dragged, her bulky heavy-clasped bag out of the glove compartment and after rooting in it began to dab at her face, patting the oversweet perfume he loathed on her neck, behind her brittle ears. He ground his teeth on the remark he longed to make. "Like Boswell and his Louisa all I wanted from you was an easy lay. But poor old Boswell and poor old me we both came out of it badly, didn't we? He ended up at the surgeon's, I at the altar. If only my disease was as curable as his!" He was sweating again. He eased his finger inside the sticky rim of his cravat. On the night it happened, if only the bloody bitch had resisted for just another few seconds, his growing disgust at his own behaviour would have driven him to desist. But maybe it was because she sensed he was about to give up that she suddenly ceased her defensive wriggling and lay warm and acquiescent beneath him. That was possibly the one thing about her he would never know for sure. Anyway, practically everything about that night was unclear. During the weeks preceding it the people and events in his life moved at a numb remove from the raw core of pain in his heart which Syd planted there the morning he rang up and gave him the news.

"I never knew Polly was keen on Frank, did you?" Syd sounded more frightened than curious, "It's incredible when you remember that he was such a good friend of yours and all! Mervyn claims they've gone to do war work in England. It was only by chance he saw the notice about the registry office in the paper otherwise none of us might have known they were intending to get married."

How contemptible now appeared the grim resolve he formed as he talked on the phone later that day to Deirdre, to take her out to the same hollow among the sand dunes of North Bull Island where he had lain with Polly so brief a time before! And what in heaven's name had he found to talk to her about as he strode across the downs beside her filled with a vengeful, violent lust that knew neither control nor discretion? That he couldn't remember now. Or didn't wish to. Was any conversation he ever had with Deirdre worth remembering? But what happened on the following day was as clear as daylight and as cold, grey and depressing as winter rain. He met her for lunch under the clock at the *Irish Times* and had to retreat into the foyer to escape the blank stares of the passers-by startled, as he was, by her strident bickering, the first sample - had he only known then! - of so much more to follow! His lips raw from her bites, his body crying out for still more of her intense blonde passion - how quickly that quenched - he pressed against the glass door through which he could see the clerks in the newspaper office looking up at them from their small pre-paids.

"You forced me, so you did, you louser" she shrieked, so loudly he wondered absurdly would that be the banner headline in next day's issue of the *Irish Times*, "I've always been a good girl and - Great Christ! - what'll my father say if it turns out you've made me pregnant? You showed no respect, or concern or feeling for me at all. Just brutal lust, that's all it was."

Was it to shut off that terrifying flow of strident outrage that he blurted out that he loved her, was carried away by his overwhelming passion for her? Or was it because he needed so badly the confidence that came to him from having a woman to sleep with that he genuinely believed he was speaking the truth? He would never get to the bottom of that now. Although, unfortunately, he had had no such difficulty with her.

"Well then if you love me as much as you claim," she said more to the delighted clerks than to him, "why don't you up and do the decent thing - marry me? There's not much sense in waiting about after what happened, is there?"

He explained that he had not planned to get married just yet, that he had little money saved, that prospects in the advertising business were not too bright on account of the shortages of paper and other materials brought on by the war. Besides wouldn't it be better to get married because they wanted to, not because they had to, so why not wait to see if her anxieties were justified or not?

"I'm not goin' to the altar bulging out of my wedding dress I'd have you know! And as for whatever plans you may have had, those can always be changed. And there's no need at all to worry about money for my father said the day I marry he'll put a thousand pounds into my hand. Now are you going to name the day or does he have to come and talk to you himself? He's no stranger to your famous Mr Myers I'd have you know!"

A complex of hesitant traffic near the church in the village of Malahide forced him to ease his furious pace. A glance at his watch sent a tremor through him. No, he wouldn't muff it like he had the question of marriage that day at the *Irish Times*. The O'Kennedy thing was too big to have anything go wrong now. Conlon can control it he affirmed, realising as he did so that an advertising man who believes his own copy is lost. Conlon would have to control his terror was more like it. For all his brashness, for all his overt nonchalance, he knew he would always be cold and frightened at times like this, a small boy aghast in a world of shrewd, edgy-voiced adults where factories suddenly close down, where the home you love is ransacked and boarded up before your very eyes. What must the criss-cross of wrinkles above his left eyebrow be like now? And the eyes themselves - round and anxious! He steered towards the drive of the Grand Hotel patiently moulding his features into the sort of vivid fixed smile he had once seen on the face of the compere of a British dance-band which played a one-night stand at the Olympic ballroom shortly after the war. The smile was a lurid mask of cheer as if it had been carved into the flesh.

From which he concluded the poor bugger was in a stab-in-the-back racket something like his own. Wearing his tight mask he drew the car to a halt at the bottom of the hotel steps. Deirdre eased her over-scented body out and straightened her tight skirt. Not looking at him she spoke down at him between her teeth. "Remember you've a big decision to make on the way back from the club. And I know you'll make the right one." She turned away and with her chin at the tilt currently popular with the photographers at Vogue went cruising up the steps from the top of which she flipped him a faint wave and called out for the benefit of the commissionaire bowing to her from beside the door; "Have fun with the boys, dear!" After which she vanished in the direction of the tea-rooms where he knew she would sit over her coffee drawing on her ash-laden cigarette and teasing Bartley, the head waiter, with flashing glimpses of her frilly panties. If the poor bastard only knew! He stared after her, watching the swing doors flicker blindingly in the sunlight until they steadied to a sheet of grey with a gleaming yellow edge that looked as sharp as the blade on a guillotine. If only she had even silently pressed his hand! Or said; "Good luck, darling!" or "Let the old bags have it!" or "Don't let it get you down, dear, it's not the end of the world!" O, anything but that gritted threat! He felt small and lonely, the stupid grin straining the muscles of his face. Without warning the volcano of his ulcer erupted in his side. Wincing his grin he steered out of the drive and drew in to the kerb across the road from a miniature park crowded with tall black trees bickering with rooks. Even the trees have to go through it! He lay quiet in his seat confronting the pain, waiting patiently for it to subside.

What a price to pay for the job of top man in the agency and two-thousand five hundred in the bank! What would a junior partnership and say five thousand in the bank add up to? Two ulcers? Still, even that would be far short of what he would need to fulfil his nagging ambition of buying Myers out. The old man was losing his grip and knew it. Fifteen thousand might induce him to retire to potter about with his roses and the skivvies on his sedate property at Foxrock. But God, where would he get fifteen thousand?

The bus he had passed on the road came down the village street towards him and stopped in the shadow of the trees. His pain began to fade to an ache that might have been anxiety rather than physical pain. He switched on the engine and drove at walking speed to avoid the bus passengers eddying into the roadway from behind the bus in the usual Irish suicidal manner. That was one way out of life's problems. And there tall amongst them was Frank Comerford, his spindly figure tight in his old earth-brown Premier-Tailors double-breasted, his hatchet face tilted to the sky still waiting for the spark of revolution to fall. "Frank!" he blurted out, immediately regretting his surprised impulse, but the yelp of the car brakes had drawn everyone's attention and Frank came warily towards the car, stooping, peering cautiously through the windscreen.

"Jasus it's Dessie!" he called out. Would a voice from heaven reply, "With whom I am well pleased"?

Dessie drew the dead weight of his limbs, the burden of his sense of doom out of the car and held out his hand, his heart suddenly sick. Where was Polly? The panic of awaiting the onset of the impact of seeing her again!

"Are you ready to take that inductive leap now and agree with me?" Frank asked, grasping his hand as if it was only last night he had been arguing the point that since everything the Church had done in Ireland was evil, the doctrines on which it claimed to base its actions must be evil as well. "No, you're still not ready." Frank stepped back appraising him, "You look more anxious than ever and you've put on too much weight."

Dessie kept his gaze hard on him, dreading and yearning for the first sight of her after all those years. Was she, in her careful way, still on the bus making sure they weren't leaving anything behind? Or just out of sight beyond Frank's sharp shoulder already staring at him? Frank moved towards him again, stooped his head and quietly, almost shyly asked: "And how's Polly?" Dessie glared at him hardly believing his ears. Frank caught his grim expression and frowned.

"I'm not prying, understand," he said in a whisper, "But surely you've seen her. On the quiet of course. Surely..."

A bitter dryness clogged Dessie's throat. "If you're trying to be funny I just don't get the joke. You more than anyone knew how I felt about her. That's a crazy way to talk of your own wife!'

"Jasus!" Frank groaned, "Didn't you know? She and I packed it in. Coming up to four years ago! I haven't seen her since."

Dessie stared at the scar on Frank's cheek waiting for the import of the words to catch up with him. From the pavement a woman's voice called; "Frank!" and he saw a stout girl, olive as a gypsy, hesitate into the roadway hovering over a small boy of about three who tugged peevishly at her hand.

"Come 'ere a minnit" Frank called to her. The woman approached, gave Dessie a sharp look, and yelped a little cry of delight. "Jesus Christ, Fanny" she bawled and threw her head back in a laugh that rippled all over her dimpled girth in which Dessie discerned the elusive ghost of the slim girl to whom he had read those lines at a rehearsal in the Boilermakers' Hall one night when he had stood in for an absent player. "Julie Connelly" he cried and avoided the shame of giving her his trembling hand by grasping her just about the wrists, squeezing tight.

"Wonders will never cease, eh Dessie?" said Frank at his side, "And what do you think of little Ivan?"

"Who is he more like, Frank or me?" asked Julie.

Dessie had a suspicion that his mind was not at present equal to engaging facts in their correct sequence. "Hello, little Frank" he said shaking solemnly the puffy stickiness of the small boy's hand.

"Hello, little Frank," echoed Frank bowing his head in a dry laugh, "God, he's still the very same. Mention Polly and the poor bugger doesn't know whether he's coming or going. And it was the same with Polly. With her it was always Dessie. Bloody always!"

"Lucky for me!" Julie laughed catching his shoulder in a tight, proprietary hug.

"All the same I had my moments!" Frank performed a feminine wriggle and patted his palm on the cluster of grey curls behind his ear, "Ah yes. At least two or three." He looked wryly downcast.

"How's Polly?" Julie asked.

"...hasn't seen her" Frank cut in too late, nodding round-eyed to Dessie to show he'd done his best.

"But she's back in Dublin" Julie said, "Been here almost three years though from what I hear she's not living with her family."

Dessie's heart gave a numb leap. He was quietly panting, unable to do anything about it, not caring that they saw. Driving through town on the trail of some account or other how often had he said to himself, When I turn the next corner she'll be there, waiting for a bus, poised on the pavement edge about to cross the road, or just standing, her clenched fist to her mouth thinking her way to some trivial decision or to some world-shaking idea. And as he came round all those corners on all those days of yearning for her, he would stare straight ahead and picture her tall and fresh as a young tree - his most recurrent comparison - her honey-gold hair waving back to the soft bun at the back of her head, her green eyes smiling out at the world she was determined to shatter violently to pieces and build again from the fragments. How often had he played that game? As often as he had cursed himself for being a sentimental idiot, a romantic hangover in a materialistic age. Yet anytime in the past three years it could so easily have been true! It could he true tomorrow. Dublin could cease to be a tense battlefield and become again the warm, relaxed place of the early days of the war when they strolled hand in hand through the elegant Georgian squares which she claimed the socialist future would preserve intact for the use of the working classes. A condemned man, he speculated, must feel something like this when told he's been reprieved.

"You must be completely out of touch with the movement" Frank said, "otherwise someone would have been bound to have told you about her. And where she's living now."

Dessie nodded his resolve that come tomorrow someone would indeed tell him.

"It was funny the way things worked out," Frank sounded as if he were about to launch into an elaborate excuse, "but when you and she - well, broke up - we two thought we could make a go of it. We saw eye to eye on so many things. And don't forget we were both members of the Party, such as it was. When Spillane sacked me for trying to organise a trade union in the firm I felt the correct way to carry out the true task of the Party was to help defeat Fascism by working in the war effort in England. Polly felt the same and for a while things were okay between us. But everything changed when I was demobbed from the army."

"You were in the war?" Dessie felt astounded at the idea of Frank in the uniform of what he himself called an imperialist power.

"Of course" Frank nodded, "There was some sense in it after Hitler attacked the Soviets. I saw the whole thing through the turret of a tank - El Alamein, Sicily, Rome, Normandy, Caen. Ended up as liaison officer with the Russians. Those nights on Semeonoff's grammar weren't wasted after all."

"Oh yes!" Dessie said politely in a flush of unexpected envy and guilt. Compared to what Frank had experienced how petty now seemed the scope of his own wartime campaigns! Securing his base in the firm through his brilliant seizure of the Cashel Cakes account, he had advanced under a barrage of catchy slogans, dirty jokes and shrewd manoeuvres to wrest Trimtown Cheeses and Asperaid right out of the seemingly impregnable fortress of the Grindley agency. Keeping his lines of communication well open he had rolled onwards under the crisp green banner with the £-sign on it to win the desperate battles fought out with the secret weapons of gossip, slander and economic analyses for Princetown Shirts, Neary's Biscuits, Micks Distilleries, Tolan's Bakeries and Jesse's Briefs until now, undeterred by the sharp wound in his side, he stood poised to launch the greatest campaign of all, the seizure of the reichschancellery of O'Kennedy Enterprises. "Oh yes" he repeated feeling he had not made sufficient politely attentive noises the first time.

"The Russians have got it all taped" Frank said shaking his head in wonderment. "They're the future and no mistake. And as you can see from the activities of the Chinese workers and peasants, the road to Paris is definitely going to lead through Peking. Anyway," he smiled sadly, "when the cheering died down, Polly and I took a hard look at our marriage and decided it had been - as the saying is - a mistake. Things hadn't improved of course by word reaching us long after the event via the usual little bird - you know, that Irish vulture - that you'd got married shortly after we left. The news went off under our own marriage as a sort of delayed action bomb. Daughter of an ex-Free State Army general we heard. No offence, but a hardened reactionary on a generous pension for his misdeeds which I believe included the Benbwee massacre. That must have been hard to swallow but I suppose he makes a good skeleton for an unoccupied cupboard. They said her name was Doreen."

"Deirdre" corrected Dessie.

"Ah yes, I might have guessed it had something to do with the sorrows. My sorrows! For the way Polly took the news showed me where her heart really lay. Only for my joining the army it would have ended much sooner. As it was there were no regrets, no recriminations, no divorce even. And then who should I walk slap into one night in Warren Street tube station on my way to a committee meeting but her nibs here."

"Ever since I played Anna Christie" laughed Julie, "I always knew I'd end up living in sin. And it's marvellous."

Frank grinned happily as he caressed the nape of her neck and smoothed his palm down her broad back like a farmer proud of the horse he was showing off at a fair. Little Ivan began to whimper and tug at his mother's skirt.

"The little fella's impatient to get to the sea," explained Julie. "You're dying to get on the beach, aren't you love?"

"I'm driving round by the seafront" Dessie told them, "Hop in and I'll drop you off wherever you like."

Frank helped Julie and the little boy into the rear seat. "See you're at the plutocrat's game now" he sniggered pushing the golf bag to one side, "But I suppose you have to take your ulcer out for a walk sometime."

"Well it makes a change from the office," Dessie smiled back at him realising the pain in his side had gone, "No walls or windows hemming you in while you're concentrating on business."

He drove quickly away from the park hurrying to be alone with his thoughts of Polly. If he could only get the damn O'Kennedy thing over and off his mind for good! Behind him, Frank kept up a commentary on the current international scene in which the term People's Republic, enunciated with ringing challenge, occurred frequently. It was like hearing an almost-forgotten language again after years of silence.

"Here'll do" Julie said when they reached the curve of the strand. "Isn't the water lovely, Ivan. It's the Irish Sea."

"And bloody wet like everything else in the joint" Frank said grinning as he helped them out of the car.

They would be in Ireland a few more days he told Dessie and would love to spend an evening with him chatting over old times. Dessie wrote down his telephone number in his notebook and under it added brief hints of the ideas that had occurred to him earlier, nodding a pretended attention to Frank's chatter. As they parted Frank called out: "I wish you looked less prosperous Dessie. Otherwise there might be some chance of getting you to commit yourself to us. No one was able to see the political and economic situation here as clearly as you. What a loss!"

Dessie drove away watching Frank's head shake from side to side in the rear mirror. Polly! Polly! his heart rejoiced as he sped round the coast road the telegraph poles, tall and black, flickering leisurely past on his left. Sand spurted away from his front wheels as he swung off the main road and drove furiously down the rough gold-flecked track to the clubhouse. He hurried inside to the men's room and washed his hands splashing cold water on his temples and winking at his quiet smile of complicity in the mirror. "She's in Dublin! She's in Dublin!" he repeated to himself exulting in the waves of joy that surged through his heart each time he said it. If only the damn O'Kennedy thing was over and done with no matter what the outcome! He strolled with careful nonchalance to the door and stood looking back down the rough road. O'Kennedy had said "about eleven o'clock" which from his shrewd study of the man he knew to mean exactly on the stroke of the hour - one of those perfectionist bastards who step on the scaffold to be dead on the stroke of eight, as you might put it. Dessie nodded to Fitzgibbon of Bast Wall Foundries who came clumping up the steps from the parking lot and headed for his favourite table in the exclusive region round behind the bar. To be dead on the stroke of eight wasn't bad considering the circumstances. He made a move for his notebook, would write it down later. No need to rush anything now. Polly and O'Kennedy both on the same morning called for every oncoming second to be encountered with acute awareness, savoured to the full, released reluctantly for the next. He patted flat the bulge of the notebook in his back pocket. It amused him that his best slogans and headlines were those he could never use, those which sprang to mind when first brought into contact with the product or service he was called on to advertise. Gem Polish puts a Real Spit on your Furniture!" "The last word in shoes - feet!" "Roman's Cigarettes, the Brand that satisfies - the undertaker!" "Sheersilk Stockings

Lead - right up to where your man wants to go." Always in a secret corner of his mind Polly smiled and approved. He turned his back on the empty road - he wouldn't use that stupid anxious-salesman ploy now - and ordered a packet of Afton Major at the bar. When the barman's back was turned he pressed his palm into the saucer of potato crisps on the counter, coughing softly to cover the noise. No harm in still using a line about O'Kennedy's Crackly Crisps being better than that crumbly mess. The clock over the bar told him it was indeed dead on eleven of clock. He felt the glow of a real smile on his face as he went to the door again and stepped out into the sunshine. Too late! McCoom, the bishop's brother, was already coming up the steps, his mouth unlatched in a smile that let you into the horrific secret of his foetid molars.

"Top o' the mornin'" McCoom said in an assumed folksiness to which Dessie gave a grunting, shrugging response. He looked beyond the dark advancing figure, down the long sandy track to check if O'Kennedy's black Plymouth was swinging in from the main road.

"Expecting someone?" McCoom asked. Dessie nodded.

"Who's inside?"

"Fitzgibbon. There may be someone else, you know, in the backroom-boys area round behind the bar."

McCoom sniggered; "We get them all in this place, don't we? All the big boys! Marvellous how they stick together, isn't it? I suppose it makes them feel more secure. Or as I sometimes think - less guilty." He peered out slyly from under his grey flecked eyebrows.

"Maybe it's just to keep an eye on each other" Dessie

said, noting that McCoom would have been old enough to have fought in the Civil War where he felt most of the guilt was generated.

"Maybe they need to and all!" McCoom grinned, "Take Fitzgibbon, you know how he got his big slice of Bamba Enterprises Inc. don't you? For putting the finger on four of his old comrades during the Free State trouble. Four key men they were and so it was a very special kind of death they got. The fellows who did it tied them up and put floursacks over their heads and took cockshots with their revolvers at the Blanchards-town Mills trade marks as if they were just getting in a bit of target practice. Afterwards, the government, which, as you know, like God, moves in mysterious ways, made sure that Fitz was made aware of the nation's gratitude. And do you know what he does now in his spare time? Plays the beloved disciple every year in the Father Michael Passion Play. I was once criticising him to my brother - you know who my brother is don't you?"

Dessie nodded and stole a glance down the track. Only a fuzz of sand blowing in from the road.

"And Andy said - that's what we called his grace as a kid - he said there's more joy in heaven over one sinner who repents - you know the text - and that I should exercise more Christian charity. Christian charity! If charity means love then Fitzgibbon's the boy for it. Not a year passes without his putting one or other of the office girls in the family way. He's a good Catholic. Won't have anything to do with contraceptives. That'd be a sin!"

Dessie jerked his head away from the unfortunate mouth gaping wide as an open sewer in a moist throaty laugh. Even his best friend - supposing he had one -

couldn't tell him. He'd swoon off before he could get close enough to whisper. And at last down the track in a cloud of sandy dust, the black snout of a speeding car boring towards them. They both watched it in silence and not until it was in the parking lot did Dessie notice it was dark-green. Murrin of the National Meat Board clambered out and hurried towards the steps. "'S'Fitzgibbon inside?" McCoom with a deep bow and a wave of the hand proffered the freedom of the club. "There's another of the big boys" he sniggered when Murrin vanished inside. Dessie waited for the inevitable character assassination. Helps to keep the hand in between civil wars. Or advertising accounts.

"Fried bread and tea is what he was reared on" McCoom said, "Was in the Fianna Boy Scouts. Out in the Rising when he was only fourteen. Course his big chance came in the Civil War when You-Know-Who hid out in his house when he was on the run from the Free Staters. They say the great man's knees were knocking so much the passers-by thought Murrin was hammering in nails. But You-Know-Who never forgets a good turn - or fails to remember a bad one - and so your man practically runs the National Meat Board where he's never inclined to chat about how the great man behaved in a crisis. Course he's not doing the meat industry much good for Murrin's only interested in horseflesh. There's not a race-meeting in the country he doesn't attend and where he gets the money he squanders so lavishly is anybody's guess. I find our new aristocracy fascinating, I really do. Especially the latest generation."

"You mean those who were too young to be involved in the politics of the past?"

"Yes" McCoom sniggered, "Those new fellows have twice the education of the older crowd and ten times the shrewdness. And they don't even have to shoot their way to power. Some of them use another kind of weapon altogether. They marry the daughters of the "big boys."

"Just get 'em laid and you have it made" Dessie surprised himself by saying. While McCoom shrivelled in on himself in a spasm of wheezy laughter he jotted down the remark - too good to miss - in his notebook wondering dare he use it as a slogan in the next Eggs-All-Ways campaign. McCoom - wheezing away - was turning out to be much more interesting than he had anticipated. The closer he was privileged to look behind the facade of Irish society the more he marvelled at the correctness of his analysis of what constituted its dynamic. Some aspect of the scene before him, maybe a hint of desert in the nearby sand dunes, certainly a sense of space and desolation, suggested a crazy parallel between the shape of Irish society and a crudely-made formula Western in which the politicians were the gunslingers - who else? - and the businessmen most of the other types you met in the bars and the brothels - the gamblers, the rustlers, the shady bankers, the land grabbers. The clergy were obviously the crooked sheriffs and marshals who'd thrown in their lot with the other two groups and the People - who else could the People be equated with if not the long-suffering, exploited Indians driven inexorably from their rightful home on the fertile plains and the hills to the confines of that great reservation - England! He almost laughed aloud.

"You always see things so clearly" Polly said on their last walk together back along the Bull Wall from the sandy downs, "But you'll never do anything to really help, will you? You're quite content to stand apart and make wisecracks, instead of decisions to commit yourself to the cause of the People. Don't you realise the damage that does to you as a person? How can you really develop your full personality if you continually hold back from what your mind tells you is the right thing to do?"

He asked her to consider the more serious damage he would do to his prospects if he were to agree to the proposition she had been making to him all evening. Hadn't she realised as yet that he really believed in the doctrines of his church, so how in conscience could he take the job she had set her mind on arranging for him on some new Communist weekly paper? He would have to join the Party, wouldn't he? That was the price to pay for the editorship. He would have to come down on the side of atheism, wouldn't he?

"And why not?" she asked, "Isn't it possible that in this century it's through the Communist Party that your God in whom we don't believe is expressing what you're always calling His inexorable will?" His roar of mocking laughter brought an angry light into her eyes. Behind the toss of her neat kerchiefed head, yellow pinpoints of light pricked the gloom along the East Wall. "The teachings of your bloody church" she said, "don't count for anything when it comes to sleeping with me, do they? The real reason you won't commit yourself is that you know this paper will have a terribly small circulation and therefore is not worthy of having your talents associated with it. And you'd really miss the satisfaction of seeing your headlines and your sickening copy - which you pretend to despise - for somebody's cornflour or somebody else's stomach powders in all the national dailies. But most telling of all, the money wouldn't be right, would it? And that makes you worse than the rotten society you prey on. Let's be really truthful and admit that most of the greed and the exploitation in it comes from an ignorance of an alternate and better way of life. But you - deliberately, slyly, cynically - look around for the highest bidder - usually a crook - and sell your talents to him." She swept past him her head averted. In his anger he shouted after her and was startled to hear his cry carry far and shrill on the wind. It was all very well for her to sneer, he raged after her. The society she condemned had given her a happy childhood, a comfortable home, an excellent education. It had cushioned her from the degradation of unemployment, of seeing her home sold before her eyes, of watching her parents die of economic shock, outrage, and despair masquerading as textbook illnesses. His last sight of her face discovered there her utter contempt for him. "Get right out of my life for good, you pimping Judas" she called. He watched her pick her way daintily along the wooden walk to the main road and run to catch a city-bound bus. She would be back, he grinned to himself. After two or three weeks, she'd be back, like the two other occasions when she had left him. He caught the next bus and hurried to the bankers social in the Engineers' Hall to pick up some girl - any girl with the usual equipment and no ideas, please to take the edge off his boredom till her return. As he entered the dancehall a girl caught at his sleeve. He looked at her in surprise. "It's a lady's choice" she explained. At the edge of the dancing area where she led him he said: "I've met you somewhere before, haven't I? Aren't you Nellie...?" She stood swaying gently backwards, her arms open to receive him. "No, my name's not Nellie. It's Deirdre." Exactly the kind of memory you are compelled to go on reliving in hell.

"But I suppose we ought to show some Christian charity" McCoom drawled breaking the silence he hadn't noticed. "The Irish are the most grudging, grasping, vindictive, ignorant people on earth and if those who rule over them display those qualities in the way they do it, then we can only conclude that the people are getting just what they deserve. And so there's no sense in criticising individual entrepreneurs and politicians is there? They're just men of the people."

Dessie stole a stealthy look of curiosity at the grey shrivelled figure musing beside him in his ridiculously outmoded Norfolk jacket and knee breeches - probably as worn by Noah in the ark - his sun-grated face drawn by its wrinkles into a perpetual cynical leer. What did he do for a living, he wondered turning his gaze once more to the bleak stretch of empty track. His name did not figure on the board of any of the companies listed in O'Neill's Directory of Directors though he had once heard Myers enumerate the solid enterprises in which his brother, the bishop, had substantial holdings. Probably the youngest of the usual football-team-sized Irish family, obviously short on initiative, no doubt the inevitable bungler, the all-time loser, aided and bribed by the other members of the family to maintain a passable standard of life that would not be a social embarrassment to them. Or to the bishop. Was that another car on its way or merely the wind whipping up the sand near the main road? He strained on tip-toe and eased back with an amused smile, watching the sand settle on the empty track. O'Kennedy wasn't coming and he felt absolutely nothing about it at all, except perhaps a vague surprise that he didn't really care. Why the hell didn't McCoom go inside or go away or just disappear down through his rutted wrinkles? He had never spoken to him before beyond passing him the time of day. He was a man constantly to be seen teetering on the edge of boisterous groups he was never invited to join, or sitting alone at a table for six a maintained smile on his horrifying mouth. He turned away from McCoom and looked wistfully towards the city. God, how ridiculous to be thinking of McCoom or O'Kennedy or anyone else while Polly was in there busy about the Party's tasks in her own quiet way, going to or coming from the inevitable meeting, as lonely for him as he was for her. His heart ached a wild cry of longing for her which came out in a pounding run down the steps of the clubhouse where he swung his throbbing face to the restless sky with its progress of sculptured white clouds. Turning he saw that McCoom was regarding him with, a creased embarrassed smile. Dessie returned the questioning gaze of the pale eyes tunnelled into the leathery face. That wizened image in a half-page layout would make a great ad for the current condition of Ireland - scurrilous, furtive, frustrated, forever immature, sick to the soul with uncomprehended hatreds and vices. He looked hard at McCoom and to his amazement felt a deep twinge of pity. No Polly in his past, no Polly in his future he rationalised desperately, knowing that the source of the emotion lay elsewhere, out of reach. Pity squeezed at his heart urging him to do something about McCoom. "Care to join me in a cup of coffee?" he asked.

"Delighted, I'm sure" an unexpected old-world charm following a start of surprise.

Dessie led the way inside and ordered two cups of coffee at the bar. "There hasn't been a call for me this morning, has there? From Humphrey O'Kennedy?" The barman shook his head and smiled slyly.

"So it's the great Humphrey you were expecting" McGoom said from the table, "Is he late?"

Dessie nodded.

"If he's more than a second late you can take it from me that he's not coming at all. Punctuality, that's his gimmick. When he had his first place, the jam factory next to the rubber works in one of the back lanes, he used to stand outside with his big watch in his hand half-an-hour before work was due to begin. Anyone who wasn't fifteen minutes early didn't last long in the place. In no time at all he was getting an extra ten minutes a day out of them. It all mounts up don't you see. He must have smelled that he'd get nothing for nothing out of you otherwise he'd be here now, sitting down opposite you his jaws working in that curious way he has when doing business, as if munching nuts. Course, you know how he got his start, don't you? After the Treaty he was told by the usual little bird..."

"...the native Irish vulture?"

"That's brilliant that is" McCoom laughed, "And so apt. As I was saying he was leaked in advance all the details of the supplies and equipment the new state was going to need for the army, police, and the civil service and he sneaked off and bought on credit all the stocks of one of the items, I've never been told which, and sold it to the government at his own fat price earning their undying gratitude as well as a fantastic profit."

"If he were here now I'd break whatever that item was over his head" Dessie said preserving out of habit the image of himself as a tough, sharp-witted advertising man. You have to do something to offset that anxious look. That story he had heard before and many similar about how this, that or the other businessman got his start - the shrewd marriage, the sudden scarcity, the fad, the strike, the stroke-of-luck, the useful leak, the loan, the windfall, even the bank robbery. Indeed there were few enterprises in the country which did not seem to have at least some of their roots in nepotism, sharp-practice, cronyism, patronage, the cynical exploitation of workers, blood even. Few seemed to have grown out of honest toil, the great man beginning humbly at the bottom and working his way honestly and steadily to the top in the usual from log-cabin to White House formula so beloved of nineteenth century America. And offhand he couldn't think of more than just a few that had sprung from a new invention or a unique creative idea or a piece of original insight into what was truly in the nation's interest. This was the general pattern of the society in which he had learned to survive and about which he told himself he had as little feeling as a doctor has about disease. Smiling, he drew from his inside pocket the neat leather case of Cuban cigars Myers had provided him with should he wish to offer one for appearance sake to O'Kennedy whom he knew to prefer Woodbines. He proffered the slim case to McCoom who chose a cigar with a child's delighted smile and lay back in his chair sniffing along it with the air of a man remembering better days.

"I'm not usually so well heeled" he said to McCoom, "My boss gave me those to impress O'Kennedy."

"Ho! Ho! Had Humphrey known there was something to be had for nothing after all" McGoom said, "he'd be here now - all ears. Sticking out at right angles. Had you noticed? They say he can hear the grass grow."

They sniggered at each other in what came so close to warm camaraderie Dessie almost forgot to notice the unfortunate mouth. He sipped his coffee, wondering about the twinge of pity he had felt for the man. For a moment out there he had seen him as Ireland, or rather as the epitome of her less endearing qualities. Was it possible that through him he was really pitying Fitzgibbon, Murrin, O'Kennedy and all the rest of those who had made over the country in the image of their own crabbed souls, who had squandered the golden opportunity that was theirs to mould the lives of the People to a form that would have done honour and reverence to Him who watched over them with love? It was amazing to reflect that the Irish and the Russian struggles had gone on at the same time yet in victory how different they were in outlook - that of the Christian Irish crassly materialistic, that of the atheistic Soviets - in spite of their terrible cruelties and blunders - dedicatedly idealistic. What a paradox! Didn't it cross the mind of any of the Irish patriots, even the clerical ones, that with the birth of the new state they were being presented with a unique opportunity to evolve the kind of Christian society Jesus would have been pleased to live in? What went wrong?

To his amazement he was gripped in a sensation almost physical by an idea that brought him to his feet tingling with excitement. Why hadn't he seen that before? Why hadn't he ever asked himself if he hadn't been born at this juncture in Irish history to fulfill his destiny which was nothing less than to reveal the whole truth of their condition to the people by writing a searching Marxist study from a Christian viewpoint of the development of Irish society from the 1916 Rising to the present post-war boom. In it he would trace the flow of power, of wealth, of privilege, turning many a hidden stone, naming names, raising embarrassing moral issues. He found himself looking down at the amazed McGoom and attempted to make his second untoward action comprehensible by bending across the table - always the brash advertising man - flicking his lighter. "How can you resist smoking that cigar?" he asked, "Don't you realise it's been rolled tight on the thighs of some beautiful Cuban girl? That's what gives it its unique flavour. Back in a sec'" he called over his shoulder heading for the washroom to be alone with his thoughts.

He paced along the white-tiled wall, past the hunched figure springing into the mirror on the verge of his vision and pacing along with him until it vanished again into the white tiles. Polly! Polly! his heart rejoiced, I've found the way back to you'. Sure as daylight he would find her, maybe even tomorrow – tomorrow! - his heart overflowed - and they would fall into each other's arms weeping tears of joy and of regret for their wasted years.

And it would be wonderful! And marvellous! And fabulous! And all the other film-poster adjectives. Oh yes, it would be all those things for a time, say a month at most.

For Polly with all her delicate sensibilities was as uncompromising as toughened steel, as clean and honest as mountain-spring water. Behind her love would lurk the contempt she would always feel for his way of life unless he brought about a drastic change in it. But the Marxist study would do that, would ensure that never again could she call him a "pimping Judas" - how those words still hurt! He would leave Myers. And Deirdre - what a scandal that would cause in the coffee-morning circuit! He would of course make her an allowance and - sweet irony - leave her the beleaguered house in Cabra to throw her fits in. He would find some means to live while he used his encyclopaedic knowledge of Irish society - he knew O'Neill's directory and the brute facts behind it almost by heart - to produce for the people the muck-raking study their long years of exploitation, of cultural deprivation, of unrealised potential deserved. A travel bureau was a business venture often in his mind as a sideline, principally as a means of rescuing his brother Bob from his dead-end job with the Turf Board. The three of them might run it together. The world was returning to normal - how else could it lay the seeds for the next war? - and tourism was bound to become big business with the great developments in aircraft. And - the explosion of his laugh in the narrow room made him jump - Polly could take charge of contacts with all the peoples' republics springing up and about to spring up all over the world. He skipped a few delighted steps. Things were looking up! Happy days were here again!

As he came back into the room he saw McCoom bearing two glasses of spirits from the counter. The Norfolk jacket swung open and he saw a small pair of binoculars hanging from a strap round McCoom's neck. He hadn't noticed before that he was wearing a pair of tennis shoes, dyed black.

"And now Mr Conlon" said McCoom placing the glasses on the table, "it's my pleasure to return the compliment." He sat down wondering how McCoom knew his name. There was a subtle change in the man's manner. He sat on the edge of his chair craning forward towards Dessie, licking his lips as if seeking an opportunity to break through into some closed circle of conversation.

"How did you manage to get this so early in the day?" Dessie asked sipping his drink which he found to his surprise was brandy.

"Friend of the corpse" McCoom joked, winking.

They sat for a time in silence during which Dessie allowed himself to come face to face with Polly in several different circumstances each ending with a swooning world-without-ending kiss. Only Shakespeare could write the copy for that meeting.

"I enjoyed our chat" McCoom said at length. Dessie declined to remark that the conversation which had passed between them was limited, to say the least. McCoom toyed with his glass, rocking one knee on the other. "I really appreciated the kind and generously friendly way you invited me to join you in a cup of coffee. And of course the charming conversation that went with it. I really appreciated the whole thing."

"Well, I don't see..." Dessie faltered.

"Please!" McCoom waved his hand, "Don't pretend you haven't noticed that nobody talks to me here."

Dessie looked at the bobbing binoculars and the dyed shoes and thought of the courting couples in the sand dunes, the girls undressing in the wind all along the beaches. Maybe it wasn't just because of his mouth they shunned him.

"Of course it's their loss" said McCoom, "For I know more than any of them about what's really going on in the business world. I have excellent contacts and nothing else to do but to observe. I bet you find that hard to believe?"

Dessie waved his hands apart in a gesture dispelling any doubts about not believing him. He knew of the many companies in which McCoom's brother had holdings and wondered if they ever had quiet chats together on matters other than spiritual.

"For instance" McCoom whispered out of his polluted mouth, "Here's something Fitzgibbon and Murrin have no inkling of, something far more profitable than whatever it is they're hatching round there by the bar. And incidentally, it's something Humphrey O'Kennedy would give his right arm, or at least his old mother's, to know about." He stabbed Dessie's knee with an insistent finger, "And this information is only for you. Not for your friends, not for your relations, not for your nearest and dearest. Just for you. Only. I have your word you'll keep it that way?"

"Certainly" Dessie almost yawned in his face. Coming up was obviously yet another of those innumerable tips, mostly worthless, or snippets of gossip that in certain clubs and bars were trotted out with a hushed air of wonder and reverence worthy of basic discoveries in science, of new ideas in philosophy or theology. He almost smiled at the notion of McCoom as the original Irish vulture.

"Well here it is," McCoom said softly, "and I know for a fact it's been divulged to only one very narrow circle, so it's practically exclusive. It seems some big man got drunk in company one night and said more than he should."

Dessie began to feel that in McCoom the advertising industry had lost a great writer of teasers.

"The government" McCoom dropped to a whisper again, "is going to take over Irishafts Incorporated."

"Oh yes" Dessie said, just for politeness sake. Who cared what happened to an ailing mining company whose prospects couldn't possibly be improved by the usual government delays, prevarications, and bunglings?

"To the tune of - wait for it - a cool thirty million" McCoom smiled slyly, "Some professors have convinced them they should have a key interest in whatever mineral wealth the country has. And of course one of the pundits keeps crying uranium. Anyway, shares in Irishafts which are down to three-and-six at the moment will reach from ninety to a hundred shillings by the end of next week. The official announcement's not due out for a few days."

He stood up, all boyish charm, his creased cheeks glowing. A whistling sprang up in Dessie's ears as if he were on a roller coaster, climbing to a dizzy height in the darkness hurtling down again out of control.

"So if you've a few half-pence to invest" McCoom said, "Now's the time. As a matter of fact you'd be a most foolish man - as I see from your look you're beginning to realise - if you didn't sink all you have on this - your shirt, your house, your car, your wife, the family skeleton! Anything you can raise money on." He winked, "But not a whisper to a living soul. We don't want to start a panic. Or a scandal. Do we? Must go!"

He held out a moist hand, the subtle constraint that had teased their relationship in the beginning now completely gone.

"Let me know how you get on," he said, "I'm in the book. Initials J. C. No, not what you think in spite of my excellent clerical connections. Just Jerome Carew."

Dessie thanked him, bade him goodbye and watched him go down the steps in an easy liquid motion, his binoculars bobbing against his narrow chest. In a few moments he had reached the nearest sand dunes along the crest of which he cruised, a black hunched figure with light skipping steps, as if performing a secret dance of his own devising. Then he was gone from sight as if into the earth. Dessie remained where he was sipping his non-tasting brandy hardly daring to move lest he disturb the brisk arithmetic clicking as on a calculating machine through his mind towards a final figure whose size made him break out in a slow rash of sweat. Already his encounter with McCoom had the shock of destiny about it, the spinal shiver of recognition. With it came a deep ache in his ulcer like a raw nerve from which the covering was being slowly stripped. There was no doubt about it! This was at last the arrival of the kind of opportunity that had teased the dreams of the lonely boy who saw a perverse destiny rampage like a maniac through his life destroying his parents and his home. From his early days in Myers and Taylors he knew that opportunities like this cropped up all the time. Following which quiet invitations were issued to house-parties in the more moneyed part of the county, down quiet by-roads and along the base of the hills out towards Wicklow, at which mild old whiskey flowed like water and some of the conversation was pure music, like the crinkle of notes, the merry ring of a busy cash register. How often had he seen sharp, hard-faced men stride into clubs and hotel lounges with a confidence - and often an attractive woman - they had never had before! And now it was his turn. Lady fortune was not only smiling at him, she was moving over to make room for him in her soft, warm bed. How embarrassingly foolish he had been just now - that stupid streak of romanticism again - to think his destiny lay in a totally different direction. But he wouldn't suffer the pain of thinking about that now beyond agreeing that romantic gestures though they were essential to dreams and dramas are in real life a luxury that most people just can't afford. He had been right earlier that morning when he felt it would be the end to start remembering Polly. But he had no time for that now - later, in a more sentimental mood perhaps, no, not even that - for he had to work out the details of his destiny which wasn't just a set of theories of society or a study of history. It was the very stuff of history itself. His history. And the next chapter was the thrilling story of the takeover of the Myers Agency. And that would only be part of a much longer whole.

Tomorrow, while his astounded broker bought a huge block of shares in Irishafts he would be arranging to gather together Deirdre's money and his own to which he would add a hefty loan, using the house as security, from Syd's money-lending brother, and throw in a thousand or two, whatever the traffic would stand, borrowed - sweet irony - from Myers himself, finally rounding off the package with whatever he could get from the three Jack Yeats pictures he got for a song from Rowkins just before the receiver moved in on him. And Deirdre would stand by him in all this. She always knew on which side her bread was buttered and how welcome a nice slice of cake was as well. Come to think of it, Dalkey wasn't all that far out of town to be worth arguing about at a time like this. He rose slowly on his trembling limbs and mopped his cold brow. Somewhere out there beyond the curve or the coast, Frank and Julie were playing on the beach with little Ivan or more likely wreathed in a veil of cigarette smoke analysing some current political situation or other. Why didn't the fools just play chess? That was far less hard on the blood pressure. Didn't they realise yet that revolutions change only the occupants of the seats of power leaving the bulk of the people more or less as they always were - only this time mourning their dead? Feudalism was elbowed out by capitalism which in its turn was being changed now into various forms of socialism. Taylor was bought out by Myers and now it was Myers's turn to be sent on his way. Couldn't they see that the only constant in history is the drive to power irrespective of whatever doctrine is being preached by whichever progressive group is driving hard to take control?

Fitzgibbon brushed past him. "How's trade?" he asked.

"Fantastic!" Dessie said following him out towards the car park. Yes, trade would indeed be fantastic before many weeks were past. For which he would offer up many prayers of thanksgiving. There was another intention he would pray for as well. He would pray hard and long that in all the twists and turns of all the streets in all the days to come his eyes would never light on Polly. Oh never, please God! Never!

Printed in Great Britain
by Amazon